P9-DZY-342

BEHIND CLOSED DOORS

SHANNON McKENNA

BEHIND CLOSED DOORS

BRAVA

KENSINGTON PUBLISHING CORP.
http://www.kensingtonbooks.com

BRAVA BOOKS are published by

Kensington Publishing Corp.
850 Third Avenue
New York, NY 10022

Copyright © 2002 by Shannon McKenna

All rights reserved. No part of this book may be reproduced in any form or by any means without the prior written consent of the Publisher, excepting brief quotes used in reviews.

All Kensington titles, imprints and distributed lines are available at special quantity discounts for bulk purchases for sales promotion, premiums, fund raising, educational or institutional use.

Special book excerpts or customized printings can also be created to fit specific needs. For details, write or phone the office of the Kensington Special Sales Manager: Kensington Publishing Corp., 850 Third Avenue, New York, NY 10022. Attn. Special Sales Department. Phone: 1-800-221-2647.

Brava and the B logo Reg. U.S. Pat. & TM Off.

ISBN 0-7582-0318-7

First Kensington Trade Paperback Printing: September 2002
10   9   8   7   6   5   4   3   2   1

Printed in the United States of America

Prologue

*T*he dream never changed.

Her father's sailboat was drifting slowly away from the shore. The clouds were growing darker. Gusts of wind whipped the dark water into a white-capped froth that sloshed up over her feet. Dread lay in her belly, as heavy as a cold stone. She watched the boat drift farther and farther. Lightning flashed. Thunder.

Then she was standing with her father in front of a tall black marble obelisk. His arm was around her shoulders, and his handsome face was pale and grim. He pointed to the obelisk. She realized that it was a tombstone.

A jolt of fear reverberated through her. It was his tombstone.

She leaned closer to read his name and the dates of his birth and death. The grooves in the marble seemed wet and dark. More than wet, they were dripping with dark liquid. It oozed out and snaked down the pale surface of the marble in long, tangled crimson rivulets. Blood.

Horrified, she looked back up at her father, but he was no longer her father. He had become her Uncle Victor, his cold eyes an electric silver gray, his teeth white and oddly sharp looking. And his heavy, muscular arm was around her shoulders, tightening until she thought her lungs would burst.

She woke up gasping for breath, a scream trapped in her aching throat, and stared wild-eyed into the dark. Trying to breathe, trying to make her hammering heart calm down.

Wondering how long it would take for the dream to drive her mad.

Chapter

1

Nine forty-six P.M. Almost time.

The monitor glowed an eerie blue in the darkened room, but the mosaic of windows on the screen remained stubbornly dark. Seth Mackey glanced at his watch and drummed his fingers against the desktop. Her schedule never varied. She should be home any minute.

There were more important things for him to do. He had hundreds of hours of audio and video to filter, and even with Kearn's jazzed-up digital signal processor filters, it still took time to run the analyses. He should at least be watching the beacon displays, or checking the other surveillance sites. Anything but this.

Still he stared at the screen, trying to rationalize away the buzz of hot excitement in his body. The hundreds of hours of digital video footage that he had on file for her wouldn't do the trick. He needed her live, in real time.

Like a junkie needed his fix.

He spat out a curse at the passing thought, negating it. He didn't need anything, not anymore. Since Jesse's death, he'd reinvented himself. He was as cool and detached as a cyborg. His heart rate did not vary, his palms did not sweat. His goal was sharp and clear. It shone in the darkness of his interior landscape, as brilliant as a guiding star. The plan to destroy Victor Lazar and Kurt Novak was the first thing that had aroused Seth's interest in the ten months since they had murdered his brother Jesse. It had rendered him a miracle of single-minded concentration—until three weeks ago.

The woman who was about to walk into the rooms monitored by the screen in front of him was the second thing.

The light and motion activated camera monitoring her garage flicked to life. He tried to ignore the way his heart rate spiked, and glanced at his watch. 9:51. She'd been at the office since 7 A.M. He had watched her on the cameras he had planted at the Lazar Import & Export corporate office, too, of course, but it wasn't the same. He liked having her all to himself.

The car pulled in, the headlights went out. She sat slumped in the car for so long that the camera switched itself off and the window went dark. He cursed through his teeth and made a mental note to himself to reprogram the default from three minutes to ten as he typed in the command that activated the infrared mode. Her image reappeared, a glowing, unearthly green. She sat there for two more minutes staring blankly into the dark garage before she finally got out.

The second two cameras snapped on dutifully as she unlocked the door and headed for the kitchen. She ran herself a glass of water, took off the hornrimmed glasses and rubbed her eyes, clutching the sink for balance. She tilted back her head to drink, exposing her slender, soft looking white throat.

She must be trying to toughen up her look with the glasses. She'd failed, in a big way. The camera he had hidden in the stove clock framed her pale face, her stubborn jaw, the shadows under her eyes.

He zoomed in on her eyes. The straight, winging brows and curling lashes were dramatically dark against her pale skin. He would have taken her for a bleached blonde if he didn't have damn good reason to know that her blond curls were absolutely for real. She closed her eyes. The sweep of her lashes was shadowy against the delicate curve of her cheekbones. Her mascara was smudged. She looked exhausted.

Being Lazar's new sex toy must be more strenuous than she had bargained for. He wondered how she'd gotten embroiled with him. Whether she was in too deep to ever get out. Most people who got involved with Lazar soon found they were in over their heads. By then, of course, it was too late.

There was no objective reason for him to continue to monitor her. Hacking into her personnel file had revealed that Lazar Import &

Export had hired her a month ago as an executive assistant. Had it not been for the fact that she was living in Lazar's ex-mistress's house she might never have come to his attention at all. Lazar's visits to that house had warranted surveillance, and they had been watching it for months.

But Lazar didn't visit the blonde, or at least he hadn't yet. She came straight home from the office every night, stopping only to get groceries or pick up her dry cleaning. The transponder he had planted in her car confirmed that she never varied her route. Weekly phone calls to her mother revealed only that the woman had no clue about her daughter's latest career move, which was perfectly understandable. A young woman kept for pleasure by a filthy rich criminal might well choose to hide the knowledge from her family. She knew no one in Seattle, went nowhere, had no social life that he could discern.

Kind of like himself.

Her big, haunted eyes were silver gray, the irises ringed with indigo. He studied the magnified image, disquieted. She looked . . . God, *sweet* was the word that came to mind, even though it made him wince. He had never before felt any moral qualms about spying on people. When he was a kid reading comic books, he'd picked out his superhero mutation of choice right away. X-ray eyes won, hands down. It was the perfect mutation for a paranoid guy like him. Knowledge was power, and power was good. He'd built a lucrative career on that philosophy. Jesse used to tease him about it.

He shoved that thought away fast, before it could bite him.

He had to stay cool and detached. Cyborg man. It was a name for a comic book superhero. He'd always liked those mutant guys in the classic comic books. They were all tormented, depressed and alienated. He could relate to that.

He'd watched Montserrat, Lazar's former mistress, with ice-cold detachment. Watching her writhe in bed with Lazar had left him unmoved, even a little repulsed. Never once had he felt guilty.

But then again, Montserrat was a professional. He could read it in her sinuous, calculated body language. She wore a mask all the time, when she was fucking Lazar, even when she was alone.

The blonde had no mask at all. She was wide open and defenseless and soft, like whipped cream, like butter, like silk.

It made him feel sleazy for watching her, an emotion so unfamiliar that it had taken him days to put a name to it. The hell of it was, the sleazier he felt, the more impossible it was to stop. He wished he could shake off the nagging sense that she needed to be rescued. He wasn't the white knight type to begin with, and besides, he had Jesse to avenge. That was enough responsibility.

And he wished she weren't so fucking beautiful. It was disturbing.

A shrink could probably explain his fixation: he was projecting deprived childhood fantasies onto her because she looked like a fairy-tale princess. He'd read too many comic books as a kid. He was stressed, depressed, obsessed, had an altered perception of reality, blah, blah, blah. Then that woman's stunning body had altered reality beyond recognition. It had shocked his numbed libido violently to life.

She drifted wearily into the range of the color-cam nestled inside the carved ebony filigree of a hanging lamp in the bedroom. The lamp had been left behind by Montserrat, who had departed so abruptly that she hadn't even taken the time to pack the personal items that she had contributed to the house's décor. The blonde had brought nothing of her own to the house, and had shown no interest in moving the pieces already in place, which was good. The lamp color-cam commanded an excellent view of the mirror on the armoire, a detail for which he had reason to be grateful. He enlarged the image until it filled the whole screen, ignoring a slight pang of guilt. This was his favorite part, and he wasn't missing it for anything.

She removed her jacket, clipped the skirt to the hanger. With the awe-inspiring resolution of the latest generation of Colbit color-cams, he could differentiate every gradation of the color of her perfect skin, from cream to pink to rose to crimson. More than worth the extra bandwidth the signal occupied. She hung up the suit, and the tail of her blouse hiked up to reveal prim cotton briefs stretched tightly across the swell of her rounded ass. He knew her routine like it was the opening credits of an old television show, and still he hung on every detail. Her unself-consciousness fascinated him. Most of the good-looking women he knew played constantly to an imaginary camera. They checked every reflective surface they passed to make sure they were still beautiful. This dreamy-eyed girl didn't seem to particularly notice, or care.

She peeled off her hose, flung them into the corner, and started her clumsy, innocent nightly striptease. She fumbled with her cuffs until he wanted to scream at her to get the fuck on with it. Then she fussed and picked at the buttons at the throat of the high-collared blouse, gazing into the mirror as if she saw another world entirely.

His breath hissed in between his teeth when she finally shrugged off the blouse. Her plump breasts were sternly restrained by a white underwire bra. It was not a sexy, rich-man's-plaything scrap of lingerie. It had plain, wide straps, was practical and unadorned—and the faint hint of cleavage it revealed was the sexiest thing he'd ever seen.

She sniffed delicately at the armpits of the blouse, which brought a grim smile to his face. It was hard to imagine that graceful, marble-white body actually sweating, though he bet he could drive her to it. She would break a sweat once she were spread out naked beneath his pounding body, her hips jerking eagerly up to meet his thrusts. Or astride him, those big, soft tits bouncing, filling his hands as he drove into her from below. He would make that ivory skin flush wild-rose pink, until tangled curls clung to her cheek, her throat. He would make her soaking wet. Every hot, sweet, slippery inch of her.

He rearranged his throbbing private parts inside his jeans and dragged his hand over his hot face with a groan. He had no business getting anything more than a purely casual, incidental hard-on for one of Lazar's toys. It was deadly stupid, and it had to stop.

Except that now it was time for the hair. God, he loved that part.

She tossed pin after pin into the china tray on the dresser, and uncoiled the thick blond braid from the bun at the nape of her neck. She unraveled the strands, shaking them loose until they rippled past the small of her back, tapering down to gleaming wisps that brushed tenderly against the round curve of her ass. His breath sighed out in a low, audible groan as she reached behind herself and unhooked the bra. His hands tingled as he stared at her plump, luscious breasts, crowned with pale pink nipples. He imagined them taut, flushed and hard against his fingers, the palms of his hands, his feverish face, his hungry, suckling mouth.

His heart began to pound as she peeled off the panties, rolling her shoulders, her neck, arching her back, enjoying the sensual freedom of being naked and alone. Unmasked. Whipped cream and butter and silk.

The downy puff of springy blond curls at her crotch didn't quite hide the shadowy cleft between her shapely thighs. He wanted to press his face against those ringlets, inhale her warm, woman scent, and then taste her, parting the tender pink folds of her cunt, licking and suckling until she collapsed in pleasure. Video and audio were not enough. He needed more data. Textures, smells, tastes. He was starving for it.

And then, the gesture that always undid him. She bent from the waist and flung her hair over her head, arching her back and running her fingers through the wavy mass. The placement of the camera and the mirror guaranteed him a spectacular view of her soft, rounded thighs, the creamy globes of her ass, the enticing divide between them.

The sight was enough to wake the dead.

Jesse. The stab of pain blindsided him.

He turned away from the monitor and forced himself to breathe over the burning ache. Don't cave in, he reminded himself. He couldn't let grief dull his edge. On the contrary, he would use it to sharpen his resolve. To turn him into a single-minded, utterly dedicated instrument of ruin. He averted his eyes, punishing himself by missing the rest of the stretch show. He'd gotten very skilled at shoving away painful thoughts and memories before they could dig in their fangs, but the blonde blew his focus all to hell. He forced himself to run over his reason for existence: to watch that treacherous bastard Lazar until he made contact with Novak. And then, open season. Payback time.

By the time he permitted himself to look back at the screen, the blonde had clothed herself in a baggy fleece sweat suit, and was logging onto her computer. He scooted over to another bank of computers and monitors, activating the hidden antenna he had planted to pick up her computer's EM frequency noise. He ran it through the DPS hardware that deciphered and reconstructed what was on her screen, and monitored her message. It was to a Juan Carlos in

Barcelona. She sent messages in half a dozen different languages, but this one was in Spanish, which he understood from growing up in the ghettos of L.A. It was innocuous enough: *how are you, I'm working really hard, how's Marcela and Franco's baby, did the job interview in Madrid go well*, et cetera. She sounded lonely. He wondered who Juan Carlos was to her. Maybe an ex-lover. She seemed to write to him a lot.

He was toying with the idea of doing a background check on the guy when a cool draft whispered across his neck. He snatched the SIG Sauer P228 that lay on the desk and spun around.

It was Connor McCloud, co-conspirator and all-around pain in the ass, who had been Jesse's best buddy and partner in the undercover FBI task force that Jesse had dubbed "the Cave." No wonder the alarm hadn't tripped. He'd bypassed it, the sneaky son-of-a-bitch. The guy moved like a ghost, despite his limp and his cane.

Seth lay the gun down, breath escaping slowly from his lungs. "Don't sneak up on me, McCloud. It could get you killed."

Connor's sharp green eyes swept the room, taking in every detail. "Hey, man. Stay casual. I brought you some coffee, but I'm thinking now that maybe you shouldn't drink it."

Seth saw the dingy room through Connor's eyes for a moment, the clutter of beer bottles and take-out containers scattered across dusty snarls of cables and electronic equipment. The apartment was getting more squalid by the day, and it wasn't smelling too good, either.

But what the fuck did he care? It was just a parking spot. He grabbed the coffee, popped the lid and took a gulp.

"You're welcome," Connor murmured wryly. "Next time I'll bring chamomile tea. And a Xanax."

"Are you sure nobody followed you here?" Seth demanded.

Connor sat down and peered into the monitor, not deigning to reply to that. "Well, if it isn't Barbie's dream house," he commented. "How much you want to bet she's a natural blonde?"

"Mind your own goddamn business," Seth snapped.

Connor's lean face settled in grim lines. "Nobody at the Cave knows about you, Mackey. Nobody will. And your business *is* my business."

Seth could think of no response to that statement that was not offensive. He kept his mouth shut and waited, hoping that the other man would get uncomfortable or bored enough to leave.

No such luck. Seconds ticked by. They turned into minutes. Connor McCloud gazed at him and waited patiently.

Seth sighed and gave in. "Was there something that you wanted?" he asked grudgingly.

Connor lifted an eyebrow. "Been a while since you contacted me. Just wondering what you're up to. Besides jerking off while you watch Lazar's new concubine, that is."

"Keep the smart-ass remarks to yourself, McCloud." Seth stabbed the print button and waited for the printer to spit out the Juan Carlos e-mail. He reached for the file, but Connor snatched it off the desk.

"Let me have a look. Lorraine Cameron, American citizen, degree from Cornell, *summa cum laude*, woo woo, smart cookie. Fluent in six languages, yada yada, appears to have lied about her professional experience on her job application. Hmm. Maybe Lazar didn't care once she showed him her tits. How are her tits, by the way?"

"Fuck off," Seth snarled.

"Lighten up," Connor replied. "You know, when this babe first showed up, I thought maybe it was good for you to have something to think about besides Jesse. But it's out of hand. You're obsessed."

"Spare me the pop psych bullshit, please."

"You're a bomb set to blow. Not that I care, but I don't want you to take me and my brothers with you." Connor shoved back his shaggy dark blond hair and rubbed his forehead, looking weary. "You're wound too tight, Mackey. I've seen it happen. A guy gets that look you've got on your face, then he fucks up, then he dies badly."

Seth schooled his face back to an indifferent mask. "Don't worry," he said, through set teeth. "I swear I'll keep it together until we flush Novak out of his hole. After that, whatever. Lock me in a padded cell if you want. I will no longer give a shit."

Connor looked pained. "That's a very, very bad attitude, Mackey."

"I've had a bad attitude since the day I was born." Seth wrenched the blonde's file out of Connor's hand and shoved the Juan Carlos e-mail into it. "Don't take it personally. And don't step on my toes."

"Don't be an asshole," Connor said. "You need me, and you know it. I have the contacts you need to make this work."

Seth glared into Connor's cold, narrowed eyes. He wanted to deny it, but it was true. Seth had the tech know-how and the money to launch their private campaign against Lazar and Novak, but Connor's years in various law enforcement agencies had garnered him a formidable local network of informants. Problem was, Connor and he were both bossy, arrogant and accustomed to command; both by nature and by profession. It made for an uneasy partnership.

"Speaking of contacts, I was down at the Cave today," Connor said. "I played up my limp. Made like I don't know what to do with myself on disability leave. Nobody has the heart to tell me I'm underfoot except for Riggs. He told me to go get my ass to a tropical beach, drink some mai tais. Watch the bunfloss bikinis walk by. Get laid, if I can."

"Did you tell him to fuck off?"

"Nah," Connor said mildly. "I'm not as casual as you are about burning my bridges. Not until I get this thing sorted out."

Riggs. Seth sorted through his memories of Jesse's memorial service. He'd lurked in the back with a miniature video camera hidden in his coat, filming the faces of Jesse's colleagues and speculating upon which one was the bastard that had sold his brother out. He remembered a thickset, balding man who had read some vapid thing that would have made Jesse puke laughing. "Was Riggs the potbelly and glasses who made the stupid-ass speech at Jesse's service?"

"I was in a coma at the time, but the stupid-ass speech has got to be Riggs," Connor replied, pulling a bag of tobacco out of his pocket. "You got any more of those warehouse raids planned?" He fished for his rolling papers, his casual tone belied by the hopeful gleam in his eyes.

Seth snorted. "You McCloud boys really get off on that, huh?"

"It's a blast," Connor admitted. "Better than sex, messing with Victor Lazar's head. Maybe I missed my calling. A life of crime has its charms. God, what a rush."

Seth shrugged. "Sorry to disappoint you, but that phase of the operation is over."

Connor's eyes narrowed. "Lazar's taken the bait?"

"Yes." Seth did not elaborate.

Connor waited. Seconds ticked by. "And?" His voice was steely.

"I'm going to Lazar's corporate headquarters tomorrow morning," Seth admitted. "He's invited me to explain to him why Mackey Security Systems Design is the solution to all his problems. The cover story to his staff is that I'm here to design a radio frequency GPS inventory tracking system, so tomorrow's meeting is just theater. Then the day after tomorrow, Lazar and I are meeting privately out at the warehouses to discuss the details of a full-out TSCM sweep."

"Ah." Connor's eyes narrowed. "TSCM. Don't tell me, let me guess. That stands for . . . technical surveillance . . . "

"Technical surveillance countermeasures," Seth finished impatiently. "Debugging."

Connor pulled out a pinch of tobacco, his face expressionless. "Wow. One hell of a stroke of luck, that he called you, hmm?"

"Not luck," Seth said. "It's called planning. Lots of people in the field owe me favors. I made sure he would hear about me and my firm when he started looking around to solve his security leak problem."

"I see." Connor stared down at the snarl of tobacco nestled in the fold of the rolling paper. "And just when would you have gotten around to mentioning this development to me?" His voice was soft and cold.

"As soon as you needed to know," Seth countered smoothly. "You aren't planning on smoking that in here, of course."

Connor finished the cigarette with a deft twist of his fingers, and scowled at it. "It's raining outside."

"Tough," Seth said.

Connor sighed, and stuck the cigarette into the pocket of his coat. "You blame me for Jesse's death, don't you?"

The brutal facts behind Jesse's death lay between them, heavy and cold. Someone at the Cave had tipped off Lazar to the investigation and blown Jesse's cover. Seth meant to find that person and rip him limb from limb. But that person was not Connor, who had been Jesse's best friend as well as his partner. Connor had almost died in that disastrous fuck-up. He would carry the scars for the rest of his life.

"I don't blame you," Seth said, feeling suddenly weary. "I don't want to make the mistake Jesse made."

"Which was?"

Seth shook his head. "Letting too many people know his business. Ever since he was a little kid. I never could break him of it."

Connor was silent for a long moment, his face somber. "You don't trust anyone, do you?"

Seth shrugged. "I trusted Jesse," he said simply.

They watched the blonde wander into her kitchen and stare blankly at her freezer for a minute, as if she'd utterly forgotten what she had planned to do. She shook herself out of her daze, took out a frozen dinner and stuck into the oven.

"We'll find the mole, Seth," Connor said finally.

Seth swung around in his chair. "He's mine."

Connor's eyes were as full of ghosts as Seth's own. "Take a number and get in line, man," he said softly. "You're not the only one who cared about Jesse."

Seth broke eye contact. He had plans for that traitor and for Novak and Lazar as well, plans that had nothing to do with due process of law. Which was why he didn't concern himself overmuch with the legality of his investigation, or rather, the total lack thereof. Once he got his hands on Novak, he needed no help from anyone in bringing him to justice. Same with Lazar. But that was nobody's business but his.

A grin dawned on Connor's face. "Check it out. The concubine's doing her exercise routine. Whoa. The guy has good taste in babes. This one's even hotter than Montserrat."

Seth looked back at the screen with elaborate nonchalance.

She was sitting on the carpet, legs spread impossibly wide, slim back straight. She flung her hair back and bent from the waist until her chest touched the ground, as graceful and flexible as a dancer.

"I don't think she's fucking him," he said suddenly.

Connor gave him a dubious look. "How do you figure?"

He shrugged, regretting the impulsive comment. With Connor's keen, thoughtful gaze fixed on him, it sounded stupid and improbable. "She never goes anywhere. She sleeps here every night. Goes straight to the office and home and back again. And he's never visited her here."

Connor shrugged. "He's a busy guy. Maybe he bangs her in his office on his desk."

"He hasn't," Seth countered. "I've covered his office. I've processed that tape. She's never been inside his personal office."

"Oh, really?" Connor's eyes gleamed with quiet amusement. "That interested, are we?"

"I'm interested in everything that has to do with Lazar." He bit the words out, cold and clear.

"Praiseworthy of you," Connor remarked. "One thing's for sure, though. If he booted Montserrat for her, she must be damn good with her mouth. Give me a call if she blows him. I'll log on for that episode."

Seth grabbed the mouse and clicked the window shut. The blonde disappeared, replaced by a little icon in the shape of a pair of glasses.

Connor shook his head in disgust. He fished the cigarette out of his pocket, lit it and took a deep, defiant drag. "Fine," he said coldly. "She's all yours, Mackey. Looks like your fantasy life is pretty much all you've got, so I'll leave you to it."

"You do that." Seth spun around as soon as the door slammed shut and called the image back.

She was curving her spine with catlike grace, hair tumbling voluptuously over her face. Then she reversed the process in a rippling movement until her back was arched, ass raised. Curve, arch. Curve, arch, in a slow, pulsing rhythm that made him dizzy and feverish.

God, he was glad that Lazar hadn't visited her. Watching that rapacious bastard grunting and sweating on top of his dreamy, soft-eyed blonde would not be pleasant. In fact, it would ruin his whole day.

He cursed into the screen, helpless to look away. Watching her made him feel alive again and he'd gotten strung out on the feeling, in spite of the fact that it threw off his precarious balance, leaving him wide open to spasms of pain he thought he'd learned to control. In spite of the fact that he betrayed Jesse every moment he spent staring at her.

Less than three weeks ago, his first waking thought every day had been on how to destroy Lazar and Novak. The risk hadn't bothered him. He just felt like an empty husk anyhow. Nothing inside him but an endless, burning thirst for revenge. With Hank gone five years now, and Jesse gone, too, there was no one left to mourn him. Or need him. It wouldn't be such a bad way to go, if they took him out with them in a blaze of glory, chapter closed, big sigh of relief from all concerned.

But since the blonde showed up, he had realized that there actually were a couple more things he wouldn't mind doing before leaving this earthly plane. Like find out if she really was any good with that full, sexy mouth of hers, for instance.

The fantasy took him by storm: her naked on her knees in front of him, his hands buried in her hair, guiding her as his swollen cock slid in and out of her lush, pink, bee-stung lips. God, that would be sweet.

Now she was doing a back bend, her body taut like an arched bow and quivering with effort, her hair coiled under her head in a luminous pool. Her sweatshirt had slid up, snagging on her breasts and exposing the soft curve of her belly. It looked velvety and vulnerable, softened by barely perceptible white-blond fuzz. He wanted to nuzzle it, rub his cheek against that smooth, fragrant warmth, memorize the scent of her lotion and soap. And tomorrow he was going to Lazar's corporate office. Tomorrow he would find out exactly what she smelled like.

The blast of excitement that accompanied that thought ratcheted him up another notch toward total sexual overload. He slammed his hand down against the desk. Pain jolted up his arm. The keyboard jumped. Empty beer bottles toppled and thudded onto the dirty gray carpet that covered the floor.

Calm down, he told himself. Concentrate. Tomorrow was all about luring Lazar deeper into the web that he had spent so many long, patient months spinning for him. Tonight was all about preparing for tomorrow. And right now, he was going to click that tantalizing blonde out of existence and get to work processing the latest data retrieved from the gulper mikes. It was going to take most of the night to filter all of it, and it was time he got started. Right now. This minute.

He tried, but his finger wouldn't push the button on the mouse.

The series of exercises was long and slow, but he never got bored.

Chapter

2

Images from this morning's dream shimmered in Raine's mind as she maneuvered through early morning traffic. The dream images seemed far more vivid and substantial than the drab, lonely half-life she was living here in Seattle. She was good at analyzing dreams— God knows she'd had plenty of practice—but ponder as she might, she couldn't come up with a plausible meaning for this one.

She was tiny, swimming in a glass aquarium. Light rippled across the fake colored rocks that covered the floor. She swam slowly through little sprays of coral, over a miniature plastic castle and a sunken pirate ship. She was naked, and terribly conscious of her nakedness. She tried to wrap her long hair around herself, but it just kept floating back up around her face in a pale, swirling cloud. A black pirate flag waved languidly in the water. The skull and crossbones insignia on it was the last image she brought to waking consciousness as the alarm dragged her awake at 5:30 A.M. Just as the blaring horn of a Ford Explorer behind her jolted her into awareness that the light was green. She had to stay in the waking world and concentrate on the rain-slicked street in front of her.

She'd been having this dream often, as long as she had been staying in the house that Lazar Import & Export had assigned to her. Staying, as opposed to living, because she couldn't get comfortable there, despite the fact that it was a beautiful place, already furnished and far too luxurious for a lowly executive assistant. It made her nervous. She had enough problems without feeling ill at ease in her own living space. She meant to look for an apartment of her own as soon as she had a second to breathe, and to hell with the extra expense.

Dreaming of herself as naked, trapped and helpless was not confidence-inspiring. She wished that she could dream of herself as something bold and fearless for a change. A pirate queen, brandishing a cutlass and yelling out her battle cry. But she shouldn't complain. The aquarium dream was a hell of a lot less stressful than the bleeding tombstone dream. It didn't leave her gasping for air, hollow-eyed with terror, aching with grief for her lost father.

Still, the skull and crossbones bothered her. There was always an image of death in her recurrent dreams. Lucky girl, she thought, with grim amusement. Way to start the day off right, with a dripping dagger, a nest of snakes, or a mushroom cloud. That daily squirt of screaming adrenaline into the bloodstream was better than coffee.

Her stomach fluttered as she pulled into the underground garage of the building that housed the corporate offices. Jeremy, the flirtatious parking attendant, gave her a wink and a wave, and she barely managed a wan smile in return. She'd gotten her job at Lazar Import & Export under false pretenses, and every day the price she paid for that deceit got higher. She'd researched the huge, diversified company exhaustively, tailoring her résumé to fit them, fabricating an employment history that she thought would appeal to them. She'd soothed her qualms by telling herself that she was justified, that it was for a noble cause. Still, Raine had never been good at lying. It made her stomach hurt. Breakfast would help, but there was no time, not even to grab a pastry.

God knows, Lazar Import & Export would be a stressful place to work even if she weren't lying through her teeth every day. It was the most vicious, spiteful, back-biting workplace she'd ever experienced. There wasn't a chance in hell of making friends with her co-workers. She stared critically at her reflection in the cloudy mirrored walls of the elevator. She'd lost weight. Her skirt was riding too low over her hips. But who had time to eat in Lazar's lair? She was lucky if she could find a moment to pee during the course of the day.

The elevator stopped and pinged on the ground floor as she was freshening her lipstick. The door slid open, a man stepped in, and the door rolled shut behind him. The elevator seemed suddenly very small. She shoved her lipstick into her purse, a light, tickling awareness rippling across the surface of her skin, like a breeze rustling long grass.

She was careful not to look at him directly, mindful of elevator etiquette, but she gathered considerable information out of the corner of her eye. Tall, maybe a little over six feet. Lean. Darkly tanned skin, she noticed, sneaking a furtive glance at the big hands that emerged from the cuffs of his suit—his very elegant, very costly suit. Probably Armani, she concluded, peeking at the cut of his sleeves. A summer hanging out in Barcelona with that shameless clotheshorse Juan Carlos had taught her a lot about the subtle nuances of men's fashion.

He was looking at her. She felt the weight and heat of his gaze against the side of her face. She would have to look straight at him to confirm it. For once, her curiosity was stronger than her fear.

Maybe it was the skull and crossbones in her dream that suggested the image, but the thought blazed through her mind the moment she raised her eyes to his.

He had the face of a pirate.

He wasn't classically handsome. His features were too harsh and craggy, his nose bumpy and crooked. Midnight black hair was cropped short. It stuck straight up, like a velvety black scrub brush. His broad cheekbones jutted out, with deep hollows beneath them. His eyebrows were thick, black slashes and his mouth was both grim and sensual. But it was his eyes that shocked her. They were black, heavy-lidded and exotic. They stared at her with searing intensity.

The eyes of a marauding buccaneer.

His gaze slid down over her body as if he saw through her prim gray suit, through her blouse, her underthings, right down to the shivering flesh beneath. His appraisal was bold and arrogant, as if he had every right to stare. The way a pirate captain might look at his helpless captive . . . before he dragged her down to his cabin for sport.

Raine tore her eyes away. Her overactive imagination promptly went crazy with the pirate metaphor, erasing the Armani and dressing him in pirate's garb; flowing blouse, tight knee breeches that showcased his . . . his assets, a cutlass thrust into a crimson sash, a golden hoop in his ear. It was ridiculous, but she felt flushed, panicky. She had to get out of this elevator before the mirrors steamed up.

To her immense relief, the door pinged and opened on the 26th floor. She lunged to exit, stumbling into the man who was waiting to enter and murmured an incoherent apology as she ran for the stairs. Walking up would make her late, but she had to regain her composure.

Oh God, how pathetic, and how typical. A hot, sexy guy gave her the eye in an elevator, and she fell to pieces like a terrified virgin. She'd blown her once in a lifetime chance to be ravished by a pirate. No wonder her love life was a non-issue. She sabotaged it before it even got going. Every damn time.

The working day began inauspiciously. Harriet, the office manager, swept by as she was hanging up her coat, her thin face pinched with disapproval. "I expected you earlier," she snapped.

Raine glanced down at her watch. It was 7:32. "But I—it's only—"

"You know perfectly well that the updated OFAC compliance report has to be finished and Fedexed by noon! And we still haven't gotten an answer from the Banque Intercontinentale Arabe about those blocked funds for the wine shipment. It's already 4:30 in the afternoon in Paris, and our distributors are drumming their fingers. Somebody has to negotiate that order for Brazilian espresso beans, and you're the only one in the office right now with halfway decent Portugese. To say nothing of the fact that the new pages of the website still aren't ready. I would appreciate it if you would take responsibility for your work, Raine. I cannot keep track of everything."

Raine muttered something apologetic, teeth clenched, and sat down, punching in the code that took her phone off voice mail.

"And another thing. Mr. Lazar wants you to serve the coffee, tea and pastries at the breakfast meeting," Harriet went on.

A jolt of terror made Raine leap to her feet. "*Me?*"

Harriet's lips pursed. "I was not looking forward to telling him you were late."

Raine's stomach fluttered with dread. "But he's never—but Stefania always—"

"He wants you," Harriet cut in. "What he wants, he gets. The coffee is already brewing, no thanks to you, and the caterers have just delivered the food. It's in the kitchen. The china and silver are already laid out in the conference room."

Stefania poked her face into Raine's cubicle. "Make sure to get the geisha girl choreography just right," she advised. "With Lazar, it's got to be aesthetically perfect. One spilled drop of coffee, and you're toast." She studied Raine with a critical eye. "And freshen up your makeup. Your left eye is smudged. Here, take my lip liner."

Raine stared down at the lip liner pencil, speechless with dismay. This was the first time Victor Lazar had publicly acknowledged her existence. She'd seen him, of course; he was impossible to miss. He swept through the office like a storm wind, scattering people in front of him and dragging them in his wake. He was as dynamic and intimidating as she remembered from her childhood, though not as tall.

The first time he'd seen her, his piercing gray eyes had flicked over her with complete disregard, leaving her weak-kneed with relief. He evidently saw no connection between his newest executive assistant and his tiny, eleven-year-old niece with the white-blond braids that he hadn't seen in seventeen years. Thank God.

His sudden interest in her now seemed sinister.

"Go, quick, Raine! The meeting was scheduled for seven forty-five!"

Harriet's razor-sharp tone galvanized her. She scurried to the kitchen, heart thudding. This was no big deal, she told herself as she unwrapped the food. She was serving coffee, croissants, bagels, mini-muffins and fruit. She would smile, look pretty and gracefully withdraw, leaving Lazar and his clients to their business. This was not rocket science. It was not brain surgery.

Oh no, piped up the sarcastic little voice in her head. *It was just her father's murderer, up close and personal. No biggie.*

She poured herself a cup of the strong, vicious brew that was always available in the staff kitchen and gulped it down so fast it scalded her mouth and throat. She had to get a backbone surgically implanted, if she really meant to go through with this. She should be pleased that Victor had noticed her. She had to get close to him if she wanted to investigate her father's death. That was why she had taken this nightmarish job, that was why she was living this surreal life. The tombstone dream had left her no other option.

For years she'd tried to unravel that hellish dream. She'd come up with dozens of logical explanations: she missed her father, had unconscious anger about his death, needed a scapegoat, et cetera. She'd studied dream psychology, gotten psychotherapy, tried creative visualization, hypnosis, yoga, every stress-reducing technique she could think of, but the dream persisted. It burned in her mind, weighing her down, derailing every effort she made to get her life on track.

A year ago she started having it every night. That was when the real desperation began. She grew dizzy, wild-eyed, terrified to go to sleep. She tried deadening herself with sleeping pills, but couldn't bear the headaches the next day. She was at her wit's end, watching her life grind to a halt—until 3 A.M. on her twenty-seventh birthday. She'd started upright in bed, chest heaving, and stared with wet, burning eyes into the pitch darkness, still feeling the cruel strength of Victor's arm clamped around her shoulders. By the time dawn lightened the windows of her room from black to charcoal gray, she had finally surrendered. The dream demanded something of her, and she could no longer say no to it. It would break her in the end if she kept trying.

She had no proof, of course. The record of events was clear and conclusive. Her father had died in a sailboat accident. Victor had been out of the country on business, then Raine's mother maintained that she and Raine had been in Italy at the time, refusing to discuss the matter further. Once, when she was sixteen, Raine had asked her mother if she believed that her first husband's death had been an accident. Her mother had slapped her hard across the face and then burst into noisy tears, pulling her shaken, bewildered daughter into her arms and begging her forgiveness.

"Of course it was an accident, honey. Of course it was," she repeated in broken tones. "Let it go. What's past is past. I'm so sorry."

Raine had never mentioned the forbidden topic again, but the silence that surrounded the past made her feel breathless and stifled. It left her so little to go on; years of running and hiding, an endless succession of false names and passports, the naked fear in her mother's voice whenever her uncle was mentioned. A lingering memory of panic and terror, tightly braided together with grief. And of course, the dream. The dream was relentless.

So here she was. In the three weeks she'd been here, she had learned exactly nothing, other than a dizzying slew of Office of Foreign Asset Control regulations, financial spreadsheet programs, container transport contract templates and website tools. She was a terrible liar and had never shown the least talent for subterfuge, but that was just too bad. She had to muddle on as best she could, fussing anxiously with her melon chunks and mini-muffins. What a fearless, audacious wild woman on the trail of truth and justice she was.

Another prickling rush of awareness raced over the surface of her skin as she was unwrapping the foil on the cream cheese. She spun around and dropped it. Cheese side down, of course.

The man she had seen in the elevator was standing in the kitchen doorway.

She swallowed, hard. She had coffee and mini-muffins to serve, she reminded herself. She did not have time to be ravished by a hungry-eyed pirate, no matter how sexy or compelling he might be. "Are you lost?" she asked politely. "Can I direct you somewhere?"

The man's hot gaze was all over her, like strong, possessive hands. "No. I can find the conference room on my own." His deep voice brushed tenderly across her nerve endings, like a slow, tingling caress.

"So you're, ah, here for the breakfast meeting," she stammered.

"Yeah." He glided into the kitchen with pantherish grace, bent down and retrieved the cream cheese. He rose up—and up, and up, towering over her five feet five inches. He took a napkin from the counter behind her, wiped off the lint that clung to the gooey wad of cheese and presented it to her. "No one will ever know," he said softly. "It'll be our little secret."

She took it, and waited for him to step back. He wasn't going to move, she realized, seconds later. On the contrary. She groped behind herself for the serving plate and somehow managed to deposit the glob of cheese without further mishap. Her heart thudded wildly.

She could smile, she urged herself desperately. She could even flirt. She was a big girl. It was allowed. But he was so close, his eyes so hot and hungry. The intensity of his masculine energy paralyzed her. She was speechless, lungs locked, unable to inhale or exhale. A hopeless cream puff.

"I'm sorry if I made you nervous in the elevator." His voice stroked her again, as soft as suede. "You took me by surprise. I forgot to be polite."

She tried to sidle away alongside the counter. "You're still not being polite," she said. "And I'm still nervous."

"Yeah?" He put both hands on the counter, trapping her in a crackling force field of masculine heat. "Well, I'm still surprised."

He leaned towards her. She wondered in a spasm of panic if he were going to kiss her, but he stopped scant inches from her hair and took a deep breath. "You smell wonderful," he muttered.

She shrank back against the counter. The condiments drawer dug into her lower back. "I don't wear perfume," she ventured bravely.

He inhaled again and sighed, his warm, fragrant breath fanning her throat. "That's why I love it. Perfume covers up the good stuff. Your hair, your skin. Fresh and sweet and hot. Like a flower in the sun."

This couldn't be happening. Sometimes her dream world seemed more substantial than the waking world, and this unspeakably bold, gorgeous man belonged in one of her more improbable dream-scapes; along with unicorns and centaurs, demons and dragons. Unfathomable creatures, unbound by mortal laws and limitations, touched by wild enchantment. Deadly dangerous.

She blinked. He was still there. Overwhelmingly so. The drawer handle still dug sharply into her back. He was very real, and not about to melt away into a puff of smoke. She had to deal with him.

"This is . . . inappropriate," she said in a soft, breathless voice. "I don't even know you. Please step back and give me some space."

He retreated with obvious reluctance. "Sorry," he said, sounding anything but apologetic. "I had to memorize it."

"Memorize what?"

"Your smell," he said, as if it were obvious.

Raine stared at him, open-mouthed, acutely conscious of the way her nipples were rubbing against the fabric of her bra, the slide of the silk blouse against her skin as breath heaved in her lungs. Her face was hot, her lips felt swollen. Her legs shook. The look in his eyes pulled at something deep inside her; a verdant, hidden place that budded and bloomed under his gaze, aching with nameless longing.

No. This longing was not nameless. She was turned on, she realized, with a jolt of horrified embarrassment. Sexually aroused by a complete stranger, right here in the staff kitchen of Lazar Import & Export, and he hadn't even touched her. This was just a dandy time for her latent, wild woman sexuality to rear its head. Her timing had always sucked.

"Ah. Mr. Mackey, I presume."

Raine spun around at the sound of Victor Lazar's cool, ironic voice. He was lounging in the kitchen doorway, taking in the scene with silver gray eyes that missed nothing.

The pirate gave him a courteous nod. "Mr. Lazar. Glad to meet you." The words and tone were polite, but the caressing roughness that had characterized his voice was gone. It was as clear and hard as glass.

Victor's smile assessed him coolly. "You've met my assistant?"

"In the elevator," the pirate said.

Victor's eyes flicked from him to Raine, lingering for an endless three seconds on her hot face. "I see," he murmured. "Very well. Since you're here . . . shall we? The others are waiting."

"Of course."

Tension throbbed in the air. The two men regarded each other, smiling identical bland, impenetrable smiles. People usually jumped at Lazar's lightest wish, but this dark stranger had his own gravitational field. He would move when it pleased him, and not before. Raine was suspended between them, afraid to move.

A faintly amused smile flitted across Victor's face. "This way, please, Mr. Mackey," he said, as if humoring a small child. "Raine, bring in breakfast, please. We have a great deal to discuss."

The pirate shot her one last, fiercely appreciative glance as he followed Lazar out of the kitchen.

No blushing or stammering allowed, she told herself sternly as she filled the silver pots with coffee and tea. No tripping over the carpet or running into doors. She had to learn to take encounters like this in stride. And while she hadn't factored a sizzling affair into her mission scenario, it wasn't necessarily such a bad idea.

That delicious, rebellious thought sent a flood of knee-wobbling panic through her. She stopped in the corridor and silently talked herself down, her arms trembling from the weight of the tray. Maybe with an act of such uncharacteristic boldness, she could prove to herself that she had the guts to act instead of being acted upon. Maybe it would be good, not just for her, but for her quest. To accomplish this impossible task, she needed to become a different person altogether. Bold, fearless, ruthless. What better place to start than her sex life? That certainly needed a massive overhaul.

She pasted a geisha girl smile onto her face and pushed open the door to the conference room with her foot. There were several people in the room besides Victor and the pirate. She smiled at each of them in turn as she poured the coffee and tea, but she was careful not to look at the pirate as she handed him his cup. Just a glimpse of his long, graceful brown fingers as he accepted it made her pulse flutter.

The conversation in the room was an indistinct wash of sound. She forced herself to focus and follow the sense of it. Any information at all could prove useful to her quest. The pirate was talking about transponders, radio frequency identification. Data collection. Smart labels and data locks and programming cycles. GPS tracking, data streaming, wireless modems. Cold, technical stuff, the type that had always flown right over her head.

But his voice was so deep and resonant and sexy. It made the back of her neck tingle, as if he were caressing it with his hands, with his lips, with his warm breath. It was incredibly hard to concentrate. Her own name jerked her to attention, making the cup she held rattle in its saucer.

". . . trust that will be convenient, Raine. Please let Harriet know," Victor was saying.

Raine gulped and laid the cup and saucer carefully down at Victor's elbow. "Let her know, ah . . . what?"

Impatience flashed across Victor's broad, handsome face. "Please pay attention. You will accompany Mr. Mackey and me on a tour of the Renton warehouses tomorrow. Be ready at three."

His face was so like her father's, at close range, but harder, more angular. His short hair was startlingly white against his olive skin.

Her father hadn't lived long enough for his hair to go white.

"Me?" she whispered.

"Is this going to be a problem?" Victor's voice was silky soft.

She shook her head quickly. "Ah, no. Of course not."

Victor smiled, and a shudder of dread raced down her spine. "Excellent," he murmured.

She murmured something acquiescent and fled, stumbling through the office cubicles until she reached the women's restroom. She hid in the furthest stall, pressed her hot face against her knees and hugged herself, trying to calm the violent trembling.

She saw her father's face as clearly as if it hadn't been seventeen years since his death. So gentle and soft-spoken. Reading her poetry, telling her stories. Showing her beautiful pictures in his monographs of Renaissance art. Teaching her to identify trees and wildflowers. He visited her in her dreams sometimes, and when he did, she woke up missing him so badly, it felt like her heart would shatter like glass under the pressure.

Get a grip already, she told herself furiously. She should be celebrating, not having a meltdown in the bathroom. This was the pirate queen's chance to strut her stuff.

But more and more, she felt like the helpless creature in her dream; swimming naked in trapped, restless circles around the limits of her transparent world. Blind to the larger implications, but still haunted by a shadow of approaching doom.

Chapter

3

"Sir? Excuse me, but there's a Mr. Crowe on the line, requesting permission to come to the island."

Victor did not turn his gaze away from the waves that lapped against the pebbled beach below the patio. He took a sip of his whiskey and savored the complex, smoky flavor. "What does he want?"

The young female attendant cleared her throat delicately. "He says it's regarding the, ah . . . heart of darkness."

A smile of satisfaction curved Victor's mouth. The perfect ending for a stimulating day. Whoever would have thought that Crowe had a poetic side? Heart of darkness, indeed. "Tell him to proceed," he said.

"Thank you, sir." The young woman retreated silently through the French doors into the house.

Victor sipped his Scotch, letting his eyes rest upon the dim silhouette of the windswept pines that adorned Stone Island. It was his favorite residence, despite the inconvenience of the eighty-minute boat ride through Puget Sound, and woe betide the person so stupid or unfortunate as to approach it uninvited. Here, in splendid privacy, he could gaze out at the Sound and contemplate the panorama of nature in all its beauty and savagery. Bald eagles and ospreys and great blue herons, dolphins and killer whales. Spectacular.

The wind was cold, daylight long gone, but he savored the pleasant burn of the fine liquor as it trickled down his throat, unwilling to go inside. He was absurdly pleased with himself. He liked the game he was playing and the element of chance that he had factored into it. His needs were changing as he aged, the need for power and control giving way to his hunger for diversion and stimulation. He must be aging backwards. Soon he would start having problems with impulse control. He raised his glass, toasting the ridiculous thought.

He looked forward to finally resolving his security problem. His patience was wearing extremely thin. Seth Mackey and his consulting firm had better be good. Rumor certainly suggested that they were. Ever since he had begun to make discreet inquiries, the name of Mackey Security Systems Design had continually cropped up. The firm was frequently used by foreign governments, government agencies, national P.I. firms, defense contractors, diplomats and famous corporate executives, and was quietly famous for its cutting edge surveillance equipment and custom designed software, as well as for demonstrated prowess at protective technical surveillance counter-measures. Best of all was Mackey's reputation for discretion, vital for Victor's purposes; as he certainly could not report the recent rash of slick, professional burglaries that had been plaguing his warehouses to the police.

The thefts themselves represented no serious economic damage to him. His profitable company could absorb a hundred times the blow without blinking. What disturbed him was the thieves' timing, precision and choice of loot; they unerringly plundered the shipments destined for his most secret and demanding clients.

It had begun some years back as a quiet import sideline, developed for the sole purpose of entertaining himself, smuggled art and antiquities and suchlike. His latest diversion was the traffic in famous murder weapons from high-profile trials, a hobby he'd fallen into almost by accident. People were willing to pay ridiculous sums for a stolen piece of violent, grisly social history. Perverse, yes, but he had always reaped big profits by taking advantage of perversity. Just another of those comforting constants in life.

One of his most recent deals had been for the hunting knife used by Anton Laarsen, the Cincinnati Slasher, on his ten-city, five state rampage. Victor had auctioned off the blade for five times what the theft had cost him in planning and manpower. It had gone to the CEO of a local pharmaceuticals firm with whom Victor often golfed, a mild-mannered, genial fellow with a sizable paunch and a passel of grandkids. Victor wondered if the man's wife was aware of the true depth of her husband's interest in deadly violence. It would be best for her if she never knew, no doubt.

Procuring such items gave him a delicious sense of having gotten away with something, a frisson of danger that kept the gray, empty feeling at bay for a little while. It was childish, perhaps, but he had reached a time in his life when he could afford to indulge himself. Or so he had thought.

In each case, he and he alone had made the arrangements for these acquisitions. Which indicated that whoever had planned and executed the extremely professional raids had access to information that could only have been obtained by electronic eavesdropping devices.

Seth Mackey's damage control plan was going to cost him. His fees were outrageous, but Victor could easily afford them. The man himself was intriguing. He was sharp, cunning and surprisingly unreadable, but Victor was a grand master at ferreting out a person's weak points. Mackey had made this glaringly obvious that morning.

Victor laughed out loud and took another sip of whiskey. Enter Lorraine Cameron, stage left. Formerly little Katya Lazar of the white-blond braids. His long-lost niece. The timing was exquisite.

The girl had surprised him. Alix, her mother, had grabbed her and run like the contemptible coward that she was after Peter's death. She'd gone to ridiculous lengths to cover their tracks, but she need not have bothered; she was no match for Victor's informational network.

Victor had no further interest in Alix, but he had followed his niece's progress with great interest. She showed potential, but had suffered from crippling shyness for much of her girlhood; and he had long ago dismissed her as an attractive but insignificant piece of fluff, content to drift from place to place, committing to nothing, achieving nothing. The fact that she had the audacity to apply for a job at Lazar Import & Export with a falsified resumé intrigued him.

There might be something strong and vibrant simmering beneath that facade of clumsy naiveté.

He wondered if Peter really was the girl's father. Given Alix's wide-ranging sexual appetites, the probability was not high, though the girl did resemble her paternal grandmother. Although now that he thought about it . . . he calculated for a moment . . . yes, it was quite possible. The girl could very well be his own daughter. Entertaining. Not that it mattered, at this point. He had sacrificed such sentimental considerations upon the altar of expediency long ago. Besides, if she were his, he would have expected more of her by now.

In any case, he would not make the same mistake with her as he had with Peter. No coddling, no spoiling. No mercy of any kind. He would temper her, bring out the proud Lazar core of her. The job had been his first test, to see if she had any stamina, and she was holding up well. She was strong in languages, a good writer, thought fast on her feet, was charming and well-spoken, and had adapted to a work schedule specifically designed to weed out the unworthy. Still, she was a nervous, cowering rabbit. Alix's doing. It would be interesting to see if he could turn her into a real woman of steel and twisting fire.

His new security consultant was certainly eager to do his part in that regard. What a piece of luck that the girl was beautiful. At least her intemperate, profligate bitch of a mother had been useful for that much. Alix had been a stunning woman in her day, and the girl surpassed her. Or would, if someone taught her how to dress.

And to think that he had actually offered her to Mackey as one of the perks of the job after the meeting this morning. Obliquely, of course, but the hungry flash of comprehension in the younger man's eyes told him everything he needed to know. He chuckled, feeling impish. Victor knew he was being a diabolical, manipulative bastard, but a man did what he must to keep things interesting; and besides, he was doing the girl a favor. Mackey was sure to prove a more inspiring sexual partner for her than the worthless specimens she had chosen so far for herself. She seemed to have inherited her father's abysmal taste in lovers. Poor Peter.

Tomorrow he would leave them to their own devices, and trust to lust. There was no way to predict or control what would happen. Thank God for the element of chance. Without it he would have slit his wrists from boredom long ago.

He would have liked to film the seduction, but it would be more logistically complicated than it was worth, in addition to being in somewhat poor taste. The girl was his niece, after all. He would concede her a measure of privacy. At least for now.

The situation was fortuitous, even aside from pure entertainment value. He needed leverage with the mysterious Mackey before moving forward with such a sensitive project, particularly after the unfortunate events ten months ago that had culminated in the death of the undercover FBI agent Jesse Cahill. He had barely managed to salvage the situation, though not in time to avoid considerable embarrassment in certain business circles. Victor loathed embarrassment.

Kurt Novak, in particular, was still nursing a grudge—but the "heart of darkness" that Crowe was bringing to him right now would change all that in the blink of an eye. It was the final detail of the plan that would put Novak right back where Victor wanted him. He smiled dreamily at the thought, looking up at the ragged clouds that scudded across the moonlit sky.

The French doors clicked open, and the attendant cleared her throat. "Mr. Crowe is here," she murmured respectfully.

The wind was picking up. Gusts of wind sent dead leaves and pine needles leaping and swirling across the flagstones like a display of naughty poltergeists, the perfect note for the transaction that was about to take place. "Send him out," Victor ordered.

Moments later, a shadow materialized behind his chair. Crowe was not his real name. Victor didn't even know his real name, nor was he acquainted with anyone who did. He was the kind of man one contacted when one wished to arrange something complicated, discreet, and extremely illegal, such as the theft of a notorious murder weapon. He was the most reliable agent Victor had ever used—and the most expensive.

He was clad in a long, olive drab raincoat, his face shadowed by a broad-brimmed hat and mirrored sunglasses, even at dusk. What little that could be seen of his face was cold and angular. He placed a steel carrying case by Victor's chair, straightened up, and waited. There was no need to check the authenticity of the item he was delivering. His reputation was enough.

The pieces on the game board in Victor's mind shifted, taking on an aggressive new formation. "The money will be transferred into the usual account tonight," he said calmly, hiding his excitement.

Crowe's shadow silently withdrew. Victor reached for the case and put it on his lap. The Corazon. The heart of darkness. He could literally feel the thing pulsing between his hands, as if he were Aladdin holding an imprisoned genie. An enlightened Aladdin, who understood power, desire and violence. And Kurt Novak was his genie.

He snapped it open. The Walther PPK was still in the tagged plastic bag into which it had been placed for the crime lab, still soiled with fingerprinting dust. Its value could not be expressed in dollars, since its price involved calling in a lifetime's worth of threats and favors.

Past, present and future were as one for an object. The famous face of the luckless Belinda Corazon floated in his mind's eye. The cold lump of steel on his lap was locked forever in an endless moment of life-stopping violence. It took a person like him, tormented by lucid dreams, sensitive to the dynamics of power, to read the gun's signature.

It was burdensome to be one of two people in the world who knew the true identity of Belinda Corazon's killer. He felt a warning flash of melancholy, and snapped the case closed, determined to forestall it. He had no reason to feel guilty, he reminded himself. La Corazon had been an acquaintance, not a friend. Like many other public figures, she had attended Victor's lavish and popular parties.

One year ago he and Novak had concluded an immensely profitable business deal, and in the subsequent flush of mutual goodwill, Novak had persuaded him to arrange a private introduction to Belinda. That was the extent of his guilt. The sum total of his responsibility.

Somehow, Novak had actually managed to seize the frivolous girl's interest. Maybe it was his gift of a triple strand of black South Sea pearls, maybe it was Novak's own poisonous magnetism.

Women's preferences were unfathomable. In any case, his charm had eventually palled upon her, and La Corazon had thought she could dismiss her swain as easily as she had all the others. She had paid with her life for her error.

Victor took a cigarette out of his antique silver holder and made a languid gesture with his hand. The doors opened and the attendant hastened to his side. She lit his cigarette with some difficulty in the blustery wind, and stood quietly, awaiting dismissal or further orders.

His practiced eye roamed over the young woman's face and body with leisurely thoroughness. He varied them often, to stave off boredom, and this one was quite new. He studied the girl's high, full breasts, her slender, athletic figure. She was a brunette with long, straight chestnut hair and, tilted hazel eyes. Enticing. The cold had caused the girl's nipples to harden. They were dark and taut, clearly visible against her clinging shirt. The wind whipped her hair, tangling it across her lovely face. He gazed at the girl's full red lips, halfway tempted to—no.

Not tonight. It was rare for him to feel this wide-awake, humming awareness. He had not felt so vibrant and alive since Peter's death. It was a moment to be savored in solitude.

He smiled pleasantly at the young woman, and struggled for a moment to remember her name. "Thank you, Mara. That will be all."

She gave him a dazzling smile and withdrew. She was lovely, really. Perhaps tomorrow he would indulge. For now, he would simply float upon the grace of this euphoria, contemplating the new pieces on his game board and how best to move them.

The game was complex, and long in the making. He knew so many intimate details about city and state officials, businesspeople and politicians that he was virtually immune to the law. And his generous donations, gifts, endowments and campaign contributions did smooth things over nicely. Victor Lazar, pillar of the community, twinkling-eyed philanthropist and thrower of fabulous parties. The faint, unsavory taint to the Lazar name just made the invitations to his parties that much more sought after. People loved to feel naughty. Yet another of life's comforting constants. The fête that would take place at Stone Island on Saturday night could prove more entertaining than ever, with these unpredictable new game pieces in play.

Yes, he had badly needed a challenge, and so did the lovely, untried Raine. She was an unknown, even to herself. It was high time she leaned the full scope of her new duties.

Seth Mackey. So that was his name. Raine mouthed it silently to herself for the hundredth time as she let herself into the house. The office had buzzed with gossip all day, and she had sucked it up like a sponge. Whenever Harriet's ramrod back was turned, the secretaries had carried on about Seth Mackey; his looks, his style, his smoldering eyes. Evidently he was a hotshot security consultant who was going to revolutionize the inventory system with radio frequency ID technology. She'd stayed an extra hour at work trying to figure out how to fit the promotional info on the new security feature into the recently updated website pages.

She unbuttoned her coat, and noticed an envelope in the mail slot. It was from the Severin Bay Coroner's Office. Her heart leaped into her throat. The first thing she had done when she arrived in Seattle was to write and request a copy of her father's autopsy. She opened it with hands that trembled.

It was just as she had been told; a ruling of accidental death by drowning. She scanned the pages, trying to stay calm and detached. Organs and tissue samples, chemical and toxicological analysis, aspirated fluids from the stomach, thorax, bladder, vitreous fluid, and more. She stared down at the sheaf of paper, feeling cold and flat and very alone. The report revealed nothing, suggested nothing. The MD who had signed it was Serena Fischer. She made a mental note of the name.

The phone rang, and she winced. None of her friends had this number. It could only be her mother. She reached for the receiver. "Hello?"

"Well. At last I catch you at home."

The hurt, petulant tone in her mother's voice made her stomach clench. "Hello, Alix."

"I've been calling and calling, honey, and you're never home!

I've left more messages than I can count, but of course you don't call back. What on earth are you doing all day, every day?"

Raine dropped her purse on the floor with a quiet sigh. After a fourteen-hour day in the Lazar Import & Export salt mines, the last thing she wanted was a conversation with her mother. She shrugged off her coat and hung it, thinking of excuses and explanations. "Oh, all kinds of things. I, ah, went on a boat trip the other day. It rained, of course, but it was beautiful. I've done some shopping. Job interviews. And I've made some nice new friends."

"Any nice new gentleman friends?"

The hot caress of Seth Mackey's breath against her throat rose up in her memory, intensely clear. She swallowed back a giggle. Seth Mackey might be many things, but she bet that "gentleman" was not one of them. Which was fine. If she got a chance with him, she didn't intend to act like a lady. "Um, no gentlemen friends," she mumbled.

"Ah." Her mother sounded disappointed, but unsurprised. "Well, I don't suppose you're trying very hard. God knows you never do."

There was an expectant pause, as her mother waited for Raine's stock response, the signal to touch off a tedious and all too familiar argument. Raine was stubbornly silent, too tired to play the game.

Alix Cameron let out an impatient sigh. "I cannot fathom why you chose Seattle," she complained. "So backwards. Always gray and damp."

"London is gray and damp, too," Raine pointed out. "And you haven't been here in decades, Mother. Seattle is very hip."

The older woman gave a doubtful harrumph. "Please don't call me that, Raine. You know it makes me feel old."

Raine bit her lip at the familiar reproof. It had been a never-ending challenge to remember her mother's changing names over the years. She'd been grateful when Alix had decided to risk going back to her original name. Much simpler than getting used to a new one every couple of months.

Raine stared down at the autopsy report that lay on the telephone table, and made a swift decision. She took a deep breath, stomach fluttering. "Alix, I've been meaning to ask you something . . . "

"Yes, honey?"

"Where is Dad buried?"

There was a horrified silence on the other end of the line. "God in heaven, Lorraine." Alix's voice sounded strangled.

"It's a reasonable question. I just want to pay my respects. Leave some flowers."

Raine waited for so long that she began to wonder if the line had been disconnected. When Alix finally spoke, her voice sounded very old. "I don't know."

Raine's jaw dropped. "You don't—"

"We were out of the country, remember? We never went back. How could I know?"

How could you *not* know, Raine whispered inwardly. She pressed her hand against the heavy knot in her stomach. "I see."

"I suppose you could find out through public registries," her mother said vaguely. "Call the cemeteries. There must be a way."

"Yes, there must be," Raine echoed.

There was a choked, sniffling sound, and her mother spoke again, her voice fogged with tears. "Honey, we were in Positano, on the Amalfi Coast. Remember the Rossini kids you played with on the beach? Gaetano and Enza? That's where we were when we got the news. Call Mariangela Rossini. She was the one who had to call the doctor to sedate me when I heard. Call her, if you don't believe me."

"Of course I believe you," Raine soothed. "It's just that I keep having this dream—"

"Oh, God! Don't tell me you're getting dreams and reality mixed up like you did when you were little! That drove me crazy with worry! Do not tell me that, Lorraine!"

"All right," Raine said tightly. "I'm not telling you that."

"Those are dreams, Lorraine! Not real! Do you hear me?"

Raine flinched and held the phone away from her ear. "Yes," she repeated. "Just dreams. Calm down, Alix."

Alix sniffled loudly. "Tell me you haven't gone to Seattle to root around in old skeletons, honey! Let the past go. You're such a bright girl, so much potential! Tell me you're moving ahead, looking forward!"

"I'm moving ahead and looking forward," Raine said dutifully.

"Don't you dare get smart with me, young lady."

"Sorry," she muttered.

It took several careful minutes to soothe her mother's anxiety and get off the phone. When she finally hung up, she clutched her abdomen and abandoned the idea of making a sandwich. As usual, lying made her stomach clench into a tight, aching ball, but there was no alternative. She was engaging in the ultimate transgression. She was going to dig up all the skeletons she could, if she had to rent a backhoe to do it.

She shrugged off her coat and hung it up, pondering her mother's words. The days following her father's death were a grief-stricken blur in her memory, and by the time she started paying attention to her surroundings again, she had been in a new country with a new name. But one thing was certain—she did not remember getting that news in Positano. Surely that was a moment that should have been etched in her mind like engraved stone, every detail vivid and immutable.

She had never seen her father's real grave. Maybe seeing that it was different from the dream image would take the menace out of the dream.

Then again, what if the reality were identical?

Her stomach flip-flopped at the implications, and she shoved the creepy thought aside. This was no time to whip herself into a frenzy. She had too little nerve as it was. She had to concentrate on the positive. The encounter with Seth Mackey and Victor had finally set things in motion. This was good. This was progress. She had to decide what to wear tomorrow.

More to the point, she had to decide what to *do* tomorrow.

The excitement that surged inside her was so strong that she jumped up, laughing out loud. She went into the bedroom and stared searchingly into the mirror on the armoire, trying to imagine what Seth Mackey saw when he looked at her. Something he wanted, evidently, but she had a hard time imagining what it was. All she saw was plain old Raine, looking pale and spooked.

It was stupid and ill-timed to fall into lust right now, poised as she was on the edge of disaster, but hey, rotten timing and poor judgment had characterized her love life ever since it began. Look at Frederick Howe, and Juan Carlos.

Those years of traveling had not been conducive to forming friendships or developing social skills. Eventually, Alix met and married Hugh Cameron, a stolid Scottish businessman. She and Raine settled in London with him, but by then the damage was done; Raine was painfully shy. The boys in her schools would have nothing to do with the tongue-tied, bespectacled girl with the tottering armful of novels.

The situation did not improve even when she went back to the States for college, and her unclaimed virginity began to weigh heavily upon her. Shortly after she turned twenty-four, she ran into Frederick Howe in Paris. He was a business associate of her stepfather's, a burly Englishman in his early thirties, pleasant and polite. He took her out to dinner, where he talked nonstop about himself. Still, he'd seemed nice, certainly safe and non-threatening. After dinner, she had taken a deep breath and let him escort her back to her tiny little rented room.

It had proved to be a huge mistake. He had been clumsy and rough, crushingly heavy on top of her, his breath sour with garlic and wine. It finished almost before it began, which under the circumstances was a blessing, since it hurt, a lot. And while she was in the bathroom washing up, he left the flat without saying goodbye.

It had taken her eighteen months after that humiliation to work up the nerve to try again. She had met Juan Carlos during a summer studying Spanish in Barcelona. He'd been playing Bach on his cello in the park; slender and beautiful, with melting brown eyes and curly Byronic locks, dressed to kill in Gucci and Prada. She was smitten with his elegance, his air of sensitivity. So different from the stolid Frederick, just the thing to soothe her bruised romantic sensibilities.

But the moment to consummate their passion was never quite right for Juan Carlos. She'd been patient with his reluctance, coaxing and reassuring him, bolstering his ego. Finally he confessed to her that he suspected he was gay.

That summer she forged a deep and lasting friendship with him. He credited her for giving him the courage to confront the truth about his sexuality, which was all very well and good; she loved him tenderly and wished him happiness with all her heart. But it left her exactly where she'd been before. Restless and confused. Climbing the walls.

Shortly after that summer, the tombstone dream began to intensify. Her pent-up sexual energy was promptly relegated to second place on her list of problems, and then forgotten altogether.

Until now. It had made a spectacular comeback, at the worst possible time. It was maddening. All her life she had been buffeted about by external events that were hopelessly beyond her control. Now she was buffeted by internal forces that were even more frightening. Her fears, her dreams, her pulse-pounding reaction to Seth Mackey.

She took off her jacket and hung it up. Fear could be faced and overcome, she told herself bracingly, as she unhooked the skirt. She was doing her best to deal with the dreams. And as far as Seth Mackey was concerned, well, that was beyond fear. He belonged to the realm of unicorns and centaurs, demons and dragons. Where even she might find herself magically transformed.

She unbuttoned her blouse and threw it onto the chair, staring into the mirror as she pulled the pins out of her hair. She really should try not to lose more weight. She was starting to look puny. Tomorrow she would put more cover-up on her undereye circles, and deepen the blusher. She shook her hair out of the braid, began to yank off the stretch lace chemise—and stopped. She tugged it back down into place, and thought about Seth Mackey's eyes. Heat rushed up into her face. There was going to be no need for blusher tomorrow.

She smiled a sultry, inviting smile into the mirror. She leaned over and tousled her hair, teasing volume into it with her fingers, and flung it back over her shoulders, letting a few locks tumble across her face. The untamed "queen of the jungle" look. A little lipstick would help, maybe. Something glossy and moist. She pouted her lips out as she pulled up the chemise, wriggling sensuously as she tugged it off. She held it out, let it dangle from her fingertips and drop to the carpet.

Now the pantyhose. They were all wrong. She needed thigh-high gartered hose, so she could sit on the edge of a chair, unclasp her stockings and slide them slowly down over her thighs while the pirate watched, his eyes tracing lines of sweet fire across her skin.

As it was, she had to bend over and peel them off, trying not to trip as she tugged them off her ankles. Probably a more experienced woman could make that look sexy, but not her. And her lingerie was tragically dull. Her generous breasts had always made her self-conscious, so she used minimizing underwire bras that made her feel more contained and less conspicuous. For the first time, she wanted something deep-cut and frilly, with lots of cleavage popping out.

Oh, well. She was new at this femme fatale business. Like any other skill, it was bound to take some time to perfect.

She cupped her breasts in the mirror, imagining Seth behind her, his hands sliding over her belly, then cradling her breasts, feeling their softness and heft. She imagined the heat of his breath against her throat, the rasp of his beard stubble as he kissed and tongued her neck and shoulder. Then *poof*, he was in front of her, bending over her chest, his tongue plunging between her breasts, licking the deep, shadowy cleft. She unhooked her bra, imagining herself bared to his sight.

It was so vivid. The scene unrolled behind her closed eyes with an almost lurid brilliance. She could actually hear his growl of appreciative pleasure, she could feel the heat and suckling wetness of his mouth as he kissed and licked her, his tongue swirling and tasting. His mouth fastened over her nipple, no longer pale pink, but flushed to deep raspberry, and hard. She wondered what kind of lover Seth was. Slow and languorous, or passionate and urgent. She wondered if he would do to her any of those things she had only read about in romance novels and erotica.

She pushed off her panties, letting them fall to her ankles. Her hand slid between her thighs as the fantasy swirled on, unstoppable; him sinking to his knees in front of her, nuzzling her navel, pressing his face against her mound. Breathing in her scent. Hot and sweet, like a flower in the sun, he had said. The words echoed in her mind, making her sigh with longing.

She touched herself, following her dream lover's movements. His hands teasing, insinuating themselves into the humid folds of slick, hot female flesh. Circling his tongue around the stiff, engorged bud of her clitoris. Her eyes popped open with a startled gasp. Usually her fantasies were rose-tinted and tenderly indistinct, but this one was urgent and hungry and explicitly detailed. It had a will of its own, and she followed it helplessly, staring at herself with wide, frightened eyes. Her face was bright pink, her lips red and parted, eyes shadowy and dilated. She looked wanton, with her panties around her ankles, one hand caressing her breasts, the other cupping her sex.

She looked like a woman half-desperate with desire.

She kicked off her panties and walked carefully on rubbery legs to the bed. She was almost frightened by the restless ache between her thighs, the wild, whimpering frustration. Need pulsed in her body, heavy and hot. She fell back against the pillows and writhed against the velvety flannel sheets, rubbing her sensitized skin eagerly against the caressing nap of the soft fabric.

Her legs fell open, and her fingers slid eagerly into the moisture between her legs. She imagined a barrage of sensual images, all the possibilities, all the positions. Maybe he would open her legs wide and press his face against her sex, sucking her clitoris with slow, tender skill. Maybe his tongue would slide up and down the soft folds of her labia, and then thrust deep into the hot, quivering core of her.

She saw him mounting her, felt the heat, the weight of his hard, graceful body pinning her down. She imagined him entering her with one swift lunge, and then the glorious friction as he slid slowly in and out of her. She would clutch his shoulders and cling to him as he thrust deeper and harder, his steely arms holding her tightly, his eyes gazing into hers, seeing her soul unveiled, incandescent, utterly his.

That pushed her over the top. She arched on the bed with a sharp cry, and came; an endless, shivering cascade of sensation, more intense than any orgasm she had ever experienced. She tugged the sheet across her limp, trembling body and slid into an exhausted sleep.

That night she dreamed once again that she was swimming naked in the glass aquarium. Her hair swirled around her, bright and luminous. But the dream changed before her eyes. The walls of the aquarium dissolved, colored pebbles became glittering sand, fake coral sprigs became huge, towering structures that glowed in the underwater gloom. The plastic castle was gone, but the sunken galleon was real, encrusted with algae and barnacles.

Whatever protection those glass walls had afforded her was gone. She'd wanted to swim with the big fish, and her wish had been granted. The feeling of limitless freedom that swelled up inside of her almost made up for the looming sense of danger as she swam deeper into the fathomless depths of the ocean like a tiny, flickering beam of light.

Chapter

4

It was pure dumb luck that Seth was all alone when he watched the sex show. If any of the McCloud brothers had happened to see it, he would have had to kill them.

She'd been asleep for almost an hour, but still he stared at the screen, his eyes still wide and burning, his cock as hard as granite. If he hadn't personally installed all the equipment, if he hadn't had reason to be almost certain that his surveillance was undetected, he would've concluded that the whole scene had been staged deliberately for him. Why else would she perform in front of the camera in a way precisely calibrated to drive him out of his fucking mind?

Except for the fact that he would bet body parts that Raine Cameron didn't know how to fake. That orgasm had been all too real.

Dear God, it had been way too long. Even before Jesse's death, his sex life had been somewhat problematic. His sexual appetites were prodigious, and he was very good in bed; he could say that with total assurance, and without vanity. What he wasn't good at was saying all the things that women wanted a guy to say, before, during and after. One ex-lover had informed him, immediately prior to dumping him, that he lacked basic social skills. He hadn't bothered to deny it. He blew it every time by telling it exactly like it was, which frequently caused women to storm off in a huff, drastically reducing or completely ceasing further sexual availability.

It was a pain in the ass, but it hadn't bothered him as much as it probably should have. He had more pressing things to occupy his mind. He was wealthy, relatively good-looking, and could be charming when he put his mind to it. If a woman stormed off, no big deal. There were plenty of others waiting to step into the vacancy.

Then Lazar and Novak had murdered his brother, and he had very suddenly forgotten that sex existed. He'd been sort of relieved by the frozen, floating feeling. Like being a disembodied brain. Not exactly peace, but close enough. It was good that his body had been cooperating in directing all of his energy into his investigation. Then Raine showed up, and all of a sudden his libido was making up for lost time.

The cell phone rang, and he jerked in his chair as if he'd received an electric shock. He checked the number on the display, disgusted to note that his hand was trembling.

Connor McCloud. Great. Just the guy to cheer him up. He enabled the digital speech spectrum inversion, punched in the code that decrypted Connor's transmission and hit "talk" with a grunt of resignation. "Yeah."

"I just got word that the gun from the Corazon murder went missing yesterday," Connor said, without preamble.

Seth waited for more explanatory info, but none was forthcoming. "Corazon?" he prompted.

Connor made an impatient sound. "You ever watch the news?"

"Uh . . ."

"Never mind," Connor snapped. "Gorgeous supermodel got wasted in her waterfront penthouse last August. Does that ring a bell?"

"Oh. Her. Yeah." Vaguely. He'd seen her beautiful face splashed across every magazine in the supermarket check-out lines. Belinda Corazon, 1980–2002. Christ, she was young. Only a zombie could have missed the Corazon murder. He almost qualified, but not quite. "What does a dead supermodel have to do with us?"

"Pay attention, for God's sake. Remember when I told you that Jesse and I were following up on rumors that Lazar was brokering stolen murder weapons from famous trials?"

Seth grimaced. "I can't believe people really buy stuff like that."

"Believe it. The world is full of sick bastards who have way too much money. The point is, I think there's a good chance that our boy commissioned that theft. And I can guess who he got it for, too."

"Who?" Seth demanded, impatient.

But Connor was being coy and mysterious. "Where's Lazar?"

"Stone Island," Seth responded without hesitation. He had personally planted a powerful, remote-controlled microwave transponder in every vehicle in Victor's fleet. Lazar's silver Mercedes had arrived at the marina at 6:59; the Colbit at the dock verified that he'd boarded the boat, and the transponder he had planted on the boat indicated that it had arrived at the island at 8:19.

"You kept track of him all day?"

"Yeah," Seth replied. "In the office till 2:45, two-hour power lunch at the Hunt Club with the Laurent Group, a meeting with Embry and Crowe from 5:30 to 6:35, then straight to the marina."

"Anybody else go to the island tonight?"

"I don't know," Seth said.

"What do you mean, you don't know? You planted cameras there, didn't you? Oh, hold on, now I get it. You were checking out Barbie's dream house instead, huh?"

"Fuck you," Seth said, through gritted teeth.

"Christ, Mackey. You sex-crazed bonehead. Are you with me on this or not?"

"I can't watch the island in real time," Seth snarled. "It's eighty-five miles away. I don't have portable power sources that can transmit that distance for more than a couple of days at a time, and security out there is too tight to sucker-up off the local power. If I want to know who came to the fucking island, I have to go out there in person, gather the data, bring it back and process it."

Connor clucked his tongue. "My, my, aren't we defensive."

"Like I said before, McCloud—"

"Yeah, yeah. Fuck me. I heard you the first time. Get your ass out there and get that data. We need to know if Lazar had a visitor between nine and ten. That would square with what my source told me."

"What else did your source tell you?" Seth demanded.

"Curious, curious," Connor taunted.

"Don't be an asshole," Seth snapped.

Connor made a snorting sound that could have been a laugh. "OK. Get this. Novak had a thing for her."

"For Corazon?" Seth was incredulous. "No way. She was too famous for a sewer rat like him. He would never have risked it."

"He risked it, evidently. Very hush-hush, of course. He sent her the crown jewels of fallen empires, solid gold death masks of famous pharoahs, the Shroud of fucking Turin, you name it. He had it bad."

"And Lazar was the guy who procured that shit for him?"

"Bingo," Connor said in approving tones. "You're a smart boy, when you're not zoning out in Barbie-land."

Seth was too intrigued to respond to the jibe. "So why weren't you guys using her as bait?"

"It was a secret affair. We didn't know, and now she's dead, so get off my case, OK?"

"I'm not on your case." Seth drummed his fingers against the table, fascinated. "So Novak was the one who really wasted her?"

"Here's another juicy detail to brighten up your night, Mackey. I'll do a recap for you, since you don't watch the news. Remember Corazon's boyfriend, the ice hockey star Ralph Kinnear? He was found at the scene, naked and covered with her blood, with his fingerprints all over the murder weapon. Didn't remember a goddamn thing."

"Ouch," Seth murmured.

"Yeah. Looked really bad for the poor schmuck, but guess what? Somebody called Kinnear's defense team right away. Gave them an anonymous tip to check his face for microscopic flakes of glass from an exploding ampule of soporific gas."

Seth digested that information for a moment. "That's weird."

"Sure was. They found the glass flakes and they found traces of the drug in his stomach, too. Ralphie's off the hook, thanks to the mystery caller. And now the gun's gone missing. Weirder and weirder."

"So you're thinking that Lazar stole that gun to sell to Novak? As a memento of his lost love? Christ."

"Yeah, it's romantic, huh? Get that data, Mackey, and let me know if Lazar had a visitor tonight."

The click of the broken connection set Seth's teeth on edge. He almost called the bastard back, just to tell him not to issue any more orders. Problem was, McCloud would probably laugh in his face. He was going straight to the island anyway. No time for stupid stuff.

That, of course, caused his mind to veer back to the most stupid stuff of all. He looked back at the sleeping woman in the monitor. Maybe Lazar had ordered her to seduce him, and she was just getting into character. That would fit with what Lazar had said after the meeting this morning—how did the bastard put it? About the mixing of business and pleasure. How the charming Raine would be glad to help him find the perfect balance, if he liked. *If he liked.* A laugh jerked out of him, so rusty from disuse that it sounded more like a cough. Lazar had seen just exactly how much he "liked." And that sucked.

It was well known that Lazar got off on providing sexual entertainment for friends and business associates. It bound them to him and gave him power over them. He had wondered what he would do if Lazar tried to tempt him that way.

Well, now he knew. Having his nose rubbed in the truth had put him in a savage, pissed-off mood all day. Raine Cameron was no innocent fairy-tale princess waiting to be rescued. His romantic fantasies were dashed.

It was better to face reality all in one bitter lump. He could no more refuse an offer to fuck Raine Cameron, no matter what she was, no matter what the terms, than he could stop breathing. Score one point for Lazar, he conceded grimly. And if he had to lose a point to that manipulative prick, he'd damn well better make it worth his while.

Now that he thought about it, the set-up was liberating. He would pull her down off her pedestal and fuck her brains out. Clear the fog of lust from his brain. He was free to indulge himself without the slightest guilt. No obligations, no courtship rituals, none of that tedious man/woman stuff he didn't have the time or energy for. He could even expect a certain professional expertise on her part, given the circumstances. That was going to be interesting. In fact, he was getting hard again, just thinking about it. Hard and hot . . . and furious.

Damn. The hotter he got, the angrier he felt. Not the cold, purposeful feeling that spurred him to avenge Jesse. This was restless and maddening, swirling in his brain like a red fog. This kind of anger was bad news. It altered judgment. It caused errors. It started fires.

He had to play it icy cold, and wait for the ideal revenge plot to reveal itself to him. Sooner or later he would get the perfect opportunity to destroy all three men responsible for Jesse's murder. Already it was an excellent sign that, out of the scant handful of qualified TSCM consulting firms that existed, Lazar had chosen him. Seth had been hoping for that, working towards it, but not counting on it.

He didn't know yet exactly what the perfect revenge would look like, but he would know it when he saw it. He was used to living in uncertainty. He'd grown up in it. Home territory.

He was grateful for the task of sneaking out to Stone Island. That would calm him down like nothing else could. The wall of security that surrounded the place was a refreshing challenge, even for him. It brought back memories of all those counterespionage missions back in his stint with the Army Rangers. Kearn, his business partner and number one techno-genius, had not yet completely solved the energy source problem for the long-range cams, so some lucky bastard always got to sneak into the sites for data retrieval. Seth didn't mind the task. In fact, he loved it. So much so that he was going to be genuinely sorry when Kearn invented the inevitable solution. Those moments sneaking around on the edge of disaster were the only real peace that he had; when past and future collapsed and he operated on pure instinct. Utterly in the present moment, untroubled by painful memories or emotions. He craved those moments the way other people craved sleep.

In fact, he liked it way too much. He knew it. Hank and Jesse had known it, too. They had tried to save him, but now they were both gone, and he was past saving.

He stared at the sleeping woman on the screen, jaw clenched. *Get your beauty rest, babe,* he urged her silently. *Tomorrow is going to be a day that you will never, ever forget.*

He started gathering up the equipment he would need to make the electronic assault on Stone Island, but his eye kept straying back to the monitor. Her white shoulder was completely exposed now. The sheet had fallen down to the curve of her slender waist. He wanted to pull the sheet up and put a blanket over her.

She was going to get chilled, sleeping uncovered like that.

"One second, please," Raine pleaded, typing desperately on the laptop. "If you're going to switch from French to German, I need to switch settings for a new set of diacritical markings. It'll take just a moment."

Victor sighed as he leaned back against the plush seat of the limo, a faint look of annoyance flashing across his face. He sipped his drink, crossed his leg and tapped his Gucci-shod foot impatiently.

Raine clicked "German" in the languages list, called up a new document and poised her fingers over the keys, hoping Victor wouldn't notice the tremor in her hands. "Go ahead."

But Victor did not resume dictating. He stared at her, his eyes sharp and penetrating. It took all of her dwindling nerve to meet his gaze. Forty minutes of close proximity with her charismatic uncle would be a challenge even if she weren't secretly plotting his downfall.

"It's rare for an American to be fluent in so many languages," he commented.

Raine blinked. "I, uh, spent a lot of time in Europe when I was young," she stammered.

"Ah, really? Where?"

She had prepared for this question, and had decided that there was no reason not to tell the truth whenever possible. "First in France, near Lyon. Then Nice for a while, and Holland, with lots of stops in between. We were in Florence for a couple of years, and then Switzerland. Then London."

"Ah. Were your parents in the foreign service?"

Why the hell wouldn't he start dictating again? Why did he have to focus those piercing eyes on her now, when she was all alone with him? "Um . . . no," she faltered. "My mother really liked to travel."

"And your father? Did he enjoy traveling as well?"

She took a deep, unsteady breath. *Keep it simple, keep it true,* she reminded herself. "My father died when I was very young."

"Ah. I'm sorry."

She nodded a brief acknowledgment, hoping to God that he would start dictating again and leave her be.

He did not. He examined her face with a dissatisfied frown. "Your spectacles. Are you capable of performing your duties without them?"

The non sequitur bewildered her. "I, uh, suppose so. I'm nearsighted, so I only really need them for long distance viewing—"

"Your vision problems are of absolutely no interest to me. Kindly do not wear those glasses in my presence again."

Raine stared at him. "My . . . you don't like my glasses?"

"Just so. They are hideous. Contacts would be acceptable." He smiled, pleasant and magnanimous.

She forced herself to close her mouth. Maybe this was a perverse psychological test. No normal executive assistant would ever submit to such an inappropriate, invasive demand—unless she were a gutless creampuff, of course. But in Victor's world, there was no "normal." He was like a black hole, bending the familiar world out of recognition.

He waited, tapping his foot, eyebrow raised.

She had stopped using her contacts and gotten these hideous glasses for the specific purpose of keeping Victor from noticing any resemblance to her mother. She took off the glasses and tucked them slowly into her purse. The world blurred and swam. The limo came to a stop, and her heart leaped into her throat.

She closed the computer and got out of the limo. She knew they were in the warehouse parking lot, but all she could see was a blur of hulking gray squares against a blinding white sky. The air smelled of petroleum and damp concrete.

She felt him before she saw him, as she had in the elevator and the kitchen, and her blurred vision intensified the shivering rush of awareness. Memories of last night's unhinged sexual fantasies spun through her mind. All her senses opened up like thirsty flowers.

The tall, dark figure moved towards them and coalesced into Seth Mackey, casually elegant in black jeans, a dark gray sweater, a black leather jacket. He was close enough now so she could see the loose waffle weave of his sweater, the beard shadow on his angular jaw. His eyes flicked over her dismissively, but she felt the strength of his interest like a hidden riptide.

The two men greeted each other, and he held out his hand to her. His face showed no trace of yesterday's teasing warmth, and his dark eyes were shadowed and grim. Probably just focused on business, she told herself. She ignored the apprehension that fluttered in her belly and pasted on a bright, generic smile.

The touch of his big, warm hand was a shock of hot recognition. It lasted no more than two seconds, and by the time he let go of her hand, her generic smile had undergone a massive meltdown and her heart was tripping madly over itself. The two men were striding towards the warehouse, and she scurried after them.

Victor turned around. "Wait here, Raine, if you please."

She blinked, and looked around at the vast, empty lot. "But I—"

"My conversation with Mr. Mackey is confidential," he said gently.

"Then why did you bring me along?" She regretted the words as soon as they left her mouth.

Victor's face hardened. "My commuting time is valuable. I maximize it whenever possible by bringing secretarial support. Kindly do not ask me to explain my decisions to you ever again. Is that clear?"

She blushed furiously and nodded, acutely conscious of Seth Mackey's quiet, intense presence, listening to Victor's reprimand. She watched them walk away, feeling helpless and foolish. Damn. The pirate queen would have thought of some quick and clever way to eavesdrop on their confidential conversation. She certainly would never have been intimidated into taking off her glasses.

Then again, the pirate queen would have been shrewd enough to stow her contacts in her purse. She knew how to plan ahead. She was bold, but crafty. Brave, but patient. She could fight when the need arose, but she didn't waste her strength or resources in useless battles. And she wasn't afraid to seize what she wanted, whether it be truth and justice, or a tall, dark, and sexy security consultant.

Raine sat down in the back seat of the limo with a sigh, and composed herself to wait. Seth Mackey didn't know it yet, but he was about to be seduced by a pirate queen.

*   *   *

"The first step is to conduct a detailed vulnerability analysis and threat assessment," Seth said. "That involves inspecting every part of your facility to identify weaknesses. Locks, doors, alarms, the telephone system, network and computer security, everything."

Lazar frowned slightly and looked around the huge warehouse. "How long will it take? My security problems are very pressing."

Seth shrugged. "It depends. At least a few days to cover the corporate headquarters and all the warehouses. Do you want to include your private residences in the threat assessment? I recommend it."

Lazar's eyes narrowed. "Let me think about that."

Seth gave the murdering bastard his very best, ultra-friendly Mr. Professional smile. "When we get down to the actual debugging, I'll call my crew for back-up. We'll start with the radio frequency sweep, then the wire and conductor check. Then we'll do a detailed physical search for hardwired mikes and remote shutdown transmitters."

Lazar held open the back door of the warehouse, gesturing for Seth to exit first. "And how do you propose to maintain secrecy under those conditions?"

The man's condescending tone made Seth feel like he was chewing glass. He turned and waited for Lazar to draw abreast of him. No way was he turning his back on that treacherous asshole. "That's your judgment call," he said. "We tend to find remote switchable devices more easily if we sweep during business hours, but your adversary could switch off the remotes, or even vaporize the microphone elements with charged, high-voltage capacitators, if he's onto your survey. It's a toss-up. Think about it."

"I see," Lazar murmured. "I certainly shall think about it."

"When it comes to the RF sweep, our spectrum analyzer is the best I've used," Seth went on. "And I've used them all."

"Oh, I'm sure your firm is everything it claims to be."

Seth pushed doggedly on with his standard promo spiel. "We use a non-linear junction detector and an infrared probe in addition to the RF sweep. We'll use time domain reflectometry for the telephones. I need a history of the system installation and a cable chart for the phone matrix as soon as possible."

Lazar nodded. "I'll have it ready for you in the morning."

They fell silent as they walked past one of the very warehouses that Seth and the McCloud brothers had shamelessly robbed only six weeks before. Funny, how even though it was all an act, his brain still clicked automatically into TSCM mode, starting the process of developing a comprehensive strategy for isolation and nullification.

God knows, this would be the easiest bug sweep his team had ever done, since he knew exactly where all the bugs were. He would find plenty of evidence to satisfy the client, plant a hell of a lot more, and make the bastard pay through the nose for the service. It was beautiful.

With this contract, Lazar was financing his own ruin. Seth liked that. It appealed to his sense of justice, and solved several pressing problems at once. He had been neglecting several aspects of his business since Jesse's death—namely, the money-making ones—and he was running through his own personal fortune at an alarming rate.

He was his own biggest pain-in-the-ass nonpaying client. Kearn and the others were at their wits' end with him. This deal would float the investigation once again—by securing Lazar's facility against Seth's own spying, thieving depredations. His mouth practically watered at the thought of bug-sweeping the Stone Island house. God, what havoc he could wreak.

He and the McClouds had enjoyed themselves hugely on those warehouse raids, and even more on the burglary of Lazar's townhouse. Once Seth had analyzed the existing security and rigged his own surveillance equipment, it had been almost too easy. Each subsequent warehouse break-in had been tougher, and more fun. With Kearn and Leslie's new ultra-sensitive thermal imaging goggles, it had been pathetically easy to see where the security guards lurked. It wasn't very sporting, maybe, but hey, he could deal with that. It hadn't been sporting to slaughter his little brother, either.

They turned the corner to the front of the warehouse where the limo was parked. The blonde scrambled out of the back seat as they approached. She pulled off her glasses and shoved them into her purse. She looked totally different without them. Soft, misty and succulent. She had been biting her lower lip so hard that it was red and puffy.

As if she'd been passionately kissed.

Lazar was talking again. Seth hauled his attention forcibly back. ". . . long will the installation take?"

Seth fished the rest of Lazar's question out of his automatic short-term memory, remembering just in time to switch back to the cover story for the blonde's benefit. "I'll need to analyze your existing inventory system, and inspect the other sites before I can tell you that."

"You can inspect the other warehouses tomorrow morning, if that's convenient," Lazar said.

"Tomorrow morning will be fine."

"Well, very good, then. I hope you will excuse me, but I have an urgent appointment downtown," Lazar said. He glanced at Raine, with a smirk that made Seth want to drive his fist into the older man's face. "Raine, Mr. Mackey is newly arrived in Seattle. Would you be so good as to show him around? Restaurants, tourist attractions, and the like?"

Raine's eyes widened in a remarkable semblance of innocent surprise. The tinge of alarm was a nice, realistic touch, Seth thought. So was the blush. "Me? Oh, but I . . . but Harriet will be expecting—"

"Harriet understands the situation," Lazar cut in smoothly. "We must welcome our honored guest. I leave that in your capable hands."

"Oh." Her eyes darted back and forth between them. She looked trapped.

Lazar extended his hand to Seth. "I'm sure you'll enjoy her company," he said.

Fury slashed through him, and he barely stopped himself from crushing Lazar's hand into a bloody pulp. He forced himself to smile politely as the other man climbed into his limo. So Lazar had sampled her charms himself. The message was clear.

He told himself to get the fuck over it. She was a professional, and it was no more or less than he had assumed from the first.

Raine gazed after the limo as it pulled away, her lower lip caught between her teeth. She looked bewildered, or maybe that was just the innocent maiden act. It was damn convincing. He had to give her that.

He shifted his leather coat, draping it across his aching hard-on.

Lascivious possibilities presented themselves to him, one after the other. There were lots of dark, secluded corners in the warehouse they had just vacated. He knew exactly which ones were out of the range of video surveillance. Places where he could pin her up against the wall, rip open her hose and drive his aching flesh deep into the hot, slick depths of her. She would cling to him, her thighs clasped around his waist, cries of pleasure jerking out of her throat with each heavy thrust.

And after he'd fucked her a few times fast and furious, after he'd taken the edge off, they could find a bed somewhere and slow down. Then it would be time for the lazy dance of lips and tongues and limbs. He would sample all the tastes and textures of her fragrant body. And then she would return the favor. He stared at her lush, faintly swollen pink lips, blood pounding in his ears like the Pacific surf.

He became belatedly aware that she was speaking. He shook his head to clear it. "Excuse me? You were saying?"

She gave him a tremulous smile. She really did look nervous. He must be her first outside assignment. He got to break her in on her maiden voyage as Lazar's whore. A red haze clouded his vision. He forced himself once again to pay attention.

". . . was just saying, um, that I'm relatively new in town, too. I've been here for less than a month, so as far as restaurants or tourist sights go, we're pretty much on equal ground."

He blinked. So that was how she was going to play it.

Whatever. He would play along for as long as he could stand it, but he wasn't going to last much longer.

"Get into the car," he ordered.

Chapter

5

Raine's nerves were so raw that the muted thump of the car door closing made her gasp. She closed her eyes and tried to calm herself down as he circled the car. She would *not* panic and run. Not this time. This was just a fling; all about pleasure, excitement, desire. It was not about forever and happily ever after. She could not afford to confuse those two utterly separate issues.

She jerked as he opened the driver's side door. The big Chevy Avalanche seemed much smaller and warmer once the dark length of him was folded into it. He turned the keys in the ignition and gave her an inquisitive look as the motor purred to life. "So?" His gaze slid swiftly down her body, then returned to her face. "Where to?"

She made a helpless little gesture. "Well, that depends."

"On what?"

"On, ah, what you want to do. What your interests are," she offered desperately.

An ironic smile flickered across his lean, dark face. "My interests," he repeated.

"Yes," she pushed on. "There's the, um, art museum, with a show of . . . I think it was Frida Kahlo, last time I checked. And the Pike Street Market, of course. The Space Needle is always a favorite. And there are some wonderful boat trips, if you haven't seen the—"

"No art. No shopping. No boats."

Raine eyed him, suspicious hint of dark laughter in his voice. "Then . . . what do you want to do?" she faltered.

A sensual smile deepened the grooves around his mouth.

Heat swept up over her chest and face. Her heart began to gallop. The silence between them stretched out. He wasn't going to move or speak, the ruthless bastard. He was going to torture her. Watch her twist in the flames with that knowing, piratical smile on his face. He was going to wait . . . and make her say it.

And he knew that she would. Those searching dark eyes saw right through her, all the way down to the sweet, restless ache that pulsed inside her, where the wild woman waited, naked and willful and wanton. He knew perfectly well how much she wanted him.

She opened her mouth, praying that something coherent would come out. "What do you want, Seth?" she whispered.

His gaze dropped to her lips. "Take a wild guess."

She closed her eyes and took the plunge. "Do you want . . . me?"

The silence was agonizing. She opened her eyes. The naked hunger in his face stole her breath.

He seized a wisp of her hair that had escaped from her knot, and twined it around his finger. It was so pale it seemed to glow against his hand. "Yes," he said. "Can I have you?"

She gave him a short, jerky nod.

There. She'd done it. She was committed, and hurtling forward into the unknown. Her heart hammered in her chest. He was so brutally handsome. She wanted to stroke the harsh, elegant planes of his face, to soothe the pulsations of red-tinged, angry energy that she felt emanating from him. Splashes of scarlet, anger and blood flashed across her dazzled inner vision, like dream images. A prickle of unease mixed into the shimmering, giddy alchemy of her excitement. Danger.

It had to be a side effect of sexual arousal, she told herself. She would not let herself panic and run. She wanted this so badly.

He turned the key, shutting off the motor. "Take down your hair."

She was glad for something to do with her trembling hands. She plucked the hair sticks out of the low chignon, slipped them into her pocket and let the coil of hair spring loose over her shoulders.

Seth gathered it into his hand and buried his face against the rippling mass. "Oh, God," he said, in a harsh, muffled voice.

She let out a startled squeak as he seized her, hauling her up and over the plastic console that divided the seats, and onto his lap. His arms tightened around her trembling body, and he stared up into her eyes. As fierce and intent as if he could read her mind.

Maybe he could. She didn't care. She could hardly feel any more naked to him than she did now. She stared back into his eyes and wiggled against him, her legs dangling over the console. Loving the hard solidity of his body beneath her. She touched his chest tentatively with her fingertips, breath fluttering. His muscles were firm and springy. His heat scorched her. He had to be running a fever. His breath was as rapid as her own as she looped her arm behind his neck and delicately touched her lips to his.

Seth made a harsh sound deep in his throat, and his arms tightened around her with steely strength. That little butterfly kiss she had bestowed upon him was permission for the real kiss to begin, a hot, devouring kiss unlike any she had ever known or imagined. She fell into it headlong, intoxicated by his voracious energy, the taste and feel of him. He smelled so good—soap and leather and wool and a unique smell all his own, warm and slightly lemony. His jaw was scratchy and rough, his sensual mouth coaxed hers open. Eager, bold and delicious.

She wanted to writhe against him, crawl inside his skin, touch everything, taste everything. He was so strong, bursting with fierce energy, and she ached with hunger for it. His thick shaft pressed against her bottom, rock hard, radiating heat.

The calluses on his hand caught and snagged against her nylon stockings as he slid it slowly under the hem of her skirt. "I can feel your heat," he said huskily. He eased her legs gently apart and his hand slid still higher, his fingertips brushing across the sensitive flesh of her inner thighs.

She pressed her face against his neck, acutely aware of every feathery stroke against her thighs. The path of his gentle, questing fingers was traced with light and heat. A sudden burst of emotion made her clench her legs tightly, trapping his hand between them. "I think I'm burning up," she whispered.

He wound his hand through her tangled hair again, tilting her face back and staring into her eyes.

"You want me," he said. It was not a question.

Raine gave him a tiny nod, as much as her trapped hair would allow. He unwound her hair from his fingers, and his hand slid higher. He pushed her legs just wide enough so that the tip of his finger brushed against her most sensitive spot. The hot sunburst of sensation made her gasp and jerk in his arms.

He laughed at her shocked expression, trailing his fingertip tenderly in teasing little circles. His eyes were bright with challenge. "It's like putting my hand into a hot cloud," he whispered. "You're already wet. I can't wait to get these clothes off of you."

Her body betrayed her, quivering with eagerness. "Seth, this is going too fast for—"

"You love it." He cut off her panicked protests with a fierce, marauding kiss and his hand slid boldly higher, cupping her whole sex. Touching her where no one had ever caressed her, not even during that terrible, botched episode with Frederick. His hand was slow and sure and wickedly clever, and his tongue thrust into her mouth as he stroked the pad of his thumb around her clitoris, tracing sensual, lazy circles through the fabric of her panties and nylons. She trembled in his arms, dazzled and lost.

A loud burst of male laughter rudely broke the spell, and they both jerked apart, startled. She stiffened, pulling away, and Seth cursed beneath his breath.

A group of men were walking towards the gate, smirking and catcalling. One of them made a thumbs-up sign at the car before they disappeared. She looked down at herself, appalled. Her hair was a tangled halo, her skirt bunched up around her waist, her face damp and hot, and probably cherry red. Legs wantonly spread, and his hand—touching her. Dear God, what was he thinking? What was *she* thinking? This tryst had spun out of control with perilous speed. She squirmed away from him, shivering. "Stop it, Seth. I am not an exhibitionist!"

"Me neither, usually." He grabbed her hand and pressed it

against his rigid penis, clearly outlined against his jeans. "Sex with an audience is definitely not my scene, but you've got me so hot, I wouldn't even care."

"Well, I care!" she said breathlessly.

"Could've fooled me, sweetheart." He cupped the nape of her neck and dragged her face to his for another rough, plundering kiss. He pressed her down against his erection as he wound her hair into his fingers, devouring her mouth. His hands were hard, insistent, right on the edge of painful, but it was a quivering, knife-edged pain. As if she were going to fly apart and only he could hold her together.

She squeezed her eyes shut, digging her fingernails into the tough dark leather of his coat. She felt intensely vulnerable, and so excited she felt she would melt apart into a shimmering cloud. She squirmed against the unyielding bulge beneath her bottom and kissed him back hungrily.

He vibrated against her with silent laughter and pulled away, his eyes taunting her. Gleaming with smug masculine triumph.

She tried to glare at him. "That's not fair," she said shakily. "This is your fault."

His eyes narrowed. "What's my fault?"

"This!" She made a frantic gesture at their entwined bodies. "It's your fault, for turning me on, making me lose my head!" She swatted him as he pulled her back for another kiss. "Stop that. Oh, God. Please, Seth."

"But you want it," he coaxed, his voice husky and seductive. "I love how you respond. I'd love to open my jeans and slide you down onto my cock, right here and now. You could ride me until you come apart. And that would just be just the appetizer, sweetheart. Just a teaser, to hold us until we get to the nearest bed. The nearest door that we can close and lock. That's when I'll really give it to you. As much as you want. Hard and fast, or sweet and slow. Whatever you want. All day long."

She stared with helpless fascination into the seductive, molten darkness of his eyes. She felt flushed and wanton, unbearably tempted to yield to him, to give him anything.

The door to the warehouse burst open. Three more men came

out and something inside her clenched up. The outrageously naughty fantasy he had woven in her mind evaporated into smoke.

She dug her fingers into his shoulders, trying to steady herself. "Hey, those guys aren't going to disappear," she whispered. "I'd— I'd rather wait for the bed and the door. Please stop teasing me."

His face lost all expression. He pulled his hand out of her hair and leaned back. "Then stop lap-dancing right now, sweetheart," he said, his voice cool and ironic. "You're making me crazy."

She scrambled back into the passenger seat, pulling down her skirt. "Sorry," she whispered, and promptly wondered what on earth she was apologizing for.

He put the Chevy into gear. She tumbled back against the seat as he accelerated out of the parking lot. The world outside the car was a fuzzy blur, reminiscent of her own interior confusion, and she fumbled wildly for her glasses, putting them on with trembling hands. She put on her seat belt, smoothed her cold hands against her crumpled skirt and tried to breathe slowly and steadily. It was a wasted effort. Her lungs refused to expand. "Where are we going?" she ventured.

His eyes flicked over her. "Where do you live?"

"No. Not my house," she said, without thinking.

"No? Why not?"

She shrugged, not eager to explain. "I don't feel safe there."

"And you think you're safe with me?"

Her spine stiffened at the derision in his tone. "No, Seth," she said, with soft dignity. "You don't make me feel safe at all."

The mocking smile faded from his face.

"That's why I want you," she said simply. "You make me feel wild. Fearless. I . . . I need to feel that way."

There it was, out in the open. The naked truth. He didn't seem to like it, judging from his grim face and the muscle twitching in his jaw.

He flicked on the turn signal. Panic leaped and pirouetted in Raine's midriff as he began to pull off the highway.

"What—where are we—"

"I saw signs for a hotel." He shot her a brief glance. "A bed and a door that locks. Wild and fearless. Whatever you want, sweetheart."

He pulled into the Marriott and parked. When she got out of the car he took her by the arm, pulling her alongside him with such restless urgency that she had to scurry to keep from stumbling.

She had set a huge machine in motion. No way to stop it now, thank God. The timid, terrified part of her wanted to cut and run, and the wanton pirate queen was triumphantly glad to have outmaneuvered it. She couldn't sabotage herself now. Not with Seth. He wasn't going to give her the option.

Her fate was sealed.

No more waiting, no more games. As soon as the hotel room door thudded shut behind them, he started wrenching off his clothes with sharp, efficient movements, keeping his eyes trained on her as if she might bolt. She followed suit, stepping awkwardly out of her shoes, shoving her glasses into her purse, struggling out of her jacket.

He unbuckled his belt and kicked off jeans, shoes, socks, underwear. He was ready, naked and waiting while she was still fumbling with her cuffs. Her gray eyes gleamed feverishly as she stared at his body, bright flags of color burning in her cheeks. She was too damn slow. She backed nervously away as he advanced on her, but his patience had run out, and as soon as her back hit the wall he started in on the blouse. Christ, he was going to buy her something stretchy that peeled off. Those fucking buttons were going to be the death of him.

His help didn't do her blouse too much good. The fragile silk practically disintegrated under his hands, and at least three buttons flew. She gasped and tried to bat his hands away, but he was already shoving the ruined garment off her shoulders, releasing a warm, heady wave of her delicious scent.

"Sorry," he said hoarsely. "I'll buy you another one."

"It's all right," she whispered. Her cool, slender hands splayed across his chest as he fumbled, cursing, with the zipper of her skirt. As soon as the fabric yielded he sank to his knees, wrenching it down around her ankles. He did the same for her pantyhose and white cotton panties, pulling them both down with one violent yank.

Seth stopped, panting. He was shaking, muscles rigid, heart racing. Losing it. He had to chill, or he was going to make a mess of it. But his face was mere inches from the soft curves of her thighs, the tangle of blond curls that hid her sex. He could see every detail, the pale and dark blond ringlets mixed together, the shadowy curves and hollows of her graceful hips, the enticing cleft of her labia.

Raine was staring down at him, her eyes huge and shadowy. Her mouth was slightly open as if she wanted to say something, but her face was transfixed by emotion, her lips quivering. Her hair glowed like the aureole of an angel, backlit by the lamp in the wall sconce behind her. She steadied herself on his shoulders, and her fingers flinched at the contact. He must be burning hot.

Her hand moved slowly, touching his throat, then his face with butterfly gentleness. She explored the bones of his jaw and his cheekbones with the tips of her cool fingers, and stroked his hair, as if she were gentling a wild animal.

The gesture sent a shaft of longing through him that cut so deep that he almost cried out. Seth closed his eyes and pressed his face against her soft belly, fighting for control.

God, he had to keep his emotions out of this, he had to remember exactly where he was and who he was dealing with at all times, or he was going to go nuts. Maybe he was going nuts anyway. He felt crazed, jagged and feverish, balanced on the edge of a knife. Every detail of her perfect body jarred him, shocked him. The skin of her belly was satiny smooth, like a baby's, and her navel a shadowy indentation, begging to be licked and kissed. And now she was petting him again, running her fingers tenderly through his hair, God help him.

He lifted up her slender, delicately arched feet one by one, peeling her hose and underwear from her ankles, and then did what he'd been longing to do from the first moment that he had seen her naked body on the video screen. He slid his hand between her thighs, forcing them slightly apart, and pressed his face against her mound. A startled cry vibrated through her body. He inhaled the sweet mélange of her scent, the hints of soap and lotion, and beneath it, the hot, heady perfume of her feminine arousal.

Her nails dug into his shoulders and her thighs trembled as he gently opened the tender folds of her labia. Inside the nest of curls, she was flushed and moist. He pressed his mouth against her cunt and tasted her, feeling the low cry that vibrated through her body. She was salty sweet, slippery and delicious, and she wanted him. He could smell her excitement, he could taste her desire. No woman could fake that, no matter how much she was paid.

That much was real, and all his. He would cling to that. For as long as he was fucking her, he would live the fantasy, and simply push reality away. It was the only way to maintain his sanity. Fortunately, he was good at it. He'd gotten a lot of practice in shoving reality away in the past ten months. He was going to need every bit of it.

He rose to his feet, his breath sawing heavily in and out of his lungs. "You're going to leave your bra on?" he demanded to know.

The pink in Raine's cheeks deepened as she reached behind herself to unhook it. She froze in place, staring at him and holding the plain white garment over her breasts.

He was impatient with the teasing game. Her mouth opened in a silent "Oh" as he wrenched the bra off of her and flung it away. She crossed her arms swiftly across her chest.

This was very different from his fantasies. He had imagined her eyes glowing with sultry invitation as she got right down to business, sinking gracefully to her knees in front of him; drawing his stiff, aching shaft into her mouth with practiced skill. Or there were a number of other scenarios, any one of which would have done nicely.

She did none of these things. She just stood there, breath jerky and shallow, her face flushed bright pink. Most of the lipstick was gone from her trembling mouth. Her mascara was smudged under her wide, dazzled eyes. One slender arm was locked across her chest and her breasts bulged over the top of it. The other hand shielded her crotch. Her body shook, a fine, rapid tremor, and she stared at his body as if she had never seen a man naked before.

Whatever. It worked for him. Having a gorgeous woman stare at his cock as if it were one of the seven wonders of the world did great things for his ego. A man's cock could never get enough female appreciation.

Seth pried her arm away from the plump, pink-tipped perfection of her tits with some difficulty. Her hand was cold and trembling, and he knew exactly how to warm it. He wrapped her slender fingers around his thick shaft. The coolness of her hand was delicious against his burning flesh, and he groaned with pleasure.

His hand tightened around hers as he showed her how he liked his cock to be stroked; long, firm pulls milking him all the way to the tip. He slid her palm around the head, moistening it with pearly drops of pre-come so that her hand could slide up and down the length of him, slick and silky. Her other hand was hovering over him as if she wanted to use it, too, but was afraid to make a mistake. She let out a terrified little squeak as he grabbed her hand and brought it up to her face. "Lick your palm," he ordered.

She blinked, and her wet tongue flicked out, licking her palm delicately. He took a deep breath, jolted by pure lust, and hung on to his control. "Again," he said roughly. "Make it really wet."

Her head bowed and she obediently licked her hand, then gasped when he pulled it down and wrapped it around his cock. He moved both of her hands with rough eagerness. "Touch me harder," he urged. "Don't worry, you won't hurt me."

Raine made a soft, wondering sound, and hid her hot face against his chest. Her fragrant hair tickled his nose, and her hands grew more confident in their grip, dragging a groan of pleasure out of him. His hands wandered over her eagerly, skimming her soft swells and dips and curves. Her breath hitched in her chest as he cupped her soft, full breasts, rolling the stiff little nipples between his fingertips.

Her hands were growing bolder, pulling him dangerously close to the brink. He had miscalculated, in his zeal to get her going. He was too turned on for this kind of play, if he didn't want to explode right now.

He reached down and trapped her hands in his. She rubbed her rosy, humid cheek against his chest, and gently kissed his flat brown nipple. Her tongue flicked out, licking his chest as her soft hands tightened around his cock. She peeked up at him shyly, gauging his reaction. "You're salty," she said, sounding fascinated. "You taste good."

That was it. He couldn't wait any longer.

Seth shoved her back against the low dresser and lifted her up onto the smooth surface, wedging his thighs between hers. She was so beautiful he didn't know where to begin. Her hair rippled down over her taut, flushed breasts, her slim waist. He ran his hands greedily over her ribs, the deep indentation of her waist, and shoved her soft, rounded white thighs wider, until he could see the glistening pink folds of her cunt inside the damp ringlets.

She clutched his shoulders for balance, fingers digging into the muscles of his shoulders. Her hands were warm now, but still shaking, and she moaned, almost inaudibly, as he trailed his fingers across her moist, sultry flesh. She was drenched and silky soft. More than ready. Her hot, womanly smell wafted up, making him salivate. Later, he was going to wallow in the luscious tenderness of her cunt, bury his face in it and lap it up like a starving man. But not yet. His cock wanted what it wanted, and he didn't feel like fighting it anymore.

Her gaze locked with his as he slid a finger inside her sheath, testing her. It was going to be a tight fit, but she was slick and soft, and clenching eagerly around his finger. She was dying for it.

He withdrew his finger slowly and circled it around her rosy, swollen clit. "You like that?"

Her fingers dug into his shoulders, her hips jerking against his hand. "Yes," she gasped out.

"You liked touching my cock?" he persisted.

Raine closed her eyes tightly and nodded.

He watched her carefully. "You're ready to take me inside of you?"

Her hips pulsed eagerly as he slid his slick, gleaming finger in and out of her. Another mute nod, and he was satisfied.

He grabbed one of the condoms he had scattered across the dresser and ripped it open. He rolled it swiftly onto himself, lifting her legs and draping them over his elbows. The low dresser was the perfect height for him to spread her out and take the plunge.

She leaned back on her elbows, her eyes glowing with tremulous hope, her soft white thighs spread out in trusting surrender. Wide open, defenseless. The look on her face made him want to cradle the delicate curve of her cheek in his hand, to touch her tenderly, reverently.

Not good. This was not what he had signed up for. It was wacked, it was crazy, and it was making his gut ache with something that felt remarkably similar to fear.

Seth pushed the feeling savagely aside, concentrating on the lust that clawed and maddened him. He positioned the blunt tip of his cock inside her, nudging it into the tender folds until it was firmly lodged. He pushed, expecting to glide into her with one slick, seamless thrust.

It didn't happen. She was incredibly tight, the tiny muscles tense and rigid, resisting him. He pushed harder, sweat dropping into his eyes, and she made a sharp, choked sound, gripping his shoulders.

None of this was going as he had anticipated. He should have been already caught up in a storm of sexual oblivion, slamming himself into the slick, eager depths of this beautiful woman, lost in the driving rhythms of wild, untrammeled, mindless sex.

Instead, he was standing stock still, teeth clenched, in an agony of reluctance to hurt her.

She sensed his frustration, and tugged at his shoulders with a tiny wince, enveloping a little more of him. The clinging caress of her body threatened his control, and he grabbed her hips and held them still. A shaky, uncertain smile curved her mouth, sending a surge of unwelcome, unwanted emotion rocketing through him.

"I'm sorry," she whispered. "I need a little more time before we, um . . . do that."

He withdrew and took himself in hand, gently caressing up and down the length of her cleft with the tip of his cock, long, soft, licking strokes that made her shudder and gasp. "You're very tense," he said.

A ripple of nervous laughter vibrated through her. "Maybe it's you who's very big."

He grunted derisively. For God's sake, he wasn't that big. His cock was good-sized, yes; certainly nothing to complain about, but it was not immense. He pulled her off the dresser and onto her feet. She stumbled, steadying herself against his chest, and looked at him with huge, questioning eyes.

"Go lie down," he snapped.

She hesitated, looking nervous and uncertain. He gestured impatiently towards the bed.

She started to say something, but the look on his face evidently changed her mind. She bit her lip and silently did as she was told.

He stared at the tangled blond hair rippling down her back, the swell of her perfect ass as she bent to pull down the coverlet. She was so docile, so unsure of herself. So different than what he had expected. It was making him angry, restless and disoriented. This was supposed to be all about sex. Pure, naked, steaming sex.

She gave him a timid, questioning look.

"Lie down," he repeated, wondering if she was ever going to take the initiative. She acted like she had no idea what to do with him.

Raine reclined on the bed and lay there like a sacrificial offering, her eyes wide and apprehensive.

Whatever. Fine. He liked being on top. It was his nature to run things, in bed and out. Probably she sensed this and behaved accordingly, like a good little courtesan. He shoved away the stab of anger that went with that fleeting thought, just in time.

Live the fantasy, he reminded himself. *Keep it together.*

She lifted her hair behind herself, spreading it out in a bright, glinting fan across the pillow, and then held out her arms to him with a shy smile.

His whole body reacted, and he didn't even remember moving. He just found himself straddling her, his heart thudding, staring down into that sweet, radiant smile, feeling famished and desperate.

Seth shoved her legs apart, trapping her beneath him instinctively, as if afraid she would try to escape. But she didn't struggle, just sighed and wiggled softly beneath him, wrapping her slender arms around his shoulders with a murmur of pleasure, as if seeking his warmth.

He pressed the burning length of his cock against her soft belly, buried his fingers in her satiny gold hair and kissed her, a starving, ravenous kiss. He wanted to devour that bright, welcoming sweetness. He wanted it all for himself. He wanted to claim it, to own it.

She twined her arms around his neck, her nails digging into his back. Her mouth was sweet and yielding beneath his. Her eager tongue ventured shyly into his mouth, her hands tangled in his hair and her slim, petal-soft body arched beneath him, silently begging him to finish what he had started. But she had already miscalculated once, and he knew himself well enough to know that once he was inside of her, he wasn't going to be able to stop, no matter what she said or did.

It was better to be sure, even if it killed him.

Raine clutched his hair and moaned as he slid down the length of her satiny body. He folded her legs up and rubbed his rough cheek against the incredibly soft skin of her inner thighs, savoring the hot smell of her sex. He loved the shocked cry of pleasure she made as he drew the swollen bud of her clit into his mouth.

Her taste drove him out of his head, the rich, earthy sweetness of her juices, the silken perfection of her secret flesh. She writhed under the slow, loving lash of his skillful tongue, her hips bucking in his grip. He held her ruthlessly still, licking and lapping at her, following the flow of energy that rose in her trembling body, pushing and coaxing. Slow and patient and relentless.

He nudged her over the top and sent her flying. He drank in her pleasure, the wailing cry, the convulsions that pulsed, wet and hot and uncontrollable, rippling through her slender body. He felt exultant, triumphant. He lifted his head, wiped his mouth and studied her. Eyes closed, panting, her body wild-rose pink and damp with sweat, still trembling from the aftermath. She was as relaxed as she would ever be.

His turn.

Seth could barely control his own trembling eagerness as he mounted her, nudging himself into her soft, drenched body. Her eyes flew open at the blunt intrusion, but she opened up, embracing him.

She gasped as he shoved himself halfway in. "Wait a second," she begged. "Let me get used to it."

He cupped her face and kissed her with pleading tenderness, making tiny rocking movements with his hips. "Relax. Let me in." His voice was rough with desperation.

She clasped her legs around his hips. "I swear, I'm trying."

He stared into her face. Her dilated eyes were gazing at him, her lower lip swollen from his rough kisses, trembling again with emotion. She reached up and touched his damp cheek, smoothing it.

She was wide open to him, utterly unmasked. Whipped cream and butter and silk, just as he had fantasized, just what he had wanted her to be. It was eerie. If it was an act, it was an unbelievably good one.

"Are you always like this?" he demanded, in spite of himself.

Her eyes opened, dazed. "Always like what?"

"Nothing." He shoved away the stab of incoherent anger, flexed his hips and drove himself inside her, all the way.

The tight, slick heat of her hugging the entire length of his cock swept away the last vestiges of his self-control. He plunged in again, hearing her sharp, breathless cries as if from a long distance. He couldn't tell if they were cries of pleasure or protest, nor could he have changed anything if he had known. He was lost, thrusting fast and furious. Locked into his own body's savage need; no hope of slowing, no chance of stopping. His orgasm bore down on him like a runaway freight train, and the explosion wrenched through him with brutal force.

Then he came back to himself, sprawled heavily on top of her. The silence in the room was deafening.

He lifted his weight up off of her. There was no sound but for their ragged breathing. Her face was turned away, only the delicate curve of her flushed cheekbone was visible. He felt irrationally afraid, as if he had ruined something as it was trying to bloom. Something as soft and fragile as a butterfly.

He rolled off her, and she drew in a great, shuddering breath of air, her breath hitching in her lungs as if she were crying. He searched for something soothing or gentle to say, but his mind was blank, wiped clean by that mind-shattering orgasm.

She rolled away from him and got up off the bed. Her trembling legs buckled beneath her. She steadied herself against the wall and hurried to the bathroom.

The door lock clicked, loud and harsh.

He hissed softly through his teeth and sat up, burying his face in his hands. When a woman locked herself in the bathroom without a word after sex, it was not a good sign.

The rationalizations started immediately—hey, she'd been willing, every step of the way. It had just gotten out of control at the very end.

When it counted the most. *Damn.*

The silence was driving him nuts. He pulled off the condom and disposed of it, then lay back down on the bed, arms behind his head. He prepared to wait, for as long as it took. No way was he going to let their tryst end on this note.

It was a matter of pride.

Chapter

6

Raine crouched in the bathtub, shaking so hard that she could barely keep her balance. She lunged up for the shower nozzle, missed it and slid back, falling with a painful thud against the cold porcelain.

Shaken to bits.

This had been nothing like her fantasies. Nothing like the rude reality she had lived with Frederick. But the Frederick episode had been stupid and embarrassing, an error to forget and move beyond. Not like this. Not earth-shattering.

Her fantasies of how sex would be with a talented lover had been soft-focus and candlelit, glittering with tints of rose and gold like love scenes in the movies. Seth had turned on all the lights and left them burning: No soft, romantic dimness for him. Every detail of him was harsh and blunt and clear, his heavy, steel-hard body, his immense strength. His big penis, probing and penetrating her. His rough commands, his restless, ravenous masculine energy.

She felt ravished, plundered. She'd had no way of knowing that it could be like this to give herself to a man. No notion of how vulnerable her helpless, writhing response to him would make her feel. And now she couldn't stop shaking, couldn't calm down. She couldn't fall in love with a man just because she went to bed with him. She barely knew him. She wasn't even sure yet if she *liked* him. For God's sake, she was twenty-eight years old. She knew better.

And he was waiting out there on the bed, as lean and hungry as a panther. God only knew what he was thinking. She had to go out and face him. She clutched the sides of the tub with white-knuckled hands, shaking in silent convulsions; she couldn't tell if they were laughter or tears. Both, maybe. She had never felt so intensely alive. Seth had ripped a veil off from the world as she knew it, and every detail glittered with unnatural brilliance. The bathroom light blinded her, the white porcelain of the toilet and sink glowed as if lit from within, the plain metal faucets blazed like sunlit platinum.

She was coming unglued.

She finally managed to snag the shower nozzle, and bit her lip as she rinsed gently between her legs, wondering if it were always going to hurt that much. She had thought that Frederick had re-lieved her at least of the technical unpleasantness of losing her vir-ginity, but she was not to be so lucky. Maybe there was something anatomically wrong with her. She wouldn't be at all surprised.

Granted, Seth was much more generously endowed than Fred-erick. But she'd been so excited. She was still shivering with unre-lieved tension, despite the stinging between her thighs. The man was addictive. Even if it hurt again, she wanted more of him.

If he was still there. It was completely quiet in the room outside.

The thought slipped into her mind with the sneakiness of a cold knife between the ribs. Maybe history would repeat itself, and she would come out of the bathroom to find the room empty.

She turned off the water, held very still, and listened.

Nothing.

She finished washing up with mechanical motions. Whether he was or whether he wasn't, she would know as soon as she opened the door. There was no point in working herself into a state.

Time enough for that later, her sarcastic inner voice commented.

She flung her hair back over her shoulders, unlocked the door, and marched out into the room.

He was there. Oh, God, was he ever. The whole lean, dark, mus-cular length of him, lounging on the bed, and managing somehow to look both relaxed and dangerous. A smile of pure joy and relief took control of her face. His heavily muscled arms were folded back be-hind his head, showing off thick, silky tufts of dark armpit hair. His big, thick penis was flushed and erect against his flat belly, swelling and stiffening before her eyes.

"You OK?" His dark eyes were keen and watchful.

She nodded, trying to wrestle down the silly smile on her face. "Did I hurt you?"

She hesitated, and his eyes narrowed, silently demanding the truth. "It's all right," she said shyly. "I know you tried not to."

He sat up, his expression darkening. "I'm sorry," he muttered.

"No, really, it's OK," she hastened to reassure him. "The first part was wonderful—"

"Which part?"

"What you did with your hands and, um, mouth," she stammered. A smile dawned slowly on his face. She blushed, and took a deep breath, forcing herself to continue. "And the rest was . . . intense. Exciting," she finished, in an embarrassed little rush. "I loved it."

The grin changed his face completely, making her realize how habitually grim his expression was. His smile lit up the room. She couldn't help but smile back at him.

He held out his hands. "Grab some condoms and get over here."

A hot glow of anticipation pulsed between her legs. "Already?"

"I just want them handy, that's all," he said. "There's no rush."

Raine licked her lips nervously. "How many?" she whispered.

His eyes gleamed with amusement. "You tell me, sweetheart."

Hah. He would learn what it meant to challenge a pirate queen. She scooped up a double handful of condoms and stalked towards him. She flung the condoms onto the bed and looked down at him with what she hoped was a cool, challenging expression.

"No, Seth. You tell *me*," she said softly.

His grin faded and was replaced by a look of total concentration. She drew herself up, resisting the urge to cover her body with her hands, and quietly bore the weight of his scrutiny.

His eyes narrowed, as if he had discovered something unexpected. "You're no butterfly," he said, almost to himself.

"What?" she asked, puzzled.

"Not a flower, either."

Raine gazed down at him, trying to interpret his cryptic remarks. "I don't understand," she said.

He shrugged, looking uncomfortable. "You're not as fragile as you look," he said brusquely. "That's ail I meant."

She felt a bright, warm stirring of pleasure. He could not have given her a compliment that would have pleased her more.

"Thank you," she said awkwardly. "I think."

"You're welcome," he replied.

For a long moment, they just stared at each other, smiling. He held out his hand. "Come here." His eyes were full of hot invitation.

She glanced down at the amazing size of his erection. He intercepted the glance and did not try to misunderstand. "Don't worry," he said. "I'll make it better for you. I won't hurt you this time."

She extended her hand. "If it's any better for me, I'll burst into flames on the spot."

He seized her hand and pulled her until she sprawled across the whole length of him. The hot shock of contact made her gasp with pleasure. She pushed herself up onto her knees, straddling his muscular thighs, and studied the details with greedy eyes and hands.

He was a banquet, a treasure trove, a sensual delight. His golden body was lightly furred by silky dark hair that lay flat and glossy against his skin. She didn't know what to touch first.

He propped himself onto his elbows and watched as her hands skimmed over him. His jaw was taut and vibrating with tension, his penis jutted proudly up against his belly. She trailed her fingers over the curves and hollows of his throat. Even his neck was thick and powerful. She petted the heavy muscles of his shoulders, her hands sliding across curves and contours, dips and bulges, the delicate tracery of vein and tendon. His body was hard and wiry, perfectly proportioned, beyond her most extravagant fantasy of the ideal male body.

She could not get enough of it.

She splayed her hands against the broad expanse of his chest, leaned over and kissed his flat brown nipples, letting her hair pool across his body. He made a low, tortured sound in his throat and started to sit up, but stopped himself, falling down onto his back with a groan. He grasped her waist, almost spanning it with his long fingers which slid over her belly, her ribs, tenderly stroking the underside of her breasts with a deliciously light, tickling touch. She followed his example with her own fingertips, brushing them across his chest, smoothing the dark hair that arrowed down to a point at his navel where his penis lay, stiff and rigid. She hesitated for a long moment and then grasped his shaft with both hands. It was hot and hard, the soft skin sliding beneath her hands, as smooth and velvety as suede.

He gasped, and swiftly covered her hands with his. "Bad idea."

"Why?" Her position, poised over him, gave her a pleasurable feeling of power, and she loved holding his penis; all that pulsing energy trapped in her two hands was wildly exciting. She gave him a bold, stroking caress, her thighs tightening instinctively around his.

His hands clamped down, immobilizing her. "Because I promised it would be better for you this time, and if you tease me, I'll lose it."

She smiled at him. "But what if that's what I want? For you to lose it? It sounds exciting."

Seth pried her hands away from his cock and trapped both her wrists in one big hand. "Too bad," he said flatly.

She tugged at her hands, but they might as well have been locked in a steel manacle. "Are you always this bossy?"

"Yes," he said, his face implacable. "Get used to it."

She yanked ineffectually at her hands. "Give me my hands back," she pleaded. "You're beautiful. I want to touch you some more."

"No. I don't trust you."

His words were light in tone, but something dark and cold suddenly yawned between them. Her teasing smile faded. She stopped tugging at her hands. They stared at each other, somber and cautious.

Raine took a deep breath, and broke the heavy silence. "You can, you know."

"Can what?" His eyes were cool, watchful.

"Trust me," she said.

His mouth hardened, and a tiny muscle pulsed in his jaw. His hand tightened painfully around her wrists, and she gasped in alarm.

"Don't go there," he said flatly. "I'm having a good time. Don't ruin it."

"Why would trust ruin it?"

He did not reply, but slowly let go of her hands. She rubbed her aching wrists, and gently persisted. "Tell me, Seth. Why can't you—"

"Drop it." He yanked her down against his chest and rolled her over, pinning her beneath him. His face was frozen, but his eyes were like pits of fire, burning with inexplicable rage.

She gazed up at him, shocked and bewildered. "But I—"

"*Let . . . it . . . go.*" His voice was soft, but it sent chills through her entire body. "Right now. Or else."

She knew this was important, dangerously important, but she dared not push it. She, of all people, knew a stone wall when she hit one. If she pushed him he was going to get furiously angry.

Raine did not know this man at all. And he was very big and strong, and fully aroused, and she was lying underneath him, stark naked.

She did not want him furiously angry with her.

"All right," she whispered.

The coiled tension in his body relaxed, almost imperceptibly. He shifted against her, lifting off enough of his weight so that she could breathe. They stared at each other, afraid to speak.

He was hiding something behind the rigid mask of his face. She read it in his eyes. An aching loneliness that spoke directly to her own.

Something turned over in her chest, sweetly painful. She pried her arms out from where they were pinned between their bodies. She cradled his face in her hands, stroking the harsh, angular lines of his jaw and cheekbone. She slid her fingers through the silky black brush of his hair and pulled his face to hers in a burst of tenderness, covering it with soft kisses; his cheek, his jaw, the corner of his mouth.

Her impulse was to soothe and comfort, but it had the opposite effect. Heat flared inside him, like a flame leaping when gasoline was thrown upon it. His arms tightened, and his mouth slanted hungrily across hers, his tongue thrust into her mouth. The hot brand of his penis swelled against her stomach, prodding her. She responded, softening and opening even as she braced herself for the stinging discomfort of penetration.

He wrenched himself suddenly up and off of her with a low curse, turning his back and sitting on the edge of the bed. "God, you are dangerous," he muttered hoarsely. "You keep driving me to the brink."

Raine pulled herself up onto her knees. "Sorry," she said, in a small, careful voice.

He twisted around and looked at her, his eyes sweeping the length of her body. He shook his head, passing his hand roughly over his face. "Listen carefully," he said. "Ground rules for the next round are, you keep your hands to yourself, and make believe my cock doesn't exist until I tell you otherwise. Got it?"

She gazed at him, bewildered. "What am I supposed to do, then?"

His grin flashed, brief and ironic. "Nothing," he said. "You let me keep my promise. You let me touch you and pet you and go down on you and make you come, over and over."

"Oh," she said in a tiny voice.

He reached out and cupped one of her breasts. "Yeah," he went on softly. "And then when you're liquid and shivering and boiling hot—" his hand slid down over her belly, then lower, "—when you're writhing and begging me, when you've forgotten your own name, then we'll try this again. Then you'll see how well we fit together."

"Oh," she said inanely. Her heart thudded heavily in her chest.

His fingers tangled themselves tenderly into the curls between her legs. He slid his hand lower and pushed her thighs apart. "Put your arms around my neck," he breathed into her ear.

She did as he asked, quivering. She already knew how this would play. He would strip her bare, and watch her with that calculating glitter in his dark eyes as he pushed her over the cliff, utterly in command of himself and of her.

Her arms tightened around his neck as his hands roved expertly over her body. She wanted him to lose control, too. She wanted him to follow her over the brink. The defiant thought took form on a deep, hidden level of her mind, even as she ostensibly yielded to him. He would never willingly let her push him so far, but she would find a way inside his defenses.

Seth buried his face against her neck, biting her just hard enough to make her gasp, and parted the soft folds of her sex with exquisite care as he licked the tender place on her throat that he had just bitten. "I'm going to make you come while I'm inside you," he told her, his voice rough with excitement. "I can't wait to feel your orgasm when I'm shoved as deep inside you as I can go, and you're clenched around me."

She moaned, her legs opening, seduced by his words and his tender, ravenous kisses. His teeth sank into her shoulder, tasting, licking her while he spread her own hot, silky juices tenderly over her labia. "That's right, baby, that's perfect," he crooned. "You're already getting ready for me, soft and wet for me."

He thrust a finger inside of her, a hiss of excitement rasping through his teeth. "Move against my hand," he demanded. "Show me how you'll move when my cock is inside you. Move!"

His voice cracked like a whip across her naked nerve endings, making her jerk in his grasp. She clutched his neck for support and tentatively rose up on her knees, acutely conscious of the blunt presence of his long finger invading her body. She sank down onto him with a shuddering moan, pushing him deep inside herself. She could barely hear his low, rough encouragement as her sheath tightened and clutched around him. She slowly found a rhythm, working herself against his clever, thrusting fingers with increasing urgency until her hips were moving sensually against his hand, craving more of the sweet, gliding friction, straining for release.

He grasped her hips with his other hand, forcing her to stop, and she struggled against him, shaking with confusion as his words penetrated her consciousness. "Not yet. Not yet, sweetheart," he was repeating. "If you wait a little longer, I can take you higher."

"I can't wait," she sobbed out, her thighs clenching desperately around his hand. "Please, Seth."

"You can't wait, hmm? Do you want me to fuck you now?"

In another lifetime, his crude language would have chilled and offended her, but she was beyond pride, beyond all boundaries. "Yes. Please. I can't wait," she pleaded, hiding her face against his shoulder.

He seized the hair at the nape of her neck and pulled her head back until she was forced to stare directly into his eyes. The full power of his forceful personality blazed out at her, and he smiled, a cool, dangerous smile, and slid his tongue slowly across her trembling lower lip. He took it tenderly between his teeth, nipping her. "You can't, but you will," he murmured, as he withdrew his finger slowly from her clinging depths. "You will, because I'm not giving you a choice."

The dark current in his voice was threatening to pull her under, into cold, unknown depths. She writhed in his tight grasp, and the fluttering surge of fear that she had felt before returned, sharper and colder. "Why are you doing this, Seth?" she asked in a shaky voice. "You can have anything you want from me. There's no need to play power games."

Soft laughter rumbled in his chest, and she felt his mocking smile against her mouth. "Two reasons," he said. "One, power games the way I play them are going to make you come . . . screaming."

"Seth—"

He silenced her with another long, savage kiss. "Two," he went on, his voice deliberate. "Two is because it's all about power in the end, angel. And if you don't know that by now, it's time you learned."

There it was, hard and cold, a gauntlet thrown down in front of her. It chilled her melting excitement as nothing else could have.

She went very still in his hard grasp, and stared into his eyes. "I think you're wrong," she said quietly.

Tension was building inside him like a deadly wave gathering force. She could see it in his narrowed eyes, in the muscle that twitched in his jaw, but still, she somehow found the force of will to hold his gaze.

A low, bitter laugh rumbled in his throat. He pushed her down onto her back and shoved her thighs apart, so suddenly that she didn't have time to react. "We'll see how wrong I am," he muttered, arching over her.

Something snapped inside her at the savage, predatory look on his face. Like a wild animal suddenly realizing the trap closing around it, she jerked out of his grasp, scrambling away in a spasm of panic.

Seth lunged for her, seizing her by the waist and tossing her down onto her back again. The bed bounced as he pinned her beneath him, and he trapped her flailing arms above her head, his eyes blazing. "Where the hell do you think you're going?"

She opened her mouth to scream, but he blocked it with his hand, his breathing ragged. His mouth clenched, as if in pain, and he closed his eyes and muttered something incoherent under his breath.

He took his hand away, but before she could speak, he was kissing her with totally unexpected tenderness. His lips moved across hers, gentle and soothing, as if he were sipping sweetness from her lips. Startled tears sprang into her eyes, and her body shook with confusion.

He lifted his head and stroked her cheek. "Shhh," he murmured. "I'm sorry, baby. I pushed too hard."

Raine tried to speak, but her lungs were heaving beneath his weight, and her lips were trembling. Tears slid from the corners of her eyes, and he leaned over and kissed them away.

"It's OK," he crooned, kissing her forehead, her cheeks. "I'm sorry. I didn't mean to scare you." He let go of her wrists, stroked her damp, tangled hair off her forehead and eased off his weight.

She closed her eyes. "Seth, I think that maybe we should stop—"

"Shhh. Don't think." He kissed her throat with seductive tenderness, nibbling her ear. "Just relax and let me do my thing."

"But I—but you—"

"No power games," he said soothingly. "Just pleasure. Just me driving you crazy, making you melt, making you come. Nothing scary, sweetheart, I promise."

Her shuddering tension was subsiding under the influence of his unexpected gentleness, his soft, pleading kisses. She could sense his sincerity; it blazed out at her like the heat of a roaring fire. But she also sensed a hidden trap behind his sensual promises.

She didn't know what it was. She didn't want to know. She let her doubts sink into the depths of her unconscious mind, spiraling down until they were lost to sight and forgotten. He was dangerous and unpredictable, but his lips were so tender and sweet against her face. Her body ached for his touch. He swamped her mind with need, blotting out reason. She had been starving for years, and he was a glutton's banquet. She couldn't resist. She had to risk it.

She turned her tear-streaked face to his and dropped a tiny kiss on his jaw, accepting his wordless apology. He said nothing, but his arms tightened reflexively around her, and she could feel the relief that flooded him, the way his breathing relaxed and slowed.

Her legs were still clamped together, and he caressed her, coaxing them apart. "Let me in, sweetheart," he urged. "I can give you so much more pleasure if you'll just relax and let me in."

He caressed the swell of her backside, pushing his knee between hers, and let out a soft growl of satisfaction as she yielded and opened to him. He slid down her body and cupped her breasts, pressing them together and rubbing his face against them with hungry appreciation. "God, these are so sexy," he said, his voice a rasp of pleasure. "I've wanted to nuzzle you and kiss you and suck your breasts since the first moment I saw you."

The shaky giggle that shook her felt alarmingly similar to a sob. "Um, thanks," she murmured.

His teeth flashed in a brief, reassuring grin, and he lowered his head and began loving her breasts. Slow, dragging kisses pulled her into a whirlpool of chaotic, melting sweetness. He licked her as if she were an exotic fruit dripping with syrup, soft and succulent. His tongue swirled in sensual circles against her plump curves, as if he could never get enough. She fell back against the pillows with a gasp, arching herself, offering him everything.

He took her nipple tenderly in his mouth and dragged at it gently with his teeth, and she cried out at the searing, bright silver wire of sensation, perilously close to pain and yet a million miles away from it. She clutched his head against her chest, shaking with pleasure as he pressed her breasts together and licked the deep valley between them. The bright overhead light came through her closed eyelids, coloring her universe a glowing, endless red. Red was the color of the wet, pulling heat of his mouth, the swollen, pulsing ache between her thighs.

She was so sensitized that the faintest touch of his hand between her thighs almost made her climax then and there. Her eyes flew open as he slid his long finger inside her. He murmured softly in approval, and slid in another one alongside it, stretching her tenderly.

His clever hand caressed her sensitive folds and furrows with tender skill, petting and coaxing her tirelessly until she crested and came, long and liquid, a wave of shimmering pleasure.

When Raine opened her eyes again, Seth was studying her, his face thoughtful. He pushed a lock of her hair gently out of her mouth and smoothed it behind her ears, and she smelled her own scent against his damp hand. "You came apart right in my hands. I felt your orgasm like it was my own," he said softly. "I love how you let yourself go."

She waited until she had control of her voice to reply. "I never have before," she whispered. "Not like this. It's you who does it to me." His grin was openly triumphant. "It's not nice to gloat," she muttered.

"Who ever said I was nice?" He slid down between her legs again, pressing them even wider.

She struggled up onto her elbows, alarmed. "Again? Already? Seth, give me a minute to rest!"

His laughter cut her off. "Forget about rest. I've barely even begun. I want more."

She clutched at his head, with the vague intention of pushing him away, but just then his tongue lashed tenderly across her most sensitive flesh, and she sagged back against the pillows with a sob of helpless pleasure.

Time ceased to have meaning. She lost count of the number of orgasms he brought her to. At a certain point, it all blended together in one endless, shuddering wave, with peaks and valleys and immense vistas. He was insatiable, ravenous; lapping at her tender flesh as if it were her pleasure that nourished him. He pushed her further than she had ever dreamed of going, until she was writhing and pleading, her hands tangled in his hair.

He gently unwound his hair, kissing each of her fingers, his eyes blazing down at her with unmistakable purpose as he rose up over her. "Now," he said raggedly, grabbing one of the condoms scattered across the crumpled sheet. "You're ready for me now, Raine."

It was true. He had leveled every barrier with his ruthless sensual expertise and the force of his fiery will. Her defenses were in ruins, even the silent, secret ones she had not known that she possessed before he had breached them. And she was glad.

She held out her arms to him. "Please."

His face was a grimace of concentration as he smoothed the condom swiftly over himself and mounted her. He pushed himself against her drenched, ravished sex with teasing thrusts that made her pant with frustration. She slid her hands down over his hips. He was slick with sweat, muscles rigid and trembling. She grasped his buttocks and pulled, inviting him into her body.

He drove himself inside her hard and deep, and she was more than ready; she was primed, silky soft and yielding and eager. All the little muscles that had resisted him before now clung to him eagerly, welcoming the intense friction of his thick shaft.

He withdrew, and thrust again with a groan of pleasure. He cupped her face in his hands. "Does it hurt now?" he demanded.

He wasn't satisfied at the mute shake of her head. "Tell me how it feels!" he insisted.

Her hips bucked beneath him as he drove himself deeper, harder, but she could find no words to say. She clutched his shoulders, squeezing her eyes shut.

"Do you like it?" he demanded.

"I love it," she gasped out, wrapping her arms around his shoulders and holding on for dear life. "I love it."

The breath escaped from his lungs in a long, sensual sigh of relief, and his mouth covered hers, kissing her with passionate tenderness. They rocked together, sighing and gasping with the consuming pleasure of each deep, gliding thrust. He slid his arms under her shoulders, dragging her still closer. "You want me to give it all to you?"

Her heart swelled at the vulnerability in his voice. It was low and shaky, ragged with desperate longing. She clasped her legs tightly around his hips. "Give me everything you've got," she urged, kissing his jaw. "I'm not fragile, remember? No butterfly. I want it all."

He stared into her eyes as he rose up onto his knees, folding her legs back against her chest. He loomed over her, his hips pulsing eagerly. His face was a taut questioning mask. She reached up and caressed his cheek, arching her back. Silently giving him leave.

He took her at her word. His control snapped, everything changed, and she was caught up in a hurricane. He shouted hoarsely as he drove into her. His slamming thrusts made her cry out, not in pain, but in savage exultation. Every part of her welcomed him, loving the slapping sounds of contact, the marvelous, sliding friction. It drove her crazy, tearing down her image of herself, releasing something deeper and fiercer, something heightened and exalted and savagely feminine.

He had lost his control and she was glad, triumphant. She wanted to claw and bite him, to tear down his barriers and see him naked and helpless before her. She stared into his face and cried out with wild, exultant joy as he exploded and wild triumph triggered her own sweet, shimmering explosion."

When she opened her eyes, his face was hidden against her neck. She pulled at his hair, trying to make him look at her, but he resisted, shaking his head and pressing his face harder against her, panting.

She clasped her arms around his neck and melted into tears, but they were soft, rippling tears that cleansed and renewed her. She held onto him as the bright storm moved through her and subsided, leaving her clear and clean, like a fragrant, rain-washed sky. The feeling frightened her. It was dangerous to be this happy. Experience had taught her that it meant she had way too far to fall.

Seth looked up, alarm plain upon his face. She laughed through her tears, dashing them away with the back of her hand. "Don't worry," she told him with a watery giggle. "I'm all right. More than all right. I'm just happy. This was wonderful. *You're* wonderful."

She was hoping that he would take her in his arms again, but he withdrew abruptly, climbing off the bed. Suddenly the air in the room felt unpleasantly chilly against her damp, flushed skin. He turned away, disposing of the condom. A vague, fearful feeling clutched at her midriff, blocking her tears at their source.

"What's the matter, Seth?" she asked.

He waited an agonizingly long time to reply, then turned to her.

"How do you let yourself go like that?" His voice was cool. Wondering.

She sat up, smoothing her hair away from her damp face, and smiled at him. "How could I not?"

"So you're like this every time, then? With everyone?"

The cold look in his eyes made her shiver, as if a cliff had appeared unexpectedly before her feet. "What do you mean, everyone?"

"Every time that Lazar sends you out to fuck one of his business associates," he said.

Her insides turned to ice. She stared at him, half-hoping she had heard wrong, knowing she had not.

She swallowed around the jagged lump that had taken form in her throat. "You thought that I—that Victor—" Her voice trailed off, breath finished. She was unable to inhale and replenish it.

"I hope he pays you well," he said. "You deserve it. You're amazing. I've never had sex like that in my life."

She opened her mouth again, but nothing came out. She shook her head, wanting to cancel, to negate, to erase, the last ten seconds.

He just stared at her, eyes cold and unwavering. He believed it. God, he had made love to her believing it.

No, not love. Not even sex. He had *fucked* her, believing it.

She shook her hair forward, hiding her breasts. Being naked in front of his cold gaze was unbearable. "God, Seth," she whispered, "I'm a secretary, not a call girl."

His expression did not change.

Raine scrambled off the bed and began searching for her scattered clothes. She yanked them on with cold, trembling fingers, not bothering to button her cuffs or to tuck in her tattered blouse. She shoved her bare feet into her pumps and lunged for the door.

He blocked her, trapping her between his powerful arms. "Wait," he said flatly. "I'll get dressed and drive you home."

She looked into Seth's dark eyes, inches from hers, and said, loud and clear, words she had never said aloud to anyone in her life.

"Fuck you."

She shoved at his naked chest with all her strength, sending him stumbling back two steps. She wrenched the door open, and ran.

Chapter

7

The patron saint of humiliated lovers must have been watching over her. A cab from the airport was discharging its passengers outside the lobby as she tore through the lobby. She made her getaway before Seth could follow her downstairs and reduce her to a state of hysteria.

She was teetering on the verge of it now, using every trick she knew to stave it off. The grizzled old cabbie could tell. He kept glancing back in his rearview mirror, his eyes troubled behind his thick glasses.

"You all right, miss?"

"I'm fine, thanks."

Her lips felt numb as they formed that terribly familiar phrase. She almost laughed, but choked it off. Laughter opened the floodgates. Then the tears would come, and then she would definitely lose it.

I'm fine, thanks. She'd been saying that for seventeen years while she was dying inside. She was not fine. She was worse than she'd ever been, which was saying a great deal. And this time it was all her fault.

What did she expect? She'd overcompensated, like always, and leaped into bed with a man without even having dinner with him, or even exchanging basic personal data. She didn't know where he grew up or what college he had attended, or even his phone number. She'd done a slutty thing. She had to deal with the consequences.

But she was so contracted with pain, she could barely breathe. Think pirate queen, she reminded herself.

Like hell. The pirate queen would be sophisticated enough to use a man for sex without letting all her barriers crumble, even when her body was flying apart with pleasure. She would have had the presence of mind to say something besides that blunt, inelegant "fuck you." Something that would've pierced him to the heart, or to the bone at least. She doubted that the bastard had a heart.

The storm was about to burst. She bore down and counted the seconds it would take to reach someplace private to fall apart, an old trick from her school days. *Eight, seven*, as she paid the cabbie and bolted up the steps to her house. *Six, five*, and it was taking too many tries to get the key into the lock, the way her fingers shook. *Four*, the key finally entered and turned. *Three*, she shoved open the door. *Two*—

"Good evening, Raine."

She shrieked, and leaped back out the door.

Victor Lazar was lounging in the foyer, sipping a glass of whiskey. "I hope you'll excuse me for helping myself to the bar. I'm familiar with the house, you see. I stocked the bar myself some months ago," he said.

"I see. It's, uh, fine," she whispered.

Hah. There it was again. Miss Nicey Nice, terrified of offending anyone even if they were stepping on her face, was just *fine*.

Victor gave her an encouraging smile and gestured for her to come in. She took a step inside. She was poised to flee, adrenaline pumping, her brain churning out any number of probable reasons that he might be here, uninvited, in her foyer.

None of them were good.

Dear God, don't let him come on to me, she thought wildly. Not that. No way. That was too much to ask. She would run, screaming; and if the dream came back, she would just beat her head against the wall of her padded cell until it extinguished itself in a bloody haze.

Anger at his presumption rose slowly up, like a bubble from the shadowy depths. She forced herself to stand up straighter.

"You don't appear to drink, judging from the state of the bar," he observed, delicately rattling the ice in his glass.

"Very little," she said stiffly.

"Or eat, either, if your refrigerator is any indication," he said in a gentle, chiding voice. "You must keep up your strength, Raine. You have no need to diet. On the contrary."

"You looked in my refrigerator?" She was startled at her own loud, incredulous tone.

He looked slightly injured. "I needed ice for my drink," he explained, draining his glass. He set it down on the telephone table. "Please, take a moment to collect yourself, Raine." He made a courtly gesture towards the bedroom, and smiled. "I can wait."

For what? she wondered frantically. She caught a glance at herself in the mirror behind him, and stifled a gasp. Her hair was a wild, tangled halo, her lips red and puffy. Her blouse was crumpled, several buttons missing, cuffs hanging sloppily open, one side tucked in, one side out. Her eyes blazed out of dark, smudged sockets.

She let her breath out slowly. So what if she looked like a madwoman. She'd been to hell and back today. This was her home, and she would not be dismissed in it like a servant. She fished in the pocket of her jacket for the hair sticks and wound her hair into a knot, stabbing the sticks through it. She took her glasses out of her purse and deliberately put them on. "What do you want, Mr. Lazar?"

If he was angered by her small act of defiance, he did not show it. His mouth twitched. "Did you enjoy your afternoon with Mr. Mackey?"

Heat rushed into her face. "I don't want to discuss—"

"I should have suggested Sans Souci for dinner, but it slipped my mind," he said silkily. "Did you go to the art museum? Or the market?"

"No," she forced out.

"So you took him directly to bed."

Raine backed towards the door. "Mr. Lazar—"

"To be truthful, I didn't mean for you to take my suggestion to entertain Mr. Mackey quite so personally."

Raine's jaw dropped. "Are you implying that I—"

"Don't be tedious," he snapped. "We're both adults. And I'm certain Mackey enjoyed your interpretation of my instructions far more than a tour of the Space Needle, or a ride on the Monorail."

Raine stared at his smug face. "You set me up," she whispered.

He frowned. "Oh, please. Whatever happened between you and Mackey is your business, Raine. And entirely your responsibility."

She flinched at the truth in his words. No one had ordered her to throw herself at Seth Mackey today, and with such enthusiasm that he had mistaken her for a professional sex worker.

The thought was so ludicrous that she started to giggle. She swallowed back the convulsions in her throat with a strangled cough.

"Are you all right, my dear? Shall I get you a glass of cognac?"

"No, thank you, I'm fine." Oh, there it was again. The pirate queen would not say "I'm fine" while being forced to walk the plank.

Victor crossed his leg over his knee and swung his foot in front of him. "Forgive me if I startled you. I came here for a reason."

She stiffened. "And that would be?"

"I am interested in your opinion of Seth Mackey. He is a relative unknown, and personally, I find him rather opaque. I am entrusting him with an extremely sensitive project, you see. I thought perhaps that your, ah, unique point of view might yield some other insights."

Raine tried to swallow, but her throat was too dry "No," she croaked. "No insights. Not a one."

He tapped a long, slim cigarette out of a silver case. "None?"

She shook her head so emphatically that the makeshift knot of hair bobbed and slid down to the nape of her neck. She pulled out the sticks. The bun unraveled down her back. "None," she repeated.

Victor's eyes flicked down, observing her white-knuckled hand. He lit his cigarette. "You should be more observant, my dear."

"Should I?" Her fingers tightened around the stick until the faceted crystal beads dug painfully into her palm.

He blew out a long, thin, stream of smoke, his eyes pale, glittering slits. "The poet William Meredith once said . . . 'the worst that could be said of any man was that he did not pay attention.' "

An image of her dreamy, inattentive father superimposed itself upon Victor's face. A buried ember of old anger began to glow inside her. "I can think of worse things that could be said," she said flatly.

Victor's eyes flashed. He tapped his cigarette into the heavy crystal ashtray on the telephone table. "Can you?"

Raine struggled to keep her face composed.

He stared straight into her eyes for what seemed like forever. "I expect you to exert yourself a bit more on the next occasion."

His offhand tone fanned the ember inside her into a white-hot glow. "Are you ordering me to have sex with Seth Mackey, spy on him, and report back to you?" she demanded.

Distaste flitted across Victor's face. "I detest crass overstatement."

"I have not even begun the crass overstatements," she hissed. "You listen carefully, Mr. Lazar. One, there will be no other occasion, because I do not want to see Seth Mackey ever again. And two, I would never spy on a person I was intimate with. Never."

Victor took a final draw on his cigarette and crushed it out briskly. "I love the conviction with which young people use the word 'never.' "

Her fists clenched at his patronizing tone. "It's very late. I'm afraid I have to ask you to leave. Right now."

Her voice broke, spoiling the effect. She held her breath, half hoping he would fire her. She would be off the hook—at least until the tombstone dream started burning holes in her sanity again.

But this time, when it did, she would be out of ideas.

Victor stood up and pulled his overcoat out of the closet.

It had worked. He was leaving. Giddy triumph emboldened her. She decided to push her luck. "And Mr. Lazar?"

"Yes?" He paused, eyebrows raised.

"I would appreciate it if you would not make yourself at home in my private space. I want to be the only person in possession of a house key." She held out her hand.

His eyes glittered with fierce amusement. "Let me give you some advice, Raine. Don't waste your time and energy clinging to an illusion of control. You'll only exhaust yourself."

She kept her hand out. "It's my illusion, and I'm clinging to it."

Victor chuckled. He pulled a key out of the pocket of his overcoat and held it out on the palm of his hand.

She plucked it off his palm with the tips of her fingers, and yelped as his fingers snapped around her hand, like a sprung trap.

Dream memories of Victor's heavy arm squeezing the air out of her lungs thundered through her mind. She pulled on her throbbing hand, trying not to panic. Out of nowhere, Seth's voice echoed in her mind. *It's all about power in the end, angel. And if you don't know that by now, it's time you learned.* She seized onto those harsh words as if they would save her life. Maybe Seth was right. Those were the rules of this nightmare world. She had to master them. Until she did, all she could do was command her own small, frightened self as well as she was able. The roaring in her ears subsided, and her vision cleared. Her trapped hand still hurt, but it was bearable.

She looked into his eyes without blinking. "Good night, Victor."

To her surprise, he let her go, and nodded at her with what looked almost like approval. "Excellent," he said softly. "Good night, Raine."

The door thudded shut behind him, and she lunged for the door, slamming in the deadbolt. She slid down against the ornately carved mahogany door until she was crumpled on the floor and gave way to deep, wrenching sobs. Seventeen years of saying no-really-I'm-fine until it was automatic, and it took a day like today to show her how foolish and vain all her efforts had been.

Don't cling to an illusion of control, Victor had said. *It's all about power in the end, angel.* Their mocking voices echoed in her head as the pitiless reality bore down on her. She had no power, no control, no illusions. She was over her head in wild white water and sinking fast. She controlled nothing; not her mind, her heart, her dreams, not even her own body. Seth had demonstrated that to her this afternoon, ruthlessly, over and over again.

Her sobs quieted to a numb silence. She pressed her face against her knees, and began to pray; she wasn't sure to whom. She wasn't at all positive there was a God, but she definitely believed in the opposing forces of good and evil. She might not have power, or control, or even a plan, but she was here in search of the truth, for her father's sake.

She was here for love. That had to count for something. In any case, it was all she had, and she was clinging to it with all ten fingernails.

* * *

The security on Lazar's town house was considerably tighter since Seth and the McCloud brothers had burgled it four months before. The increased security wasn't much of a challenge, though, considering how he and his team had rigged the data retrieval. It was almost too easy.

Seth thought about that first burglary raid as he slid through the bushes like a shadow, far out of range of the infrared motion detectors. He shouldn't have been thinking at all; he should be in the zone of pure focus, but anything was better than thinking about Raine.

He'd been surprised at how smoothly the four of them had worked together to coordinate the electronic assault upon Victor Lazar; the planting of the vidcams, phone transmitters, laser gulpers, and wall resonator mikes, all while staging a simulated burglary. They'd worked like swift, silent parts of the same machine, no ego in the way, thoughts running on the same groove. Quick learners, too, even though they weren't trained gearheads like him. A good team. They saved their annoying personality quirks for their leisure time.

He fumbled in the darkness as he set the microwave frequency he needed to activate the resonant bug in Lazar's office. He tuned the receiver for the return broadcast, cursed behind his teeth when he got it wrong, and entered it again. He was going to have to hurry to finish inside the time frame he had set himself. He hated hurrying.

He'd run through the routine, visualizing every move in advance, but he needn't have bothered. His concentration was blasted to shards. A nighttime data sweep was a sneaky, ninja-type job that usually chilled him, but it wasn't working tonight. His brainwaves weren't smoothing into undulating alpha curves; they were as jagged as the teeth of a broken pocket comb. Every muscle in his body was rigid; his head and neck and balls all ached, and every time he started to calm down another phalanx of sexual images would roll over him, leaving him breathless and flattened.

He had plenty of tactile data on Raine Cameron now, but the joke was on him—he couldn't control the data flow. It came at him in a torrent; her scent, her velvet softness, her smile. This was hell on earth. Worse than before he'd slept with her. Exponentially worse.

The video had done it to him. He'd been on edge already after Raine stormed out of the hotel room; then he got home, logged on and saw Lazar waiting in her house, sipping his drink in fucking *real*-time. All his instincts screamed at him to get the hell over there and protect her. Then cyborg man had risen up and taken control. That kind of behavior would get him killed prematurely, leaving Jesse unavenged. Besides, what did she have to fear from her own pimp? Fantasy time was over. Time to wake up and face reality.

So he'd clenched his teeth, planted his ass and waited for her to get home. One thing was for sure. If he had to watch Lazar fuck her, then it was a damn good thing he had nothing in his stomach.

The conversation that took place, from 9:35 to 9:47, had astonished him. Raine Cameron was exactly what she appeared to be; a bewildered, overworked new secretary in a big import/export firm.

So why the provocative set-up? Why was she ensconced in the ex-mistress's love nest? Why had she fallen into bed with him, as if she knew that it was expected of her? It didn't add up. Nothing added up.

He'd monitored Lazar's Mercedes to the marina, satisfied himself that the boat was bound for Stone Island, and replayed that twelve minutes of footage until it looped endlessly in his mind. He paced around, kicking the cheap furniture, punching the walls.

He had to do something, or he would go nuts. Something sneaky and challenging, preferably dangerous. A data retrieval sweep was pretty tame, but what the hell, it was better than stealing hubcaps.

This was asinine. He had more important things to worry about. So he'd nailed a beautiful woman, hurt her feelings, and then pissed her off. Whatever. That sequence of events was normal for him.

But this was Raine, his red-hot fairy tale princess.

His ugly final words to her echoed in his mind as he slipped through the bushes and alleys. She'd opened him up and he hadn't expected it. He couldn't afford to be naked and vulnerable in front of one of Lazar's women. His instinct had been to shove her away, as fast and as hard as he could.

He headed back to Oak Terrace and set the audio data to run through the processors. It was going to take the voice recognition filters a while to sift through the massive data load of frequencies that the gulpers had gathered and polish up any matches it found with the frequencies of Lazar's or Novak's voices. He and the McClouds had planted virtually undetectable carrier current transmitters in Lazar's town house phones, neatly circumnavigating the problem of the digitally encrypted phone lines, but he hadn't yet pulled off the same trick for Stone Island. Phone calls from that location were still an unknown quantity, representing a gaping hole in his surveillance coverage. Which bothered the hell out of him.

Oh, God. He couldn't sit around in that cramped, suffocating place and watch data crunching. He had to get out into the wide, glittering night. He felt dangerous and wired. Two head-banging, mind-blowing orgasms should've chilled him out, but he was more wound up than ever. He bolted for the Chevy and set off, speeding through the streets, mind racing. Incoherent and out of control, streaming with data, images and feelings, fire and smoke.

Connor McCloud's words echoed through his mind when he saw the exit that would take him to Templeton Street. *"They get that look you've got on your face, then they fuck up, then they die badly."*

Seth didn't slow down until he parked half a block from her house. He wondered if the events of this afternoon, plus whatever idiocy he might yet perpetrate tonight, qualified as an official fuck-up.

He slid down on the seat until his face was in full shadow, stared up at her house, and concluded that it did. Look at him, lurking in the dark like a stalker. At least at this hour, nobody was likely to notice him and call the cops. That would be the crowning indignity.

From this vantage point, he could cover both front and back entrances plus monitor the lights in the living room, bedroom and bathroom. From this distance, thanks to Kearn's evil genius, he could just flip on the receiver he'd built into the Chevy's dash and watch every move she made on his laptop, without even the benefit of a phone line.

Better yet, he could disable her alarm, pick all three locks, and walk right in. It made him furious, how vulnerable she was. Which made no sense, since her lack of defenses was entirely to his advantage. Nothing made sense tonight.

The hypothetical scene played in his mind. She would be furious at first, but he would plead and grovel until she softened up. He knew exactly how to turn her on: Having once gotten through her barriers, he knew the way now like he was born to it. He knew how to get under her guard just as he knew how to disable her alarm and pick her locks. He had great instincts when it came to sex. They had never failed him—at least not while he was actively engaged in it.

Afterwards, of course, was another story. But he wouldn't worry about that now. One step at a time, for God's sake.

First the words and the charm. Then the kissing and cuddling, until Raine calmed down and started to cling to him, sweet and trusting. He would pet her and nuzzle her until she started to secretly wonder if he were ever going to do anything more. And when he felt the subtle signs of that restless energy building inside her, that was his cue.

Then he would lay her out on the bed or couch or carpet, whatever was closest, and pleasure her with his mouth until she had forgotten why she was mad at him. Until she was writhing, slick, wide open. Begging him. Delicious. Easy. Like taking candy from a baby. He had the means, he had the power, but when he reached for the door handle, something strange happened. He just . . . stopped.

He had no choice. The control tower in his head had been taken over in a surprise coup. An unfamiliar command team was running everything. Strange thoughts took form in his mind, bewildering him. Just because he could pick her locks didn't mean necessarily that he should. After today, the least he could do was guard her house, ensure her one night of genuine safety. He even felt too inhibited to just flick on the receiver, power up the X-Ray Specs program and watch her, the way he'd been watching her for weeks. It felt all wrong tonight. She'd given him everything she had to give, and he'd taken it all and paid her back with . . . oh, shit. Whatever. He felt bad, he was sorry. Enough already.

It was stupid. A pointless tribute that she would never appreciate. She would never know what it cost him to leave his magic tricks in the bag and just sit there in the dark, helpless and inert.

It was bizarre. He had never been chivalrous in his entire life. That was Jesse's department.

Even a fleeting thought of his young brother was a mistake. He was helpless to push away unwanted thoughts tonight. They raced

through his mind, tumbling over each other, maddened by their un-
accustomed liberty.

Memory triggered memory. Even minor ones made his gut cramp.
Jesse's dirt-colored hair that stuck straight up in a case of perpetual
bed head. His green eyes, shining like the headlights of a car. His
hundred-mile-an-hour intelligence, his zingy one-liners. His extravagant affection for the whole world, even when it kicked him in the
teeth.

Seth's heart had already been heavily armored by the time his
mother DeAnne hooked up with one of her ex-boyfriends, Mitch
Cahill, and moved the guy into their apartment. Then DeAnne
compounded her mistake by getting the bright idea that now that
there was a father figure around, she could go collect Seth's little
five-year-old half-brother from where he'd been living with her
mother in San Diego. Seth had only seen the snot-nosed, motor-
mouth little kid a couple of times since he was born. A couple of
times had been more than enough for him.

Seth had hated Mitch on sight, and sullenly resented the bug-
eyed, scrawny kid who followed his eleven-year-old brother around,
getting in the way of business, and in general annoying the shit out
of him. But Jesse was like a fly that kept landing on his nose. He
couldn't be chased away. Seth still remembered the horrified alarm
he'd felt on the day when he realized that Jesse loved him. Not because he was lovable, because he wasn't; he'd been out-and-out
mean to the clueless little geek. Not because he deserved to be
loved, because he didn't. Seth went out of his way to be obnoxious
to everyone.

No, Jesse had loved him because Jesse desperately needed to
love someone. It was just the way he was made. He'd loved De-
Anne, too. He'd even loved Mitch, his brutal, worthless, stinking-
piece-of-offal excuse for a father. Managing to love Mitch was a
fucking miracle.

Jesse had needed to love like he needed to breathe, and Seth had
just happened to be in the line of fire. After a while, in spite of himself, he started to feel protective and proprietary about the little guy.
He would kick the shit out of anybody who messed with him,
shoplift clothes and shoes for him when his stuff wore out, make

sure he got something to eat when Mitch and DeAnne were too stoned to feed him. Little things like that, but they took on their own momentum, and before he knew it, Jesse was all his. His headache, his responsibility. Nobody else around the place was sober enough to give a rat's ass about the kid.

His bond with Jesse was not an official one. The liaison between DeAnne Mackey and Mitch Cahill had been a common-law marriage that figured on no public registry. DeAnne stoutly claimed that Jesse was Mitch's son, and she had nagged until Mitch changed Jesse's last name to Cahill. Seth remembered those arguments all too clearly. *"But I'm not going to give my name to that other thieving, smart-mouthed punk of yours, so don't even bother asking."*

Hah. As if he had wanted it. Asshole.

After her death, Seth had dodged the help of those public agencies supposedly dedicated to his welfare, but he still hung around the neighborhood, to keep an eye on Jesse and protect him from Mitch.

It hadn't been easy. Jesse had been hard to protect. He loved stupidly, indiscriminately. He forgave friends after they'd stabbed him in the back, he lent money to thieves and crackheads, he fell in love and got stomped on more times than Seth could count, but he just kept on flinging his heart into harm's way with a reckless courage that had never failed to stupefy his brother.

He hadn't thought of their bond as love, because in those days, the word *love* did not figure in his working vocabulary. He'd thought of it more as a monumental pain in the ass, having to look after that feckless little jerk. But in the moments in which Seth allowed himself to consider such things—mercifully few, and usually only when he was drunk off his ass—he knew why he'd hung around. He, like Jesse, needed at least one person to love. A hard, controlling sort of love, but it was the best he had to give. The best he had ever given.

Jesse should never have gone into law enforcement. He was too trusting, too tender-hearted. He should've become a pediatric nurse, a goddamn kindergarten teacher. Seth had tried so hard to protect him from the world, but the world was big and sneaky and treacherous, and Jesse had been dead-set on saving it from the bad guys.

If Jesse were here, he would tell him to stop jerking off and cut the pity party. And seeing him parked in the dark outside a woman's house like a lovesick teenager would have made Jesse laugh his head off. Seth could see him in his mind's eye, cackling and pointing his finger. *Hah. It's your turn now, bro, and about fucking time, too. Let's see you act all superior now, sucker.*

Seth's eyes stung, and he scrubbed at them with the back of his hands as he stared up at her bathroom window. He wondered if she were crying again. He'd refrained from watching that part of the show. All twenty-two minutes and twenty-six seconds of it.

Maybe she was taking a bath. He could imagine her stretched out in the tub, her lush curves dripping and gleaming as she sudsed herself up. In a hundred and ten seconds, he could be inside with her.

Helping her bathe.

His hand drifted over onto the door handle. He clutched it until his knuckles ached, and slowly let it go. The guys up in the control tower in his head were armed, dangerous, and not to be fucked with. It was martial law up there, the moralistic bastards.

He slumped down lower. His head pounded, and his gut gnawed. He should have grabbed something to eat. He'd been too keyed up before the meeting, too sex-crazed while Raine had been in his grasp, too upset afterwards. The coffee and doughnuts he'd eaten that morning were a million years ago for a six foot tall, two-hundred-and ten-pound guy with a raging metabolism.

He should have bought the woman lunch before falling on her like a starving wolf, but he'd been so jacked up and frantic. Afraid she would change her mind and slip away from him somehow. He hauled his laptop out, feeling sullen and chastened. No excuse for not getting some work done while he sat there in the dark. He wondered if a violent attack of conscience was a condition that passed relatively quickly, like heartburn, or whether it was a chronic type of thing. Like acne.

In any case, there were limits to his new scruples. Martial law or no martial law, if Raine walked out that door, she was fair game.

If she walked out that door, she was his.

Chapter

8

Bedroom, stairs, kitchen, dining room, living room. She was wearing a groove in the carpeting. She'd tried a hot bath, yoga, herbal tea, relaxing music, but whenever she stopped moving, her body popped up again as if she were on springs. She could only hope this overdose of adrenaline would see her through another grueling day at work.

Work. Her mind raced around in frantic circles. How could she go back to work? How could she put on her makeup and pantyhose and trot off to the office as if it were a normal day—yes, sir, no sir, anything you say, sir—after this crazy night? How could she stick close to Victor Lazar and cultivate his favor if he really had set her up to be seduced and humiliated?

That triggered a fresh bout of reliving every second she'd spent with Seth Mackey. She'd been so wanton, so needy. Thinking of him made her catch her breath and press her shaking thighs together, even though her body was exhausted and sore from his hard use. Even though she was burning with shame. She'd been so stupid.

By the time the clock ticked over to 2:30 A.M., she gave up on sleep, and put on her jogging clothes. She would tear around the block a few times, unload some of this nervous energy.

She did a few stretches on the porch, and broke into a jog, darting between pools of shadow cast by the bushes. The breeze smelled of rain and dead leaves. The darkness was more menacing than usual, but she chalked it up to her mood. She needed to ground herself, and then she could start the process of disguising herself as a normal person.

She heard the muffled pop of a car door opening. Her heart leaped into her throat. She spun around and broke into a dead run.

She heard light, running footsteps behind her. "Raine, hey—"

She recognized his voice, but she'd gone too far down the road to panic to turn back. She gathered her breath for a scream, and Seth clamped his hand over her mouth. "It's just me, you idiot. Calm down."

She sank her teeth into his hand. He yanked her braid back, forcing her to release his hand. She lunged for his eyes with her keys.

He blocked her hand and pinioned it behind her back. "Don't fight me!"

"You scared me!" she hissed. "Let me go!"

He maintained his hard grip on her wrist and braid. "I'm sorry I scared you—"

"Oh, thanks!" She thrashed against him, furious.

"—but there *is* no good way to get a woman's attention on a dark street in the middle of the night. Just give me a few seconds."

Her heart was beating so fast she felt almost faint. "A few seconds for what?"

He lifted her hand up to his face, the one that had the keys clutched in it like a dagger. He brushed the back of her hand across his cheek, an awkward, uncertain gesture. "To apologize," he mumbled.

She went limp with shock. "Apologize?"

"Yeah."

She twisted in his arms. He loosened them just enough for her to swivel around and look him in the face. His eyes gleamed in the dim light of the streetlamp. Pirate eyes, dark and watchful. The night shadows made the planes and angles of his beautiful face seem even more inscrutable. "That's crazy," she whispered. "After what you said—"

"Yeah, I know. It was terrible, I was wrong, I'm the scum of the earth. What the hell are you doing out here? Jogging? Are you nuts?"

She brushed aside his diversion without even noticing it. "Let me get this straight. You mean you've changed your mind? You no longer think that I was paid to sleep with you?"

"Right. Exactly. You got it."

She was alarmed by the little burst of joy that went through her. It proved beyond all doubt that she had an inexhaustible source of blind, self-destructive stupidity inside her. "What changed your mind?"

He glared at her. "I thought it through."

"You thought it through," she repeated, surprise giving way to anger. "Good for you, Seth. How perceptive of you. How sensitive."

He stiffened. "Lazar set you up, Raine. He offered you to me like a cigar. What was I supposed to think?"

So it was true. Just as she had suspected. She filed that chilling bit of information away for future thought. "And you took what he offered," she pointed out. "That makes you just as bad."

He started to say something, and stopped himself. He shook his head, and pulled her against him, hard. "I wanted you."

"That's gratifying, I suppose," she faltered, squashed against the solid wall of his chest. "But it was so amazing, what we shared today. And then—and then you—"

"Yeah, I know," he broke in. "I was an asshole. I'll apologize forever if you want. Let me grovel. Here, watch this. Gold medal, Olympic groveling." He sank to his knees, still clutching her waist.

Raine batted at his head. He ducked, weaving back and forth, but not really trying to evade her blows now that the nervous energy had gone out of them. After a moment, she subsided and just stood quietly in his grasp, staring down into his dark eyes. A hot, trembling sensation was spreading throughout her body. Her fingers had gotten threaded through his hair somehow. She was almost petting him.

He was working his black magic on her already, clouding her mind with his sorcerer's tricks. Making her forget what a bastard he had been, how much he had hurt her feelings. She dug her fingers into his thick hair and tugged it, hard. He winced, but did not yield. His chin was pressed against her navel, and he gripped her hips, the intense warmth of his big hands sinking through the fabric.

Her throat was vibrating, her whole body was vibrating, as if she were about to shake apart. "Let me go, Seth," she whispered.

"No. I'm not letting you go until you accept my apology."

She covered her face with her trembling hands, smelling the scent of his hair upon them. "It doesn't work that way. You can't coerce me into accepting your apology."

"Watch me." His voice was low and stubborn.

"We'll freeze out here. Don't be ridiculous."

"I'll keep you warm." He pressed his face against her belly. The heat of his breath spread through the zippered sweatshirt.

She was shaking so hard now that his hair sliding between her fingers was her only point of reference, the only way to tell which way gravity was supposed to pull in this shifting universe. Her anger was draining away. It leaked out as if she were a sieve, leaving her hollow and desolate. She just wasn't designed to hold anger for very long. It was a structural flaw in her basic personality.

Canny as he was, he felt the exact instant that she softened. He rose to his feet, opened the back door of the Chevy and pushed her smoothly inside. He followed her in and shut the door. The lock snapped down. They sat together in the dense darkness, silent but for their ragged breathing.

He pulled her shivering body onto his lap, tucked her head into the curve of his neck, and hugged her hard. She felt his mute, painful apology in the quivering tension of his muscular body.

She also felt the pulse leaping in his throat, the heat of his erection against her thigh. Maybe that was all this was about. He hadn't gotten enough this afternoon, the insatiable bastard, and he thought he could just apologize and have some more. Anger flickered inside her, but she was too tired to fan the flame. It guttered and died. She was burned out, content to lie against him, exhausted.

He nuzzled her neck with small, soothing kisses, and his heat radiated into her body, making her sigh and stretch, almost purring. What an odd sensation it was to be held like a baby in his strong arms, surrounded by his heat. She felt protected, cuddled. It was an illusion, of course, but a lovely, delicious one. She wanted it to last.

But it was stupid to relax. Seth was a maze of contradictions. Tenderness and cruelty, seductive persuasion and ruthless coercion, wound together so tightly that it was impossible to pull them apart.

Every barrier she put up he brushed aside as if it were tissue paper. She didn't have the strength to construct another one tonight.

"Don't you make a fool of me again, Seth Mackey." She pressed her mouth against the hot, velvety skin of his neck and nipped him, hard enough to make him wince. "Don't you dare."

His arms tightened until she could barely breathe. "I won't."

She wiggled in his arms. "Hey. Ease up," she protested.

"No."

"Just let me breathe," she said. "I'm not going anywhere."

His eyes were doubtful, but he loosened his grip. Very slightly.

She pried herself out from under his chin. "Don't think that just because I'm letting you hold me means that you're off the hook."

His teeth flashed. "Wouldn't dream of it." There was an infinitesimal purring sound, and her zipper gave way. He shoved her sweatshirt open, and his hands slid inside, moving over her body.

She batted them away. "So that's what this is about? You just apologized because you want to fuck me again?"

He paused. "That word doesn't sound right coming out of your mouth." His tone was vaguely disapproving.

She let out a startled laugh. "Oh, really, Seth? Did I offend you?"

He cuddled her against his chest. Her cheek scraped against the wool of his sweater. "Never mind," he muttered. "Come back here."

"How long have you been here?" she asked him.

"Since about twelve-thirty."

"Two hours?" She struggled into a sitting position, startled.

He shrugged, rubbing the wisps at the end of her braid against his cheek. "Yeah. What of it? God, your hair is soft."

She tried to pull her braid away from him, but he kept a tight, jealous grip on it. "Why didn't you just . . . come to the door?"

He sniffed her braid. "I figured you'd tell me to fuck off again. You were royally pissed with me, and it is the middle of the night, after all."

"So why?" she persisted. "Why stay out here in the dark?"

"Why not? Why does anybody do anything? Do I have to have a reason? I felt bad. I wanted to be near you. Maybe I wanted to do penance, or something weird like that."

"Penance," she repeated. Her lips began to twitch. "If it's penance, then it's not enough."

"What would be enough?"

She pushed at his chest and twisted until she was perched on his lap facing him. "Let me think about it for a while."

He snorted. "Bad idea. Don't think, Raine."

"Yes, it would be awfully convenient for you if I didn't, wouldn't it?" she said. "Too bad my brain doesn't have an off switch."

He stared at her for a moment, his eyes unreadable pools of shadow. He slid his hands under the hem of her shirt. "Do you know how sexy you are in that jogging stuff?"

"Oh, please," she snapped. "Don't even. You can't distract me with cheap flattery like that, not after you—"

"Yeah, I know," he cut in. "I'm a rude son-of-a-bitch, we've established that. Let's move on. I'd rather talk about how soft your skin is underneath this shirt. How I want to slide my hand in, and touch your belly . . . like this. God, so soft. Like flower petals. I've never felt anything like it. I could pet you for hours and never get bored."

The lazy caress made sweet shivers race across her skin. With the rough hunger in his voice and a few simple words, he created images in her head, unleashed sensations in her body; and melded them seamlessly together into a promise of pleasure that was seductive and voluptuous and sweet. She had told him that her brain didn't have an off switch, but she had lied. It did. He had found it. And he knew it.

"You are dangerous, Seth Mackey," she whispered.

He pushed a wisp of hair out from her mouth and dropped a light, butterfly kiss on her jaw. "Maybe." He tasted her lips again, and then deeper and hungrier, his lips seeking and coaxing, then demanding.

She turned her face away from his kiss, her heart pounding. "You're not a nice man."

"No," he agreed calmly. "I never pretended to be."

"I should have picked somebody tame to experiment with," she murmured, almost to herself. "I'm out of my depth with you."

He nuzzled the side of her face. "Too bad, sweetheart," he muttered. "You picked me, and you hooked me. Now you've got to deal with me, whether you like it or not. I'm not easy to get rid of." He cupped her face in his hand, the rough, callused spots scraping lightly against her skin as he explored the contours of her cheekbone. "How much experimenting have you done?"

"Hmm?" She was muddled and distracted by his caresses.

"You said you should have picked someone tamer than me. What does that mean? How much sexual experimenting have you done?"

He smoothed her hip, and she jerked as his fingers feathered along the cleft of her bottom, tickling and teasing. She forced herself to concentrate. "Um, not a lot," she admitted.

"How much exactly? Be honest. If you're lying, I'll know."

His fierce attention made her feel hunted. "That's really none of your business."

"That's where you're dead wrong. Since yesterday, everything about you is my business."

She tried to think of a response to that outrageous statement. Nothing forceful came to mind, just a sense that she'd best choose her battles with him very carefully. He had enormous charisma and stamina, and she was too vulnerable and depleted to oppose him.

She might as well let him win this one. At least on this front, she had nothing to hide. Indeed, she had practically nothing to tell.

She let out a long, slow sigh. "Just the one time," she offered.

His body went extremely still. "One time?"

She winced at the ugly memory. "Yes. In Paris. I was sick of being a virgin, so I decided to—"

"How old were you?"

She lost her train of thought, and flailed for a moment. "Oh, twenty-four, I guess. Almost twenty-five. It was a little over three years ago. I was at the Louvre, and I ran into this man that I knew—"

"Jesus. Twenty-four." He sounded almost horrified.

"You were the one who said you wanted to hear this," she snapped.

"Go on, go on. I won't interrupt you again," he assured her.

"Anyhow, I ran into this man I knew, and, well, he seemed nice. Kind of dull, but pleasant. And safe, I guess. He was in Paris on business. We had dinner, and I decided it was time. So I let him escort me back to my flat."

"And?" he prompted.

She winced again. "And what? I let him—well, we, um, did it."
"And?"

Her face was burning. "God, don't you ever let up?"

"Never," he said calmly. "Tell me."

"Well, it was terrible." The words burst out of her in an embarrassed little rush.

Seth was eloquently silent. "What constitutes terrible?" he asked.
His voice sounded deeply curious.

"Oh, please—"

"Just tell me, so I won't ever do it to you."

She laughed, but it felt more like a sob. "You couldn't. It was over in less than a minute, and it hurt. He—he ran out on me while I was washing up. I came out of the bathroom and he was gone."

He hissed in disgust. "What a prick!"

She smiled at the fury in his voice. "I'm over it."

"No foreplay, no petting, no oral sex, no nothing?"

She blushed even hotter. "Seth, please—"

"Don't be prissy," he snapped.

She sighed. "He couldn't wait. He just wanted to . . . you know."

"Yeah, I do know. And how. But that's no excuse for botching your first time. Jesus. What a flaming asshole."

She kissed his forehead, touched by the genuine outrage in his voice. "It's all right," she whispered. "The second time made up for it."

He pulled her close, in a fierce, possessive grip. Raine let her head fall back with a soft sigh of pleasure as he nuzzled her neck.

"What's the bastard's name?"

She froze as his question sank in. "Why do you want to know?"

"Want me to kill him for you?" His voice was supremely casual.

A cold fist clamped around her stomach. "Not funny, Seth."

"Whoops. Sorry. How about some broken bones? Ribs, kneecaps, fingers?" His teeth flashed in the dimness. "You choose."

"That won't be necessary, thank you," she said stiffly. "I'm over
          1d boorish and bad in bed is not a capital crime,
        w that, don't you?"
      ge, sweetheart." His voice was as soft as a kiss, and

he slid his hand beneath her shirt and trailed his fingertips across her belly again. "Being mean and boorish to you has just become one."

He was making her very nervous. She clapped both hands over his hand, and held it still. "Seth, you *are* kidding, aren't you?"

He pulled her into his arms again. "Sure I am, sweetheart," he said soothingly. "Only one time. Jesus. I wish I'd known. I would have been so different with you."

The warm caress of his breath against her ear sent a melting, shimmering sensation racing across the surface of her skin. "I liked the way you were," she told him. "All except for the last three minutes."

His lips dragged across hers, demanding and seductive, and his arms tightened. "So you forgive me, then?"

The intensity in his voice put her on guard. "I'm not sure yet."

"Make up your mind, babe, because I'm burning up here."

"Don't you dare push me, Seth Mackey," she said, with as much austerity as she could muster. "You are still on shaky ground."

He laughed. "I'm at my best on shaky ground, sweetheart."

She knew that the long, sweet, skillful kiss was calculated to make her helpless and giddy, but even when it worked, even when she felt his triumphant smile against her mouth, she couldn't be angry at him. He stroked her hair back and gazed into her face.

"I'm sorry about what I said, Raine. I wish I could take it back."

His sincerity made her heart ache, hot and soft. Made her want to cover his face with soothing kisses as if he were a baby, to make up for the loneliness she sensed behind his rough facade. She wrapped her arms around his neck and pressed her face against his hair.

Her soft embrace provoked a frightening flare of heat in him. He spread open her jacket and shoved her T-shirt up over her collarbone, rough and urgent. She twisted against him in protest. "Seth, don't."

Her breathless words lost their meaning as his warm hands stroked and soothed. "Just this. Just let me rub my face against your skin. I'm starving for it. So soft. I love the smell of you. Please, Raine. I need this." His voice was a pleading rasp, and he caressed her breasts through the spandex sports bra. His tender, ravenous mouth tongued the hollow of her throat, licking the soft skin above her bra.

It was easier to just let herself believe that he was giving her a choice, she thought, as he discovered the zippered front of the sports bra and growled in approval at the convenience. He yanked it open, folded the flaps back and bent his head to her naked breasts.

That was it. She was lost. He held her breasts, one in each big hand, suckling both nipples in turn, licking the plump curves. His breath was a warm caress that generated a wild chaotic heat. There was no stopping him. He could take whatever he wanted, and make her beg him to keep taking and taking, until he'd taken everything.

He lifted his head. "Quit Lazar."

"What?" She was disoriented, the moist skin of her breasts cool where his suckling mouth had been. "What?"

"You heard me. Quit the bastard. It's not a healthy place for you. Don't go back there at all. Don't even call. Just blow them off."

She shook her head, bewildered. "I can't just—"

"The place is poison for you, Raine. You know I'm right."

Hah. If he only knew. Her mind raced, seeking a plausible excuse. "I can't just leave. Where would I go? Even this house belongs to—"

"Come with me. I'll take care of you." He slid his hands under the waistband of her leggings and delved inside her panties, his fingers tangling in the warm nest of curls between her thighs.

She squeaked, grabbing his wrist with a nervous laugh. "And what do you want in return for taking care of me? Do I get to be your, um, mistress, or something? Your little love slave?"

His tongue slid along her open lips, probing and dancing against hers, drinking in her nervous, panting breaths. His hand probed deeper, his gentle fingers seeking the wet, silky heat hidden in her soft folds, and finding it. "That sounds good," he said huskily. "Mistress, love slave, either one works for me. Never had a mistress before, but it sounds like fun."

"Oh, please, Seth. I was just kidding. I can't possibly—"

Her words cut off in a sharp gasp as his hand thrust deeper. "It would be perfect," he said. "I want to look after you, I want to protect you, and I want to have sex with you. Every chance I get. Front, back, sideways, up against the wall, in the shower, everything. Call it whatever the fuck you want. Just come with me."

"Seth, slow down," she said, wiggling. "Wait. I—"

"Humor me," he muttered, biting her throat. "Please, Raine. It'll be OK. I've got lots of money. I'll make it worth your while."

His words were like a splash of ice water. She shoved him away and yanked his hand out of her leggings. "You bastard!"

"What?" He sounded completely bewildered.

"Worth my while? All that carrying on about how you're so sorry, you were wrong about me, and now you're trying to . . . to buy me!"

He let out a sigh of disgust. "Raine—"

"Let me out of this car." She flailed in his tight embrace.

"I wasn't calling you a whore." He pulled her back against his chest. "I just phrased it wrong. I guess I figured having money might be relevant information to put forward while trying to persuade a woman to abandon her livelihood and become my mistress. All I mean is that you'd be covered financially. Money is not a problem for me. Got it?"

She stopped struggling, but her whole body still shook with anger. "You are rude and crass," she informed him.

"Yeah. I've been told that I lack social skills," he said sourly.

"You were told right."

"OK. Sorry. I swear to God, I didn't mean to insult you again. It's the last thing I wanted to do. Forgive me. Please. *Again.*"

The frustration in his voice was very real. She studied his taut profile for a long moment, nodded and slowly took his hand in hers.

His sigh of relief was audible. "OK. Rewind, erase, and let's take this again from the top," he said. "Never mind my money. Forget about it. Do it for the sex. Do it for pleasure, Raine. You know I can satisfy you. I can make you come until you pass out. And I will. Remember how it was today? You all spread out on the bed, sweet and sticky like taffy, with your legs draped over my shoulders? You liked that, didn't you? That's how it'll be. All the time. As much as you can take."

His hand slid into her leggings again, easing them over her hips. His hands were cupping her bare bottom. The reality of her situation finally hit her. All night she'd been lecturing herself about how stupid she'd been to throw herself at a stranger. Seth Mackey was still a stranger, and here she was, nearly naked in his car, about to be ravished all over again. God, was she ever a slow learner.

"Wait," she tried to say, but his tongue was thrusting into her mouth, his hand between her legs. She clenched her thighs around his probing fingers and he murmured something in a low, approving tone against her trembling mouth. She struggled in his grasp, but he held her still, his thumb circling her clitoris. He was as slow and deliberate as he was ruthless, driving her before him straight into the heart of unknown sexual sensation.

She came, violently. Hot bursts of pleasure jerked through her repeatedly, jagged and intense.

She lay in his arms, astonished. Seth cradled her limp body, and drew his hand out from between her thighs. He raised it to his face, inhaled, and licked his fingers, one after the other. "That was heaven."

A burst of shivery, tearful laughter shook her. "That's my line."

He untied the laces of one of her running shoes and pried it off. "Say it the next time I make you come."

"Wait, Seth. I don't think we—"

"You're so juicy and sweet down there." He struggled with the laces of her other shoe. "I want to go down on you. Right now." The shoe thumped to the floor. "I could eat you for hours."

His feverish intensity alarmed her. "Seth, wait. Wait," she protested, pushing at his chest. "Slow down, please."

"Stop fighting me." He seized her wrists in one big hand and started to pull her leggings off. "Relax. I'll make it good for you."

It infuriated her that he wouldn't listen. She slammed her elbow into him, and he let out a startled grunt. She froze, horrified at herself.

He stared at her. "What the hell was that about?"

She swallowed over the hard, painful lump in her throat. "Don't use your strength against me."

Raine shoved against the rigid circle of his arms, and he opened them, leaving her shivering and wobbling on his lap. She steadied herself against his shoulder, conscious of her near nudity, breasts bared, leggings yanked halfway down her thighs; at a total disadvantage. She searched for words to make sense of this tangle of incomprehension. Nothing came to mind.

"You liked it, Raine," he said slowly. "I was making you feel good. I don't know what the goddamn problem is."

"You use your strength too much," she said, fighting back tears. "I want you to slow down. I can't control anything. It scares me."

He peered into her eyes as if he were trying to read her mind. "Why should you control anything? What the hell do you think needs controlling? It was working great. You came like crazy. It was awesome."

"Please," she whispered. She reached out, touched his cheek with shaking fingers. "Just ease off, Seth. I can't bear it."

He leaned his head back and closed his eyes, shaking his head in helpless frustration. "Damn. I really don't want to wreck this."

The baffled hurt in his voice pained her. "You didn't," she blurted out. "You haven't. But I can't just let myself go like you want me to. Or at least . . . I shouldn't."

"Why not?"

She threw up her hands. "Because I don't know you!"

He lifted his head. "So? You know how much I want you. You know how good I can make you feel. What more do you need to know?"

The abyss between their points of view staggered her.

"This afternoon, we both made stupid assumptions. We crashed and burned, and it was awful. I can't let that happen again," she explained, in an earnest little rush. "I'm not the kind of person who can have anonymous sex with a stranger. It was . . . a mistake."

"A mistake?" His voice was dangerously soft.

"No! I mean, yes. I mean, it was wonderful to make love to you, but it was a mistake to make love to a stranger. I don't want you to be a stranger, Seth. I can't make love to you again until I know you better."

His silence was unnerving. "What do you want to know?"

She threw up her hands. "Anything. The usual things."

He let out a short laugh. "There's not much that's usual about me, Raine."

"Unusual ones, then," she said desperately.

"Be specific. What exactly are you interested in?"

"Oh, stop making this difficult," she snapped. "Where are you from? Where did you go to school? What's your family like? What do your parents do? What's your favorite breakfast cereal?"

"I hope you're not expecting any pretty stories."

She was taken aback by his flat tone. "No. Just the truth."

He laid his hands on tops of her thighs, stroking her skin. "I grew up in L.A." he said. "I don't know much about my father. Neither did my mom. All she could tell me was that his name was Raul, he spoke only Spanish, and I look just like him, only taller. They didn't communicate much, except in bed. That's the sum total of my knowledge about him. My guess is that he was her supplier, and she was screwing him to get whatever her drug of choice was at the time."

She stared at him, aghast. "Oh, God, Seth."

"She OD'ed when I was sixteen, but with all the junk she did, she was pretty much dead to me a few years before that. There was a sort of a stepdad for a while, but he meant less than zero to me. I raised myself, more or less."

She wrapped her arms around his neck. He stiffened as she pressed her cheek against his hot face. "Don't get mushy on me," he muttered. "That's not part of the deal."

"Sorry." She pulled away. "How did you survive?"

"I don't know. I ran pretty wild. Got into lots of trouble. Fights, lots of fights. I'm good at fighting. And sex, of course. I started real early with sex." He hesitated. "I'm good at that, too," he added.

He paused, trying to gauge her reaction. She waited patiently.

"My mom liked pills, and my stepdad liked booze, but my drug of choice is adrenaline. I'm good with my fists. Good with a knife, too. I was a talented thief. I can pick locks, I can hotwire cars. I was into drag racing for a while, that was a lot of fun. I was good at that, too. And I was an awesome shoplifter. Never got caught once."

He waited. She gave him an encouraging nod, petting his hair.

"I never did deal drugs, though," he said. "Watching my mom turned me off to that but good." He stroked his knuckle over her cheek, a slow, lingering caress. "Am I scaring you yet, Raine?"

His tone was almost taunting, but she heard the message behind it as loudly as if he were shouting it. It could not be easy for a man like him to tell her such painful and intimate things. His blunt words were a sacrificial offering. She was moved by the gesture.

He didn't scare her. He broke her heart, maybe, but she wasn't intimidated in the least. In some ways, his childhood had a lot in common with her own. The alienation, the loneliness. Probably the fear, too, though she was sure he would rather die than admit it.

She stroked the short, soft hair at the nape of his neck and rubbed her face against his scratchy cheek. She smiled at him.

"No," she said softly. "You're not scaring me at all. Go on."

Chapter

9

Raine's words sent another tremor of raw emotion through him. He was jacked up and out of control tonight, his armor suddenly cracked. The grisly details of his past were nobody's else's goddamn business, but the words had just fallen out of him. She was the one with almost no clothes on, but he was the one who felt naked.

He splayed his fingers around the yielding softness of her waist and tried to remember if he'd ever discussed his hard-luck childhood with any of his other women. It wasn't much of a turn-on, as conversational topics went. Seemed to work for Raine, though. There was always the possibility that she was pumping him for info for Lazar, but when he looked at her shadowy eyes, her soft, trembling mouth, he doubted it.

Her hands were so gentle, petting his face. It distracted him.

"OK," he muttered, trying to gather his thoughts. "So one day I'm burgling this guy's house, and he pops up out of nowhere and sticks a Para-Ordnance P14-45 in the back of my neck. Turns out he was a retired cop, a guy named Hank Yates. He roughed me up a little, just to teach me a lesson, and he started to haul me down to the station—"

His throat closed down. He swallowed, and stopped. He couldn't go into how Hank had grabbed him by the scruff of the neck to shove him into the car, and realized that the smart-mouthed, thieving kid was burning with fever and coughing up blood. In the end, he'd taken Seth to the emergency room instead of to juvie, where he'd been diagnosed with pneumonia brought on by untreated bronchitis. When he recovered, the gruff, self-righteous old bastard had felt so bad about having smacked a sick kid around that he'd taken it upon himself to rescue Seth from a life of crime. God, how embarrassing.

What a royal pain in the ass that had been. Hank had been a stiff-necked authoritarian, a solitary widower who had long ago alienated his own grown children. He and Seth had clashed violently at first, but after a very stormy period, they had both recognized that they needed each other. Hank had meant well, and in his own way, Seth was grateful to him. Particularly because with Hank's help, Seth had been able to make sure that Jesse got a fighting chance, too.

At least until ten months ago.

Raine was patiently waiting, still stroking his face. He struggled to remember at what point he had left her stranded in the tar-pit of his childhood. "Where was I?" he demanded.

"Hank was about to take you to the station," she reminded gently.

"Oh. Right. Well, he didn't. He decided to straighten me out instead, and after a while, I decided to let him do it. I was just smart enough to realize that there wasn't much of a future in my lifestyle."

"Yes?" she prompted. "So?"

"It's a long story, but basically he just bullied me and hassled me into getting my GED. Then he bullied and hassled some more until I ended up in the Army. Hank was an Army man."

God, it had been so long since he let himself think about all this stuff. His brain was churning out memories all on its own, like watching an old movie. He could actually hear Hank's gruff voice.

"Come on, kid, where else are you gonna learn that tech stuff that you like? They'll help put you through school, too. Can't beat that. Got eighty thousand bucks stashed in a mattress someplace to go to Stanford? Got any rich relatives? Gonna rob a bank? No. Stop. Don't answer that."

But Seth was already grinning. "Bet I could, you know."

"That ain't funny, kid."

"Who's joking? Who's laughing?"

He shook himself again. This weird inability to concentrate was pissing him off. "Where the hell was I?" he snapped.

"The Army," she reminded him.

"Oh. The Army. Yeah, they made me take all the tests, and figured out that I actually had a brain underneath all that attitude. They sent me to Rangers school, and I ended up in the 75th Rangers regiment. And bam, I was hooked. I did my time investigating threats to national security. Counterintelligence, anti-terrorism, anti-espionage, you name it. The discipline was pure hell on earth, but I knew if I was a good boy they would let me play with their toys. It was actually worth it to me. So I stuck with it."

"Good for you." She kissed his forehead.

He grabbed her wrists, gripping them hard enough to make her squeak. "Get this straight, Raine. I'm not telling you about my childhood to make you feel sorry for me, because I don't feel sorry for myself. I'm telling you for two reasons. The first is because lying is a big waste of time."

She hesitated. "I agree."

"Good. I'm real glad we're on the same page with that one. The second reason I'm telling you my life story is because, if I understood correctly, you won't have sex with me again until I do. And I want to have sex with you again. Soon. Right here, in fact. You cool with that?"

A tremor went through her body, but she didn't pull away. "Um, yes," she said softly.

"OK," he muttered. He let go of her hands and seized her waist again. "I wanted that to be perfectly clear. No more misunderstandings."

"Crystal clear." She gave him an encouraging nod. "Go on."

His hands slid down and settled on the swell of her hip. "So to make a boring story short, I ended up serving part time in the Reserves. I enrolled at UCLA on the GI bill. Got some scholarships, scraped together the tuition somehow. Got a degree in electronic engineering, teamed up with some other egghead geeks, and Mackey Security Systems Design was born. My status as an ex-thief gives me a unique edge when it comes to designing surveillance and countersurveillance systems security, but I don't tell potential clients that. I play up the Rangers angle instead. It tends to inspire more confidence. So I'd appreciate it if you kept it to yourself."

Her shadowy, appreciative smile made his cock pulse and throb painfully. He had to wrap this up and get back to seducing her before he exploded. "There it is, babe," he concluded. "My life story. I'm damaged goods, but I can fake it when I have to. Money covers up a lot of warts."

She cuddled up against him. "You're very cynical."

He snorted. "Yeah." He splayed his hands wide and gripped the warm, smooth cheeks of her beautiful bare ass. "So? Anything else you need to know about me before I make you come again?"

She twisted in his arms, and her soft breasts pressed against his chest as she hugged him, kissing his jaw. "I'm so sorry about your mother," she murmured, her voice catching.

He turned his face away from her soft kisses. "Don't feel sorry for me, because I'll take advantage of it, I promise you," he said roughly. "I'm an opportunistic bastard, and don't you ever forget it."

She leaned her forehead against his, and shook with a whispery little laugh. "If you're so opportunistic, then why are you warning me?"

"Damned if I know," he muttered. "Somebody's got to, I guess."

She was so intent on her questions that she barely noticed that he'd tugged her leggings completely off and was peeling off her socks. "Are you still in touch with Hank?" she asked.

"Hank died five years ago. Liver cancer." He tossed her discarded clothes to the floor.

"I'm sorry," she said. "So now—isn't there any family out there for you? An aunt, or uncle, a grandparent? Nobody?"

He hesitated. "No."

"But . . . there did used to be someone?" Her voice trailed off into a questioning silence.

His split-second hesitation had been a mistake. She was quick and smart, and listening so carefully that she had sensed the ragged black hole inside him where Jesse used to be. The one place he was utterly unwilling to go.

Diversion time.

He seized her ankles and placed them on the seat, pushing her back until she was crouched in front of him, thighs splayed. He leaned against her, pressing her thighs even wider. "Story time is over for today, sweetheart."

Her head fell back against the seat with a breathless gasp. She lifted her hips, offering herself to him. His leather coat creaked in the hushed darkness as he hunched over to suckle her breasts. She reached up and clutched his jacket, gasping as he slid his finger tenderly inside her, stretching and opening her. "Are you sore?" he asked. "I was pretty rough on you today."

"I'm all right." Raine gripped the front of his sweater and moved herself against his hand. "I love what you do to me. Please don't stop."

"How about my offer?" He played with her sensitive folds, in sync with the eager movements of her hips, spreading her moisture tenderly around. "You going to blow off Lazar and come away with me?"

Subtle sounds were loud in the stillness of the car: unbuckling his belt, the buttons popping open on his jeans, the rustle as he ripped open a condom and fitted it over himself.

Her fists were trembling, clenching hard onto his sweater. "I don't need a protector, Seth," she whispered. "I can take care of myself."

She let out a sharp sigh at the first blunt, probing contact of his cock. He nudged the head of his shaft tenderly up and down her cleft in a slow, controlled caress. "That's not how it looks to me, sweetheart."

Her hips pulsed against him, but he held her still, pinning her against the seat, circling his penis around her swollen clit. Making her squirm and whimper and wait, until they were both sure she wanted it as much as he did. He wanted there to be absolutely no doubt.

"It sounds like you're saying I should be protected from you." She let out a nervous little laugh as he lifted her into position.

He nudged his cock slightly deeper as he captured her mouth in a hot, demanding kiss. He bit her lush lower lip, and slid his tongue into her mouth, mimicking the shallow, teasing thrusts he was making with his hips. "Yeah, you probably should be protected from the likes of me," he said, not even bothering to hide the dark triumph in his voice. "But you're not, Raine. And you know what?"

"What?" she begged, pulling at him, her eyes dazed. "What?"

"That's just your tough luck, babe."

He thrust himself inside her with one deep, hard lunge.

She almost screamed. He was so thick and hard and hot, the rough penetration both exciting and painful. He'd been right, she was sore from yesterday's encounter, but so aroused that she hadn't wanted to risk him stopping, or slowing, or holding back in any way.

She wanted all of him, everything. She needed it, now and forever. Only Seth had the power to drive away her fears. Only this white-hot blaze of pure desire would do the job.

She grasped his upper arms, but they were too thick with muscle and slippery with stiff leather to get a good grip, so she seized fistfuls of his sweater again. First she was upright, pinned between him and the sweat-dampened leather seat. Then he shoved her down onto her back and folded her legs up over her chest so that his thrusts had his whole weight behind them.

The world focused down to this cramped seat and Seth's heaving body. He blotted out all the light and sealed her into a tumultuous velvet darkness. Cars passed occasionally, their lights dancing erratically across Seth's rigid face. She barely noticed, and did not care. All she knew was his weight, his breath, his strong hands, the plunge and slide of his thick shaft inside her. The fire he had unleashed stormed and raged inside her, driving her higher and deeper into herself. She was glowing, molten, hotter with every stroke.

He took all she had to give, but he was generous too, pouring a current of sexual electricity into her body, transforming her with his magic. It was ravishing, perfect. She wanted it to last forever, but they were already speeding over the brink together, crashing to the finish.

As soon as Raine could form a coherent thought, she realized that her throat hurt. She had been yelling and screaming. She wondere ⅃ if anyone had heard, and realized that she didn't give a damn.

They clutched each other for a long time, damp and pant˙

"God," Seth finally said. "I'm soaked."

She kissed his forehead, tasting his salty sweat against her lips. "Should have taken off your jacket, silly."

"Didn't think of it."

She tightened her arms and legs around him, cuddling him against her breasts and stroked his damp hair. He heaved a sigh of contentment, and she squeezed her eyes shut, trying to impress the moment of perfect intimacy upon her memory. She wished she could extend it to infinity, but reality was encroaching, the way cold air crept under even the warmest blanket.

He dropped a kiss on her shoulder and raised his head. "Go pack a suitcase. I'll take you to a hotel for now, but I'll rent something for you as soon as real estate agencies open. What part of town do you prefer?"

She stiffened. "Wait, Seth. Hold on. I don't think—"

"Don't think what?" His voice was sharp.

"I don't think I'm cut out to be a mistress."

"OK, fine. Forget about being my mistress. Come with me anyway. Be whatever the hell you want. You can find your own apartment. And you can find a better job in ten minutes. Pack your bags now, though. It'll be dawn soon, and this neighborhood is about to wake up."

His words indicated that her decision was foregone, but his watchful stillness said otherwise. He waited, his penis still shoved deep inside her. She wiggled beneath him. She could barely move.

If she went with him now, and let him claim her, protect her, define her whole existence, she would be just as pinned. Just as helpless. He was overwhelming.

It was so tempting. She wanted to laugh at the irony. From a famine to a glutton's feast. Frontwards, backwards, sideways, up against the wall, in the shower. She saw herself sprawled beneath ⌐eth's big, beautiful body, having multiple orgasms until she was ˎ bliss. What a day job that would be. She could tell the ghosts ˎ that she'd had no choice. Sorry, guys. Never mind the ˎnd justice. She'd been swept off her feet and right

off that easily. Seth couldn't protect her her own head. Her nightmares, her past, her ˎ save her but herself.

She looked into his narrowed eyes, sensing how badly he wanted to protect her. It brought hot tears to her eyes. She tightened her arms around his neck and kissed him in silent gratitude.

"I'm sorry, Seth. I can't go with you," she said.

Tension gathered in his body as he readied to do battle. "No," she said, more sharply. "No means no, Seth. I can't quit my job right now. And I can't go with you. Thank you for offering to help me, but no."

The tenderness on his face had vanished. It was taut and angry. "Why not?"

She touched his cheek, wishing with all her heart that she dared to confide in him. "I have my reasons," she said quietly.

He flinched away from her hand and withdrew himself from her body. He closed his jeans and rummaged around, gathering her things. He tossed the tangled wad of clothing at her. "Get decent."

She clutched them to her chest, chilled at the biting tone in his voice. "Is that all you have to say?"

"If I beg like a dog, will it change your mind?"

She shook her head.

"Then get to it. I have work to do."

"At three in the morning?"

"Yeah." He offered no further explanation.

She began to turn her clothes right-side out and pull them on. Sweat was cooling on her body, making it harder. He waited, grim and silent, until the laces were tied and the zippers zipped. He snapped the locks open and got out of the car. "Out you go."

"Seth—"

He reached in, grabbing her arm and pulling her after him. "You've got your house keys?" he demanded. "Let me see them."

She fished them out of her pocket, shivering in the cold.

"Go on inside. I want to see the door locked before I leave."

He got into the car, and she stood there on the street, frozen in place. Her legs shook so hard that she didn't dare move. She was afraid she would fall on her face. The motor hummed to life. His window rolled down. "Get your ass into the house, Raine."

His harsh tone jarred her nerves. "Don't order me around, Seth."

"If I have to carry you in there, I will, but be aware that it is going to seriously piss me off."

She backed away, holding up her hands, unable to bear the cold look on his face any longer. She scurried into the house, locked the door behind herself, and peeked out the window. He saw her, nodded, and pulled away. She watched his taillights disappear down the street.

She sank down onto the carpet. Her shoulders shook, but with what emotion she wasn't sure. The situation seemed to call for tears, but she had cried so much recently, she was all cried out.

Then it occurred to her that after all the passion and intensity of that encounter, he still hadn't given her his phone number.

She had to laugh after all.

Chapter

10

Victor took a sip of his brandy and stared up at the sky. The moon emerged, making a brief appearance in the ragged window in the clouds. It illuminated the water for a few seconds, and vanished again.

It was long after midnight, but he could seldom sleep when the moon was this close to full. The wind had an icy nip, but he felt so exultant, he didn't care. His niece wasn't a rabbit, after all. She needed work, but the raw material was there. Maybe she really was his daughter. She certainly didn't get her spirit from poor Peter, and Alix was all noise and bluster, not spirit or strength.

His campaign to toughen her up appeared to be working splendidly. The encounter with Mackey had done her a world of good. She had actually defied him, the naughty girl. She had thrown him out of her place. How marvelous. His whole body was pleasantly wide awake, humming with excitement. Tonight was a night to celebrate.

He tossed back the last of his brandy and went inside, handing the glass to the hovering attendant. "Send Mara to my suite in ten minutes," he said briskly.

Her soft knock sounded before he had finished undressing. He let her wait outside the door as he donned his robe and sat down in his favorite chair, positioned for a clear view of both the window and the mirror. "Come in."

She stole into the room, barefoot, her long dark hair tousled around her shoulders. She was wearing a short robe of crimson silk, belted at the waist. She walked towards him slowly, a sultry, expectant smile on her face, and stopped a few feet from his chair, awaiting further instructions. His staff was very well trained.

He studied her at great length, liking what he saw. "Take off the robe," he ordered.

She tugged the belt loose and shrugged. The robe slipped off her gleaming shoulders, the smooth fabric caught for one delicious, suspended moment upon her taut brown nipples. It snagged even more briefly upon the curve of her hips, and pooled silently around her feet.

Gilded toenails, he noticed. He liked that detail. He did not like the toe ring, but that could be overlooked for now. He would mention it to the housekeeper tomorrow. "Turn," he said.

She gracefully did so, lifting her hair and arching her back. Her muscles rippled and flexed, and her breasts were perfect. The sharp, humming energy in his body coalesced. The moment was right.

Victor gestured for the girl to kneel in front of him, and then leaned back to watch as she sank to her knees, smiling at him with seductive promise. She reached confidently inside his robe, grasping his aroused penis with cool, smooth hands.

He was pleasantly impressed with her technique. The girl was skillful and sensual. The pacing was perfect, the ratio of depth to pressure very enjoyable; he felt no teeth. The way she used her hands in tandem with lips and tongue was perfect. She was bold yet graceful, managing to be beautifully carnal in the act of fellatio while avoiding the pitfall of vulgarity, never an easy task. She made no unpleasant noises with her mouth. Above all, she displayed an unforced, pleasant enthusiasm for the task. He appreciated that, whether real or feigned.

He shifted his attention to the mirror, enjoying the picture she made. The dip of her waist swelled into buttocks that looked as if they had been polished to marble smoothness. Flawless. He would inform his housekeeper to give her a bonus. He lit a cigarette. Mara's eyes flicked up in a questioning look. He nodded, indicating that she should continue.

The dimness of the room suddenly struck him as oppressive. He flipped on the light, but this proved to be unfortunate, as it highlighted the fact that Mara's forehead was somewhat low, her nose a bit too narrow. Her makeup, under the light, seemed harsh.

He closed his eyes, blocking out the sight, and found himself thinking of his niece. Her tryst with Mackey must have been a good experience. Or, at least, extremely intense; the only kind of experience worth having, in his opinion. He wondered idly if Mara was still capable of blushing. He opened his eyes and observed her. Watching his penis slide in and out of her glossy crimson mouth, he rather doubted it.

The conflicting thoughts weighed upon him, threatening both his mood and his erection. He tried to dismiss them, but a startling thought was taking shape in his mind, so ludicrous it was impossible to ignore.

He was jealous of his clumsy, ignorant, blameless niece. She was poised on the brink of miracles and disasters. Anything could happen to her. Anything probably would. The danger and intensity of her life was worlds away from the flat emptiness that he faced every day.

He closed his eyes, deliberately allowing the warm, wet suction of Mara's skilful mouth to coax him over the crest. He came, in a long, painful shudder. A crashing silence descended on him.

When he opened his eyes, his cigarette was a teetering tube of ash. Mara was wiping her mouth, trying to hide the apprehension in her eyes. He twitched his robe shut. "You can go," he said curtly.

She rose to her feet. She looked faintly hurt, but was far too professional to make any protest. She left without a word.

He stared out the window. The cold inside him deepened.

Summoning Mara had been a mistake. Sometimes sex alleviated the cold; sometimes it intensified it. Unfortunately, in the initial stages of sexual excitement, it was impossible to tell which of the two it would be. He should probably give up sex altogether, he thought, with a fierce stab of regret. It was no longer worth the risk. Self-denial was tedious, but at this point, self-indulgence usually was, too.

He experienced a flicker of discomfort at how cold and abrupt he had been with Mara. She had done her best, and the situation was not her fault. She was being very well paid to get her feelings hurt, however. He brushed the thought aside, poured a glass of whiskey and sipped it, gazing at the desolate beauty of the moon on the water.

He knew what would happen now. The cold would deepen into a hollow ache. The ache would spread out, cracking him open until he was staring into an abyss of emptiness. On nights such as these, the moon was a cold, unfriendly eye that witnessed all, remembered all, forgave nothing. Sometimes he was tempted to medicate away the ache and the emptiness, but he preferred even intense discomfort to the fog of drugs or alcohol. He should not even try to sleep tonight. In such a mood, a dream was sure to afflict him. He wondered if Raine had inherited the Lazar gift of dreaming.

It was a most inconvenient birthright for a man such as himself.

He needed something absorbing to entertain him, if sex was no longer a viable diversion. He'd been on tediously good behavior since the wretched Cahill affair, and this moratorium on illegal activity galled him. Perhaps it was time to turn back to collecting. Not the treasures he had down in his vault, though many of them were indeed priceless. His real hobby was collecting people.

He had always had a talent for finding and exploiting people's weaknesses. The stolen murder weapons were just a new variation on an old theme, binding people to him with secrecy and collusive guilt. He loved the power, the sense of control.

His collection was vast and varied, but lately he had gotten bored with collecting public figures and pillars of the community. For some time now he'd been toying with the notion of collecting more dangerous, unpredictable creatures for his private zoo. Exotics, as it were. Such people's key secrets were uglier, more dangerous. Rather like his own.

That was the impulse that had gotten him involved with Kurt Novak. Novak was the most exotic creature he had ever attempted to collect. It was like swinging a poisonous serpent by the tail—one had to keep the centrifugal force in constant motion. Once collected, however, Victor would have a lever with Kurt's even more powerful father, Pavel Novak, a Hungarian, and one of the richest and most influential bosses of the burgeoning Eastern European mafia. That was a prize too intriguing to resist, with infinite possibilities for entertainment and profit.

His last attempt had been foiled by Jesse Cahill's untimely interference. Novak had been infuriated by the whole affair. Trapping and murdering the undercover agent had barely appeased him.

Victor had sincerely regretted the necessity of Cahill's death. Murder was never to his taste, and Cahill had been a likeable young man; but he had known who he was dealing with. He had rolled his dice, and lost. He was glad that he had not been present at Cahill's execution. Novak's tastes were baroque, to say the least of it.

He had seen it in his dreams, however. Most unfortunately.

To set the new game in motion, he had to gamble on one of his dreams. He seldom did so, because of the unpredictable nature of his uncanny gift. It could betray him at any time. Therein lay the risk—and the reward. His mind seized hungrily onto the idea, giving him instant relief from the ache and the emptiness. He had been formulating this plan carefully for months, ever since the Corazon dreams began.

He lit a cigarette and reached for the phone.

The scrambled line clicked open on the fourth ring. "Hello, Victor. I'm surprised you have the gall to call me at this hour."

"Good evening, Kurt. I trust you've been well?"

"Just because you suffer from insomnia doesn't mean you have to impose it on me." His cool, clipped voice was faintly accented.

"I apologize, but some conversations are inappropriate to conduct by daylight. They lend themselves naturally to the darkness."

Novak grunted. "I have no patience for your mysterious ramblings tonight, Victor. Get to the point. This is a secure line, I trust."

Victor smiled up at the luminous clouds. "Of course, Kurt. Have you heard of the recent disappearance of the Corazon pistol?"

Novak's sudden attention leaped through the phone lines like a surge of electricity. "Did you have something to do with that, Victor?"

Victor took a drag on his cigarette, savoring the intensity of the other man's interest. Dangling raw meat in front of a deranged animal such as Novak was the very best kind of sport. "I confess that I did. You can't imagine how many favors I had to call in to procure this object. I stressed a system of contacts that took an entire career to build."

"I can imagine it. What I can't imagine is why," Novak remarked. "But I suppose you will enlighten me. In your own good time."

"As an investment, of course. There are any number of possible buyers, but I wanted to offer it to you first, of course. I am well aware of the strength of the feelings you had for the young lady."

Novak was silent for a long moment. "Have you gone completely insane?" he inquired, in a conversational tone.

"Not at all. I just thought you would like to be advised before the gun disappears forever into some anonymous private collection. It's your decision, of course, but you should be aware that the pistol is linked to another object which I am sure will be of even greater interest to you. And to your father, incidentally."

"Which is?"

"A videotape," Victor said softly.

"Yes?" Novak prompted him impatiently. "Spit it out."

Victor closed his eyes, calling up the images. He began to speak in a low, dreamy voice. "She peers through the peephole, and is displeased to see who is behind it. She tells him to go, but her visitor is undeterred. He unlocks the door himself and pushes in, shoving her to the floor. Her long black hair is wet. She is wearing a silk robe. White. He tears it off. She is naked beneath it. Everything in the room is white, even the bouquet of tulips on the credenza beneath the mirror. She sees the thing he pulls out of his coat . . . and begins to scream."

He paused. Novak said nothing. He went on.

"Her lover comes out of the bedroom, naked, holding a Walther PPK which he clearly does not know how to use. The mystery guest pulls a strange little pistol out of his pocket, points it and shoots, directly in the man's face. He clutches his throat, falls against the wall and slides to the floor still alive and unmarked to serve later as a scapegoat. The mystery guest turns back to the young woman, who is struggling to her feet." He paused. "Need I go on?"

"How?" Novak hissed.

"It doesn't matter how," Victor chided him. "What matters is that several copies of that tape exist, in various places, with instructions as to how to dispose of them should I meet an untimely end. Not that I doubt your friendship, Kurt."

"So you were the anonymous caller who ruined my perfect revenge." Novak's voice was poisonously soft. "I wanted that man behind bars for life, Victor. For daring to touch her."

"Even I suffer from occasional attacks of altruism," Victor murmured. "It seemed a bit excessive to throw Ralph Kinnear to the wolves, as well."

"Do you know who you are dealing with, Victor? Do you really dare to play with me?"

"The last time you misbehaved, your father was adamant that you keep a low profile from now on, no?" Victor asked. "His organization is having image problems as it is. To have his wayward son implicated in the grisly murder of a famous supermodel would be sure to distress him. Imagine the media furor. The mind boggles."

Novak was silent for a moment. "How much do you want for the tapes?"

"Don't be banal, Kurt. This isn't about money. The tapes are not for sale. They will remain in my private collection. Forever."

In the charged silence that followed, he felt something working in his system like a drug, the triumphant rush of a well-executed maneuver in a game of power. There was no videotape, nor had there ever been. He had to be careful with his phrasing when he used information that he had gathered from a dream; chronology was often sacrificed for the sake of colorful symbolism. Over the years he had learned to compensate for this variable.

"What do you want, Victor?" Novak's control was back, his voice as neutral as if he were asking what kind of brandy Victor would like.

"I want to resume my privileged place in your business circles, Kurt. I ask only that you cover my expenses. If you want the pistol, of course. Five million should be sufficient. And of course, the matter will remain between us."

"You are crazier than I am." There was grudging admiration in Novak's voice. "I will set up a meeting for you with my representative."

"I went to a great deal of trouble to procure this item for you, Kurt," Victor said softly. "I would like to meet with you personally."

Thus entering into that select circle of people who had seen Novak's new face. The next step in the game. He waited, breathless.

"Do you, really, Victor?" Novak asked slowly. "You realize that what happened ten months ago cost me a fortune. I was forced to remove myself from circulation, to reconstruct my face. I have no interest in doing business with people with such inadequate security. If this blows up like last time, I will destroy you."

"Understood," Victor murmured, smiling up at the moon. His good mood was utterly restored. Nothing like a death threat from a deranged megalomaniac to chase away nagging ennui.

"By the way, I've been meaning to ask you. That lovely creature you have installed in the house on Templeton Street. I've been admiring her. She's different from your usual style."

An unpleasant shock tingled through Victor's body. "What about her?" he asked lightly.

"You're not the only one who minds his friends' business. I'm looking at photographs as we speak. She has that luminous, unspoiled air. Exquisite, but if I were you, I would increase her clothing allowance."

"She's thirty-three, Kurt," Victor said, advancing Raine's age by five years. "You like them when they still have that teenaged glow."

"Thirty-three, hmm? Odd. She looks ten years younger."

"Thirty-three," Victor said firmly.

"She's fucking another man behind your back, you know," Kurt said, with relish.

"Indeed?"

"This very night, my friend. Less than an hour ago. She looks like an angel, but she's a dirty little slut like all the rest. In the back seat of a sports utility vehicle, right out on the street. Her brawny young stud puts it to her quite roughly, my sources report. And she was very noisy in her appreciation. Keep that in mind the next time you visit her, and maybe she won't have to look elsewhere for her satisfaction."

"How kind of you to pass that along."

Novak could surely scent his dismay, like the cunning beast that he was. Of all possible scenarios, this was one he had not foreseen: that Novak would take an interest in his niece. Most unwelcome.

"Of course, if you would like for her to realize the error of her ways, I would be delighted to instruct her," Novak offered softly. "You know that is my very particular specialty."

"And deny myself the pleasure?" Victor let out a short laugh. "No, thank you, Kurt. I will deal with the situation personally."

"If you change your mind, let me know. You're more squeamish than I about such things, but we can establish the parameters in advance, if you like. There won't be a mark on her lovely body, but I guarantee you, the young lady will never defy you again."

A sickening image of Belinda Corazon's blood-spattered white carpet flashed through Victor's mind. "I'll keep that in mind," he said.

"You know how well I'm willing to pay for my amusements, Victor," Kurt added. "This would be worth a great deal to me. I might even be persuaded to part with that derringer that you so admired in San Diego last year. The murder weapon in the famous John F. Higgins murder-suicide in 1889, remember? I paid two hundred thousand, though it was worth twice the price. Think about it. And as to that other little matter . . . you'll hear from me soon."

The phone clicked. The line went dead.

Victor laid the phone down, shocked to feel the physiological signs of fear in his body. Cold sweat, tremors, abdominal discomfort, all of it. He had almost forgotten the feeling, it had been so long.

He had not been afraid for someone else for longer than he could remember. It alarmed him to realize that he actually cared about the girl. It was one thing to toy with Novak himself. He was a disappointed, bitter old man, bored with his life and his wealth, with nothing to lose.

It was quite another to expose his niece to Novak's poisonous regard. Well and good to speak of toughening and tempering, but she was by no means ready to take on such a malicious opponent.

He was obscurely comforted by the fact that Mackey was so taken with the girl. He would make a formidable bulwark for her, if his primitive masculine instincts were aroused. As they clearly were.

Noisy sex in the back seat of a sports utility vehicle, indeed. On a residential street. His mouth curved in an unwilling smile.

Naughty little minx. She was shaping up nicely.

"Well, well, well. Look who's finally decided to grace us with her exalted presence." Harriet strode toward Raine's cubicle, heels clicking in a sharp, staccato rhythm.

Raine laid her purse on her desk and glanced at her watch. She was an hour late, but after what she'd been through lately, she simply didn't have the energy to be anxious about it. "Good morning, Harriet."

Stefania appeared behind Harriet's shoulder. "Look, boys and girls," she said with a sugary smile. "It's the flavor of the week. I hope you had a relaxing afternoon yesterday while we finished your work."

Raine turned to face them as she unbuttoned her coat. A cool, detached part of her mind reflected that only two days ago, this situation would have made her want to throw up. Now the two women seemed like mosquitoes, buzzing at her from afar. Annoying, but largely insignificant. "Do you ladies have a problem?" she asked quietly.

Harriet blinked. "You're late."

"Yes," Raine agreed. "It was unavoidable."

Harriet quickly found her stride. "I'm not interested in excuses, Raine. I'm interested in—"

"Results, yes. Thank you, Harriet, I've heard that lecture more than once. Now, if you will excuse me, I'd be much more productive if you all would let me get to work."

Harriet's face darkened. "Perhaps you think you're quite special now that you evidently enjoy a private relationship with Mr. Lazar, but you should be aware that—"

"I don't think anything of the kind," Raine said wearily. "I'm just not in the mood to be bullied."

"Well!" Harriet's face flushed a deep, unpleasant red.

"Perhaps her majesty would be interested to know that she missed her ferry," Stefania said. "We'll have to call Mr. Lazar and tell him you won't make it to Stone Island until the taxicat at the marina is free to run you over. He'll be without secretarial support for the entire morning. I can assure you he *won't* be pleased."

"Ferry? What ferry?" Alarm pierced through her protective fog of weariness and indifference. It sank in like a knife.

Harriet felt it, and smiled a thin, triumphant smile. "Oh, yes. Your services have been requested at the island. Mr. Lazar often works from there. When he does, the support staff takes the ferry to Severin Bay, where they are met by his private boat and taken to Stone Island."

"If you'd gotten to work on time, you could have caught the 8:20 with the others," Stefania said. "As it is, you'll have to wait for the taxicat. It'll still be quicker than driving up to Severin Bay."

"So we'll be doing your work today as well," Harriet snapped. "Don't bother taking off your coat. The car is waiting downstairs."

A half-hour later she was at the marina, shivering in the cold wind that swept over the water. Trying to persuade herself that she was ready to face Stone Island, and with it, the swirling miasma of panic that surrounded it in her memories.

Her mother had lied when she insisted that they had been in Italy on the day of her father's death. She was sure of it. She closed her eyes and tried for the hundredth time to remember that day.

She must have hugged and kissed him goodbye when he'd climbed aboard his little sailboat. Probably she'd begged to be taken along, like always, but he almost never had. He liked his privacy, so he could daydream, gazing at the islands, taking nips from his little silver flask.

It hurt that she could not recall that final farewell. It should be indelibly stamped on her memory, but it seemed to have been scribbled over with heavy black ink instead. All she felt was anxiety, edging closer and closer to panic. It was going to be hard to fake being nonchalant and professional today. After years of stifling inaction, everything was happening at once. She was changing so quickly she barely knew herself from one moment to the next.

That made her think of Seth's early morning visit and her own wild, uninhibited response. Naked and sweating and straining beneath him in the back seat of his car. Screaming her pleasure right out loud. Oh, yes, she was changing, all right, at the speed of light. Heat suffused her face. She turned it to the icy cold breeze to cool it.

"Good morning," someone said.

She spun, startled. A handsome, stylish blond man in his late thirties was looking her over with obvious masculine interest, his eyes hidden by mirrored sunglasses. He smiled. Raine smiled back, wondering if she ought to recognize him from somewhere. He had deep dimples, a winsome, charming smile. She would surely have remembered him, if she had seen him before.

Seconds ticked past. Raine could think of absolutely nothing to say to him. He continued to stare, and his smile was objectively attractive; but he emanated a strange energy, like nothing so much as a sound shield of white noise in a psychiatrist's waiting room. She could barely hear herself think over the static.

The man moved closer to her, and for no reason, she thought of Medusa, the mythical snake-haired woman whose gaze turned men to stone. He was closer now. Too close. She could see her own reflection in the lenses of his glasses. Her eyes looked big and frightened.

The corners of his narrow, ascetic mouth tilted slightly up. She was intimidated, and he seemed to like it.

Anger flared inside her, but the interchange was too small and too subtle to protest. Without saying a word the hateful bastard had made her feel like prey. "Excuse me," she murmured, backing away.

"Wait, please. Have we met?" His voice was friendly, the faint European cadence impossible to place.

She shook her head, frozen in place. "I don't think so."

Idiot, she told herself, furious. Miss Nicey Nice just gave him an opening and made her sound doubtful and vulnerable. Cheep, cheep, cheep, said the fluffy baby bird, as the snake stretched open its jaws.

"You work for Lazar Import & Export, no?"

That, too, was an unpleasant shock. He knew too much already. "Yes," she said. She backed away further.

He followed her, undaunted. "That explains it. I have done business with your employer in the past. Surely I have seen you. Parties at the island. Or meetings, receptions." He grinned. His teeth were white and straight. Unnaturally perfect, like a cartoon character's.

"I've only worked for Lazar for a few weeks," she said. "I've never attended any corporate social gatherings."

"I see," he murmured. "How odd. I have the strongest feeling that I have seen you before. May I offer you breakfast?"

"Thank you, no. I'm catching a boat in a few minutes."

"For Stone Island, I presume," he said. "Allow me to escort you in my boat. It will be much faster. In this way, I can do Victor a favor and at the same time have the pleasure of your company at breakfast."

Her programmed impulse was to smile politely and offer some stammering excuse. She stopped herself, took a deep, calming breath, and jammed the program. "No," she said.

"May I see you again some other time?"

"No," she repeated stupidly.

He took off his sunglasses. His eyes had dark, purplish shadows around them that set off their jade green color with a weird intensity. "Forgive me if I embarrassed you," he said. "I am often too forward when I see something I want. I take it you are not, ah, free?"

"That's right," she said. "I'm not free." She hadn't been free from the first breathless moment that Seth Mackey had fixed her in his hungry gaze in the elevator. Only two days ago, and it felt like forever.

But she would never be free for this man. Under any circumstances. Not in this lifetime, or the next.

"I am desolate," he said softly.

Miss Nicey Nice smiled before she could block her automatic smile muscles. The catamaran was arriving. She glanced at it, counting the seconds until she could escape this man's vicinity.

"Would you be so good as to give your employer a message?"

"Of course," she said politely.

His gaze swept her, from head to toes and slowly back up again. "Tell him the opening bid has just doubled. Those exact words."

She felt like an animal frozen in the headlights of an oncoming car. "May I tell him who the message is from?" she asked faintly.

He reached out and touched her face. She jerked back with a

gasp, her eyes focusing on his outstretched hand. The last joint of his index finger was missing. He had touched her with the scarred stump.

"He will know," the man said softly. "Count upon it."

There was a glint in his jade-colored eyes, like a flash of ancient glacial ice. He gave her a cold, unfathomably remote smile and strolled away. She stared after him, frozen into place.

If she'd known Seth's phone number, she would have rushed out, bought herself a cell phone, and dialed it. Just hearing his gruff voice would make her feel safer. Even if he yelled at her again, it would be comforting. But she was on her own.

The noise of the people disembarking jarred her back into reality. She hastened down to board the boat. Why was she so intimidated by a stranger indulging in a harmless flirtation? There was nothing so terribly sinister about the encounter. She was imagining things.

Calm reason did not bring the butterflies in her stomach into line. *The opening bid has just doubled.* What could it mean?

Nothing good, of that she was absolutely sure.

She swallowed hard and turned her face to the cold wind again. Being Seth Mackey's mistress had never sounded so good.

Chapter

11

"**R**ise and shine, dude."

Seth's arms jerked up, shielding his face. He dropped them, muttering a disgusted curse when he saw what he'd done.

Not since his early Army days had he woken up flinching away from a blow. He focused on Connor McCloud, holding out a steaming cup. "What the hell?"

"Whoa. Aren't you just a little ray of sunshine today."

Seth swung his booted feet to the floor and grabbed the coffee. McCloud's penetrating stare was making him uncomfortable. He hated being studied like a rare bug.

"That couch is not long enough for you," McCloud commented. "Use the bed, for Christ's sake. Is Lazar still out at the island?"

Seth glanced at his watch. "Forty minutes ago he was."

Connor stuck his hands in his pockets. His eyes were worried. "You keeping it together? You look like shit."

Seth gave him a freezing stare. "I'm fine."

Connor shrugged. "Just checking. Just wanted to let you know that your video Barbie is headed out to Stone Island too."

Scalding coffee splashed over Seth's hand and sprayed across the floor as he lunged for the computer. "Where is she now?"

"Hey. Relax. My guy at the parking garage told me the limo was headed for the marina. He overheard the Lazar staff that left an hour before bitching about the blonde being late and missing the ferry. That's how he knew. I just got the call about ten minutes ago."

"Why the fuck didn't you call me then?"

"I was already on my way," Connor's voice was calm, but steely. "You planted vidcams at the marina, right? So settle down. Open them up. Let's see if she's still there."

Seth typed feverishly into the computer, flipping the marina vidcam windows open one after another until he finally found her, almost out of range, hanging over the railing of the deck that overlooked the marina. The wind had tugged some long, wispy curls out of her braid. The camera caught her delicate profile, gazing out into the infinite sky like an ad for expensive perfume. She fished a tissue out of her pocket, wiped rain off the lenses of her glasses, put them back on.

"Come on, man. It was inevitable," Connor said. "Lazar had to want a piece of that sooner or later."

"Shut up and let me concentrate," Seth snarled. He rested his elbows on the desk and dug his fingers into his hair, calculating the time it would take to get down to the marina to stop her. But she'd refused to be rescued last night. Why would she change her mind now? He rubbed the grit out of his eyes, and grappled with senseless panic.

"Hey. Seth. Check out the guy in the trench coat."

Seth jerked his attention back to the screen. He wished his body would stop pumping him full of useless adrenaline. Pure torture, being all jacked up and revving, with no saber-toothed tiger to grapple with, no river of molten lava to run like hell from. Just a computer screen to stare into, with mounting horror and disbelief.

"Holy shit. Are you thinking what I'm thinking?" For the first time ever, Connor's voice was totally devoid of irony.

"No way," Seth said.

"Way." Connor scooted closer to the screen. "The face is different, yeah. He's had surgery, someone really good. But his vibe gives him away. He oozes slime."

"This guy's taller. Thinner. And the hairline is different from Jesse's video footage," Seth countered.

"So he's wearing lifts, lost weight and shaved his temples."

Raine backed away. The man advanced with a predatory jackal's smile. Seth leaped to his feet, skin crawling. "I'm going down there."

"You're too far." McCloud's voice was flat and matter-of-fact. "Sean and Davy are both closer than we are. Besides, he's probably got six bodyguards armed to the teeth covering him."

Seth's fist slammed down, making the keyboard leap and rattle.

"You were the one who pushed for the cold, patient approach, man," Connor reminded him. "Calm down. Look at him. He's feeling confident, flirting with her, letting the whole world get a good, long look at his new face. He's getting cocky. This is good news."

"Good news? What's good about it? She's there, he's there, we're here. This is not good news. This is fucked!"

Connor dropped into a chair and stared at the screen. "I could call the Cave," he said slowly. "Nick lives down near the marina. I trust Nick. They're the cavalry, Seth. If we can't call them, we can't do shit."

"Brilliant," Seth snarled. "The last time you called the Cave, my brother was slaughtered and you spent eight weeks in a coma."

Connor's haunted eyes slid away from Seth's. "I don't get it. Those guys are my friends. We've risked our lives for each other."

Seth's fingers danced over the keys, opening a new window as Raine backed out of range. "Shut up, McCloud," he muttered. "You're making me cry."

The mystery guy lifted his hand to her face. Raine flinched, and they both stopped breathing, noticing the missing last joint on the index finger. Proof positive.

"He's ditched the prosthetic," Connor whispered. "Arrogant prick."

Seth shook his head. "He just took it off to creep her out."

"It worked," Connor said.

Seth flipped open the other windows one by one, following Novak until he walked out of range and disappeared.

The group of people getting off the catamaran climbed up the stairs to the deck, hustling past Raine. She stood there as if hypnotized. Someone jostled her, and she jumped, looking around like a bewildered, lost little girl. She hurried down the stairs to the dock.

"The day's got off to a hell of a start for your girl," Connor commented. "Off to the island to service Lazar, all cuddly and tight with Novak. Who knows what else the day will hold?"

Seth ignored him. He fought off nausea as he watched the catamaran pull away from the dock. Moving away, getting smaller. No stopping her now.

". . . yo, Seth. Anybody home? You in there?"

"Huh?" He swung his focus back to McCloud's frowning face.

"I was just saying that this could be an interesting slant. If Novak is interested in her, which he obviously is, and who can blame him, then we've got another lead. Maybe one of us should ask her out. Find out what she knows. Plant a transmitter on her. Excellent, huh?"

"She doesn't know anything," Seth growled.

"You don't know that. I'd even give her a try myself."

Seth spun around so fast he knocked the mouse off the desk.

"You have first refusal, of course," Connor added hastily. "I know you've had your eye on her, but if you don't have the heart for it, I could shave and comb my hair and give her a whirl. No hardship. She's hot."

"McCloud—"

"Or I could pass her on to Sean," Connor said thoughtfully. "He's better-looking than me, and he likes juicy blondes with great tits as much as the next guy. I don't think Sean's ever fucked information out of a woman before, but hey, there's a first time for everything."

Something snapped. Everything got weird and faraway, as if there were a blood-red filter across his eyes. Space and time distorted. He flew through the air in slow motion, slamming into Connor. He knocked him off the chair, onto the floor. Electronic equipment crashed down with them. His hands were around Connor's corded throat, squeezing. Connor's hands were jammed against his own jaw. He was talking, his voice thick and strained. The words began to register.

"D—don't, Seth. Don't do it. Chill, man. You don't want to get into it with me. Big waste of time and energy for us both. St—stop."

The red haze subsided. Connor's face emerged through it, slowly. Strained, but controlled. Squinting. Watching him like a hawk.

Seth forced himself to relax and let go. He rolled up into a sitting position and dropped his face into his shaking hands.

Connor dragged himself upright. "I think you threw my back out," he said. "And you've wrecked some of your gizmos."

Seth didn't even look up. "I'll fix them," he said dully.

"Oh, thanks for your concern. Don't trouble yourself. I'll be fine."

Seth's hands dropped. He stared down at the dingy gray carpet. He groaned and covered his face with his hands again.

"You've had her already, haven't you?" Connor demanded. "You sneaky son-of-a-bitch. Why didn't you tell me?"

Seth met his eyes, and looked away quickly.

"Aw, shit." Connor flopped back down onto the floor. He shoved back the tangled mass of hair that had fallen across his thin face and stared up at the ceiling. "Look, if you want out, just say so. Take her off to a desert island. Do whatever it is you do with her, I don't give a flying fuck. Just stop screwing with my investigation."

"It's our investigation, McCloud, and I haven't screwed anything."

"Nah, just Lazar's mistress," Connor spat back. "If that's not screwing with the investigation, then—"

"She's not his mistress. Lazar offered her to me. She knows jack shit, so don't push me. You won't be able to talk me down a second time."

Connor jerked up onto his elbows. His astonishment was satisfying, but he had good recovery time. "I wouldn't bother," he snapped. "I'd just proceed directly to beating the living shit out of you."

Seth's hands clenched into fists. "Like hell."

"Then you'd have a big macho ego crisis about being flattened by a guy with a cane. Fucking pathetic. I want to spare you that, you know? Being as how you're such a sad, sorry son-of-a-bitch already."

Seth stared at him for a long moment, and then looked down. He suppressed a snort of reluctant laughter.

Connor scooted on his ass across the floor to retrieve his cane, and struggled to his feet. "Let's beat our chests some other time. When all this is over, we'll do some sparring. Find out whose balls are bigger and hairier. Until then, peace. Deal?" He held out his hand.

Seth got to his feet. He reached out and gripped Connor's scarred hand. "I'm holding you to that."

The two men stared at each other for a long moment.

"You were deliberately messing with my head, weren't you?" Seth asked. "Don't do that again, McCloud."

"I wanted to see how far out of your mind you really were," Connor said coolly. "I feared the worst, but this is worse than the worst. You're not just obsessed. You're in love."

"Bullshit," Seth growled.

"Is it? Whew." Connor mimed wiping the sweat away from his brow. "You don't mind if we use her as bait then, right?"

"Do not get anywhere near her. Do not factor her into your plans, do not even think about her, McCloud. She is out of the game. Got it?"

"Get real," Connor said sagely. "She's out at the island with Lazar. She's chatting up Novak. And now she's screwing you. How much more in the game can she be?"

Seth shook his head, feeling hunted and desperate. "She's out of it," he repeated.

"Hey. Take it easy," Connor said gently. He brushed the grit from his jeans and shook his head, letting out a muffled crack of laughter. "What a joke," he muttered. "Why should I feel sorry for you? You're the one who just got laid. We'll see how far out of it she is when we hear what Novak said to her. The gulpers at the marina caught it, right?"

Sean clenched his teeth. "Yeah."

"Good. Go get it, then. And, uh . . . how long has it been since you've showered and shaved? You look like a derelict, man. You skulk around the marina looking like that, you'll get arrested for vagrancy."

"Fuck off, McCloud," Seth said wearily.

Connor swatted him on the shoulder with a grin. "That's my boy."

Raine's mind expanded, hushed and awestruck, as the dark hulk of Stone Island grew closer. A sense of silent immensity extended in every direction from the place. Wind sighed through the pines, and swollen clouds hung heavy in the sky. The morning fog was beginning to lift, revealing the familiar shape of the shore. The scent of moss, damp wood, algae, pine and fir filled her nose.

Clayborne, Victor's personal assistant, was waiting for her on the dock. He was a middle-aged man with a pencil-thin gray mustache on his long, twitching upper lip, and a manner of perpetual anxiety.

"Finally," he fussed, waving for her to follow. "Come along. We needed your French during business hours, and it's past seven in the evening in Morocco. What on earth kept you?"

"Sorry," she murmured absently. The house rose up before her eyes as they ascended the path, a sprawling but still somehow graceful structure. It was deceptively simple from the outside, sided with wood shingles that had mellowed to a glowing silver-gray.

The scents of the luxurious interior shocked her sense memories to life. Bowls of lavender and pine potpourri were in every room, and the walls were faced with fine cedar paneling. Alix had always complained about the rich smell of the wood, claiming that it gave her headaches, but Raine had loved it. The scent had lingered in her things for months after they had run away. She still remembered how bereft she had felt that day in France when she had buried her face in the folds of her coat and realized that the perfume of cedar had faded entirely away.

Clayborne led her directly to the bustling office on the second floor, shoved her behind a desk and began to fire instructions at her at full speed. Just as well. She was grateful to him. There was so much to do, and all of it in such a tearing, anxious hurry that there would be no time to work herself into a state. It was the perfect way to hold memories at bay.

At some point, sandwiches and fruit were left on the sideboard, but nervousness got the better of her and eating seemed unthinkable. The house beckoned and whispered to her. If she turned her head fast enough, she would catch a glimpse of her former self: a silent scrap of a girl with big, startled eyes magnified behind coke-bottle glasses.

Wind sighed and moaned outside, whipping the pines into a frenzy. Raindrops trickled down the windows by her desk, and bit by bit, the frantic activity and the roar of white noise ceased to shield her from the memories.

There had been no other children to play with on Stone Island when she was small. Her father was closeted in the library with his books, or out sailing with only his silver flask as a companion, and more often than not her mother stayed at the apartment in Seattle. Raine had made friends with silence, with trees and water, stones and gnarled roots. The whole island was her own private fantasy landscape, inhabited by dragons and trolls and ghosts. Later, amid the noise and chaos of changing cities and languages, the remembered silence of Stone Island had become like a dream of paradise to her. That fantasy world pulled at her now, whispering in a thousand hushed voices.

Towards the end of the day, Clayborne bustled into the room. "Raine, go to the library, please," he said importantly. "Mr. Lazar has correspondence that needs to be Fedexed as soon as we get back to the mainland. Go on, hop to it."

She grabbed her notebook and set off, and was halfway there before she realized that she hadn't asked where the library was. A stupid lapse, but too late to fuss about it now.

It was strange how she had forgotten how lonely and chilly Stone Island was. The only warm, colorful thing about the place had been Victor. Compared to her father's detached melancholy and her mother's self-absorption, Victor had been a hot blast of dynamism and danger. She stood in front of the library door, her hand trembling.

Too much dynamism and danger. She pushed the door open.

The familiar room reached out and twined sensuously around her, pulling her in. It was lined with books from floor to ceiling, with tall windows between each bookcase. The windows were adorned by borders of stained glass, designs of curling vines and morning glories, rain-spotted and glowing with the deep blue of early evening.

She stole in to the empty room, drawn by a shelf of photographs that bore the look almost of an altar. There was a photo of Victor and her father as a skinny boy of twelve. The eighteen-year-old Victor was wearing a thin tank top. His muscular arm was flung over his little brother's neck, and a cigarette dangled out of his mouth.

There was a faded pencil portrait of her grandmother, a pretty dark-haired girl with pale eyes, and a photo of her when she was a handsome older woman, from which the portrait that hung over the credenza was copied. Raine studied a school photo of herself, in the sixth grade at Severin Bay Middle School. She remembered the itchy lace on the collar of that hateful green velvet dress.

The last photo was of her father's sailboat. She stood in front of it, along with her mother, Victor and an unknown man. The strange man was dark-haired and handsome, with a thick mustache. He was laughing. Something about him made the back of her neck prickle, but the thought would not rise to the surface. It flashed away, like a fish disappearing into dark water, accompanied by a pang of sharp, sick anxiety. She forced herself to pick up the photo and examine it.

It was a rare sunny day, and her mother was glamorous and beautiful in a yellow halter sundress, her hair tied back with a silk scarf. Victor's arm was flung over Alix's shoulders, and his other hand was ruffling Raine's hair. She remembered the bathing suit with the green frogs on it, the green frog sunglasses that matched it. Victor had yanked on her braid for some reason, hard enough to bring tears to her eyes. Then his cool, dragging voice, faintly accented, echoed through her memory. *"Oh, for God's sake, Katya, toughen up. Don't be a crybaby. The world is not kind to crybabies."*

She'd blinked the tears back, glad to have the sunglasses for a shield. She could at least pretend not to cry.

The same frog sunglasses were sitting next to the photograph. She reached for them, convinced that her hand would go right through them like a hologram. They were real. Cold, smooth, hard plastic. She stared down at them, marveling at how small they were.

It started in her stomach, a sick roiling. Fear, spiraling wider, higher. Running, screaming. Water. A dizzy green blur. Blind panic.

"Katya," came a low voice from behind her.

She spun around with a sharp gasp. The glasses dropped to the carpet with a thump. No one but her mother knew her former name. No one had addressed her by it in sixteen years.

Victor Lazar stood in the door, his hands shoved deep into the pockets of his fine wool trousers. "Sorry, my dear. I didn't mean to startle you. I seem to be making a habit of it."

"Yes, you are." She breathed deeply, trying to stop trembling.

Victor indicated the photo still clutched in her hand. "I was referring to the photograph. The little girl is my niece, Katya."

"Oh." Raine placed the photo on the shelf. The obvious next move was a polite inquiry as to his niece's well-being. She didn't want to draw more attention to the photo, but with every second that ticked by, her lack of comment drew more attention to it than any comment ever could. "She's . . . a pretty little girl," she faltered. "Where is she now?"

Victor picked up the photo and looked at it. "I'm afraid I don't know. I lost touch with her many years ago."

"Oh. I'm sorry."

He nodded towards the glasses that lay on the carpet. "I kept those as a memento of her. The same ones she is wearing in the photo."

She scooped them up and put them back in their place. "Um, excuse me," she stammered. "I didn't mean to—"

"Think nothing of it." He gave her a soothing smile. "Speaking of spectacles, I see you are still wearing your own."

She was ready for this one. "I'm afraid I don't see well enough to do my work without them."

"What a pity," he murmured.

She summoned up a businesslike smile. "So. Shall we begin? I need to hurry if you want the letters Fedexed tonight, so—"

"How goes your fiery romance with our mysterious security consultant?"

She pressed her trembling lips together. "I thought I made myself clear last night. I have nothing to say about—"

"Oh, come now. Last night you told me you never wanted to see him again. He must have made a very strong impression indeed."

"I am not interested in discussing Seth Mackey. Now or ever."

"He is using you, too, you know," Victor said. "Or if he is not, he soon will be, the world being what it is. Does he deserve such stoic loyalty from you just because he is capable of giving you an orgasm?"

He was doing it again; twisting the world around himself like a black hole with his low, insinuating voice. Making her doubt herself.

"What you ask is inappropriate," she said. "This whole conversation is inappropriate."

Victor's laugh was beautiful, rich and full. It made her tight, nervous voice sounded ineffectual and prissy. It made her feel dull and humorless. A fool for not agreeing with everything he said.

He pointed at the photos. "Look here, my dear." The faint Russian flavor in his voice intensified into a perceptible accent. "See this? My mother. And this boy here, my little brother, Peter. Nearly forty years ago I ran away from the Soviets. I worked and schemed, made money for the bribes and the papers to bring my mother and brother here. I built this business for them. To do this I made many compromises. I did many, many inappropriate things. One must, because the world is not perfect. One becomes accustomed to it—if one wishes to be a player. And you do wish to be a player, no?"

She gulped. "On my own terms."

Victor shook his head. "You are not yet in any position to dictate terms, little girl. The first step toward power is to accept reality. Look the truth in the face and you will see your way more clearly."

She clenched something deep inside herself and resisted the pull of his charisma. "What on earth are you talking about, Mr. Lazar?"

Her voice was clear and sharp. It broke his spell.

He blinked, and an appreciative smile flashed across his face. "Ah. The voice of truth. I talk too much, do I not?"

She wasn't touching that one. Not with a ten-foot pole. She kept her mouth shut and concentrated on inhabiting her world, not his.

He chuckled and placed the picture back on the credenza. "No one has had the nerve to tell me that in years. How refreshing."

"Mr. Lazar . . . the letters?" she reminded him. "The ferry will be here soon, and I—"

"You are welcome to stay here tonight, if you wish."

Her skin crawled at the thought of a whole night at Stone Island with no one but Victor for company. "I wouldn't, ah, want to put your staff to any extra trouble."

He shrugged. "My staff exists to be troubled."

Your world, not his, she repeated to herself, with a deep, calming breath. "I would prefer to go home tonight."

He nodded. "Good night, then."

She was bewildered. "And the dictation?"

He gave her a charming smile. "Another day."

The man at the marina flashed through her mind. "Oh, yes. Mr. Lazar, I met a man this morning who gave me a message for you."

His smile hardened. "Yes?"

"He was a well-dressed blond man in his thirties. He wouldn't tell me his name. He was missing a forefinger on his right hand."

"I know who he was," Victor said curtly. "The message?"

"He said to tell you that the opening bid had doubled."

The humor and charm that animated Victor's face was gone. Beneath it was cold, hard steel. "Nothing more?"

She shook her head. "Who was he?" she asked tentatively.

"The less you know, the healthier you will be." In the fading light, he looked suddenly older. "Do not encourage this man, Raine. Avoid him in every way possible if you should see him again."

"You don't have to tell me," she said fervently.

"Ah. You have good instincts, then." He patted her shoulder. "Trust them. With trust, they grow stronger." He picked up the frog glasses, turning them over in his hands. "Another thing. Take these."

"Oh, no, please." She backed away, alarmed. "They're a memento of your niece. I couldn't possibly—"

He pushed the glasses into her hand, closing her fingers around them. "You would be doing me a service. Life marches on, there is no stopping it. It is very important to be willing to let go of the past, no?"

"Ah . . . yes, I suppose so," she whispered. She stared down at the glasses, afraid that the strange panic would seize her again.

They lay quiet in her hand. Cool, inanimate plastic.

"Good night, Raine."

It was a clear dismissal. She hurried out of the room. God forbid that the boat leave her here, stranded on an island full of ghosts.

She thought about Victor's cryptic words on the ferry, with icy wind whipping through her hair. *Let go of the past.* Hah. Her hand dug into her pocket and closed around the frog glasses. As if she hadn't tried. As if it were that easy. Her life got more complicated by the day. Now she had the mysterious blond man to watch out for, as well as Victor.

And then there was Seth Mackey. Her knees buckled, and she grabbed the railing. She shouldn't get involved with Seth. He was a wild card, strong and restless and arrogant. He could derail her. But he countered the sad, lonely chill Stone Island had given her. He was a roaring furnace of life-giving heat. She craved it, even if it burned her.

Her heart hurt when she thought of the halting, bare-bones story he had told her of his mother's death. She ached for the pain he'd tried so awkwardly to gloss over. It made her furious. She wanted to punish anyone who had ever hurt or neglected him, to protect the innocent little boy he had once been. Tears sprang into her eyes. She thought of Victor's long-ago words at the dock.

Toughen up, Katya. The world is not kind to crybabies.

All her life she had tried to follow Victor's hard advice. She was finally realizing the truth. The world was not just unkind to crybabies. The world was unkind to everybody.

She blinked as the wind blew the tears out of the corners of her eyes, mourning for all that foolish, wasted effort at self-control. The lights on the shore melted and swam into a soft wash of color. So did something inside her chest that had been brittle and frosted for years. She let it melt, with a dawning sense of wonder. More tears slipped out, and she let them fall. She might as well cry. It didn't necessarily mean that she was weak. It meant that her heart wasn't dead.

And that was good news.

He was going to kill them. Both of them. Then he was going to kick his own ass, hard, for having been stupid enough to collaborate with such dickheads as the McCloud brothers.

Connor stopped limping up and down the room, and flopped into a chair with a disgusted sigh. "Get over it, Mackey. She's the best bait we're ever going to find. You saw the tape. You heard them talk. He wants her. We could wrap this up quicker than we thought if—"

"She froze him out. He may never approach her again."

Davy McCloud grunted and crossed his long legs. "Nah. Not Novak. Now he probably wants to teach her a lesson."

Seth's stomach rolled. "That's why she's leaving town. First plane to anywhere out of SeaTac tonight."

The two brothers exchanged long, knowing looks. "Oh yeah?" Davy asked. "Gonna tell her everything?"

Seth spun around in the chair, and rubbed his reddened eyes. His mind swam with grisly images of what that man had done to Jesse before he killed him. He couldn't stop the images, couldn't block them. Couldn't let Novak get his hands on Raine. Couldn't.

"Look at it this way," Connor said, in the voice of one trying to reason with a lunatic. "She's bait whether we use her or not. Now you have a God-given excuse for sticking to that chick like glue. It's all you ever wanted to do, so get into it, already. Enjoy it."

"No. I want her out," Seth repeated. "It's too dangerous."

Connor shook his head. "You can't pull her out of this without ripping out all the stitches, Seth," he said gently. "Don't fall apart on me. I need your techno magic to pull this off."

"Do not condescend to me, McCloud," he snarled.

Connor just stared at him, his pale gaze calm and unnerving.

He hated admitting he was wrong. It made his jaw hurt. He closed his eyes and tried to organize his thoughts. "I have to be right on top of her. Guarding her," he conceded grimly. "Not just tailing."

The two brothers exchanged long, silent looks, and Seth turned away. It reminded him too much of Jesse. Not that there had ever been much silence when Jesse was around. Jesse had never shut up.

God, he was so angry. At the McCloud brothers for still having each other when his brother was dead. At Jesse for getting himself killed like an idiot. At Raine, for getting herself mixed up in this fucking snakepit when she obviously didn't know enough to come in out of the rain.

What maddened him most of all was the image of Jesse in the back of his mind, doubled over laughing. One would think that the ungrateful little jerk would appreciate his big brother's efforts to avenge him. But no. In death, as in life, Jesse just had to be original.

He opened up one of the black plastic cases full of Kearn's gizmos. He grabbed a cell phone, pried it open, and started messing with it.

"What are you doing?" Davy asked.

He sifted through the transmitters in the case. "Putting together a present for my new girlfriend," he said. "A cell phone with a

Colbit beacon in it. I'll dust the rest of her stuff, too. I want to know where she is at all times, when I'm not with her. Which won't be often."

Davy looked thoughtful. "Novak's less likely to make a move if you're always lurking around."

"Tough shit," he snarled. "Whenever I'm not with her, one of you guys will be watching. Armed and ready to kick ass. Is that clear? Now get out. I can't concentrate with you guys breathing down my neck."

Davy nodded in farewell and slouched his tall body out the short door frame. Connor started to follow, but he turned back, his eyes full of reluctant sympathy. "Look at it this way. The sooner we wrap this thing up, the sooner you can settle down and have ten kids with her."

"Fuck off, McCloud." The words popped out, an automatic reflex.

For the first time, he wondered why he reacted like that.

Connor nodded as if Seth had said goodbye, or later, dude, or have a nice night. "Take it easy," he said. "Keep in touch."

Seth turned back to his preparations, but the image Connor had put in his head quivered like a freshly shot arrow in a wooden post.

He had never contemplated fathering a child. He was a textbook example of a guy who would make a rotten father. He was rude and crude and arrogant, he had a mean streak ten miles long, his moral development was questionable, to put it mildly, and he lacked basic social skills. Other than crusty, irascible old man Hank, he had no models for fatherhood. Except for Mitch, of course. That said it all.

As for the things he was good at, well, the list was short and telling. Spying. Stealing. Fighting. Sex. Kicking ass. Making money.

Not the best skills for a babbling baby to learn at its daddy's knee.

He'd grown up fully aware that his life bore no resemblance to what he saw on TV sitcoms and commercials for life insurance and breakfast cereal. Cynical little bastard that he was, it hadn't taken long for him to start suspecting that TV's perfect normal world didn't really exist anyway. He was comfortable with his own dark, gothic underworld. He knew its rules, its pitfalls. He didn't pine after fairy tales of marriage and family and cozy domestic bliss.

Oh, he kept it together, more or less. He was registered to vote, he had served his country in the armed forces, he paid his taxes, they had his picture down at the DMV. But his public persona was a means to an end. Hank and Jesse had been his points of reference, ambassadors to the world of normal. Without them, he was lost in space. So far off the grid, he didn't even appear on the screen.

He'd gotten so good at shoving thoughts and feelings away. Now look at him. Fantasizing about Raine, pregnant. Holding his baby in her arms. The feelings that image provoked were so strong, they terrified him. Fear, for how unspeakably vulnerable that would make him. Anger, because anger always followed on the heels of fear. Anger of the ugly, gut-wrenching, teeth-gnashing variety.

Anger and fear were a hell of a recipe for fatherhood. Better if he stuck to kicking ass and making money. He'd inflict less damage on the world that way. He forced himself to concentrate. What was he doing? Gathering the hardware to take to Templeton Street. Right. Revenge and ruin. Now there was something he could wrap his mind around. There he was on solid ground. Stick to what you know, the experts said. He threw his bag into the Chevy and drove through the streets, trying not to think about Raine or Jesse.

He needed to think about ruin and revenge. Cold, careful and methodical. Novak wanted Raine. Seth wanted Novak. The formula was simple. She was bait. Once he'd killed Novak, he would be free to take out Lazar, and that would be the end of the matter, unless some tight-ass tried to prosecute him for it. In which case he would fade discreetly out of sight and live the rest of what would pass for his life outside the bounds of respectable society. The prospect held few terrors for him. He'd spent half of his life there anyway. The rules weren't all that different. He had several alternate identities already set up and waiting for him: passports, credit histories, the lot. He had money socked away in out of the way places, and when it ran out, no problem. There was plenty of lucrative work in the underworld for a man of his skills.

But he couldn't take a woman with him there. At least not a certain type of woman. Keeping a woman was definitely an on-the-grid proposition. Women liked family reunions, Christmas cards. Babies.

It occurred to him that he hadn't been such a terrible brother to Jesse. Maybe he wasn't the type to remember birthdays, but he'd always been there when the chips were down, ready to kick ass.

God. What was he thinking? A guy didn't qualify for domestic bliss because he could kick ass. Any thug on the street could kick ass.

No, there was some other, far more mysterious set of credentials.

The conclusion he came to as he parked in front of Raine's house was that the mysterious list of credentials probably did not include spying on a woman, or bugging her apartment, or planting transmitters in her stuff, or deliberately not telling her that she was the chosen prey of a sadistic arch-villain. It probably centered more on tedious, inconvenient crap like following rules, respecting boundaries, telling the truth like a good little Boy Scout.

Too bad. The truth was too dangerous to tell. So much for his newfound moral scruples and his attack of conscience. He smiled grimly as he inserted the pick gun into her lock. He was cured. Hallelujah.

He stole into the dark house and wandered through it. She had left no visible trace of herself in the place, just a bright, humming awareness of her presence. Her refrigerator was empty, cupboards bare. It was the first time he had been inside since she'd been living there. He smelled her everywhere—whispers of her soap, her lotion, her own sweet, ineffable smell. He sank to his knees by her bed and buried his face in her pillow, aroused to the point of pain.

He logged onto his computer and deactivated all the wall sensors and vidcams in the house's interior. He needed total privacy for what was going to happen in that room tonight. No witnesses, no records.

The smart thing to do now would be to go out and sit in his car until she got home, and then ring the doorbell. Ding-dong, lah-di-dah. Good evening, don't you look lovely tonight. Mr. Civilized, faking social skills. Another lie, on top of all his other deceptions.

Fuck it. Why pretend? She was on to him, anyway. She knew what kind of man he was, ever since he'd taken her to bed. And he liked it that she knew. Twisted and dangerous though that was, he liked it that at least one person on earth had a clue who he was inside.

He settled into the chair and pulled up the vehicle beacon display. The Stone Island boat was finally heading towards Severin Bay. He pulled up the ferry schedule, calculated the length of a ferry ride, then the cab ride. Then he was going to find exactly what part she was playing in this game. He'd never fucked information out of a woman either, but hey, like Connor said—there was a first time for everything.

Chapter

12

Maybe she could keep down chicken soup, if she was lucky, and some stale crackers.

Raine leaned back against the seat of the cab, exhausted. Her body was beginning to protest going so long without food, but a mental inventory of her larder was not inspiring. She didn't have the energy to contemplate shopping, or cooking, or a restaurant. Even the idea of sorting through a pile of take-out menus seemed too much to face.

She had to nurture herself better. She couldn't run on nerves alone. Each day was getting crazier than the last. The loony bin and the padded cell lay at the end of that road.

She wandered through the house once she got home, throwing off her coat and kicking off her shoes as she went. She didn't even bother to flip on the lights. The brief attack of hunger was already passing, and now she felt too tired to eat. She headed for the bedroom. First a shower, to warm her up, then her floppy fleece pajamas, and then—

"Where the *fuck* have you been?"

She leaped back from the door, cowering against the wall of the corridor. Her heart thudded against her ribs. The eerie blue glow of a laptop screen seeped through the bedroom door.

Seth, of course. Who else. She reached in the door and flipped on the hanging lamp.

The wingback chair he was slouched in looked too fussy and small for his long body. He was all in black like the cat burglar that he was; black jeans, a black sweatshirt, his thick scrub brush of black hair sticking every which way, like he'd been running his hands through it all day. His eyes were shadowed with exhaustion, but they blazed at her with unnerving intensity.

She shook so violently she had to clutch the doorjamb to stay upright. "You scared me practically to death!"

He made a few keystrokes and snapped the laptop shut. He slid it into the bag and glared at her. Not shamefaced in the slightest. As if she were the one in the wrong. The outrageous, presumptuous bastard.

"That settles it." She marched into the room. "The next man who scares me out of my wits jumping out of the dark at me—*dies*. I'm sick of it. Do you hear me? No excuses, no explanations. I am not speaking figuratively. Do you understand that, Seth?"

He didn't even blink. "Yes."

"Yes?" Her anger bubbled and fumed. "That's all? Just yes?"

He got to his feet. "Yes, I understand that. Let's move on to what the fuck you've been doing for the past sixteen hours."

She was so furious, his looming and glowering didn't even intimidate her. "What business is it of yours? You have no right to ask! You have no right to even be here! I should be calling nine-one-one!"

"After yesterday, I have every right."

The cool conviction in his voice maddened her. She wished she hadn't discarded her shoes. She needed the extra two inches to face him down. "Let me explain something to you, Seth, because we're not communicating very well," she said. "If I had a boyfriend, I would of course include him in every aspect of my life. I would call him, and e-mail him, and leave cute little text messages on his cell phone. I would keep him informed of where I'm going, when I'm getting back—"

"Yeah. Exactly. That's what I—"

"But I don't have a boyfriend, Seth!" she yelled. "I don't have a phone number, I don't have a beeper number. I don't have a clue! What I do have is a problem. A big, nasty-tempered problem who invades my privacy and jumps out of the dark like a horror movie monster! A man who thinks he owns me just because we slept together!"

"For the record, that wasn't just sleeping together."

"Oh no? What was it, exactly?" she demanded. "Enlighten me, please. Remember, I don't have your vast experience in these matters."

"It was . . . it was more." He shoved his hand through his hair and shook his head. "It blew my mind. And there was no sleeping involved. In fact, I haven't actually slept since I met you."

"Oh, please. I'm so flattered! I'm so incredibly hot in bed, you just can't help yourself? Sleep deprivation has driven you so far out of your mind that you feel justified in breaking into my house? What is it with me, Seth? Why does everybody seem to think that the normal rules of civilized behavior don't apply with me? Have I got a sign on my back that says 'anything goes?' "

His breath hissed through his teeth. "Christ, Raine. I've been sitting here on a bed of nails wondering what that bastard was doing to you, and you're mad because I forgot to give you my phone number?"

She stared at him. "How did you know I was at the island?"

"I called the office! If you'd been there, I would have asked you out to dinner! But you weren't there! You were off at Lazar's fucking private island!"

She sat down on the bed and dug her toes into the thick carpet. "Why would you think that Victor would hurt me?" she asked gently.

"Oh. It's Victor, now, not Mr. Lazar, hmm?"

She brushed his words away with a wave of her hand. "Don't be ridiculous, please. Just answer the question."

"He handed you over to me yesterday like you were a professional, Raine," he said hoarsely. "He threw you to the wolves, and he did it for fun. *For fun.* Why not again, if that's how he gets his kicks?"

Her mouth dropped open. He had been worried. Frightened for her. She was so touched that for a moment, she forgot how angry she was. "Victor Lazar did not force me to go to bed with you," she told him gently. "I had already decided on my own to seduce you, if I could."

He snorted. "If you could. Hah."

She lifted her chin. "I went with you because I wanted you. I am not as helpless and stupid as you seem to think. Today, I negotiated contracts for Taiwanese pharmaceuticals, Indonesian teak flooring and textiles, Baltic timber and Norwegian cheese. I also formatted the annual report and typed letters and e-mails to the entire world, in five different languages. It was a very normal working day, Seth. I was not called upon to provide sexual entertainment for Victor or anyone else, so put your mind at ease."

He opened his mouth, but she held up her hand. "I'm not finished yet. You have to follow the rules. Like knocking on locked doors, for instance. That's not too much to ask. And this jumping out of the dark and scaring me to death, that's a terrible habit. I won't tolerate it."

"Like a dog pissing on the rug?"

She forced herself not to laugh at his sour expression. "Exactly," she said. "People should try to follow the basic rules of civilized society. Particularly . . . lovers."

The silence in the room was absolute. His gaze bored into her face, as focused as a laser. "Does that mean we're lovers, then?"

This was the moment of truth. She had felt it coming since his visit that morning. It was time to either dive off the cliff into deep, unknown water, or turn and run like hell. She squeezed her eyes shut, head spinning with a tingling rush of vertigo. She opened her eyes and jumped. "I don't know, Seth," she whispered. "Are we?"

Two swift strides, and he was upon her. "Hell, yes."

His hard grasp made her stiffen up; it was too much, too soon, and she was still angry and confused. The world dipped and spun. She was on her back, on the carpet with Seth arched over her. He unraveled her braid and fanned her hair out around her head. He pushed her legs apart and settled his hard body against her.

She shoved against his chest. "Seth, hold on. Wait!"

"Relax." He tugged her blouse out of the waistband of her skirt, sliding his hand beneath it. He growled with pleasure as his hand found warm skin. "What's the problem? You said we were lovers, right?"

She seized his wrist and yanked it out of her blouse. "Sex is not all that means, you dog!"

His eyes gleamed. "Woof," he said. "What else does it mean?"

"Lovers do things together! They rent videos, they ride Ferris wheels, they go out for pizza, they play Scrabble. They . . . they talk!"

"Talk?" He lifted his head and frowned, his eyes puzzled. "We talk all the time, Raine. I've never had such talkative sex."

"That's just it!" She wiggled, flailed, but couldn't budge him. "Two minutes alone with you, and I'm flat on my back. Every single time!"

A slow, knowing grin spread over his face. "Is this your way of telling me you want to be on top?"

It was too much. She had been pushed around all day, she was still buzzing with adrenaline, and that smug, self-satisfied look on his face was unbearable. Pressure built up and snapped, faster than she could think or reason. Her hand lashed out and slapped his face, hard.

They stared at each other, stunned. Raine looked at her stinging hand as if it were not her own. Seth seized her wrist and pinned it over her head without speaking. His eyes were hard with controlled anger.

"Oh, God," she whispered. "I wish I hadn't done that."

"Me too." His voice was low and menacing. He settled more of his weight upon her, squashing her breathless. "That one was for free. Do not ever, *ever* hit my face again. Is that clear?"

She licked her dry lips and tugged at her trapped wrist. "Seth, I—"

"Is that absolutely clear?"

She nodded. Long, silent moments slid by. They were frozen, immobile. As if waiting for a bomb to explode.

Raine pushed at his chest, trying to make room for her lungs to expand. "You're playing power games again," she said. "Please don't."

"This isn't a game. You're pushing me, Raine. You're testing me, and I'm just laying down the rules."

"Your rules," she said.

"That's right." His face was implacable. "My rules."

"That's not fair."

"What's not fair? You wanted to follow the basic rules of civilized behavior, right? Civilized people don't hit each other. Simple enough. Or do the rules only apply to me, and not to you?"

"You just broke into my house, you manipulative bastard," she hissed. "Don't you dare throw my words back in my face! And I'm not the one who's pushing. You're the one who's pushing me. You never stop. Move, please. Right now. I can't breathe."

He shifted his weight off, and propped his head on his elbow. "But it turns you on when I push," he pointed out. "I feel what makes you hot, and I follow what I feel. That's how I make you come. By pushing you to the place that you need to go."

It was hard to frame the elusive thought into words with his eyes boring into her face, scattering her wits. "But it drives me nuts!"

"I love driving you nuts." He lowered his face to kiss her.

She shoved him away. "I mean nuts in a bad way, not in a good way! I've never hit anyone in my entire life, Seth! I'm a total creampuff pacifist, and you—you made me hit you!"

He studied her face for a long moment with a keen, assessing look. "That is such bullshit," he said finally.

She blinked at him, bewildered.

"Don't give me that confused, innocent look. Your creampuff act is just a mask. I can see right through it. I see right into you, Raine."

"Do you?" She squirmed beneath him, restless."What do you see?"

"Something shining. Beautiful and strong and wild. It pulls on me, makes me ache and burn. Makes me want to howl at the moon."

His heated words licked at her like flames. Her body relaxed with one last shuddering sigh, and she gave in and twined around him, pliant and soft. "Don't push so hard," she pleaded.

"Stop resisting," he coaxed, his lips nuzzling, nipping at her throat. "I could take you so incredibly far if you'd just let yourself go. Let me drive, Raine. I swear, I know where I'm going."

She let out a choked burst of breathless laughter. "How can I trust you if you don't trust me? Look at us, Seth." She gestured at his body, still pinning her flat. "I only weigh about a hundred and twenty pounds, and you—"

"No, you weigh less. Your fridge has nothing but mustard and a couple of wrinkled apples in it. Do you ever eat, or what?"

His critical tone grated on her nerves. "The contents of my refrigerator are nobody's business," she snapped. "My point is, you don't have to pin me down. I'm not quick enough to run away from you, even if I wanted to."

"You don't want to?"

She opened her mouth, and closed it, unwilling to give him another opening. Simple honesty won out. She didn't have the presence of mind to tell him anything but the naked truth.

"No. I don't want to run away from you," she said quietly. "I want you to let go of my wrist. I want you to let me breathe."

The manacle of his strong fingers slowly relaxed. "I don't want to get hit again," he warned.

"I promise, I won't," she assured him.

He pulled her onto her side so they were lying on the floor facing each other, and studied her face as if she were a puzzle he were trying to solve. "I'm sorry I broke into your house," he said, in a stiff, formal tone. "I'm sorry I scared you."

She put her hand to his face, caressing the place where she had struck him. "I appreciate the apology." She echoed his formal tone.

"I did it because I was worried about you," he added, frowning.

That broke the spell. Raine laughed in his face. "Don't ruin a good apology by justifying bad behavior."

His cautious smile faded quickly. "Does this mean that I'm your boyfriend, then? Officially?"

Another blind leap. She didn't know what those words meant to him, coming out of the alien landscape of his mind, but something hot and soft was moving in her heart. She couldn't draw back. She could see in his eyes how badly he wanted the strange, awkward declaration.

Don't cling to an illusion of control, Victor had said. For once, she agreed with him. It was time to give her heart a chance to run the show. Things couldn't possibly get any crazier than they already were.

"OK," she said gently. "You're my boyfriend, if you want to be."

He let out a long, slow sigh, and hooked his leg over hers, pulling her closer so that the whole length of her body was touching him. "I want to be. God. Do I ever want to be."

"All right, then." She petted his tense jaw with a soothing hand and smiled at him. "You are. It's official. You can relax."

Seth arranged her hair between their faces, right next to his nose, so he could stroke it and smell it. "I know I come on too strong," he said, his voice hesitant. "It's a really weird time in my life."

"Do you want to talk about it?" she invited gently.

"No." His tone was like a gate clanging shut in her face. She flinched away, feeling thrown back on herself.

He pulled her back against him, cursing softly. "I'm sorry, Raine. I can't talk about it. I'm intense, yeah, but I'm not dangerous."

"No?" She turned her face away, avoiding his kiss.

"No. Not to you." He caught her face in his hands and insisted on the kiss, his thumbs tenderly stroking her cheek. She savored the hot, delicious flavor of his mouth, the intimate thrust of his tongue.

What Seth said was untrue. She would give anything for this passionate, ravishing tenderness from him—and that made him deadly dangerous to her.

He lifted his head, smoothing her hair off her forehead. "I got you a cell phone today."

That was so unexpected, she could think of nothing to say.

"You'll send me cute little text messages now?" he prompted. She closed her gaping mouth. "Is that what you want?"

"That's what I want." There was a touch of embarrassed defiance in his tone. "I'm your official boyfriend now, and I want all the perks that go with the job. You cool with that?"

"Um, yes," she murmured.

He cupped her head in his big hand and kissed her again, but the kiss had changed. There was a soft, pleading sweetness to it, as if he were silently begging her for something which she could not help but give him. Something that would break her heart to withhold.

He pulled away and stared into her face, his eyes troubled.

"What's the matter?"

"I'm nervous," he said bluntly. "I don't know much about the steady relationship thing. I feel like a bull in a china shop."

She laughed softly and stroked the deep little frowning groove between his eyebrows "Just be nice. Be gentle."

"It's not the sex I'm worried about," he snapped. "And I've always been gentle with you."

"Just because you don't leave bruises doesn't mean you're gentle. Conan the Conquerer."

He stroked her hair, smoothing it all the way out to the tips. "Hey. Give me a break. I want you bad. You're so fucking beautiful, I just want to carry you off to my beastly lair and make love to you forever. On my bearskin rug."

She touched his face with her fingertips and stared into his eyes, speechless. She could feel him gathering his seductive powers, weaving a spell to make her helpless with desire. He grabbed her hand, pressing hot kisses against her palm, and rubbed her knuckles against his cheek. "You're not throwing that Conan the Conqueror crack in my face again," he said. "This time you'll tell me how much you want me. I want to hear you ask for it, pretty please."

She drew back anxiously. "That sounds like another power game," she said. "Seth, I don't—"

"Shhhh." He placed a finger over her lips. "No, not at all. You've got me wrong. I just want to show you something about yourself. Something beautiful. You'll like it." He explored her trembling lower lip with his finger, staring at her with hot, fascinated eyes.

A bold impulse flashed through her. She drew his fingertip into her mouth and suckled it. He jerked as if an electric shock had gone through him, pulled his hand from her mouth and began to unbutton her blouse with fingers that shook. "Goddamn buttons," he muttered.

She laughed up at him. "You don't like my clothes, do you?"

"No, I do not. You're like a box with too much packing tape."

"Poor baby. Such frustration," she teased.

"Watch what you say, if you care about this blouse," he warned.

He got it open and flung it away, rolling her to her side to unhook her bra. He lifted it off with reverent slowness, caressing her breasts,

rubbing the taut tipples against his palms. A flurry of peeling, unhooking and unzipping followed, and she lay before him naked.

He stared at her body, running his fingertips over her belly, dip-
ping into her navel and then tangling tenderly in the soft nest of hair
at her crotch. "Do you ever touch yourself?" he asked.

Raine was so startled, she couldn't reply. She stared at him, her
mouth open, a hot blush sweeping up over her chest and face.

"Come on, sweetheart. Do you?" he coaxed.

"Doesn't everybody?" She tried to sound nonchalant.

"I don't give a shit about everybody. I'm interested in you."

Her embarrassment melted away in the heat that radiated from
him. "Of course," she said simply.

"Touch yourself for me." His voice was husky, pleading.

"But—don't you want to—"

He pressed her hand against the hot bulge in his black jeans.
"God, yes. The next time. But first I want you to open up for me, all
on your own. No pushing." He settled between her legs and pushed
her thighs wider. "Check me out, Raine," he murmured. "Civilized
self-control personified. Didn't think I was capable of it, did you?"

"Is this another one of your power games?" she demanded.

"No way. It's a gift. To make up for hitting me."

She shook with nervous laughter, and tried to wiggle away from
him and his wicked satyr's smile. "Damn you, Seth. That's not fair."

He lunged for her, grasping her waist and holding her still.
"Please, Raine," he said softly. "You're so beautiful. And it's so intimate, so secret. I'm starving for it. Show me that you trust me that
much." He dropped a gentle kiss on her belly, her hip, and let his
hands slide, slowly and lovingly, all the way down the length of her
thighs. He gripped her knees and pushed them wide again. "I want
to know what goes through your head, what you fantasize about. I
want to see that beautiful cunt get flushed and hot and soft and delicious. I want to watch you make yourself come. That's my idea of
heaven."

She couldn't answer, couldn't speak. He reached for her hand and
pressed her fingers gently against her sex. "Show me."

She squeezed her eyes shut and did as he asked, shy at first, but
his magic was so potent that her inhibitions melted down into hot,

sweet syrup. Her bedroom disappeared. They could have been any-where; floating together in the silent heart of a white orchid, swim-ming in a tropical sea. She abandoned herself to the dance of shifting energy between them. He taunted her with his eyes, with his rigid self-control. She taunted him with her body and her desire.

A fierce, joyful power swelled inside her. She played with the soft, secret folds of her sex, her body arching and heaving, offering him everything. The feeling unfurling inside her no longer terrified her. It was a burning cloud that expanded in her chest, her belly, in her womb. Hotter, higher, brighter. She wanted to push him to the very edge of his self-mastery, but still he sat there, watching and waiting. His eyes glittered, feverish. Flags of hot color burned on his high cheekbones.

"Tell me what you're thinking now," he demanded.

"I'm not thinking. I'm feeling," she said shakily.

"What do you feel?"

"You." She slid her fingers inside herself and writhed.

"What am I doing to you?"

"You're . . . touching me. Kissing me."

"Am I licking you?"

"Yes," she moaned. "Yes." Her hips began to jerk, frantic.

"And now?" His voice was low, hypnotic. "Is my cock inside you?"

"Please, Seth—"

"Am I fucking you now?"

"Yes!" She moved faster, following the swelling surge of pleasure.

"Say it," he told her. "Say the words. What am I doing to you?"

"You're . . . inside me. You're fucking me," she gasped. The crude words launched her, made it all burst and fly apart.

She cried out and dissolved, shivering all over.

She rolled onto her side and curled up, panting. Reality slowly crept back, and along with it, embarrassment at what he must think of her. Displaying herself like that. She felt more vulnerable than ever.

Which had surely been his intent.

Her eyes flew open at the sound of his belt unbuckling, his fly unzipping. He peeled the black shirt off his lean, beautifully muscled torso, and flung the garment away. He pried off his boots and socks, tossing them into the corner, and hooked his thumbs into the waistband of his jeans. He smiled at her wickedly. "My turn."

She licked her lips. "You're driving me nuts, Seth."

He pulled his jeans and underwear off. His penis sprang out, jutting hungrily towards her. He sprawled next to her, pulling her against him. "Is that good or bad?"

She put her arms around him tentatively. "I don't know yet," she said in a small voice.

"I didn't push you that time," he protested. "You did it all yourself."

"Yes, you did too push," she said quietly, petting the thick muscles of his shoulders. "I don't think you even know what it would feel like not to."

He slid his arm behind her shoulders, pressing his hard chest against her breasts. His eyes were wary and troubled. "So you think I'm, uh, weird in bed, then?"

Raine almost laughed at the doubt in his voice, but stopped herself just in time. "I don't have any basis for comparison," she said softly.

His arms tightened. He kissed her forehead. "Keep it that way."

She ran her hands over the ridges of his muscular back, exploring him with eager, fascinated fingers. "Besides, this isn't a bed," she pointed out.

"You can't see the mirror from the bed," he said. "I like the mirror. It's another great view of your gorgeous, bare-ass naked body."

She looked at the mirror, and blushed again. He followed her gaze, rolling onto his side and pulling her against him so that her backside was pressed against his hard, hot penis. He nudged her legs open, crooking her knee, and slid his hand between her legs with a low, rumbling groan of pleasure. "Beautiful," he said. "You're ready now. Ask me for exactly what you want, Raine. Come on. Out with it."

She closed her eyes and pressed herself back against his bold caress. "Why do you do this to me, Seth?" she pleaded. "You've always got something to prove. It makes me feel vulnerable."

He nuzzled her ear, pulled her earlobe between his teeth and nipped it. "Face it, babe. You *are* vulnerable."

His tone infuriated her, as if he were stating something too obvious to bother mentioning. She tried to pull away from him, but he just pushed her flat onto her belly and rolled on top of her.

He locked eyes with her in the mirror. "Too weird for you, huh?" His voice challenged her, soft and taunting. "You'd like it better if I was a nice, tame, normal guy?"

He pushed her thighs apart and slid his finger inside her. She strained beneath his weight with a soft moan. He slid his hand out and thrust again, with two fingers, deeper. Preparing her.

She couldn't think, couldn't speak, clenching around his fingers. "I like the way you are," she admitted, in a halting voice. "But I don't know how to give you what you want. It's a language I don't speak."

He bit her neck. "It's not that complicated. I just want you to know what you want. So I can be sure that I'm giving it to you. It may not seem that way, but I really am making an effort to be civilized."

She laughed. "Civilized? You call yourself civilized? Seth, you are a wild animal."

His eyes lit up like a wolf in the moonlight, making her shiver again. She sensed that her words had unleashed something that might have been better off left confined. He grasped her hips and pulled her up until she was on her hands and knees. The picture she made, made her blush even hotter, redder. Seth loomed behind her, his thick penis pressed against her bottom. He stroked her with his strong hands. "That's what you want from me, isn't it? You love it that I'm a wild animal."

The position made her feel too vulnerable. She murmured something incoherent and tried to scramble away, but he was too quick. He slid his strong arm in front of her hips, arching over her and holding her in place. "Trust me," he said soothingly. "This is what you want."

She shook her head, frantic. "No, Seth. I feel too—"

"Wait," he urged, his hands petting and soothing. "Give it a minute. Let me touch you . . . like this. Spread your legs wider.

That's right. That beautiful ass, open like a peach, all juicy and sweet. I won't do anything you don't like, Raine. I promise you'll love it."

His fingers slipped tenderly along the delicate folds of her sex, and blissfully sensual tremors shook her at his skilful touch. He pushed her legs wider, murmuring his approval when she didn't resist.

"You'll love it like this," His voice was a hypnotic rasp of desire. "You know why? Because you're a wild animal too, Raine. Just like me."

He slid his thumb tenderly around her clitoris. She moved against his hand, seeking deeper contact. She had thought that the submissive position would make her feel weak and helpless, but it didn't. Not at all. It slid into focus and flooded her with heat. She felt savage and hungry, full of fierce, primal yearning. All the energy of nature woke up inside her, charging her with its pure, wild potency.

She felt strong. Furious at him for his arrogance, for teasing, for making her wait. She arched her back, seducing him with her body, with her naked, honest animal self. She looked into his eyes, saw his helpless response. For a bare instant, she had a fleeting sense of just how much power she could wield over him. If only she knew how.

"Beautiful, sweetheart," he said hoarsely. "Arch your back for me, raise your ass in the air. Give it all to me."

She obeyed him, deep in the grip of his sensual enchantment, and content to be there. He could push her all he wanted, drive her all the way to bittersweet, glorious climax. She would die if he didn't.

She almost wept with relief when he fished the condom out of his jeans, smoothing it over himself. She pulsed her hips against him with a sob of eagerness, desperate to have him inside her. He grasped her hips and splayed his big hands across them, holding her still.

"Don't worry, sweetheart. You'll get as much of me as you want. Just let me tell you when."

"Don't play games now, Seth. You're killing me. I can't take it."

"What did I tell you?" he said softly, caressing the swell of her hip. "I knew you'd love it. My beautiful wild animal."

He nudged his thick shaft a little deeper, and she braced herself, pushing back. "I know your secret. Beautiful animal. You're so wet and soft. You love it when we do it like this. Don't you?"

She tried to speak, but her throat was vibrating, and would not obey any mental commands. She gave him a jerky nod.

He flexed his hips, pushing deeper, his breath ragged in the silent room. His slowness maddened her. "You like that?" he demanded.

She heaved back against him with an impatient gasp. "Yes."

"You want more? How do you want it? Deeper?"

She looked in the mirror and was lost in his dark gaze, in the pulsing magnetism of his sexual power. "Deeper," she whispered.

His fingers dug into her bottom. "Harder?"

She nodded, opening and reaching for him with every part of her whole self. "Yes," she demanded emphatically. "Harder. Now, Seth."

He thrust deep, his body slapping against her backside, jerking a sharp cry out of her throat. "Like that?"

"God, yes." She sought his rhythm and lifted herself up to meet him. With each stroke she was more soft and wet and wanting.

"Look at us," he demanded. "How your tits swing forward every time I put it to you hard, like . . . this." He punctuated his statement with a hard thrust. "God. It's the most gorgeous thing I've ever seen."

She stared at herself, dazed. The sight was more erotic than the most uninhibited sexual fantasy she had ever permitted herself. Her hair hung over her face, her breasts dangled and swayed, her legs were opened wide, her bottom high. And Seth behind her, as beautiful as a god, his muscular golden body driving into hers, gleaming with sweat.

He was so sexy, so strong; his big hands dark against her white flanks, the tendons standing out on his throat. He studied their image in the mirror, fascinated, one brown hand sliding up to caress her breasts, the other delving into her damp puff of blond pubic hair.

She watched herself, astonished. Her face was rosy, wanton, almost frightened. And as she watched, he reached around and pulled her up against him, her head flung back against his shoulder, open and arched back like a bow. He pulsed his hips against her with slow, controlled strength while his long fingers coaxed, caressed, undid her. Sent her flying over the top in an erotic cascade of hot, bursting pleasure.

When she could frame a coherent thought again, he had pushed her back down onto her hands again, and was thrusting hard and deep. "So beautiful," he muttered. "Your cunt clutches at me like a wet little fist when you come. I love it. You are unbelievable, Raine. Red hot."

Amazingly, the fierce desire began to spiral up again. She arched back and worked herself against him frantically, frightened at the intensity of the explosion gathering inside her. He followed, his instincts unerring, gathering speed and force and giving her exactly what she needed to detonate the charge. One final hard, relentless push, and she hurtled, headlong and yelling, into another orgasm.

He grabbed a handful of her hair, winding it through his fingers. "Open your eyes," he urged. "Watch me while I fuck you, Raine."

She opened her eyes, gasping for breath. "Oh, stop being a cave man," she snapped. "The hair-pulling is over the top, even for you."

He grinned, tightened his grip on her hair and pulled her head to one side, biting her on her damp neck. "You love it," he said, watching her with each hard thrust. "Me Tarzan, you Raine."

The goofy little line was so out of context in the dark, complex dynamic of their love play that it shocked a peal of helpless laughter out of her. Her laughter melted instantly into tears, and she collapsed forward, laughing and sobbing. She heard his voice against her ear, but couldn't understand his words. Then his anxious, pleading tone sank in.

"Don't cry on me. Raine, for God's sake. Please. I can't handle it."

"That's just tough," she said, laughing through her tears. "If you don't like it, go find some girl who doesn't care as much."

He pushed her down until she was lying on her belly and covered her gently from behind, curving around her and surrounding her with his warmth. The carpet scraped against her cheek, the tears unraveled her. The sensations thundering through her body were almost too intense to call pleasure. He surged into her, tight and hot and unbearably intimate, his arms locked around her as he finally let himself come. His hips pumped furiously, his energy blasting through her body, lighting her up like a torch.

When she opened her eyes, she was lying on her side, her face wet, still shaking with tiny sobs. He stroked her hair, her shoulders, hugging her against him tightly. Nuzzling her neck with little, pleading kisses. She breathed deeply, and let the shuddering vibration subside.

Sweat began to dry upon them. He withdrew himself, got to his feet without a word, and went into the bathroom.

She tried to move, but couldn't. Her will was severed from her body. She just lay there on the carpet, limp and spent. She listened to the water run in the bathroom sink, her hair draped over her face. The door opened. He crouched down beside her, lifting the hair off her face and turning her face so that he could look into her eyes. She smelled her own fruit scented hand soap on his hands. Rosehip Raspberry.

"I'm wiped out," she whispered. "I can't move."

"You need food," he said.

She grimaced. "Wilted apples with mustard? Ick."

"Not. I ordered out," he announced, his voice triumphant. "There's bread, potato salad, turkey, pastrami, roast beef, ham. Sliced cheddar and Swiss. Some of that bottled fruit tea stuff. And brownies."

She actually managed to lift her head at that. "Brownies?"

He slid his hands beneath her shoulders and knees, and scooped her easily into his arms, looking pleased with himself. "Yeah. Two kinds. Double fudge walnut and chocolate cheesecake swirl." He carried her to the bed and laid her down. "I'm going to make you a sandwich. Then we'll try to get some sleep."

She narrowed her eyes. "I don't remember inviting you to spend the night in my bed," she said without real force.

"Official boyfriends get to spend the night," he said, tucking the duvet carefully around her. "It's one of the perks of the job. Part of the standard contract. It's also covered under the rules of civilized society. It's very bad form to throw a man out the door after he's made you come . . . was it three times? Or four?"

Raine betrayed herself by giggling. "I really should throw you out. Just to teach you a lesson."

"Yeah. You and what ten big guys with Uzis and duct tape?"

She giggled again, and he followed up his advantage with a kiss that bloomed swiftly into something hot and sweet and sinuous. He drew back with difficulty, his breathing uneven. "Besides, who would feed you sandwiches and brownies if you threw me out?"

"You're terrible," she told him. "You really are an opportunist."

"You're learning, babe. You're learning." His grin slowly faded as he gazed into her eyes. "If you really wanted me to go, I'd feel it. I'd go. I don't stay where I'm not wanted. But you want me to stay. Just like you wanted me to take you on the floor just now. Like a wild animal."

She sat up, stung, and the duvet slipped down to her waist. "Don't you dare tell me what I want, Seth Mackey."

He reached up, touching her bared breast, and she smacked his hand away. He shrugged, aggrieved. "I just followed your cues, that's all I meant. I didn't mean any offense."

She pulled the duvet up over her chest and slanted him a narrow look. "I thought you did that to punish me. For calling you an animal."

His eyes widened, horrified. "Punish you? Fuck, no!"

"That's how it felt," she murmured. "At least at first."

"You call screaming multiple orgasms punishment?"

She almost laughed at the bewilderment on his face. "The orgasms are beside the point."

"The hell they are! If that's your idea of punishment, then I'd by God like to know what constitutes a reward!"

"Seth—"

"It would probably kill me," he went on, his voice incredulous. "My head would explode. And I didn't know being called an animal was an insult, either. On the contrary, I kind of liked it. It turned me on."

She grabbed a pillow and swatted him with it. "Oh, please. Everything turns you on," she snapped.

He jerked the pillow out of her hands and climbed onto the bed. He pushed her onto her back, straddled her and seized her chin, forcing her to look straight into his eyes. "Look, sweetheart. If I'm too weird, or too rough, or too over the top for you in bed, I'll tone it down. The sex doesn't have to be wild and crazy all the time. If you want it sweet and soft by candlelight, that's fine. I'll give it to you sweet and soft."

"You will?"

"Sure. Sweet and soft is fine with me. I like it all ways. Anything you can dream of, that's my fantasy. Got that?"

She nodded. He stood up, looking relieved. "Now relax while I go fix you some food." He grabbed his jeans and tugged them on. "What do you want on your sandwich? Spell it out for me, babe. Don't make me guess. I don't want to lose any more points with you. Before I know it I'll be thrown out the door for pissing on the rug."

"Oh, stop it," she snapped.

"Little of everything? Mustard, mayonnaise, or both?"

"Both are fine."

"Lemonade or peach tea?"

"Lemonade, please."

He looked as if he wanted to say something more, but stopped himself. He picked up the pillow, tucked it tenderly beneath her head and smoothed her hair over it. "I won't be long."

The door closed after him, and she slid down beneath the duvet, shivering in the cool sheets. She stared up at the ceiling fan, and struggled to comprehend what was happening to her.

And if it was a good thing or a bad thing.

Chapter

13

Boyfriend. He was Raine Cameron's official boyfriend.

He rolled the word around in his mouth, trying it out. Sure, it was just a cover, but what a kick-ass cover it was. What better cover for a bodyguard than the role of jealous, possessive new boyfriend? No one would think twice about him hanging all over her. They'd take one look at Raine's gorgeous tits, her soft pink lips, her glowing eyes, and assume that he was madly in love with her. Who could blame him?

He felt giddy and wired as he padded barefoot through her house. He pulled the small bag of equipment out of the top shelf of the coat closet where he had stashed it, stopped and listened carefully for sounds of movement from upstairs. Nothing.

He opened up his kit, sorting through Colbit beacons of various sizes and ranges. One slid unobtrusively into an unused pocket of her wallet. Another screwed into her pen. He ripped open the seam of the lining of her purse with his penknife and slipped one into the hole. He took out the sewing kit in his case, sewed the hole deftly shut and stitched another one into the hem of her raincoat.

That was enough for now, along with the cell phone. He could get more creative and ambitious later on, when he had the time and the privacy. He winced as he caught sight of himself in the mirror in the foyer. He sure didn't look like an official boyfriend. Wild hair, beard shadow, bare chest. Smelling of sweat and sex. One of his ex-lovers had once told him that he would be really handsome if he could manage to be a little less scary looking. When he demanded to know what the hell she meant by that, she'd hedged and stammered, regretting the thoughtless statement. Finally she said she thought it was his eyes.

The relationship hadn't lasted much longer. In fact, now that he thought about it, that might have been the very last night. He stared at his eyes in the mirror. They looked pretty much like they always did, if a little more bloodshot and shadowed than usual. Raine hadn't complained about them yet, thank God.

He padded into the kitchen and proceeded to build four massive sandwiches with the same methodical attention to detail that had made him such an excellent thief, spy and techno nerd.

Hot damn. Official boyfriend. He had never voluntarily sought the title from anyone in his life. He'd always been brutally honest with his lovers about his preference in keeping things light. He liked sex just fine, but he could rarely be bothered with the rest of it. Jesse had teased him about that. Teased him hard, like he thought it was a real problem, though they usually ended up laughing about it. Jesse had thought that Seth's difficulty with trust and bonding with women was because of his relationship with his mother, blah blah, snore, zzzzz. Jesse had been heavy into psychobabble for a while. College had that effect on some guys who had more brains than were good for them. Usually Seth had managed to tune him out.

He braced himself for the burning stab that came along with thinking about Jesse. It didn't happen. Or rather, the feeling was there, but different. More like a hand pressing down hard on his heart. A hot, hard ache. Almost . . . bearable.

He'd enjoyed a whole lot of women, some of them very thoroughly, but as soon as they invited him to Mom and Dad's silver anniversary bash, or whatever, he was outta there. Which was doing them a favor, really, since it always went to hell anyway. Inevitably the day arrived when he opened his mouth, let whatever he was thinking come out of it, and kaboom. Screaming, tears, and scenes that ended with *go to hell, you rude, insensitive bastard.* Doors slamming, tires squealing, and him standing there with his dick in his hand, back to square one. Big bummer.

The hell of it was that he never quite knew what exactly had set them off. It was a mystery.

God, what an idiot. He was a wild animal, dreaming about being domesticated. He stood in front of the refrigerator door, mustard dripping off the knife and onto the floor. Stupefied by the realization that he would say anything, do anything to keep this woman close to him. He was even willing to meet her parents. He stared at the splotch of mustard on the floor tile, transfixed. He would even put on a big show for them. Lie about his background, clean up his language. He would suck their goddamn toes, if that was what it took.

He was losing it. This wasn't about a cover, and he didn't even need Jesse to tell him so. He was terrified of wrecking this thing. It was so tenuous, so fragile. And it was all that was holding him together.

He shook that alarming thought out of his head, and gathered up plastic spoons and napkins. He stopped. Montserrat had liked candles. Chances were there were still a few of them floating around. He'd seen her loading up her witchy candelabras all the time.

He found five crimson candles in a kitchen drawer, along with a box of matches. He shoved it all under his arm, loaded himself up and carried it all up to the bedroom.

Raine had fallen asleep, one hand cradling her flushed cheek. Her plump, childlike cherry-red mouth was slightly open, lashes sweeping the bluish shadows under her eyes. She was so beautiful, and she looked so exhausted. The protective tenderness that rushed through him made the plate of sandwiches shake.

He laid it on the bedside table, sank to his knees and lit a candle. He dripped hot wax onto the plate and set the candles in it. He liked them. Like a little wine-red grove of trees. They smelled faintly of honey, just like she did. He stroked her hair with his fingertips, hating to wake her. "Hey," he said softly. "Sustenance."

"What?" Her eyes fluttered open. She looked dazed.

"It's your new boyfriend," he informed her. "Bearing dinner."

She propped herself up on her elbows, saw the candles. Her

smile of delight was so bright, it hurt. She was so easy to please. He had to look away for a second, blinking away a stinging dampness in his eyes.

She gasped when she saw the plate of towering sandwiches. "Good God. Who's going to eat all that?"

He grunted, amused at her innocence. "Don't worry about it. I'll polish off whatever you don't want."

Not since Jesse had been too little to forage for himself had he prepared food for someone else. Breakfast stuff and sandwiches were pretty much the extent of his culinary repertoire, but Raine seemed to enjoy it. They feasted, sitting cross-legged on her bed. She got around an entire sandwich, and watched, fascinated, as he devoured the other three. Then he got the bright idea of feeding little pieces of brownie to her by hand, but that backfired on him because it was a flaming turn-on to place crumbs of fudgy cake in her soft mouth, to feel her hot tongue greedily licking off the crumbs and glaze, to watch the pleasure blooming on her face.

"Sugar orgasm," she moaned. "Give me another piece, quick."

"Cheesecake or fudge?"

"I want to finish with the fudge, so make sure that's the last piece you give me." She opened her mouth, accepting another mouthful. "Who would have thought that such a strange day would end so well?"

He tucked another gooey crumb between her lips, and his whole body tightened as she licked the chocolate off. "Are you referring to the sex, or to the brownies?" he asked.

Raine stretched and smiled in a way that made his cock swell up again, poking dangerously close to the opening of his unbuttoned jeans. "Why? Are you feeling insecure and competitive?"

He was foolishly delighted with himself for making her smile. "I would never ask you to choose one over the other," he assured her. "I'll keep you well stocked with both."

She trailed her fingertips over his torso. Her eyes dropped, widened. He looked down, realizing that he had exceeded the waistband limit. His flushed, swollen cock was poking its head out hopefully.

"Don't worry," he said thickly. "I know you're tired. I won't bother you again. I just want to hold you while you sleep."

She swirled her fingertip tenderly around the head of his cock, her eyes fascinated. "Bothering me? Is that what you call it?"

He stared down at her circling finger, fighting for self control.

"Bother me again, Seth," she whispered. "Just bother me sweetly and softly. Like you promised. OK?"

He was off that bed in an instant, scooping paper, cutlery, condiments, all to the carpet. Stripping his jeans off and sheathing himself in a condom, in flat-out record time.

She lifted the duvet, inviting him into the dark, fragrant warmth of her secret female self. It made him drunk, crazy-wild with lust and longing. Sweet and soft, he repeated to himself, thinking of his promise, the candles, the chocolate. Sweet, soft and romantic. That was what she wanted from him, and that was what she'd get. The duvet floated on his back as he mounted her, as light and puffy as a cloud.

She was so silky-soft and warm and strong, cradling him. Her slender arms wrapped around his neck and her legs twined around his. Sweet and soft, he repeated to himself. Official boyfriend-type sex. Not power games, or moon-crazed animal, or Conan the fucking Conqueror, or any of the other assorted craziness that his perverse sexual imagination could churn up at a moment's notice. He wanted to hold her, as close as he could. He wanted to make her feel incredibly good.

He wanted to make her feel safe.

It was the hardest thing he had ever done, keeping it slow and soft. Her perfume went to his head like a drug, and the candlelight turned her hair to swirls of bronze highlighted with glinting flashes of gold. She was so gorgeous, he could have come just staring at her face. He had to close his eyes, grit his teeth to hang onto his self-control.

She was wet and soft from the last time, and damn lucky for him; he was so desperate, he could never have survived a bout of foreplay. She let out a low, shaky moan as he prodded and pushed himself inside her. Their eyes locked, speechless. He was humbled. Awestruck at the mystery of it. It had never occurred to him before how intimate that moment really was. How enormous the act of trust on her part.

He had never thought of sex in terms of trust. Only of pleasure, his duty to give it, his due in return. A simple and straightforward exchange. He had followed his instincts in pursuit of pleasure all his life, but now they were leading him down paths that he had never trod. Sex with Raine was like nothing he had ever known.

He started rocking inside her, and suddenly they were kissing as if the world were about to end and her arms were wrapped around his neck. His strokes got deeper, and soon she was taking all of him, slick and deep, her hips jerking up to meet his.

He pulled away from that mind-melting kiss, laughing. "Cool it," he protested. "You said sweet and soft, but if you go crazy on me, what the hell am I supposed to do?"

"Oh, shut up." She pulled his head back down to hers.

Her hips heaved and bucked beneath him, and he used his weight to hold her in place, letting her churn and struggle and strain against him. Creating something firm and strong for her to break herself against, like a wave crashing on a rock, an explosion of foaming ecstasy, and he was the rock. He held her back, not letting her rush, or panic. Coaxing her towards where she needed to go, not driving her. Letting her pleasure unfold, over and over, blooming sweeter and hotter every time. He made her come, over and over, sweet and slow and careful. The hot, clutching pulses of her orgasm milked him ever closer to his own, but not too close. Not yet. Not until she felt safe enough to let go completely, to launch herself and fly. Not until he had fashioned a net to catch her, as big and soft and beautiful as the whole sky.

Raine lay beneath him, limp and exhausted with pleasure before he finally let himself go. Pleasure rushed and pounded through him, so hard and furious that he lay there, clutching her and trembling for a small eternity before he even remembered who he was.

The last thought he had, after he got rid of the condom, was of how incredible it would be to make love to her without latex. Usually it didn't even cross his mind. He hadn't had unprotected sex since he was too young and dumb to know better, two-thirds of a lifetime ago. How amazing it would be to bathe his naked cock in her scalding heat, to explode inside her. To fill her with himself, his seed.

Seth refused to let himself examine that thought, electing instead to slide into real, deep sleep. For the first time in what felt like forever.

At first, it was the classic contradiction; the horror of surprise side by side with a terrible sense of inevitability. Her father, pointing. Herself, leaning to look. Blood oozing out of the marble, like the credits in old B-grade horror movies. She looked up, and it was not her father, it was Victor, smiling. He grabbed her braids and yanked on them hard, making tears spring into her eyes. "Toughen up, Katya. The world is not kind to crybabies." His voice boomed in her head, loud and metallic.

She was at the Stone Island dock, dressed in the green frog bathing suit. Her hair was braided tight for swimming, and her mother was wearing a yellow sundress, laughing. The big dark man with the mustache plucked her green frog glasses off her nose, and was holding them too high for her to reach. Taunting her, dangling and yanking. Dangling and yanking. The sunglasses were prescription, and without them everything was blurry. The mustached man was laughing like it was all so funny, but it wasn't at all. Tears of frustration gathered in her blurred eyes, no matter how she tried to blink them back, and Victor was sure to scold her again if he saw them.

Her father's sailboat was floating away from the dock. He was waving goodbye, and even with her blurred eyes she could see the bleak sadness in his eyes. It crushed her to see him so defeated. He gestured at the three laughing adults, getting smaller and smaller.

"Remember." He was too far for her to have heard him, but the word reverberated in her head as if he had spoken it directly in her ear.

This was it, she knew it. She would never see him again. He was getting smaller, only his shadowy eyes could be seen, like the eyeholes of an aged skull. Panic exploded, and she was screaming after him, begging him to turn back, come back, she would save him, she would think of something, she would do anything if only he would please, please come back and not leave her all alone—

"Raine! Jesus, wake up! It's only a dream, baby. Wake up!"

She struggled wildly against the strong arms that were holding her. Then it all slipped into focus. Seth. Sex, chocolate, candle flames guttering in a pool of blood-red wax. The island. Another dream.

She collapsed against his warm chest and dissolved into tears, but they didn't last as long as usual. His fierce embrace radiated heat through her body, relaxing her. The tears subsided, and she wiped her eyes with the back of her hand. "I'm sorry I woke you," she said.

"Don't be an idiot," he said. "That was a hell of a nightmare."

She nodded, resting her hot forehead against his chest.

"You want to tell me about it?" he prompted.

"No, thank you."

He hugged her tighter. "It might help. So I've heard."

She shook her head. He kissed the side of her face that wasn't pressed against him. "Suit yourself," he said. "If at some point you change your mind, I'll still be interested."

"Thank you," she whispered.

He pulled her back to him, fitting her into the crook of his shoulder. "Are you going to be able to sleep?"

"No," she admitted. "Not for a while. Maybe not at all."

"So this is a chronic thing."

His matter-of-fact voice made the whole thing seem less dreadful. He flipped on the bedside lamp and studied her damp face, his eyes somber. "Can I help? Is there anybody whose ass I can kick for you?"

She snuggled deeper into his warmth, kissing the thick bulge of his bicep, and shook her head. "You can't save me from this problem, Seth," she said quietly. "But I love you for wanting to."

He stiffened beneath her, and she realized, with a twinge of alarm, that she had used the scary L-word. She'd heard that it made men panic, when used prematurely.

Stop clinging to an illusion of control, she reminded herself wryly. He wasn't running or screaming. That was promising.

"So," he said, his voice elaborately casual. "What happens now?"

She kissed his chest. "Now you sleep, and I stare at the ceiling."

"No. I mean, with us."

She propped herself up on her elbow and smiled at him, threading her fingers through the hair on his chest. "You can start by promising to never leap out of the dark and scare me, ever again."

"Give me a key," he suggested. "When you come in, just say 'Honey, I'm home,' and if I'm there, I'll say 'How was your day, dear?' "

She was taken aback by the bold request. "It seems almost redundant to give you a key, Seth," she hedged.

"Your neighbors might get nervous if they see me picking your locks all the time. Besides, official boyfriends get issued keys."

"They do?"

He frowned. "Hell, yeah." He looked annoyed at her hesitation.

Raine stared down at the pattern of hair on his muscular chest, contemplating the idea. It flew in the face of all the rules, but those rules didn't correspond to the crazy reality she inhabited. She was destined for chaos. She took a deep breath, and followed her heart, not her head. "I'll give you the keys that Victor gave me," she offered.

He jerked up onto his elbow. "What?"

"He was waiting for me when I came home last night," she said.

He gestured impatiently. "What did he want?"

"He wanted me to spy on you," she said. "He's curious about you."

"So? What did you tell him?"

"I told him no," she said simply. "I told him to leave. What else could I do?"

"You could quit," he said curtly. "You could tell him to fuck off. You could get the hell out of town, that's what you could do!"

She looked down and shook her head.

He cursed, and flopped down onto his back, staring up at the ceiling. "You're driving me nuts, Raine. Bad nuts, not good nuts."

She studied his scowling face, puzzled. "Doesn't it bother you that Victor wants to spy on you?" she inquired.

He slanted her an impatient look. "Not particularly. I'd do the same if I were him. I knew the guy was a sleaze. It comes as no shock to me. Want me to dream up some stuff for you to tell him, just to keep him off your case?"

"No, thank you. I don't want to play his game at all."

His face hardened. "Then what are you doing here?"

She shook her head again. "Seth—"

"I have to know. You don't want to play Lazar's dirty little games, and yet, you can't leave. You say you have your reasons. So what are they?"

His voice slashed across her nerves, already jagged from the nightmare, and her fragile calm began to crumble. She thought of her father's sad, hollow eyes as he drifted away. Tears came, in a hot, uncontrollable rush, and she covered her face with her hands.

Seth made an impatient sound. "I'm not going to be put off by sniveling, Raine. What the hell is it with you and Lazar? Out with it."

The words came out of their own volition. "He killed my father."

He didn't react, or exclaim, or look shocked. He just studied her, his eyes thoughtful, for a long moment. He reached out and brushed the tears off her cheeks with his knuckle. "You want to run that by me one more time, babe?" he asked gently.

She pressed her hand against her mouth as she tried to sort out what she dared to tell him. One wrong word and the whole thing would burst out of her, uncensored. "It was years ago," she whispered. "I was eleven. My father . . . worked for him. I don't know the details. I was too small. It was passed off as a boating accident. We ran away, never came back. My mother refuses to talk about it."

"So what makes you think that Victor—"

"This damned nightmare!" Her hands fell, and she let him see her tear-blotched face, her humiliating desperation. "I've been having it ever since my father died. He shows me his gravestone and the letters start to gush blood. I look up, and there's Victor, laughing at me."

"No proof? Nobody else accused him at the time?"

"No," she whispered. "We just ran. My mother and I."

He gently smoothed away her tears with his knuckles. "Sweetheart," he said carefully. "Could this just be about grief?"

She flinched away from him. "Do you think I haven't asked myself that question for seventeen years? At this point, I no longer care. I have to do this, or I'll end up in a mental ward. It's that simple."

He scowled. "Do what? What exactly do you have to do?"

She threw up her hands. "Find out what my father knew that got him killed. Look for clues, motives. I never said I was Wonder Woman."

"I thought your parents lived in London."

She shot him a startled glance, and he shrugged impatiently. "I hacked into your personnel file," he explained.

"Oh," she murmured. "Hugh Cameron is my stepfather. After my father was killed, we wandered all over Europe for five years. Then my mother finally calmed down enough to settle in London with Hugh."

"What's your father's name?"

This was the one detail she wasn't ready to tell him, or anyone. Some instinct blocked the words at their source. She tried to hide the tremor that went through her. "His name was . . . Peter Marat."

It was true, as far as it went. Peter Marat Lazar.

"You studied literature and psych at Cornell, right?" he asked.

"You really studied that file, huh?"

"Of course I studied it. My point is, what does a secretary who studied lit in college think she's doing investigating a seventeen-year-old murder? Do you have the slightest idea how to go about it?"

She looked away from him. "I've done some reading," she said.

"Reading. Huh."

Exhaustion rolled over her, in a crushing wave. "I'm not doing this for fun, Seth," she said. "I'm compelled. Maybe I'm mentally unsound after all those traumatic nightmares. I wouldn't be surprised, but it wouldn't change a thing. I've still got to do what I've got to do."

"What have you got to do?" he demanded. "What's the plan?"

She hesitated. "I'm sort of making it up as I go," she admitted. "It's a good thing that Victor has taken an interest in me—"

"Like hell it is," he snarled.

"For my purposes, it's excellent," she corrected. "I was lucky to get called to go to Stone Island yesterday. I'm looking for memories, for clues and signs. I'm present, I'm paying attention. I'm doing my best. The dream won't let me do anything else."

"So what you're saying is that you've got no plan at all."

She let out a doleful sigh. "That's about the size of it."

His hand slammed onto the pillow, hard enough to send feathers wafting into the air. "That is the craziest, stupidest, most totally fucked thing that I've ever heard in my life."

He was glaring at her, angry enough to spit nails, and she felt wonderful. Telling him had raised a crushing weight off of her. She was as light as air, about to float up off the bed. "Oh, yes," she agreed cheerfully. "It's really stupid. Believe me, I know."

"Lazar is a killer shark," he said roughly. "How can anybody be so stupid and naïve and still be walking around alive?"

She smothered a giggle, then tried to look thoughtful and serious. "That's a question I've asked myself more than once," she said. "The only answer I can come up with is pure, blind luck."

"Luck doesn't last, babe," he growled. "You need back-up."

The brief rush of euphoria began to fade. "I'll think of something."

"No, you won't. You'll be on the first plane out of SeaTac tomorrow morning. No way am I letting you—"

"Seth." She cut him off, putting her hand against his hard chest. "You're forgetting something important. It's not up to you."

Their eyes locked. She grappled with him, on a plane of awareness she had only discovered since they had become lovers, and realized something surprising about herself. Seth was extremely strong, but she could bear the weight of his disapproval, even his anger.

Seth's eyes narrowed thoughtfully. "No butterfly, huh?"

She shook her head. "Not anymore."

"Forget about the bastard, Raine. Cut bait and run. Find someplace where you can live a normal life."

She blinked for a moment, and let out a startled laugh. 'What's a normal life, Seth?" she demanded.

He looked blank. "Um, a house in the suburbs?" he offered. "Two point four kids, PTA meetings, summers on the lake? Minimalls, multiplexes, bake sales, Little League? Credit card debt?"

Her lips curved in a rueful smile. She shook her head mutely.

He shrugged, defeated. "Whatever. I give up," he muttered, pulling her close. "I wouldn't know normal if it bit me on the ass."

"We're two of a kind," she told him.

He buried his nose in her hair. "I like the sound of that."

"I'm glad something pleases you, at least." Her voice was muffled, with her nose squashed against his collarbone.

He pushed her down onto the bed and rolled on top of her. "Nothing I can say will make you get on that plane tomorrow?"

"I've already tried running away," she said simply. "For seventeen years I've tried it. I promise you. It doesn't work."

"OK, then. This is how it's going to be tomorrow." His voice was hard and businesslike. "I'm taking you to work tomorrow, and I'm picking you up. You're not leaving the office without telling me. Call me, e-mail me, beep me, whatever. Do not set foot out of that place without letting me know, not even for a cup of coffee."

"But I—"

"Lazar wanted you to spy on me, right? Go for it. Seduce me, sleep with me, spy on me. Study every inch of my body, count every hair on my head. You're just trying to make your boss happy, right? The perfect excuse. That's what I call a win-win scenario."

She was dismayed. "Seth, I think you're overreacting."

"My clueless girlfriend tells me she's trying to single-handedly take down a powerful, ruthless guy for murder. Then she tells me she has no proof, and no investigative experience. Then she tells me I'm overreacting. Tough shit, babe. This is the price you pay for confiding in me. Do as I say, or I will make your life so difficult, you'll end up giving in anyway, but you'll be exhausted and pissed off, too."

A foolish smile spread helplessly across her face. She didn't mind one bit how protective and paranoid he was. She would work out the thorny details of coping with him as she went along. It was worth it, for that warm, soft feeling in her chest. "OK," she said, rubbing her cheek against his scratchy jaw. "I'll keep you informed, if you want."

"I want," he growled, sliding back under the duvet. He arranged her so she was draped over him, her hand resting on his heart.

"Seth?" she murmured.

"Hmm?"

"I know you think I'm a lunatic, but I feel so much better now that I've told you all this."

"Oh yeah? Well, bully for you. I feel like shit."

She hid a smile against his chest and snuggled closer. Her thigh brushed against his penis. Hot and hard. She reached down and stroked him from the base to the tip. He was hugely erect. Again.

He groaned. "Don't get me started. Hands off. Sleep time."

She took her hand away reluctantly. "Is this, um, normal?"

"You know how I feel about normal, sweetheart."

"You know what I mean."

"Ah. You're referring to my perpetual boner, I take it." He kissed the top of her head. "Well, I've never had any problems getting it up, but I have never had so much trouble keeping it down until I met you."

"Oh. I'm, ah, flattered."

"Don't mind him." His lazy voice had a hint of laughter in it. "Ignore the savage beast, and eventually he'll calm down."

"You can sleep like that?"

His chest vibrated with silent laughter under her ear. "Let me worry about that," he said. "Get some rest, for God's sake."

To her surprise, she realized that she actually could. She was warm and relaxed, curled up on top of him, resting on his strength. For the first time, she wasn't all alone in the dark with her monsters.

What a crazy day. So much had happened, all at once. She had a boyfriend. She was giving him a key to her house. She had confided her darkest, most painful secrets to him. He warmed her, charged her with wild energy and euphoria, maybe even courage and luck.

They were hurtling forward at three hundred miles an hour with no brakes, and she didn't even want to slow down.

She'd never had a dream so delicious, so awash with sensation. Warmth and wetness, luscious heat and light and shifting colors. Touches, melting and swirling. Divine pleasure, as if a god were making love to her. Then the seamless slide into consciousness, the faint morning light that seeped into the room pressing on her eyes. She tried not to wake up, to make the beautiful dream linger and last, but the pleasure didn't fade. It got stronger. She opened her eyes cautiously.

The comforter was folded up from the bottom and flung up over her chest—and Seth was lying between her legs.

Licking her.

She jerked, startled, and he gripped her hips in his hands, murmuring something reassuring. She flung aside the comforter, and he lifted his head just long enough to give her a smug, satisfied grin. "Good morning," he said, putting his mouth to her again.

She writhed at the delicious intimacy. "Seth, you're obsessed," she whispered.

He laughed, and her sex vibrated with the resonance of his voice, the sweet, tickling heat of his breath. "Yeah," he admitted. "I love giving you head. The taste of you drives me out of my mind." He lifted his head and stared into her eyes. "That a problem for you?"

"Dear God, no," she gasped. His tongue slid up and down her labia, circling her clitoris. He drew it into his mouth, sucking on it with exquisite care. "I just think that you—oh—"

"That I'm what?" he demanded.

"That you're the p-perfect boyfriend," she stammered.

She couldn't speak, or think. She let him work his erotic magic, lapping and toying with her with sensual tenderness, his tongue flicking and dancing across her sweetest, hottest spot until he pushed her relentlessly over the crest. Spasms of bright, hot rapture shuddered through her.

He rested his head against her thigh for a long moment before he sat up. He wiped his face and gazed at her with an odd combination of lust and wonder. "Good morning," he said again as he got up.

Raine sat up and stared at his body. His wiry muscles were so long and lean and elegantly proportioned. To say nothing of the thick, engorged penis that bobbed enticingly in front of him. "Good morning," she replied, suddenly shy. Wild woman inside her was jumping up and down, pointing to his fierce erection, and saying, *"Mine. That's mine, and I want it. Give it to me. Now."* She struggled to express the impulse in socially acceptable terms, but her brain wasn't functioning very well. She gestured towards his groin. "Seth. Do you want to, um—"

"Of course. But you're new to this, and we went at it like a couple of minks last night. I don't want to overdo it. I'm not a total maniac."

"I am," she said baldly.

His eyes lit up with hungry anticipation. "It won't be sweet or soft. That's not where I'm at right now."

The words hung between them, a blunt warning, and a challenge.

"That's all right," she said. "That's not where I'm at, either."

Wild woman capered and howled with delight as he grabbed a condom from the shrinking stash on the bed stand, ripped it open and smoothed it over himself. He grabbed her ankles, dragging her until her bottom was at the edge of the bed, then pushed her onto her back. He spread her thighs up, folding her wide open like a full-blown flower.

His hands gripped her knees, opening her. His eyes bored into hers. "I don't want you to go back to that asshole's office today."

He was seeking to assert dominance over her with his fierce masculine energy, but his vain efforts just aroused her more. "I'm sorry you feel that way," she said. She gripped his arms, pulling him down to her. "Come on, Seth. Don't be coy."

"Open up for me," he said softly. "All the way. Ankles for earrings." He pushed her thighs still wider and spread the lips of her sex open delicately with his fingertips. "Perfect. Show me that sweet sexy thing, all buttered up just for me."

"I'm ready," she urged him, arching her back.

"I know you are, sweetheart. I've got your sex juice all over my face." He slid his hand beneath her bottom and gently nudged the blunt tip of him inside her. "God, look at you."

"Do it," she snapped. "Don't be a tease."

She cried out at his first deep thrust, but not in pain. He stopped, alarmed. "You OK?"

She yanked him closer. "I'm fine, I'm great. I love it. Please, Seth."

"You got it," he muttered. "Nothing fancy today, sweetheart."

He gave her exactly what she wanted, a deep, surging rhythm that caressed every part of her swollen, aching sex, to her very depths. He arched over her, the thick, heavy muscles of his shoulders taut and corded, his face rigid with concentration. Sobbing breaths gasped out of her with each plunge, and she clutched his arms and urged him on. Neither wanted anything other than that rhythm, just more of it. Hotter and faster, deep and furious and relentless, until they both exploded.

He collapsed and draped himself over her, trembling. "My God," he said. "It's always like this with you. It scares me."

She reached down and ran her fingers lazily through his sweat-dampened hair. "What scares you?"

He pulled out of her and folded down to his knees, hooking his arms under her legs. He clasped her hips in his arms and rested his head on her belly. "You're scaring me," he mumbled.

"Seth," she murmured, wiggling. "I'm all wet."

"Yeah, and I want to rub it all over myself. Your perfume makes me crazy with lust." He inhaled, a deep, hungry whiff.

She giggled at his foolishness. "I told you, I don't wear perfume."

"I'm not talking about perfume from a bottle. I'm talking about *your* perfume. All the scented things you use, soap and lotion and stuff, they add to the mix, but they're only overtones. The basic perfume is like—" he stopped, burying his nose in her navel and breathing deeply, "—like a cross between honey and violets. Violets after a rainstorm. But warmer, hotter. Softer. Mix the smell of sex into it, and I'm a dead man."

She struggled up onto her elbows and gazed at him, touched. "Why, Seth. You're a poet," she said softly.

He looked alarmed. "No way. I'm just stating the plain facts. They just happen to sound poetic by accident."

"Oh. I see," she murmured. "God forbid that I should think you had a lyrical, poetic side."

He scowled at her as he pulled off the condom, wrapped it up and disposed of it. "Yeah," he muttered suspiciously. "God forbid."

Raine sat up, gathering her courage. "Seth, next time—"

"What? What did I do wrong this time?"

She was startled by the sharp edge in his voice. "Nothing at all," she said hastily. "You did everything incredibly right. I just wondered if the next time you'd let me try . . . um, you know."

He shook his head. "I don't dare guess. Spit it out, sweetheart."

She took a deep breath and closed her eyes. "Oral sex," she whispered. "You're always doing it to me, and I'd like to try doing it to you. But I've never tried it. So I probably wouldn't be any good."

When she finally opened her eyes, he was gazing at her with a look of almost comical dismay on his face. "God, Raine. You don't have to ask. Do whatever you want with me. Do that, and I'll be your slave. Anytime, anywhere, and I'm not kidding. Right now, if you want."

She blushed, and shook her head. "I'm already late. Next time."

"I won't let you forget." He lunged on top of her, pinning her onto the bed. "There's just one more thing I have to know before we face the day. How do you like your eggs?"

She stared at him blankly. "Eggs? I don't have any eggs, Seth."

"Sure you do. I got breakfast stuff last night, along with the deli stuff. Eggs and bacon and orange juice and toast and coffee. With real cream. You need to get some more meat on your bones."

He looked so pleased with himself, she had to laugh. "You were feeling pretty confident last night, huh?" she asked, caressing his face.

"Don't hold it against me." He rubbed his cheek against her hand like a cat, then grabbed it and kissed her palm. A warm, glowing feeling heated up her chest. It had been so long since she'd had any reason to feel happy in the morning.

She glanced at the clock, and winced. "Actually, it's really late. I'd better just pop into the shower and run. I have to—"

"They can goddamn well wait until you get some breakfast into you." His voice cut harshly over hers. "You've been opening your veins for that place for weeks. Enough already."

She was unnerved by his uncanny grasp of all the details of her life. "How do you figure that?" she asked hesitantly.

"All I have to do is look at you."

She winced. "That bad, huh?"

"Cut it out," he said. "You're drop-dead gorgeous and you damn well know it. But you need to eat more. And I'm the one who's driving you to work, anyhow. I'm not doing it until you eat."

Her eyes wandered from his scowling gaze, down over his naked, gorgeous golden body. "Do you want to shower with me?"

His frown vanished, and his gaze heated up. "Oh, yeah. Only more than I want to breathe. But you know exactly what would happen. And I want you to eat breakfast."

Sensual images rushed through her mind of soapy hands slipping and sliding over flushed skin, clouds of steam rising as he pinned her against the slippery tile. Hot water pouring, pounding.

He backed away from her, shaking his head. "You are dangerous, babe. Go quick and take your shower, or I'll fuck you again right now."

She scurried into the bathroom and turned on the shower. She stood beneath the stream of water, amazed and grateful to feel no residue of terror or grief from a nightmare clutching at her. She was rested and relaxed, her muscles loose, filled with energy. Joyful.

She was actually hungry. She'd never felt hungry in the morning in her life. Lately, she'd begun to forget what hunger felt like altogether. But right now, bacon, eggs, toast and orange juice sounded like heaven. She danced beneath the water, humming as she worked shampoo into her hair. A dark shadow loomed on the other side of the glass door. Seth slid the door open, his eyes raking her soapy body.

"I tried to be good," he said. "I tried to be self-controlled. I tried to be civilized and restrained. I tried to resist temptation."

Raine rinsed foam out of her eyes and blinked at him. "Oh? And?"

He stepped into the shower and reached for her. "I failed."

Chapter

14

"You remember the drill?"

Raine leaned across the seat and kissed him. "Don't worry, Seth."

She meant the smile to be reassuring, but it had the opposite effect. It made him uncomfortably aware that she wasn't taking him seriously enough. If she knew the whole truth, she'd be scared to death.

"I didn't ask if I should worry. I asked if you remember the drill."

The hard edge in his voice made her pull away, eyes wide and wary. He took a deep breath and tried to soften his tone. "Not one foot out the door of that place without contacting me. Got it?"

"Yes. You have a lovely day, too, Seth. Have fun inspecting the warehouses." She smiled over her shoulder at him, and was promptly swallowed into the revolving glass doors of the building.

He fought down the urge to run in after her, and distracted himself by keying her transmitter codes into the handheld monitor. He adjusted it until the cluster of signals were showing in the grid, spatial data streaming in a continuous flow of changing coordinates alongside the flashing icons. He punched up McCloud's number.

Connor answered on the first ring. "Yeah?"

"I need to know everything you can find out about a guy named Peter Marat," Seth said. "Get Davy to run a check. He worked for Lazar about seventeen years ago until he mysteriously drowned."

"What's the connection?"

"He's Raine's dad. She wants to prove that Lazar snuffed him. An apparent sailboat accident when she was a kid."

There was a brief silence. "The plot thickens," Connor said, in a mock ominous tone.

"Just get on it. One of you guys has to cover her while I'm in Renton. I'm heading out there now. She's at the office. I planted five Colbits on her yesterday. Here are the codes. Got a pen?"

"Hold on a sec . . . yes. Go."

Seth read out the transmitter code sequences. "Key up one of the monitors and get your ass over here, fast. I don't want her uncovered. Get Sean to tail Lazar this morning."

"Yeah, sure. No problem. Hup, hup. You know, Seth, when all this is over, you and I are going to have a serious talk about your social skills."

"No, we're not."

Seth broke the connection and edged the car back into the dense morning traffic. A window dresser was putting up Thanksgiving decorations in a shop, and he stared at him idly while he was waiting for the light. A wicker cornucopia with squashes and corncobs spilling out, a papier-mâché turkey, mannequins dressed in pilgrim garb. His stomach clenched. Jesse had been killed in January. The winter holidays without Jesse were staring him in the face. He wasn't ready.

Not that holidays had been any big deal to them when they were kids, on the contrary; but they had taken on more significance once they started hanging out with Hank. The holidays had been important to Hank, like some kind of emotional link to his long-dead wife, so he and Jesse had played along, grumbling all the way. Every year they'd buy a pre-roasted Safeway turkey, pumpkin pies, stuffing, all the rest of that holiday slop. They'd scarf the stuff off of paper plates and spend the night listening to Hank's old Julie Andrews and Perry Como Christmas albums, knocking back shots of Jack Daniels until Hank started getting maudlin about his lost Gladys. That was their cue to take him by the armpits and haul him off to bed. It had gotten messy and sad towards the end, when Hank was so sick, but it was as much of a family as any of them had, and they were all three of them grateful for it.

For some reason, in the last few years after Hank died, he and Jesse had kept up the habit of hanging together on the holidays. They usually opted for Mexican or Thai rather than the insipid traditional stuff, but the shots of Jack deep into the night were a memorial to Hank. The first Christmas after his death had been depressing, but they'd gotten through it. They'd cracked a lot of lame jokes, clenched their teeth, tossed back the whiskey, and faced it down together.

He had no idea how he was going to face it down alone.

The swishy guy in the store window was arranging the pilgrim maiden's long yellow hair. Seth was comparing the Dynel floss to the warm gold of Raine's hair when the idea came to him. The perfect way to get through Christmas unscathed.

He could kidnap Raine and take her away to the coast with him. Find a hotel room with an ocean view and a Jacuzzi tub and spend the whole holiday in an endorphin-induced haze. Ply her with champagne, hand-feed her oysters on the half shell in between bouts of hot, juicy sex while rain pounded against the window, and surf pounded on the shore. White foam surging across the sand in sensual, rhythmic pulses.

Hell, yes. He almost shouted with glee. That would be one righteous mother of a distraction. Jesse would have been proud of him.

He could persuade her. He could play her like an instrument. She was so sweet, so affectionate. It would be awesome. He could hardly wait. He got so excited, thinking about it, that for a minute or two, he completely forgot what the hell he was here for.

Jesse, Lazar, Novak. Bloody retribution. Christ, what was he thinking. Everything was subject to this investigation. Everything.

Still, a part of his mind clung stubbornly to the idea of himself and Raine, the hot tub, the pounding surf. Maybe he could get this fucking nightmare wrapped up by then, and Christmas at the coast with her could be his reward. Assuming he lived through it.

Horns blared. Someone howled an obscenity. The light was green, and he was still staring at the pilgrim maiden's vacuous smile. He laid his foot on the gas and forced himself to remember what Jesse's body had looked like when Novak was done with him.

Just the image to shake a guy's priorities right back into place.

*   *   *

"Can you wait for me?" Raine asked the cabbie. "I won't be long."

The cabbie slumped down in his seat and rummaged for a paperback book. "The meter's gonna be running," he informed·her.

"That'll be fine," she assured him.

She rechecked the Lynnwood address on the scrap of paper and walked slowly up to the bungalow. She rang the bell. The door opened and a white-haired woman peered out from behind the chain. "Yes?"

"Dr. Fischer?"

"That would be me."

"I'm Raine Cameron. I called you this morning regarding the autopsy report of Peter Lazar."

The older woman hesitated, and unhooked the chain. "Come in."

The doctor seated her in a little parlor, and brought out coffee and a plate of sugar cookies. She sat down on the opposite end of the sofa.

"So, Ms. Cameron," she said briskly. "How can I help you? I would have been happy to answer your questions on the phone."

"I didn't have the privacy I needed, unfortunately. I want to ask a few questions about this report." She fished out the manila envelope that the Severin Bay Coroner's office had sent her.

The doctor's eyebrows snapped together as she scanned the sheets of paper inside. "This was pretty clear and straightforward, as I recall. It was ruled an accident. I remember it quite well. I was the only doctor in the area who had a specialization in pathology, so I was called upon to do autopsies in surrounding communities fairly often. We didn't have many incidents of suspicious death in a place as small as Severin Bay, though. They tended to stick in one's memory."

"Do you remember actually doing the autopsy?" Raine asked.

"Yes. It was all just as the report states. Toxicology samples indicate that he'd been drinking heavily. There was a blow to the back of the head, presumably from the boom of the sailboat. There was a nasty storm that afternoon, and we've all seen that happen. There was water and air mixed in the lungs, and water in the stomach. Indicating that he did indeed drown, if that's what you're wondering."

Raine searched for words. "Was there any reason to think that the death could have been . . . anything other than an accident?"

The doctor's lips thinned. "If there was, I certainly would have indicated it in the report."

"I'm not questioning your professionalism," Raine assured her. "I'm just, well—is it conceivable that someone could have hit him? Was there a mark on the boom that corresponded to the head wound?"

"I suppose theoretically that someone could have hit him," the doctor said grudgingly. "But several eyewitnesses saw him leave Stone Island alone, and the blow didn't break the skin. I can't imagine that there would be any corresponding mark on an aluminum boom. Particularly since the boat was capsized for hours afterwards."

Raine placed her barely nibbled cookie on the saucer, fighting down the clench and roll of impending nausea. She rose to her feet, hanging on to her control. If she were going to have a panic attack, she certainly didn't want an audience. "I appreciate you giving me your time like this, Dr. Fischer," she said faintly. "I'm sorry if my questions seemed out of place."

"Quite all right." Dr. Fischer followed Raine back to the foyer and took her coat out of the closet. She handed the coat to Raine, and started to speak. She stopped herself, shaking her head.

Raine froze, halfway into her coat. "What?"

The doctor twisted her hands in the pockets of her cardigan. "I don't know if this is relevant, or useful to you. But you're not the only one who was interested in the results of that report."

Raine froze into place, forgetting that her arms were twisted behind her into the sleeves of her coat. Dr. Fischer reached out and took the coat lapels, pulling until the coat sat straight upon Raine's shoulders. She gave Raine a little pat, as if she were a child. "Two FBI agents came to me, asking very much the same questions as you did. They seemed frustrated that Peter Lazar had gotten himself drowned. Convinced that I didn't know my job. Arrogant jerks, both of them."

Raine tried to swallow, but her mouth was too dry. "What did they want from Peter Lazar?"

"Well, they weren't sharing any details with me, but there was a good bit of rumor and speculation at the time."

"About what?"

The doctor's face tightened, as if she regretted opening up the can of worms. "Oh, the wild goings-on out at Stone Island, among other things. The place was aptly named, they say, for the quantity of drugs that went through the place. There were some truly legendary parties out there. Very few local people were ever invited, but everyone loved to tell tales. Most of it sheer nonsense, I'm sure, but you know how people are. And Alix made a splash, with her glamorous wardrobe and her celebrity attitude. Everyone loved to gossip about her."

"Did you know her?" Raine asked cautiously.

"By sight," the doctor said with a shrug. "She got her medical care in the city."

Raine hesitated. "Those agents," she ventured. "Do you remember their names?"

Dr. Fischer's eyes crinkled up. "You're in luck. The card they gave me got sucked into the void years ago, but I remember one of the names just because it was similar to that of an old college boyfriend of mine. Haley was the older one. Bill Haley."

Raine reached out and clasped the other woman's hand. "Thank you. You've been very kind."

The doctor squeezed her hand, but did not let go of it. She held on, staring at Raine's face with focused concentration until Raine began to fidget. "I take it your identity is a deep, dark secret?"

Raine opened her mouth, but nothing came out.

The doctor touched the heavy blond braid that lay on Raine's shoulder. "You really should have cut and dyed your hair, dear."

"How did you—how—"

"Oh, come now. Who else would take such an interest in Peter Lazar, at this late date?" the doctor said gently. "Besides, you're the image of your mother. Though you strike me as . . . warmer, somehow."

"Oh, God," she whispered. "Would anyone who knew her notice the resemblance?"

"It would depend upon their powers of observation."

Raine shook her head, appalled at her own idiocy. She had tried a brown wig, at first, but the effect of dark hair with her pale face had been so obviously fake that she'd concluded that it would draw more attention than it would deflect. Besides, the shaggy, layered bronze mane of hair her mother had worn back in '86 was nothing like her own plain twist or simple braid. And her mother had said so often that Raine was so dowdy, no one would ever guess she was Alix's daughter. With her big hornrimmed glasses, she'd felt safe enough.

What a cretin. Victor's powers of observation were colossal.

"I examined you once, you know," Dr. Fischer commented.

Raine gaped at her. "You did?"

"The school nurse at Severin Elementary School was a friend of mine. You were always in the infirmary in the afternoons with bad headaches, telling her wild tales about ghosts and goblins and dreams. She was worried about you. She thought you needed to see a psychiatrist, or a neurologist. Or both."

"Oh," Raine murmured, struggling to remember the incident.

"She'd already contacted your mother, and had evidently hit a blank wall." The older woman's eyebrows furrowed at the memory. "So she asked me to drop by and take a look at you."

Raine waited. "And?"

"My diagnosis was that you were an intelligent, sensitive ten-year-old with a lively imagination and a very high-stress family situation." Dr. Fischer patted Raine's shoulder and let her hand rest upon it. "I was so sorry about your father. And all my sorry was for you. Not for the rest of that rabble out on the island. If you'll excuse my saying so."

"It's all right." Raine blinked back a rush of tears. "I would appreciate it if you would not tell anyone about me."

"Good heavens, no," Dr. Fischer said emphatically. "I'm pleased to have the opportunity to help you, since I couldn't back then. Good luck, Ms. Cameron. Let me know how things go. And, ah . . . do be careful."

Raine hurried for the taxi. "I will," she called.

She got into the cab, embarrassed. Some pirate queen she was, blubbering at the slightest act of kindness. It didn't mean she was weak, she reminded herself. Just stressed. She swallowed, calming her shaking, vibrating throat.

"Where to?" the cabbie demanded.

"I'll know in a minute," she told him.

She used the cell phone Seth had given her to call directory assistance, and began the search for Bill Haley. They drove around the residential neighborhood in big circles, waiting on hold, transferred from here to there. At great length, she was informed that he was heading up a task force at a different location. She dialed the number the receptionist gave her, asked the switchboard operator for Bill Haley, and sat back to wait, clenching her stomach against the butterflies.

Her luck was changing. She could feel it. This morning, she had looked Harriet in the face and told a barefaced lie without blinking; she was leaving for a doctor's appointment, so sorry for the inconvenience, bye bye. The scary part was, she'd actually enjoyed the look on Harriet's face. Maybe it was the delicious breakfast Seth had insisted on cooking for her. He had dosed her eggs with pixie dust.

Thinking of Seth brought on an uneasy pang of guilt. She'd promised to tell him every move she made, but the request was bossy and paranoid. He was tied up inspecting the inventory system today anyway, so why distress him? She couldn't afford to waste her energy in a dispute over being accompanied or not. Besides, her errands were innocuous enough. It wasn't like she was meeting a stranger at midnight under a bridge.

Seth's protective instincts made her feel cuddled and cherished, but he had a life, and far better things to do with his time than tag around after her. She had to be bold, to catch this new wave of courage and momentum and ride it for as far as it would take her.

The Muzak version of "Silver Bells" abruptly clicked off. "This is Bill Haley's office," a woman said. "How can I help you?"

"My name is Raine Cameron. I'm calling with some questions about a case that Mr. Haley was working on some years ago, involving Peter Marat Lazar, in August of 1985."

"And what is the nature of your interest in the case?"

Raine floundered for a second, and then followed her instincts, as she had last night with Seth. "I'm Peter Lazar's daughter."

"Hold on," the woman instructed.

Raine clutched the phone, her head spinning. She had spoken the truth, for the first time in seventeen years, to a faceless woman on the telephone. Now three people on earth, including her mother and Dr. Fischer, knew her true identity. When Bill Haley knew, it would be four.

The Muzak version of "White Christmas" clicked off. "Mr. Haley would be glad to talk to you. When can you come?"

"Right now?"

"That's doable. Hurry, though. He has a meeting at twelve-thirty."

Her hands shook as she scribbled down the directions. She was electrified by the thought that there might come a day when she would no longer have to lie to anyone about anything.

Oh, God, it was going to feel wonderful.

He would never have thought that angel face capable of lying. The painful, exposed honesty trembling in her voice last night; he'd bought it completely. This was the kind of stuff that happened to a guy when he started thinking with his dick. Other men were used to it, maybe. For him, it was an unpleasant novelty.

He dialed McCloud, staring at the cluster of signals on the beacon display screen. Raine was not safely ensconced in the Lazar Import & Export corporate office. She was on southbound I-5, moving through Shoreline. He'd stopped at Oak Terrace to grab some fresh clothes and equipment, and punched up the beacon display to check on her. So he could relax. Hah.

McCloud picked up on the third ring. "Why didn't you call me when she skipped out?" Seth snarled.

"Because you were busy, and I had the situation under control," Connor said calmly. "At least until just now."

"Yeah? What's that supposed to mean?"

"It means that Raine's been holding out on you, buddy. I just talked to Davy. Nobody by the name of Peter Marat has ever worked for Victor Lazar." Connor clucked his tongue. "I'd hold off on the wedding invitations until you figure out what she's up to."

"You are annoying the shit out of me, McCloud."

"That's my specialty. Back to your blonde. I've been chasing her around all morning. Her first visit was to a retired doctor named Serena Fischer. Davy checked her out, tells me that Fischer is a GP who used to practice in Severin Bay. She was there for about twenty minutes."

"Now what is she doing?"

"This is the interesting part. I tuned in to her cell phone. She's going to see my boss. She's on her way to Bill Haley's office right now."

Seth's mouth fell open.

"She's that good, huh?" Connor's voice was coolly speculative. "Been spilling tales while you've been boning Blondie, Seth?"

"Fuck, no." He was too stupefied to be angered by the accusation.

"Hmm. You're never going to guess what else she said to Donna, when she called the Cave. You sitting down?"

"Don't be coy," Seth snarled.

"She said she was Peter Lazar's daughter. Peter . . . Marat . . . Lazar. Congratulations, Mackey. You've been giving the high hard one to Victor Lazar's niece."

An icy claw gripped Seth's gut, and squeezed. He sat down. Hard.

Connor's voice was relentlessly matter of fact. "Davy ran another check. It all happened pretty much like Raine said, except for the trifling detail of the last name. Victor's younger brother Peter drowned in '85. He had a daughter, name of Katerina. The kid and her mom skipped the country and haven't been heard from since."

Connor paused, expectant, but Seth was struck speechless.

He grunted and went on. "That's not all. Sean tailed Lazar's Mercedes around all morning, listening to his cell phone. There's going to be one of those depraved VIP shindigs out at Stone Island tonight. Victor's been calling members of his club of illicit collectors, plus his favorite exclusive escort service, for the late-night entertainment. Sounds like a big deal. It'll be interesting to see who comes."

Seth struggled to follow him. "Uh, yeah. Real interesting."

"And the most interesting tidbit of all was a phone call to Lazar's supposedly secure private line in his office. Love that little drop-in bug you slipped into his phone. Davy monitored a twenty-five second phone call from an unidentified person who simply said that the meeting for the 'heart of darkness' would be on Monday morning."

Seth rubbed his hands over his stinging eyes. "No location?"

"Nope. Bummer. Mystery caller said more details would be forthcoming."

"Shit," Seth muttered.

"Yeah. We're going to have to improvise, like I always figured. Anyhow, back to Blondie. I can't follow her to the Cave. I'm no good for covert surveillance down there. I've asked Sean to cover—"

"I'm on my way," he cut in. "Don't let her out of your sight."

"But she knows you," Connor objected. "She doesn't know Sean. Come on, Seth—"

"She won't see me." He cut the connection and shoved the phone into his pocket with trembling hands. He had to play it cool. No red haze. It would run him off the rails, and he would be fucked.

Victor Lazar's niece. Holy shit.

Right now would be a good time for his inner cyborg to take over and run the show, but there was nothing left of him but a pile of parts. Circuits blown, wires smoking, all tangled together with flesh and bone and pulsing blood. Raine Cameron Lazar had taken him to pieces.

"Lucky that you came when you did," Bill Haley told her. "I'm retiring, you see. This time next week, I'll be salmon fishing up in the Inside Passage. Please, sit down."

"Congratulations on your retirement. I'm glad I caught you," Raine said. Bill Haley was a twinkling-eyed man in his sixties, with chubby, Santa Claus cheeks, bushy brows and curly iron-gray hair.

"No need to prove that you are who you say you are," he said. "Damn, but you look a lot like your mom."

"I've been hearing that a lot lately," Raine said.

He steepled his fingers together and gave her an affable smile. "So, Ms. Cameron. What is it that you think I can do for you?"

"I heard that you took an interest in my father's death," she said. "I'd like to know why."

Haley's smile faded quickly. "You don't remember much of that time, huh? How old were you? Nine, ten?"

"Almost eleven," Raine said. "And I remember just enough to make me really nervous."

Bill Haley studied her face. "You should be nervous," he said bluntly. "It was very convenient for Victor Lazar that his brother had that accident. Victor had his fingers in all sorts of pies back then. Peter had finally agreed to testify against him." Haley tapped his pen against the desk, studying her reaction. His eyes no longer seemed to twinkle. They had taken on a sharp, metallic glint.

Nausea clutched at her belly again. She willed it to subside. "Please go on," she said resolutely.

"There's not much more to tell. With Peter's testimony, we could have nailed the bastard in '85, but Victor ran off to Greece, and before we knew it, Peter was floating face down in the Sound. Uh . . . sorry, miss."

"It's OK." She waited.

Haley shrugged. "After that, Victor got smart. He cleaned up his act, went mostly legit. We haven't been able to get a hold on him since. He's very slick. Very careful. And very connected."

She clenched her hands together in her lap and braced herself. "Do you believe that Victor had my father killed?" she asked bluntly.

Haley's face lost all expression. "There was no proof that Peter's death was anything other than a boating accident. That's just the way it is sometimes. Nothing we could do. Particularly since Peter's wife and daughter vanished. We never got to question them." His eyes fixed on her in a cold, probing gaze. "But here you are. Did you see or hear anything on that day, miss?"

There it was again, the swirling, nauseous panic, the blur of green. Screams, echoing. She swallowed hard and fought it down. "I . . . don't remember," she faltered. "My mother insists that we weren't there."

"I see." He tapped his pen against the desktop, a rapid tattoo. "Your uncle, does he know you're asking around about Peter?"

She shook her head.

Haley shrugged. "Be a hell of a lot better for you if he never found out, if you ask me."

"I know that," she said stiffly.

"You watch your back, miss. People who take too much of an interest in Victor Lazar's business have a bad habit of dying young. And being closely related to him isn't much of a safeguard. Obviously."

"Obviously," she repeated softly.

The grim silence that followed signaled a close to the conversation. A faraway, mechanical part of her brain dealt with the business of shaking hands and thanking Bill Haley for his time. The same part kept her from walking into the people in the corridor outside.

She finally had something concrete to corroborate her dreams. That was progress. But if trained agents of the federal government, with all their experience and all their vast resources had thrown up their hands in defeat, what could she possibly hope to accomplish?

Raine bumped into someone, and veered away, mumbling an apology. She had to keep on as she was. Infiltrating. At least she wasn't crazy or delusional. She was on the track of something horribly real, no matter how elusive. That was something to cling to. A man was turning to stare at her as she walked past. She shot him a brief glance, just long enough to register information without seeming interested. A split second after she looked away, her stomach began to roll.

There was no reason for it. She'd never seen him before. She reviewed everything she had caught in the swift, photographic glance. Tall, protruding belly. Thinning dark hair, clean-shaven, bifocals. Nothing particular about him, other than his expression. Not one of masculine appreciation. He'd looked horrified.

She turned to look again. He was striding down the hall away from her, very fast. Almost running. Ducking into a doorway, the same one she had just exited. Bill Haley's office.

She turned around and kept walking, shivering with the rising panic. It was like a whirlpool inside her, a sick, out of control feeling.

The green blur, the screaming. This was senseless. Why was she having a panic attack after catching a glimpse of an innocuous middle-aged man? Maybe she really was going nuts.

The best option was the simplest and most direct one, she told herself. She could go back to Haley's office, knock, and ask the man if they knew each other from somewhere. Either they would or they wouldn't. Raine turned, and took a slow, reluctant step in that direction.

There was a loud snap. She felt a stabbing pain in her hand. She pulled it out of her coat pocket. She'd been clutching the frog glasses so tightly that one of the earpieces had broken off. The metal joint had dug into her palm, hard enough to draw blood.

Trust your instincts, Victor had said. *With trust, they grow stronger.* She shoved the glasses back in her pocket and hurried towards the stairwell. As soon as her legs got moving, it was all she could do not to draw attention to herself by breaking into a dead run.

Chapter

15

"Ah. There you are. Harriet told me you were absent for a doctor's appointment. I trust you're feeling better?"

Raine looked up from the cell phone into which she was trying to punch a message to Seth. She slipped it into her pocket, message uncompleted, and forced herself to return Victor's solicitous smile.

"I'm fine, thank you," she assured him.

"My personal physician would be happy to see you at any time."

"No, really, I'm quite all right," she repeated.

"So glad to hear it. I trust you're fit enough to go out to Stone Island this afternoon, then. I need your help on an urgent project."

She heard Seth's reaction in her mind, and winced inwardly at the thought. "I—ah, well, on such short notice, I really—"

"Don't worry about packing. Everything will be provided. The car is waiting to take you to the marina. I will join you at the island after I take care of a few small items of business. Be brisk, please. There's a great deal to be done." He strode away without waiting for a response.

She stared at his retreating back, dismayed. Harriet sashayed over to her desk and leaned down with a big fake smile. "Don't worry," she hissed. "Everything will be provided."

Raine lifted her chin and glared right back, sick to death of the pointless, toxic hostility of that place. "Don't you get tired of being such a cast-iron bitch, Harriet?" she demanded. "Doesn't it wear you out?"

Her voice carried farther than she'd intended. Shocked silence spread out, like the electromagnetic pulse of a hydrogen bomb. Not a piece of paper moved. Even the phones stopped ringing. The whole office waited for the sky to fall.

Harriet yanked Raine's coat off the hook and flung it at her. "Your carriage awaits," she spat out. "Get out of here. Don't come back."

It took the whole ride to the marina for her heart rate to slow down to normal. She calmed herself by fiddling with the cell phone, composing and sending a message to Seth. *Going to Stone Island. No choice. Don't worry.* She added three little heart icons. Goofy little messages, that was what he said he wanted. Useless, too. Of course he would worry. She had to push that fact away and concentrate.

She was met at the dock, not by Clayborne, but by a stunning brunette with hazel eyes who introduced herself as Mara. They passed right by the main stairway that led to the second floor office, to Raine's bewilderment. "But aren't I—doesn't Clayborne need me in the office?"

"Clayborne's not here. None of the office staff are here." Mara started up a spiral staircase, which led up to the tower bedroom that had once been her mother's. Raine's apprehension climbed a notch.

"Then why did Mr. Lazar tell me—"

"Ask him, not me." Mara pushed open the bedroom door.

The room was brilliantly lit with a makeup mirror. A rack of plastic-covered clothes hung in front of the bed. Raine turned to Mara, bewildered. "But Victor told me he had a project he wanted—"

"You're the project, honey," said a thin, short-haired woman. She and the plump white-haired lady beside her rose to their feet, eyes narrowing as their professional instincts leaped to life. "Out of that horrible outfit, and into the shower, please. We've got to get your hair shampooed so I can blow the curls out."

Raine shook her head. "But I—"

"Just do it," Mara said flatly. "There's a huge party tonight. You've got to look good, so let's get on with it."

"But—"

"You do have contact lenses with you, don't you?" Mara asked.

"Ah, yes, I have them in my purse, but—"

"Thank God." The white-haired woman rolled her eyes and began unraveling Raine's braid.

There was no stopping them. They plucked, steamed and peeled, massaged and moisturized her. Her hair was washed, conditioned, rinsed, trimmed, dried, straightened. It seemed a waste of energy to resist. It was part of Stone Island's spell. Part and parcel of the bizarre transformation she underwent, day by day.

Even the lingerie was provided. It was the most beautiful stuff she'd ever seen—midnight blue lace panties, lace-trimmed thigh-high stockings. She looked around for a bra, but Mara shook her head.

"Not with the dress you'll be wearing. You won't need one."

"Me?" Raine looked nervously down at her bare chest, trying to imagine what kind of dress she could possibly wear braless, but there was no time to fret about it. She was plunked down in front of the big makeup mirror. Lydia, the short-haired woman, coiled her hair back into a smooth, intricately knotted chignon at the back of her head, while the plump woman, whose name was Moira, began with the makeup. She made approving little noises as she dabbed on cosmetics with a slow, delicate hand. She brushed Raine's face with a translucent powder and stepped back with a triumphant smile. "Done."

"Now the dress." Mara rummaged through the things on the rack and pulled one out, tossing it on the bed. A long, voluminous skirt spilled out from the plastic wrapping, gleaming against the white lace coverlet. It was a deep, peacock blue taffeta, shot through with subtle rainbow tints. The garment was two pieces, the billowing skirt and a tight, boned corset top, strapless and scalloped at the neckline, angling down to a rounded V at the bottom. Raine finally understood the lack of a bra. The close-fitting bodice was a bustier in itself. It pushed her up, offering a daring expanse of her white chest, and lots of deep, shadowy cleavage. Lydia scowled as she fastened up the hooks. "You're thinner than I was led to believe."

"Sorry." Raine almost laughed at her accusing tone. "I haven't had time to eat lately."

"If you don't eat, you'll lose your looks," Lydia scolded, threading her needle. "Hold still while I fix this."

They twitched and tucked, stitched and tweaked, spritzed and sprayed. Finally they led her before the mirror on the armoire.

She tried not to gasp, but she was truly shocked at the way she looked. The color of the dress set off her skin, making it pearly and luminous. The makeup was subtle, but it brought her face into focus, accentuating her high cheekbones. Her straight brows were plucked into an elegant shape, opening up her face. Her eyes seemed huge. Even her big, full mouth, which she had always felt made her look childlike and vulnerable, looked different. Sensual and curvy. She looked glittery, luminous. Almost . . . beautiful.

She had never considered herself beautiful. Pretty, maybe, in a washed-out sort of way, but beauty was Alix's undisputed territory and Raine had sensed from an early age that it would be dangerous to encroach on it.

The knowledge that she was beautiful gave her no pleasure, however. It was a possible advantage, maybe even a weapon, if she had the stomach to use it. Alix had used hers. Often, and without mercy.

The thought chilled her. Beauty did not make her feel powerful. At least, not here. On the contrary, she felt even more vulnerable in the sensual, beautiful gown. Victor was playing with her.

The dress was the color of the last light of evening in a clear sky. It reminded her of an illustrated volume of fairy tales she'd read as a child. Bluebeard's bride had worn a dress like this one, except for the addition of puffed leg-of-mutton sleeves. The same peacock color had clothed her on her voyage of horror and discovery through her new husband's grim, bloodstained castle.

She shuddered. Mara misinterpreted it and reached behind her.

"There's a wrap, if you're cold," she said. She draped a stole of the same peacock taffeta across Raine's shoulders. Rainbow highlights shifted, shimmered. Raine dragged her gaze away from the mirror and looked at the expectant faces of the three women. She manufactured a smile. "Thank you. You're all very talented. I look wonderful."

"Come with me now," Mara said briskly. "Mr. Lazar said to bring you to the library when you were ready."

She followed Mara through the corridor. The taffeta skirt billowed around her, brushing sensually against the floor. Cool drafts sighed across her bare shoulders and exposed neck, making the stole float behind her like fairy wings. Mara opened the door to the library, gave her a brief nod of farewell, and melted away into shadow.

Raine wafted across the crimson carpet. The library was lit only by a stained glass hanging lamp that illuminated the photographs on the shelf below and the portrait of Raine's grandmother from above. She stood in the center of the roiling serpentine pattern of the Persian carpet, swathed in an enormous, dreamlike silence.

She stared up at the portrait. Her grandmother's painted image seemed to stare down, her pale gray eyes gleaming with subtle amusement. Raine realized that she had the same eyes and brows. The brows were slightly different, now that Moira and Lydia had plucked and tamed them, but the basic effect was the same.

She wished she had called Seth, but the cell phone was still in her purse in the tower room. She had no evening bag to match the dress to carry it in. She'd been so afraid of Seth's reaction, but now, dressed up and led here like a virgin sacrifice, his anger seemed the least of her worries. She stared at her reflection in the window. Darkness had fallen, and the skin of her exposed throat and shoulders looked shockingly pale in the dim room. Trapped in this spooky dream world, the thought of Seth was a lifeline to reality.

Currents of air whispered across her shoulders. She sensed the library door opening, though it made no sound. Her senses had dilated, like eyes opening. There would be no more jumping and squealing in surprise. She knew exactly who had just come in the door.

She stood in the center of the blood-red vortex of the carpet's strange pattern and waited quietly, staring at her grandmother's image. Victor's reflection moved closer. He placed his hand on her shoulder for a moment, then removed it.

He gestured towards the portrait. "You're very like her, you know."

She let out a long, silent sigh. He knew who she was, he had always known; and the awareness of his knowledge had crept up upon her so gradually, it had no power to jolt or alarm her.

The world shifted and settled quietly, like a garment fluttering down around her. She turned to him. "Am I? People keep telling me I look exactly like my mother."

Victor dismissed her mother with a casual flick of his hand. "Super-
ficially," he said. "Your complexion is like Alix's, but your bone
structure is much more pronounced and delicate. Your lips are fuller.
And your eyes and eyebrows are pure Lazar. Look at her."

They stared up at the portrait for several moments.

"You share more than just her name," Victor said. "May I call you
Katya? It would give me great pleasure."

Her automatic desire to be accommodating and agreeable crashed
up against this new, solid woman planted in the center of a red vortex. The new woman won the struggle with surprising ease. "I
would prefer to be called Raine," she said. "My life is chaotic. I wish
to maintain as many lines of continuity as possible. Otherwise I'll
lose myself."

Displeasure flickered in his eyes. "That disappoints me. I had
hoped that your grandmother's name would be carried into the future."

Raine held her ground. "We can't always get what we want."

Victor's mouth twitched. "Now that, my dear, is God's own
truth." He offered her his arm. "Come. It won't be long before our
guests arrive."

"Guests?" She lifted her chin, and did not take his proffered arm.

His smile radiated warmth and approval. "I take too much for
granted, eh? Since we had not formally established your status as my
beloved, long-lost niece, I could not discuss my plans with you. It is
a relief, no? To finally be who you are?"

"Yes," she said, meaning it with all her heart. "And your guests?"

"Ah. My guests. It is just a gathering of friends and business associates for dinner. The original idea was to host a simple meeting of
my collectors club, for dinner and drinks, and a showing of some recent odd acquisitions of mine. I am a collector of art and antiquities,
you see. But once you arrived, the idea of the party became more
grandiose."

"I see," she murmured, still baffled. "But why all this? The dress,
the hair. Why do you want me at your dinner party?"

"Isn't it obvious?"

"I'm afraid not."

Victor smiled, and brushed his knuckles across her cheek, a light, glancing touch. "Vanity, I suppose. I'm a childless man. I can't resist the opportunity to present a beautiful, cultured, intriguing young woman to my friends and associates as my niece. Think of it as your debut."

She stared at him.

"I know it's foolish," he said with a shrug. "But I am growing older. One must seize these opportunities while one can."

She swallowed over the lump that was growing in her throat. "How long have you known about me?"

Her heart twisted at how similar his smile was to her father's. The high cheekbones, the deep smile lines, the sharp, sculptured cut of his jaw. "I've known where you were since the day your mother took you from this place. I never lost you for so much as a day."

She could barely breathe. "All that running," she whispered. "All those fake identities. All for nothing."

"Alix always did have a tendency to overdramatize. It was my responsibility to keep an eye on you, as I did not trust Alix to do so. She is . . . well, self-absorbed would be a charitable way to put it."

Raine winced at the casual contempt that Victor's tone revealed.

He went on. "I set up red flags in the Lazar Import & Export computer system to alert me if anyone using any of your aliases ever made a move to contact me. Imagine my pleasure when I logged on one morning and saw the automatic message in my inbox. Raine Cameron had sent her résumé to my personnel department. How fascinating."

"I suppose you wondered why I didn't just contact you directly," she said cautiously.

"Lazars tend to be subtle and devious," he said with a winsome smile. "It's a family trait. Naturally, I assumed that you wished to learn more about the events of that terrible summer when Peter died."

Her stomach clenched. Victor's smiling face revealed absolutely nothing. "You're not angry?"

He shook his head. "Not at all. It's a tribute to my brother that you care enough to look for the truth. I'm proud that my only niece is courageous and enterprising."

Her mouth was so dry it was sealed closed. She stared at his smile, probing with all her senses for the trap that had to be hidden beneath his gentle, approving words.

He took a step towards her. "I'm grateful to finally have a chance to say this to you, face-to-face, my dear. I was out of the country when Peter drowned. I was devastated by his death. He was despondent. He should not have been sailing alone. What I regret most of all is the tension that was between us. Much of it due to your mother. Alix liked to stir the pot. No matter what people say, I loved my brother."

The words vibrated between them, low and impassioned.

Raine's throat began to quiver. She wiped away tears carefully with her fingertips, locked in an inward struggle to cling to the message of her dream, to Bill Haley's words. *Her world, not his,* she repeated silently to herself, like a charm against the pull of his charisma.

He gave her a crooked smile. "You are not convinced."

She did not answer, and he began to laugh. "Honesty is so rare in my life these days. Like a splash of icy water. Refreshing. Well, my dear, whether you believe me or not, can you put your doubts aside long enough to enjoy a pleasant evening with my friends?"

"If you'll excuse me, I need to make a phone call first."

He gestured towards the phone on the table. "Be my guest."

She paused. This was not a conversation he could overhear.

He smiled at her hesitation. "You wish to call your young man, I take it? To reassure him that you have not been lured into some salacious orgy? I have anticipated you, my dear. I have already invited Mr. Mackey to this gathering."

His eyes gleamed at her stunned expression. "He jumped at the chance when he heard that you would be a member of the party. He is the jealous, possessive type, no? Think of it. You, out here overnight, subject to who knows what depraved appetites. Ah, dreadful. It was sure to drive such a young hotblood into a jealous frenzy. So I told him to come to dinner, to put his mind at ease. I hope I did well. That he will not bother you."

"Oh, no. Not at all," she assured him. "I'm very glad he'll be here."

Her knees were practically rubbery with relief. Seth would be furious when she was introduced to him as Victor's niece, but he would understand once she explained the circumstances. And he was powerful enough to keep her from being sucked under Victor's spell. He would keep her warm, grounded and real. She would be as safe as it was possible to be in this uncanny place, with Seth at her side.

Victor's gaze swept over her, and he nodded in approval. "It will be amusing to see his reaction when he sees you like this." He made a sweeping gesture at her. "You are breathtaking, my dear."

She blushed. "Thank you."

"That reminds me." He turned to the wall and removed an antique Japanese scroll, revealing a safe beneath. He keyed in a series of numbers, waited, keyed in a second series. The lock clicked open.

He opened it, rummaging through several items, and drew out a flat black velvet box. "Your mother always coveted this, but I would not allow Peter to give it to her. I did not consider her an appropriate custodian." He placed the box in Raine's hands. "Go on. Open it."

She lifted the lid, and gasped. It was a fire opal, a teardrop shape, set in gold and a brilliant, milky swirl of tiny diamonds. She moved it in the light, old memories stirring inside her. The pearly smooth surface of the opal flashed in the light, pulsing with blue, green and violet fire.

"I remember this necklace," she whispered.

"You played with it sitting on your grandmother's lap," Victor told her. "You were her joy. The necklace is called Dreamchaser."

"I thought there was a tiny rainbow trapped inside the stone," Raine said, touching it reverently with her fingertip. "A live rainbow."

"It's a family heirloom. A gift from your great-great-grandfather to his bride. At last, it comes to you."

He clasped it around her neck. The chilly gold of the glittering chain made her shiver. The past was reaching out cold fingers to touch her. It called out in soft, whispering voices, like faraway music.

Victor turned her until she was looking at herself in the mirror. The pendant was the perfect length for the peacock gown. It nestled at her cleavage, sumptuous and elegant. Perfect.

"I don't know what to say," she stammered.

"Dreamchaser will remind you to look beneath the surface. To seek the passion and fire behind a deceptively plain exterior. Not that you need to be reminded." Victor laid his hand upon her shoulder. "Please, wear the necklace often. All the time, if you can. It's been waiting for you for years. Your grandmother would be glad that you have this. She would have been proud of your beauty and your intelligence. And your courage."

She clasped the pendant in her hand. Tears flashed down her cheeks, and she flicked them away, trying not to smudge the makeup. Victor's piercing gaze saw right inside her, all her fears and weaknesses, her hunger for love and approval. It was so hard to resist. No one had ever been proud of her that she could remember. Alix was disapproving and competitive. Hugh, her stepfather, barely knew she existed.

She knew it was a trap—and she almost didn't care. Almost.

Victor kissed her forehead gently and offered her a handkerchief. She dabbed at her eyes and gave him a cautious smile. He smiled back. A smile that saw too much, understood too much. He offered her his arm. "I would be pleased to show you my collection, but there's no time tonight. Perhaps tomorrow. If such things interest you, of course."

"Thank you, yes. That would be fascinating," she murmured.

"Come, let's take a tour of the house before our guests arrive. Allow me to reacquaint you with your childhood home."

She reached out and took his arm. Trap or not, lies or not, she couldn't make her scars and fears and needs disappear by sheer force of will. All she could do was to watch them flowing like water, swirling and changing with every instant that went by.

"Yes, please," she said. "I would love to."

Chapter

16

Of all scenarios, waltzing into a dinner party at Stone Island as the date of Victor Lazar's long-lost niece was the last one he could have envisioned. Seth tied up at the Stone Island dock, and forced himself to concentrate on arming the custom-modified infrared motion-detector security device on his boat. If anyone came within two meters of the boat in his absence, a device attached to his waistband would vibrate, and a video camera would snap to life, recording everything.

Attention to detail was everything in this kind of work, but he kept staring into space, forgetting where he was, breaking out in muttered profanity. He wanted to confront her, but he was bound by his own secrets. Secrecy had never felt constricting before. It had always felt like power. Now it made him feel helpless and maddened.

Three days ago, he would have crawled naked over broken glass for an opportunity to walk right through Stone Island's wall-of-thorns security. But his mind was reeling, his focus blown. He kept trying to come up with a plan for tonight, but he couldn't think, couldn't plan. He was going to have to wing it. Look what he was reduced to. Victor Lazar was a fucking genius.

The house was lit up like a Christmas tree. It felt strange to march right up to the place without sneaking. The flagstone path was lit by strings of ice-white lights draped from tree to tree. He felt exposed, despite the SIG Sauer in the shoulder holster beneath his coat.

A huge fireplace was roaring in the main reception hall. There was a jazz combo in the corner of the room, and a saxophone was crooning. It was filled with people in evening dress. He recognized a local politician out on the terrace, carrying on an animated conversation with a lovely young woman in a short fur jacket. The young woman gulped champagne, threw back her head and laughed. Too bad Connor wasn't here, with his encyclopedic knowledge of the local movers and shakers. All Seth knew was that Victor had all kinds of people in his pocket, the only common denominators being wealth, power, and a secret weakness that Lazar had learned to exploit. Just as he'd done to Seth. He was just as compromised as any of these poor, champagne-guzzling bastards.

"Ah! There he is. Our intrepid security consultant. Come in, come in." Lazar hurried forward, seized Seth's hand and pumped it heartily. "So glad you came. Raine will be delighted. She despaired of you coming when the last boat arrived."

"I came in my own boat."

Victor's eyebrows arched. "Ah. And well you should, if you have the means. Where is that girl? Ah, there she is, chatting with Sergio. My dear! Your guest of honor has arrived!"

But Seth could no longer register what Lazar said. The world disappeared, the air was sucked out of his lungs. All he saw was Raine.

She was a fucking goddess, decked out like that. Supermodel gorgeous, Hollywood gorgeous. Ice princess, big-money, unattainable gorgeous. She'd always been sexy and delicious, even in her frumpy little business suits and hornrimmed glasses. She was adorable in her baggy fleece pyjamas, and she was heart-stopping when she was naked, with her hair rippling right down to her ass.

But he had never imagined her like this. The blue corset thing molded every curve, lifting up her pale breasts and offering them to the eye. Sex goddess and ice princess, rolled into one. Some wickedly expensive looking jewel was nestled between her perfect tits. Her hair was weirdly perfect, swept back in a complicated bun. She was a fairy-tale princess out of his comic book fantasies. She glowed like a star.

He hated it. It made his jaw clench and his dick harden. It made him want to wreck something, punch walls, hurl plates. He wanted to drag her into a corner and rip off her glittering veil of illusions. Remind her that she was his beautiful wild animal, not this remote, perfect being. She was earth and sweat and blood and bone, she was hunger and need and howling at the moon. Just like him. Part of him.

She rushed towards him, with a smile so sweet and welcoming that it made his gut cramp. All she was missing was the fairy wings and the fucking tiara and—he had to get a grip. Right. Now.

"Seth! I'm so glad you—"

"You didn't call."

His tone stopped her cold. Her eyes went wide and uncertain. "I know. I'm sorry. It was an intense day. I can explain—"

"I just bet you can."

She recoiled, the welcoming light gone from her eyes, and he hated that, too. People were sensing the tension between them. They were pausing in their conversations and looking over curiously.

Keep it together, Mackey, he told himself. Don't piss on the rug.

"Is something wrong?"

Victor Lazar's smooth, oily tone made Seth's hackles rise. He choreographed the muscles in his face into a polite smile. "Not at all," he said, from behind clenched teeth.

"I'm so glad you could make it. Tonight is a special night for us, Mr. Mackey. After seventeen years, I'm finally reunited with my beloved niece. The people who are important to her must celebrate with us."

"Your niece, huh?" His voice was dangerously thick. He stared into Raine's eyes. They were naturally large and tilted. Accented with cosmetics, and wide with apprehension, they seemed enormous. "Your niece," he repeated slowly. "That is just . . . incredible."

Raine's mouth tightened. A blush raced across her translucent skin.

"Doesn't she look splendid?" Lazar's eyes rested upon her with a proprietary pride that made Seth want to spit.

"I liked her better before."

His voice came out flat and loud. Raine winced, visibly. *Tough shit,* he told her with his eyes. He was only flesh and blood. If she wanted to poke sharp sticks at him through the bars of his cage, she'd better expect him to snap and growl.

"Lazar women tend to be unpredictable," Lazar said coolly. "You'll get used to it, I expect. If you manage to hold her interest, that is."

"Victor!" Raine's voice was shocked.

Seth locked gazes with the smug, silver-eyed bastard. The red fog was coming over him, his blood was pounding in his ears, loud and heavy. He became aware that Raine was tugging desperately at his arm. "Seth, please," she pleaded.

"Raine, why don't you take your guest to the bar and get him a nice, relaxing drink?" Victor suggested. "Dinner will be in a quarter of an hour. I'm afraid you missed the hors d' oeuvres, but the dinner itself will be just as excellent. Mike Ling is cooking tonight, stolen from the Topaz Pavilion for the night. Pan Asian fusion. I hope you enjoy it."

Seth held out his arm to Raine. "Sounds delicious," he said, through gritted teeth. "Come on, sweetheart. Show me to the bar."

She took his arm with the tips of her fingers, and they moved silently through the lavish room. He knew he should be paying attention, gathering data, but he was helpless, inert. All he could feel were the tips of her fingers, burning through the fabric of his jacket.

He got himself a beer, got her a glass of champagne, and steered her to a secluded corner by the window. They stared at each other, as if they were afraid of each other.

"You're furious," she murmured, staring into the champagne.

"Yeah." He took a swallow of beer. "You've been lying through your teeth ever since you met me. Lying makes me sick."

"I did not lie to you."

The cool, righteous tone in her voice jerked an ugly laugh out of him. "Yeah? Peter *Marat?*"

"That was the only thing that I withheld, and you can hardly blame me. Try to understand, Seth. I've only known you for four days, and I'm doing something that scares me to death—"

"To death, huh?" He picked up her pendant, and she flinched back when his fingertips lingered at the velvet heat of her cleavage. He held it to the light, admiring the flashing colors. "Very pretty," he commented. "I bet putting this thing around your neck scared you right out of your mind. What did you do to earn it, sweetheart?"

She jerked the opal pendant out of his hands. "Don't be crude. It was my grandmother's." She stepped back and wrapped the glossy blue shawl across her chest. "You're being ugly, and I hate it," she said in a small, clear voice. "Please stop."

"I can't." It was the naked truth. "I'm for real, babe. What you see is what you get. Which is more than you can say for yourself, Raine Cameron Lazar."

Her cheeks flushed a deeper pink. She lifted bright, defiant eyes to him and drained the rest of her champagne in one long swallow. "We'll talk about this later," she said. "It's almost time for dinner. Can you manage not to make a scene in front of Victor's guests?"

"What's it worth to you?" he taunted.

Her lips went white. "Please, Seth."

There was something haunted and pinched in her face, behind her radiant veil of glamour. It tugged at him, despite his anger. Made him feel like a bastard, kicking a puppy. "Later," he muttered.

"The others are going into the dining room. Shall we?"

He bowed and offered her his arm. "At your service."

He sat down next to her at the table, a fake, tense smile on his face. He finally understood the value of social skills. They were simple, pure technique to fall back on when you were about to lose it, but could not afford to. Like fighting. You studied kicks, punches, parries and falls until they were second nature. Then when somebody tried to pound the shit out of you, self-defense was smooth and automatic.

Social skills. Kicks and punches. Same damn thing.

Raine had no idea how she managed it. She smiled and spoke in Italian to Sergio, the museum curator on her left, about medieval art; she conversed with the distinguished older man across the table about his consuming interest in collecting historical weapons. She laughed and smiled and chattered social nonsense, all with a seething volcano sitting in the chair next to her. The food was exquisitely prepared, but she didn't remember eating or drinking, although she must have done so.

After the fruit, dessert and coffee, people began to wander into the main room where the showing of Victor's new acquisitions would take place. A buzz of anticipation was rising. Victor strolled over to them and tucked a wisp of hair back up into her coif. With every nerve raw, she clearly sensed Seth's rage roaring up like a flame at Victor's possessive, avuncular gesture, even though he made no overt sign of it.

Victor's smile showed that he felt it too, and was amused by it.

"Perhaps you young folks would like to be left to yourselves. I plan to show you my entire collection tomorrow, Raine, so there's no need to bore Mr. Mackey with it. Give him a tour of the house, if you like."

"A tour of the house sounds fine to me," Seth cut in, his arm closing around her shoulders. "Great place you've got here. I'd love to see it."

"Very well, then. Come down for drinks later on, if you care to." He kissed Raine's cheek, gave Seth a nod, and walked into the hall.

Seth pulled her out the front door. She scurried to keep up with his long strides. "Where are you taking me?" she demanded.

"To my boat."

She pulled back and dug in her heels. "Your boat? I can't just leave, Seth. I have to—"

"My boat is the only sheltered place on this whole island where I can be reasonably certain that our conversation won't be overheard or recorded. If we don't scream at each other, that is. Which at this moment, I can't guarantee."

"Oh," she whispered.

It was even colder when they drew near the dark water that lapped against the dock. He helped her onto the boat, steadying her as she teetered on the fragile high heels. She stood in the door of the cabin and watched as he untied the boat and started up the motor.

He took them out into the dark water, twenty, thirty, fifty meters, and cut the motor. She scrambled out of his way as he entered the cabin. His heat began to warm the place the minute he followed her in.

He switched on the lantern that was bolted to the table and did something with a keyboard and monitor attached to the cabin wall. He turned to her, folding his arms. "OK. We're out of range of any directional mikes Victor could point at us. Let's hear it."

She huddled inside her thin stole. "Hear what?"

"Why you broke your promise. Why you didn't tell me what you were doing today?"

She sank down onto the cushion of the bench, and twisted the crumpled blue taffeta of her skirt, organizing her thoughts. "I knew you would be working all morning," she began slowly. "I didn't want you to worry. And overreact."

"I see." He waited.

She closed her eyes against his intense scrutiny, and allowed herself to feel the true depths of her exhaustion. "I wasn't ready to tell you, or any other person that I was Victor Lazar's niece," she admitted. "I'm very glad you know now, though. Anyone who wants to can know now, since Victor knew all along. And I thought I was being so crafty."

"Tell you what, babe. It didn't look so terrible, all decked out in the ball gown with Grandma's necklace on. Victor's pampered darling. You took to it pretty smooth, if you ask me."

"I didn't plan that!" she protested. "He sent me out here to work, Seth! I got shanghaied by a gang of women who wrestled me down and dressed me like a doll! I didn't know what else to do, so I went with it!"

"Let's see how you turned out. Come on, open up the shawl and let me take a look."

He yanked the stole open. It slipped to the floor, and he stopped her lunge to catch it, seizing her upper arms. She jerked away at the rough contact, but his grip was hard and fast. "I love what that dress does for your tits," he said. "So did every other man in the room. Did you see them all staring, Raine? You must have. Did you like it?"

"Don't, Seth." She touched his face, trying to get him to meet her eyes, but he was staring fixedly at her body. He grabbed the bottom of the tight bodice and yanked it down. The tops of her breasts spilled out over the neckline, her nipples taut and puckered from the cold.

She tried to slap his hands away. "Stop it, Seth! You have got to stop wrecking my clothes!"

"No problem, princess. Uncle Victor will buy you another one." Seth's hands slid hungrily up over the front of her bodice, cupping her breasts and rolling her nipples between his fingers.

"It's not like that," she protested.

"Oh no?" His hands slid down, cupping her bottom. "I like this skirt. I'd like to fuck you with all that shiny stuff rustling around you, and your nipples poking out of that corset. This dress was made for sex. Most dresses a guy just wants to rip off so he can get on with it, but this one, whoa. This one can stay on, no problem."

She grabbed his wrists and tried to drag them off of her. "Stop it," she hissed. "Don't you dare touch me when you're angry. I—"

"And check out the sparkler. The crowning touch." He held the opal pendant up to the light. "Victor's princess was a good girl today, huh?"

"I told you, it belonged to my grandmother, and it was a—oh!"

He snapped the jeweled clasp and flung it behind him. It bounced off the wall with a ping and clattered to the floor. "Now if you'd get your hair down and wipe some of that paint off, I might even recognize you."

That was it. The outrage inside her coalesced. She launched herself at him with a shout of fury. Seth let out a surprised grunt as he fell back onto the bench. She landed on top of him. The boat rocked wildly. "Goddamn it, Seth," she hissed. "You listen to me."

He opened his mouth. She clapped her hand over it. "I said *listen!*"

His eyes bored into hers for a moment. He gave a short nod.

She was so startled at his acquiescence that for a long, panting moment, she could think of nothing to say. She squeezed her eyes shut and searched for words. "You say you can feel what I really want, no matter what I might say to the contrary, you arrogant bastard. What I really want right now is for you to calm down and listen to me like a rational, civilized man. Not a lunatic with rocks in his head. Can you do that for me, Seth? I challenge you to do that for me."

He stared up at her for a moment, and the smile lines around his eyes crinkled. He nodded, and his face changed beneath her hand.

He was smiling. She lifted her hand away.

"This position really does it for me," he said softly.

She looked down. She was straddling him, resting against what had become a very prominent erection. He radiated heat even through all the layers of fabric. She scrambled to her feet.

"Don't even," she snapped. "Forget it. I'm not finished!"

"Go right ahead. Tell me some more stories." His eyes were still fixed on her breasts, which were still over-flowing their bounds extravagantly. "The view's great from here, no matter what you say."

"I was not lying to you, damn it!"

"Keep it down, babe."

"Stop goading me, then! And don't call me that!" She rearranged her bodice until it more or less encompassed her breasts. "I never lied to you. The only thing I withheld was my father's real name, and—"

"Pretty goddamn important detail, if you ask me."

"As I was saying," she went on icily, "everything I told you is true, and a matter of public record. Check on my story all you want."

Their eyes locked, and she stood there quietly for long, silent minutes and let him probe her with his burning gaze. She didn't allow herself to look away or flinch.

He seized a handful of her skirt and tugged her till she swayed towards him. "So where'd you go today, sweetheart?" His voice was soft and challenging. He pulled until she was standing between his legs, clasped her hips with his big, warm hands and waited for her answer.

She was cautiously encouraged by the gentle physical contact. "I went to see the doctor who signed my father's autopsy report," she told him. "She told me that there were two FBI agents investigating Victor at the time. She remembered one of their names. I tracked him down, too. My father was going to testify against Victor back in the summer of '85. He drowned before he had the chance."

Seth's eyes narrowed thoughtfully. He made no comment.

Her mouth tightened as she thought of the interview with Bill Haley. "The guy wasn't very encouraging," she said. "He basically told me to keep my head down and be a good girl."

"That was damn good advice," Seth said. "Say the word, and I'll start up this motor and get you the hell away from here. For good."

Raine closed her eyes and let herself imagine it, for one wistful, weary moment. She shook her head. "No. The dreams will never stop if I run. I'll spend some time with Victor tomorrow, and see what happens. He wants to show me his collection. Whatever that is."

Seth stroked the slick taffeta that covered her bottom, a remote, calculating look in his eyes. "His collection? Is that so?"

She nodded, steadying herself on his shoulders. Exhaustion rolled over her, and she swayed closer. He pulled her gently down until she was perched on his lap, his arms clasped around her waist.

She should be furious with him. He had behaved very badly but now he was nuzzling her bosom and kissing her neck, the slick, seductive bastard. She was too tired and dizzy to protest. She leaned against him, soaking up his sustaining heat. An idea came to her.

"Seth?" she whispered.

"Hmm?" He kissed the top of one of her breasts, then the other, then buried his face in her cleavage. "What?"

"I was wondering if you could . . . help me."

"Help you what?" His head lifted. He frowned at her.

"Gather information," she said softly. "I'm just blundering along. I know that you have a lot of experience in—in—"

"Sneaking around in the dark? Engaging in morally questionable activities to find out things that are none of my goddamn business?"

She nodded eagerly. "Exactly. I could really use some pointers."

He nuzzled her shoulder. She could actually feel the quality of his concentration, buzzing like electricity as he pondered her request. The boat rocked gently back and forth like a cradle as she waited. Water lapped against it in a slow, gurgling rhythm that measured his silence.

He looked up. "I'll do it. But you have to do something for me."

Heat swept up into her face. He let out a harsh laugh. "No, sweetheart. Not what you're thinking. I'll have that no matter what deal we cut. We don't negotiate with that coin. Got it?"

She nodded, waiting for the blush to subside before she dared to speak. "What is it that you want from me, then?" she ventured timidly.

His hand slid over her bare back, stroking her as if she were a wild animal that might bolt. "A favor. You said Victor wants to show you his collection tomorrow, right?"

Butterflies began to flutter in her belly. "Yes," she said slowly. "Why?"

"There's an item in that collection that I want to track. I don't want to steal anything. I just want to gather information."

Things clicked quietly into place, and she acknowledged with her conscious mind what she had sensed from the beginning. "It's just like I thought," she said softly. "You're not here to upgrade Lazar's inventory system, are you, Seth? You've had your own agenda all along."

His face was expressionless. He didn't try to hold her when she slid off his lap and backed away. "Do you want my help or not, Raine?"

She hated the cold, implacable tone in his voice, but she was lost, and he was the only path she could see. "Yes," she whispered.

"What I want from you is simple. I want you to plant a tracking device on one of the items in Victor's collection. The transmitter is tiny, about the size of a grain of rice. No big deal."

She plucked the stole off the floor and wrapped it around herself, shivering. "Why can't you just sneak in and plant it yourself?"

His lips twitched. "I'm good, but I'm not that good. That vault is a steel-reinforced concrete armored room with ultrasonic Doppler and passive infrared motion detectors, just for starters. I could probably pull it off, but not without a lot of planning. And I'm on a tight schedule."

She gulped. "A tight schedule for what?"

"Are you up to it?"

She wobbled on her spike heels, and steadied herself against the table. "You want me to . . . plant a tracking device," she repeated softly. "But why? What's the item that you want to track?"

"Is that a yes?"

She sank down on the bench opposite him and crumpled a handful of peacock blue taffeta anxiously in both hands. "I don't know if I could pull a thing like that off," she told him, with utter sincerity. "I'm not very slick or devious, and I'm not a very good liar."

"You're learning, babe. You're learning every day."

His words stung, but when she looked into his face, she saw no mockery or irony at all. He looked somber and watchful.

It occurred to her that if she were to say no, she could find herself in more serious trouble than she had ever imagined. Raine forced herself to examine that ugly possibility. She pushed the thought away.

She might be fooling herself, but her deepest instincts told her that Seth would never hurt her. At least not intentionally. And if this was the devil's bargain that fate saw fit to offer her, fine. She would take it, and be grateful. She took a deep breath. "OK. I'll do it."

He nodded. "Good. Listen carefully, because we're not going over this again after we leave the boat. It's a Walther PPK pistol. It might be in a carrying case, it might be in a plastic bag, in which case it'll be harder to plant the transmitter. Improvise if you can. If you can't, you can't. Don't take stupid risks. If it's not smooth and simple, let it go."

"What's special about this pistol?"

"It's the murder weapon in the Corazon case."

Her mouth dropped open. "But—oh, no. Oh God. What is Victor doing with a thing like that?"

A grim smile curved Seth's mouth. "That, sweetheart, is a question that a whole lot of people would love to have the answer to. I'm not one of them, though."

"No?"

He shook his head. "I don't give a shit how he got it or why he wanted it. All I want is to know where it goes from here. Not one word of this once we're off this boat, Raine. It's like we never mentioned it."

"I understand," she said. "Why do you want to track this thing?"

"Don't worry about it, babe."

She bristled like an offended cat. "I'd rather you snap at me than condescend to me."

"Fine. I'll bear that in mind the next time you ask for information that's completely irrelevant and useless to you."

"You don't trust me at all, do you, Seth?" she challenged him. "You know all my secrets, but you won't give one inch with your own."

His eyes glittered at her, implacable. "Live with it. You want to take Victor down? Then do as I say, and don't ask questions. Because you need help, sweetheart. You are a walking disaster on your own."

Her face reddened, and she tore her gaze away, stung. She wanted so badly for him to trust her, and it was a stupid, useless, hopeless wish. She huddled into her stole. "Now what?"

His eyes slid down her body, lingering on her breasts. "Victor invited me to this party to entertain you." He grabbed her wrists and tugged her gently to her feet. "I want to fulfill my function."

She sighed. "Seth, are you capable of thinking about anything besides sex for more than thirty seconds at a time?"

"I used to be," he said ruefully. He sank to his knees and lifted the billowing skirt. The rough, callused places on his palms snagged and caught at her delicate hose as he swept his warm hands up her thighs. "My concentration skills used to be unbelievable. You trashed them, Raine. So make use of what's left of me. You might as well."

She threaded all of her fingers into the thick, silky brush of his hair, quivering as he put his hand between her legs. He stroked her lace-shielded mound in a feather-light, teasing touch.

"Let's seal our bargain right here," he suggested. "You won't be cold when I'm done with you. You'll be hotter than hell. All that fancy makeup will melt off, and your hair will fall down, and you won't even remember what happened to your underwear."

She stared into his eyes, resisting the dark magic of his voice. In this cold, manipulative mood, she sensed that he wouldn't yield his self-control to her for a second. He probably wouldn't even bother to take off his clothes. She would be the naked one who ended up in a trembling, sobbing heap. She wanted him, but on her own terms. She had to change this unbalanced power dynamic. For his sake and hers.

"Not here," she said, in a cool, sharp voice.

His fingers stopped in their probing caress. "Why not?"

"I don't want it like this. On the floor, or standing up. I like my comforts," she said haughtily.

His eyes narrowed. "Excuse me, princess."

She clutched the stole around herself, shivering. "Don't call me that unless you mean it," she snapped. "My room up in the tower has a kingsize four-poster bed. Hand-embroidered linens, cashmere blankets and a white lace coverlet."

He grunted. "Cool. Guys like me go nuts for white lace coverlets."

He reached around for the leather jacket that was hanging on a hook, and she took the opportunity to scoop the broken pendant swiftly into her hand. She kept it hidden when he turned back, careful not to threaten the fragile new equilibrium between them. He draped the jacket over her shoulders and wrapped his arms around her. She huddled against him, scrabbling until she found an inside pocket.

She slipped it into the pocket and pulled the zipper shut.

No matter what Victor might or might not be guilty of, that fiery opal was her only link to her grandmother. She'd be damned if she would throw it away just to placate Seth. This was the opening move in her grand campaign to stop being pushed around. By everyone.

Chapter

17

The walk back up to the house was utterly silent. He clasped her shoulders, his mind racing with the effort to justify his crazy impulse. It was an incredible gamble, but irresistible. The symmetry of it felt so right; that this chance should present itself to him just in time, and by Victor's own flesh and blood. Poetic. His instincts screamed to seize the moment, get on with it, so he could find out once and for all if there was something on the other side or not. And he wasn't misleading Raine by promising to help, either. If he got his revenge, by definition she would have hers, too. The desired end result for both of them was the same. He could close this thing, and she could finally be safe.

Yeah, right. Pitting her against Lazar and Novak was one hell of a way to keep her safe. Or himself, either, for that matter. He might've just signed his own death warrant, but what the hell. If she couldn't be trusted, then she didn't need rescuing anyway, and he was used to thinking of himself as a dead man.

She led him up a spiral staircase though he could barely see in the stygian darkness. At the door, he pushed her behind him and peered in, scanning the place carefully before he let her enter.

He knew that this house was full of eyes and ears, but even if he hadn't known, he would have sensed them. He could actually feel a camera's cold, unblinking gaze against his skin.

He locked the door, opened his bag and mounted the portable squealer onto the door frame. One of Kearn's bored-on-his-coffee-break inventions, handy when you wanted privacy. He pulled out the probe monitor, and began to methodically sweep the walls.

Raine sat down on the bed. "What are you doing?" she asked.

"Sweeping for bugs." He grabbed a fragile-looking antique chair and climbed onto it, hoping it would bear his weight.

Her eyes widened. "You think that—"

"I don't think. I know. That's why he invited me here. He wants to watch us, and probably film us. For posterity."

"I don't believe that!"

Under other circumstances, he would have laughed at the prim horror in her voice, but he was too concentrated on his task. "Victor likes to watch," he said bluntly. "And I know exactly how much money he's willing to spend on toys like this."

He found the first bug in the ceiling fan: remote 399-030 MHz free space transmitter. There was another in the track lighting. There was a 490-mm modulated sodium optical bug in one of the overhead lightbulbs. There were four pinholes spaced out high in the wall with video cameras mounted behind the cedar paneling, impossible to get to without a hammer or an axe. He pulled a stick of gum out of his pocket, chewed it until it was soft, and plugged up the holes.

He used the VLF probe function to test for carrier current signals, of which he found two—the clock and one of the bedside lamps. He dismantled them both. Lazar obviously believed in overkill.

At the risk of seeming paranoid, he took out multi-function thermal imaging goggles, fitted a 99% obscuration IR filter and switched on the night vision function to scan for laser diode infrared emitters. There were two. That devious bastard.

He dismantled those, and turned around slowly in the middle of the room for a long time, scanning the walls and ceilings. Essentially, he was feeling around with his own internal antenna, using pure instinct.

Negative. Unless he was losing his touch, the room was clean.

He turned back to Raine, and held out a bristling handful of dismantled surveillance gadgets. "There's a lot you don't know about your precious uncle, princess."

"Don't call me that," she said sharply. "You found them, right? We'll have our privacy. So there's no harm done." She looked around at the dismembered lamp, the gutted clock. Her face convulsed, and she dropped it into her hands, shoulders heaving with silent laughter.

"What's so goddamn funny?" he demanded.

She lifted her face. Bright spots of red glowed in her cheeks. "Everything. This place is surreal. I feel like Alice down the rabbit hole."

"I'm glad you're amused," he growled.

Her hands dropped to her lap. "I don't see why you're so wound up." There was a hysterical tremor in her voice. "Everyone's family has a"—she choked back a giggle—"a problematic uncle."

"Problematic? You call this *problematic?*" He opened his hand and let the stuff drop, clattering across the parquet floor.

Raine threw up her hands, shaking with helpless laughter. "I'm just trying to cope, Seth. If you'd make an effort to do the same, I would really appreciate it. Try and look on the situation as . . . a test."

He let out an ironic grunt. "Like the underground fantasy comics I used to read when I was a kid? I'm in the castle of the evil sorcerer king. If I solve the riddle, I get to fuck the beautiful princess. If I don't, I get fed to the dragon, chunk by bloody chunk."

She shook her head, regal and aloof. "No, you tasteless clod. You get to *marry* the beautiful princess, and live happily ever after with her."

He stiffened, and his ears started to buzz. "Oh," he said stupidly, staring at her. He swallowed. "So that's how the story goes?"

"Yes. Standard fairy-tale format. Knights errant aren't usually crass, rude, suspicious, sexually obsessed commitment-phobes."

"I must've read the wrong comics when I was a kid." He stared at her, hypnotized by the way the bedside lamp backlit the wisps that had finally begun to escape from her hairdo, illuminating them like a delicate golden crown. "I guess if the guy's gone to all that trouble to slay the dragon and solve the riddle for that princess, then he's ready to settle down in a split-level suburban home with her."

"Having normalcy fantasies again, Seth?" she asked sweetly.

The rosy lamp painted her with smudgy velvet shadows. He couldn't wait another second to lick and nuzzle every single sweet curve. "Fuck normal," he said. "I solved the riddle and I want my prize. Get that dress off, your Highness. Let me see what I've won."

She rose to her feet and backed away. "Wait a minute, Seth."

He trapped her against the cedar paneling, loving the way the corset crammed her breasts together and offered them up to his eyes like luscious fruit. "Why wait? I was summoned to service you, right? Let's play a sexy game, Raine. You get to be the beautiful, pampered niece of a shady multimillionaire, and I get to be the brainless, muscle-bound stud with a perpetually hard cock who's been summoned to the island hideaway to fulfill her every erotic whim. What do you say?"

She splayed her hands against his chest, but not to push him away . . . more as if she wanted to assure herself that he was real. She licked her lips, her eyes glowing with catlike interest. "I'd say the set-up is kind of trashy and unrealistic, but it has possibilities."

He stroked the tops of her breasts tenderly with his fingertips. "Sounds like the plot of an awesome porno flick."

Her soft mouth tightened. "I wouldn't know. I don't watch that kind of thing."

The Miss Priss tone bugged him, and he yanked the bottom of her corset again. "Oh, no? Too nasty for you, your Highness?" he crooned.

She twisted and slapped his hands away. "Don't," she said sharply. "Your mean streak is showing, and it's making me angry. Get that sleazy tone out of your voice and wipe that dirty look off your face, or I'm not playing."

Her words hung in the air. His hands dropped to his sides. He felt almost as abashed as he was aroused. "Weird," he muttered.

"What's weird?" Her face was wary.

"I just found out something kinky about myself. Your tough-talking bitch goddess persona really turns me on. I'm as hard as steel." He seized her slender hand and placed it upon the aching bulge in the front of his pants. "Have pity on me," he murmured, with a coaxing grin. "I'm desperate. I'll be good. I'll be nice. I'll do anything."

She drew in a jerky breath, half-laughing, and measured him with her fingertips through the fabric of his pants. "That's fortunate, considering what I have in mind."

"Want to play out my fantasy?" he asked eagerly.

She slid from between him and the wall. "I've got a better one."

A huge grin took over his face. "By all means, let's hear it."

"Go stand in the middle of the room," she ordered.

He did as he was told, curiosity and arousal building up to explosive force. She began to circle him, her gaze sweeping up and down the length of his body. He turned his head to follow her.

"I'm a pirate queen, and I've conquered your vessel," she told him.

He spun around, astonished. With that sensual smile and that look in her eye, she was a creature he'd never seen before. Mysterious and unpredictable. His perilous princess, swathed in midnight and moonlight. "Whoa," he breathed. "You're really going for it, aren't you?"

"Oh, yes. I almost made you walk the plank, but when I looked you over, when I saw those muscles, the shape of that butt, that bulge in the front of your pants, I decided that it would be a sad waste of a prime piece of male flesh."

"Was I the captain of the captured ship?"

She flung the stole onto the bed. "Does it matter?" She lifted her arms gracefully as she circled him, as if casting a spell. The movement lifted her bosom another tantalizing inch out of the bodice.

His eyes followed her, transfixed. "It does to me," he admitted.

Her shoulders lifted in an indifferent shrug. "All right. Be the captain, if you like. But it makes no difference. You're just my slave now. And the more you cling to your lost power and control, the more you will suffer. Let go, slave. Give in to your new destiny.'"

His mouth dropped open in a soundless laugh. "Wow. Cruel, heartless pirate queen. I'm in truly deep shit now, huh?"

"Yes, you are," she coolly agreed. "My brawny pirate henchmen, who worship me, have dragged you down to my cabin. Your very existence now depends upon how much pleasure you give me. So get ready to exert yourself . . . sailor boy."

His grin reached around to the back of his head. "When I make you scream with pleasure, will they rush in and kill me?"

"They have their orders," she murmured coolly. "They're used to my indulgences. Take off your clothes."

Raine's voice, usually so musical and lilting, had suddenly acquired the sharp snap of authority. He leaped to obey her, fingers trembling with eagerness, and yanked off his clothes. He had a moment of doubt when she caught sight of the SIG Sauer. She blinked, but made no comment as he unbuckled the shoulder holster and placed it on the bedside table. She made an impatient gesture. He forgot about the gun and finished stripping with feverish haste, leaving his clothing in a tangled heap on the floor.

He stood in the middle of the room, stark naked and hugely erect. She began circling him again, close enough so he could smell her delicate perfume, like a mix of warm honey and violets after a rainstorm. He felt the insubstantial kiss of her breath on his shoulders, the back of his neck. Then she was touching him, her cool fingers brushing across him, measuring, petting, teasing. Cupping his balls, gripping his cock. Sliding her soft hand with agonizing slowness. Squeezing. Oh, God, this was going to kill him.

"Very nice. Big and strong and vigorous looking," she murmured. "I haven't seen such a fine specimen in a long time."

He tried not to groan. "Seen a lot of them, hmm?"

"Oh, more than you can imagine." Her hands were getting warm as they brushed over his ass, gripping the hard muscle with an approving sigh. "All colors and shapes and sizes. I'm insatiable, you see. I keep them for as long as they arouse me. It's in your best interests to try very hard to please me, if you wish to stave off that inevitable day that you bore me, and I decide to make you walk the plank after all."

"I'll do my very best," he promised.

"Wise lad," she murmured, her cool hands sliding tenderly over his chest, feeling every bump and hollow. "Lie down on the bed."

Grinning seemed out of place in her fantasy scenario, but he had no control over his face. He didn't care, though. He had abandoned his brain, he was in free fall. She could do anything she liked with him. He spread-eagled himself on the bed, and grinned up at her like an idiot.

Raine sauntered up to the bed, reaching back to unhook her skirt. "Do I need to tie you, or are you going to be a good boy?"

He was almost tempted. His eye fell upon the SIG on the bedside table. A tiny crumb of sanity returned, just in time. Bondage games in Victor Lazar's lair were a little too dangerous even for him to contemplate.

"I'll be good for now," he said. "I can't speak for later."

He groaned, almost in pain, when she let the skirt drift to the ground. It billowed and crumpled like a parachute. She kicked it away, and he stared, openmouthed, at her pale, perfect thighs, the deep blue stockings, the barely-there panties made of midnight colored lace. It all matched the outrageous blue corset thing that must have given a raging hard-on to every man at that dining table tonight.

She turned around and leaned over to unbuckle her stiletto heeled shoes. Deliberately giving him a long, mind-blowing look at her round, rosy buttocks, tenderly framed by the cock-teasing scrap of lace. She flung them away, straightened up and slowly hooked her thumbs into the panties. She tugged them down, inch by inch, until they cleared the curve of her thigh and dropped, revealing the soft puff of blond ringlets. She seized the bottom of the corset thing, paused and gave him a slow, sultry smile. She tugged it down until her taut pink nipples popped over the edge.

It was the look on her face, more than anything, that dazzled him. Fey, potent sexual magic. It made her radiant. She was a she-wolf in the moonlight; a wild, beautiful animal discovering the full extent of her power over him. She climbed up onto the bed and curled her legs under herself, trailing her fingers across his body.

He reached for her, and she slapped down his hand. "Ah, ah, ah," she purred. "Don't presume, slave. Do as you're bid."

"Next time, I get to conquer your vessel," he told her.

She slapped his hand away again. "You're always conquering my vessel, you big bully. Behave yourself. Or do I have to summon my brawny pirate henchmen to subdue you?"

"You're driving me nuts, Raine," he groaned.

"Good nuts, or bad nuts?"

He shook his head, helpless, and she laughed. "It's high time you knew how it felt," she whispered. Her fingertip trailed down the steely, throbbing length of his penis. "My pirate henchmen love it when I torture my love slaves. Sometimes, when they're very good . . . I let them watch."

"What the hell?" He surged up into the sitting position.

She shoved him back down. "Ah, ah, ah. Careful, slave."

"You hot little bitch." A feverish red flush suffused his face. "I'm going to make you pay for this."

"Really?" she taunted. "Does the image bother you?" She seized his penis, murmuring in approval at his involuntary gasp. She stroked him, squeezing gently, and shocked a helpless groan out of him. "Hmm. Well, it doesn't seem to bother you," she said, in mock puzzlement. "If I didn't know any better, I would think that it really . . . excited you."

"I thought you said you weren't an exhibitionist."

She laughed at him softly. "I'm not, you idiot. This is just a fantasy." She swung her thigh over his neck and straddled him, lowering her sex to his mouth. "Now shut up, sailor boy, and put your tongue to better use."

He needed no further urging. She could reach inside him and drive him to a screaming frenzy every time, without even trying. But he had tricks of his own. He was going to use every last one of them.

Seth trapped her hips in his hands and pressed his face against her delicious cunt, wallowing in her, lapping at her with tender ferocity. He could never get enough of the sweet-salt flavor of her labia, the damp blond ringlets that shielded it, the tender, swollen little bud of her clit. Her slender, strong body flexed and arched above him, her hips jerked. She cried out wildly as she exploded, shuddering as waves of pleasure rocked through her.

He caught her, and lay her gently on her side. The fierce, conquering energy that had sustained the pirate queen's personality had been rendered down like molten gold in the forge of pleasure. She was liquid, helpless. Her hair was breaking loose of its moorings, and he plucked out the pins, combing through it carefully with his fingers until he'd found them all. They'd done something to her hair to take the curl out. He hoped it wasn't permanent. It was still beautiful, but he liked the long ringlets better than this too perfect, satin-smooth floss.

He got up, rummaging quietly through his bag until he found the box of condoms. Raine was curled on her side on the bed, one stocking on, one off, breasts still spilling seductively out over the top of her corset. He sheathed his throbbing cock in the condom. Whatever she had in mind, he wanted to be ready for it. And if she had no further ideas, no problem. He had plenty of ideas of his own.

Raine smiled with misty pleasure, eyes still closed, when she felt his fingers at her back unhooking the tight bodice. She breathed a sigh of relief when it came loose. The thing did great things for her figure, but it was not the most comfortable garment she'd ever worn.

He rolled her onto her back, parting her legs and peeling off the remaining stocking. His callused fingertips rasped tenderly up the length of her legs in a long, appreciative caress. She stretched and like a pampered kitten, arching and wiggling with voluptuous pleasure even before his fingers brushed across her damp sex.

"Did I pass?" he asked.

"Hmm?"

"Will the sexpot pirate queen let me live to love another day?"

She reached out to caress the jut of his erection, already conveniently sheathed in latex, she noted with interest. "It depends on your stamina," she said sternly. "You didn't think that the pirate queen would be satisfied with one little orgasm, did you?"

"That orgasm was not little. It went on and on." He lifted her up until she straddled him. "Show me who's boss, pirate queen. Ride me."

Raine was still shaky from the aftermath of her last orgasm, and she braced herself against him, splaying her hands across his hard chest. The unfamiliar position made her feel clumsy and uncertain.

Seth took control smoothly, lifting her up and nudging himself inside her. It was always a shock, the heat and solid hardness of him pushing, forging his way in. But she was relaxed, her sheath soft and moist from his tender skill. She enveloped him easily, with a shuddering moan of pleasure. She touched his face and found it hot and damp with sweat. The unguarded look in his eyes moved her, and she collapsed across his chest, wrapping her arms around his neck.

In that moment all their power games, playful or otherwise, were revealed to her for exactly what they were. Superficial games, to distract them from the strength of their feelings. She didn't feel conquering, or conquered. She felt unveiled. She knew herself better in that moment than she ever had before, her fears and her hunger and her loneliness. All of it was brilliantly lit, out in the open for them both to see.

She saw him, too, in an infinity of poignant details: the mole on his shoulder, the sweeping winged pattern of his heavy eyebrows, the seams carved around his wide mouth. The sharp-cut line of his full, sensual lips. Seth's dark eyes were full of the terrible knowledge of their mutual vulnerability, just as her own must be.

It filled her with tenderness, a burning ache. She hid her face against his shoulder and lost herself in the surging, voluptuous tempo of his body beneath her. It wasn't power she surrendered to as she clenched herself around him. It was wonder. Breathless, knocked flat, heart-swelling wonder, leaving her soft and helpless.

He wound his fingers through her hair and gently tugged until she lifted her head. The dark intensity of his gaze reached inside her and saw everything she was. Accepting it, wanting it.

"Hey." He rolled her onto her back, still joined, pressing her into the crumpled sheets. "You never told me the rest of the story."

Raine clutched his shoulders and arched, opening herself to accept more of him. "What? What story?"

"What happens to the pirate queen and the captured sailor."

"Oh." She laughed, breathless and charmed by his mischievous grin. "I, um, don't know the rest yet," she admitted.

"I do. Sailor stud is so insatiably hot in bed, he fucks the pirate queen senseless. Totally blows her mind. Nobody's ever given her such good head before. She loses it. She gets swept away. She falls in love."

He had never used that word before. The scary word. The L-word.

Raine clenched her arms and legs around him and licked her lips, tried to remember how to speak. "That's terribly dangerous," she said. "She shouldn't compromise her power like that. It's sure to be her ruin."

"Yeah, I know, but the poor chick can't help it. She just goes nuts when he touches her like this." He reached between them and rolled his thumb tenderly around her clitoris, making her gasp and heave against him. "She loves it when he thrusts his cock inside her, all the way, like this, and stirs her around . . . and around, like a nice, big stick . . . see? Hitting all her sweet little love buttons, inside and out. She's just got to have it. He's too good. She's hooked. . . ."

She cried out, losing the thread of the story as the deep thrusting of his shaft within her combined with his clever, skilful fingers to provoke another sensual explosion inside her.

When she opened her eyes, he was waiting patiently, staring down at her. He folded her legs up and rose up onto his knees for a better view as he withdrew. He slid just the head of his cock up, down, all around her clitoris, in a tender, highly stimulating caress.

Raine tried to make her trembling lips form words. "She's sexy and insatiable, yes, but she's tough, too," she said shakily. "She wouldn't let herself be controlled by sex, no matter how amazing it is. She's more than just an overheated body. She has a brain, you know. Otherwise she wouldn't be top dog."

"Yeah, but don't forget. She has a heart, too."

Raine stared into his eyes, speechless.

Seth nudged himself inside her body once again. "That's what gets her, see. Her heart. Sailor stud finds the key to it. He gets past her armor, sees all her secret wounds. He understands why she's such a scary, bad-ass babe, why she thinks that she needs all that control. He finds the vulnerable woman inside, and for the first time ever . . . he makes that woman feel safe."

"Oh," she gasped.

He slid a hand beneath her buttocks, lifting her so he could wedge himself still deeper. "But it goes both ways," he said. "Sailor stud is in bad trouble. He's never had it so good, see? He's almost willing to just surrender. Almost willing to settle for a life of humiliating captivity, just so he can have that red-hot, sex-crazed pirate queen lather him up and ride him into screaming oblivion every night. And before he knows it, crash, bam. He's in love with her, too."

She reached up, gripped his shoulders and hung on for dear life. "A disaster," she said. "What a dilemma."

"Hell, yeah. It's nightmare for the poor bastard. His heart is being squeezed in a fucking vise." Seth slid inside her in a slow, heavy lunge.

Raine squeezed her eyes shut. "What . . . what does sailor stud decide?" She held her breath. The fate of her whole world might hang upon his answer. Or then again, maybe not. Maybe it was just another game for him. She couldn't know, or guess. She could only feel.

She opened her eyes when she felt his hand against her face, and was immediately lost in the intensity of his dark gaze. He pushed a lock of hair out of her eyes. His fingers brushed her cheek, soft and reverent. "I don't know the rest of the story yet. I'm making it up as I go along, too, Raine. Just like you."

His shaky, uncertain tone made her heart turn over with terrified joy. "Well, um, the pirate henchmen are getting restless," she said, trying for an airy tone. "They're crazed with jealousy for sailor stud—"

"Because pirate queen wants him all to herself. She won't let them watch. Not even once." His eyes dared her to argue with him.

"Not even once," she conceded gently. "The door to her cabin is locked, and she covers up all the spy-holes in the wall."

"So they know their perfect world is threatened. Their goddess, their whole reason for being, has been seduced away from them." He scooped the nape of her neck into his big, warm hand, smoothing her hair over the pillow. "They want things the way they were before. They want their goddess back, but she's changed. You can't turn back time. You can't stop a force of nature. You can't stop love."

"No," she whispered, in total agreement. "You can't."

He moved inside her, melting her heart with the powerfully erotic sweetness of their lovemaking. He draped her arms over his neck, sliding his arms beneath her shoulders.

"Hold on tight," he said. "Listen carefully. This is how it goes. Pirate henchmen hatch a plot to tie up sailor stud hand and foot and throw him overboard, but pirate queen gets wind of it at the very last moment. She dives into the ocean with her dagger clenched between her teeth, grabs him before he sinks, and cuts his bonds. Even though the crew has mutinied, and she knows that she and sailor stud will be left out there in the drink . . . shark chow."

She tried to smile, but her mouth was trembling "Oh, come on," she protested. "She would never do that. You're pushing it, Seth."

"He gives truly excellent head," Seth explained. He pulled out of her and slid down the length of her body, splaying her legs wide, and proceeded to illustrate his point. He took her clitoris delicately between his teeth and flicked his tongue across it, skilfully, without stopping.

The pleasure went on and on, and finally she seized as much of his short, silky hair as she could grasp and tugged. "OK, OK," she pleaded. "She'll jump into the sea, she'll fight sharks with her dagger, she'll do anything, I promise. Just come back inside me, please. I need your arms around me."

Seth rubbed his face against her thigh and nuzzled her navel, kissing his way slowly up her body with hot, wet, sucking kisses. He got distracted when he reached her breasts, and stayed there, suckling and licking until she was writhing with delirious frustration, struggling to yank him up to where she needed him.

Finally, he was back on top of her, covering her with his heat. He pushed inside her, panting, and stopped, looking perplexed. "So what happens to them? Do they drown, or get chomped by sharks, or what?"

Raine jerked beneath him in protest. "God, no! How could you even say such a thing?"

"Sorry. I'm a cynical realist. So sue me."

She thought for a moment, and looked straight into his eyes. "They wash up in a tropical paradise, and in primeval splendor on coconuts and mangos and barbecued fish," she said. "They spend the rest of their lives frolicking in the surf, playing on the beach and making passionate love in a ten-room hut made of palm fronds."

"Oh, yeah?" There was an anxious frown line between his eyes.

She pulled his face down to hers and kissed it gently. "Oh, yeah," she said softly. "He spends his time spearing fish, gathering fruit and making garlands of tropical flowers for her."

He looked doubtful. "Garlands of flowers? Come on, Raine."

"Keep in mind he's not the only one who gives excellent head."

He grinned. "OK. Garlands of flowers. You want 'em, you got 'em. Big, smelly piles of them."

"They sit beneath the swaying palms in the evening, watching the sun set," Raine said softly. "They leave the violence and ugliness of the world behind. They let go of the pain and betrayal in their past, and give themselves to each other, body, heart and soul. No more power games, no more lies, no more manipulation. Just passion and truth and tenderness. He gives it all to her, and she gives everything to him."

Emotion vibrated between them like a taut silver wire.

"That's a good ending," he whispered. "That ending works for me."

"It's not an ending, Seth." She covered his face with tiny kisses. "It's a beginning."

They stared into each others' eyes. Both lost, both terrified. Only he could save her, only she could save him. She was swimming with sharks, a dagger between her teeth. Tears sprang into her eyes.

His arms tightened. "No," he pleaded. "Please, sweetheart. Have mercy. I'm too far out to sea tonight. You cry on me, and I'll lose it."

She pressed her face against his neck, burying her tears where he couldn't see them. "I wouldn't mind if you lost it," she whispered. "You're safe with me, Seth. I'll hold you together."

"Please, don't." He hid his face against her hair. "Not here. Not in this house. Not so close to him."

Seth was right. There was a loaded gun lying next to their bed. This was not the time or place to make that fearless dive into the infinite.

"Distract me, then," she ordered him. "Quick."

He cradled her face and kissed her. "OK. Ah, sunsets on the beach. Garlands of flowers. I give it all to you, you give it all to me." His hand trembled as he stroked her hair. "No more games."

She kissed him back, holding him as close as she could. "All right. Give it all to me, Seth," she whispered. "I want all of you."

They pulled away from the perilous brink of the unknown. They gave themselves up to wild, soaring pleasure instead. And it was enough for now, surging and melting together into the swirling red heart of their own private tropical sunset.

Chapter

18

The monitor that should have shown four different camera angles of the tower room was blank and dark.

Victor turned away with a chuckle. He wasn't disappointed that he would not witness the intimacy between his niece and her lover. It would have been inappropriate anyway, though the thought made him laugh at himself. Such scruples, all of a sudden. How odd.

On the contrary, he was quietly pleased that the young man was astute enough to protect his privacy, and Katya's. He could not think of the girl as Lorraine, or even Raine, no matter what she preferred. Wretched name. Alix must have chosen it. It smacked of her taste.

Yes, intelligence and territorial instincts were exactly what he wanted in a self-appointed and highly motivated bodyguard for his niece, now that Novak had been so bold as to indicate an unhealthy interest in her. All Victor needed was to find some way to ratchet up Mackey's protective instincts to a higher pitch without compromising his own all-important security. A challenging puzzle, but he was confident that the solution would present itself soon.

Mackey was not a bad match for Katya, he reflected. He was seething with repressed anger, of course, but most men were if you scratched their surfaces. He was smart, successful and aggressive. Careful background research had revealed that his childhood had been of the squalid urban variety, but he had pulled himself out of the tar somehow. He was a self-made man, which Victor respected. Rather like Victor himself. Rough around the edges, but what he lacked in polish he made up for in sheer ruthlessness. And Katya was more than strong enough to handle him, whether she knew it yet or not. All she needed was a whip and a chair, and a little bit of practice.

The intercom made a melodious ding. He clicked the line open.

"Mr. Lazar, it's Riggs again." Mara's husky alto voice was as soft as the brush of costly sable across his skin. "I told him several times that you didn't wish to be disturbed, but he's at the Severin Bay Marina, asking to be brought over to the island."

A glimmer of an idea began to take form in his mind, chasing away his irritation at Riggs's presumption. "Wake up Charlie. Tell him to go pick Riggs up. Then bring him here, to me."

"To the control room?" Mara sounded discreetly astonished.

"Yes. And Mara?"

"Yes, sir?"

"You have a lovely speaking voice," he told her.

There was a long, startled silence. "Ah . . . thank you, sir."

He lit a cigarette and settled himself to wait, letting his mind clear to examine possible solutions to his dilemma. All too soon, he heard the heavy clump of the man's boots outside the door. Then the subtler click of Mara's heels. The door opened, and the stink of bourbon that exuded from Riggs's pores reached across the room. The man was much reduced, and failing fast. His usefulness was drawing to a close.

Mara's heels clicked delicately into the distance. Victor did not even bother to turn from his view of the video monitors. "It is un-characteristically stupid, even for you, to come here," he said.

"You ignore my messages." Riggs's voice vibrated with tension. "I didn't know what else to do."

Victor snorted.

"You don't seem to understand how dangerous the situation is. She saw me today! Peter's daughter was at the Cave, talking to Haley, ask-ing questions! She has to be taken care of, Victor. I should have done it seventeen years ago, but Alix . . . God, I'm sorry, but it just has to be done. I know she's your niece, but you have to admit—"

"I do not have to do anything." Victor's tone cut off Riggs's monologue, and he panted, waiting like the whipped dog he was for permission to continue speaking. Victor took a leisurely drag on his cigarette. "Perhaps what happened seventeen years ago has given you a mistaken impression of me, Edward. The truth is, I really do prefer not to kill members of my own family, if I can possibly avoid it."

"You didn't mind throwing my team into Novak's trap, though," Riggs snarled. "Didn't lose any sleep over that decision, did you?"

"Ah." Victor blew out a perfect smoke ring, watched it disintegrate. "Still sulking about that, are you?"

"Cahill died in that fuck-up. Badly. McCloud was in a coma for two months. He's still gimping around like a cripple. Two of my best agents, damn it. That whole thing really sucked for me, Victor. Yeah, you could say that I'm still sulking."

"We've been through this, Edward. I didn't hurt those men. Novak did. Besides, you should have controlled your men better. You shouldn't have let them get so close," he chided. "You inconvenienced an extremely important client of mine. Take responsibility for your part in that fiasco, my friend."

"I am not your friend," Riggs rasped.

Victor spun in his chair and smiled at him. "Are you my enemy, then? Think before you answer, Edward. I make a very bad enemy."

Riggs's throat worked. His bloodshot eyes were desperate and haunted. "Victor, you don't understand. She saw me. And she reacted."

Victor's smile was pitiless. "Your problem."

"It's your problem, too!"

"Not at all. I have nothing to lose, really," Victor reminded him. "But you have so much. Your career, your reputation, your standing in the community. And let's not forget your lovely wife, your daughters—"

"Are you threatening me?"

Victor clucked his tongue. "Threatening? Is it threatening to take a friendly interest in a colleague's personal life? It's been such a pleasure, following the progress of your charming girls. I was so happy for you and Barbara when Erin graduated from the University of Washington. Lovely girl, with that long dark hair, and such grace-ful bone structure. She takes after your attractive wife. So intelli-gent, too. Highest honors in art history and archaeology, if memory serves. Magnificent young woman. I congratulate you."

"Stay the fuck away from my family." Riggs's face was purple with impotent fury.

"And the little one, Cindy. More lively than Erin. I confess, she's my personal favorite. She's given you some sleepless nights, hasn't she? Oh, I'm sorry, Edward . . . I forgot. All your nights are sleepless now."

"Goddamn you," Riggs muttered.

"Pretty little Cindy, just starting her sophomore year at Endicott Falls Christian College, and on a full band scholarship, too. I hear she's quite the talented saxophonist. Three-zero grade point aver-age, they tell me. In my opinion, she could apply herself a bit more. But she's such a party girl. Youthful high spirits, and all. Girls will be girls."

Riggs dropped into a chair and turned away, but Victor was re-lentless. "And Barbara seems to be burying herself in community service lately. Or is all this philanthropic activity just her way of compensating for the fact that she's married to a whoring, murdering drunk? She must sense the truth, even if she doesn't know it con-sciously. Women always do."

"No," Riggs moaned, putting his head in his hands. "No."

"I'm sure that even after sixteen years, Barbara would be very much interested in the content of certain high-resolution video footage that I possess. Hours of you fucking my ex-sister-in-law, and in the most imaginative ways, too. Bizarre positions—oral, anal, what have you. And you, a law enforcement agent with a perfect family." Victor shook his head sadly. "Come to think of it, your daughters might be startled by that video footage as well," he added.

"You fucked her, too, you hypocritical bastard," Riggs hissed.

"Certainly. Who didn't? But I tired of her in about ten minutes. She was empty, Edward. Knock, knock, but there was nobody home, eh? Not like Barbara. Now there is a woman of substance. Worth the trouble. Wasted on you, if you ask me."

"Do not speak my wife's name." Riggs sounded defeated.

"Ah, Alix." Victor clucked his tongue. "She may have been an avaricious slut with no scruples, but she served her purpose well."

Riggs sat down heavily in front of the video bank, took off his glasses and rubbed his reddened eyes. Victor concluded that he had pushed far enough. Time for a new tactic. He got up and poured a glass of scotch from the decanter on the sideboard. Riggs's head rose at the sound of liquor gurgling into the glass, like a dog coming to point.

"What do you want from me this time?" he asked dully.

Pathetic. Yes, Riggs's usefulness was definitely near the end.

Victor handed Riggs the glass. "To start with, you can relax. Don't take it all so seriously. Life is to be enjoyed, not agonized over."

Riggs took a swallow and wiped his mouth. His pinkish eyes were watery. "Stop playing with me."

"Oh, Edward. Since you're already inside my den of iniquity, you might as well take advantage of some of the luxuries that I can provide for you. Look at the monitor on the far right, second from the top. Go on, take a look."

Riggs lifted his head and looked. He leaped to his feet, snatched his glasses out of his breast pocket and slapped them onto his nose, leaning closer. "Mother of God," he whispered.

Victor turned away to hide his smile. Sometimes it was almost painful how easy people were to manipulate. How predictable their fears and appetites made them. "Her name is Sonia," he said. "I've had her in mind for you for some time. Judge Madison certainly seems to enjoy her attentions, no? She'll be free soon, if you care to indulge. Sonia won't mind working a double shift. His Honor isn't known for his staying power. She'll be available in, oh, probably less than an hour, if you care to wait. The time it will take for her to freshen up."

Riggs scanned the other monitors, his mouth sagging. He chug-a-lugged the liquor left in his glass and cast a longing glance at the decanter. "Trying to get your claws into me even deeper, huh?"

Victor's laugh was mirthless. "They couldn't be any deeper than they already are. I just thought to offer you a bright spot in the midst of the daily round of lies, betrayal and self-loathing."

Riggs's head snapped around. The look that flashed from his eyes was one of pure, concentrated hatred. Victor registered it with a clinical sense of relief. Perhaps Riggs still had enough juice left in him for one last task. He wasn't quite ready yet to be ground into fertilizer.

"So, Edward? What do you say? Whoops . . . look at that. His Honor has already finished, poor man. He'll be asleep in minutes. Care to indulge?"

"Fuck you," Riggs said, through gritted teeth.

"Oh, come now." Victor picked up a silver-framed photo. It was an enlargement of the one in the library. The sunny day at the dock, with Alix, Katya, Riggs and himself. "You know that I've always been rather hurt that you don't come to my parties."

"Why do you keep that goddamn photo around? It's dangerous!"

Victor placed the photo tenderly back on the shelf. "To keep you honest, Edward," he said softly.

"You are one crazy, twisted son-of-a-bitch."

Victor shrugged. "Perhaps. Since you won't take advantage of my hospitality, let's move on directly to the favor I want from you."

"Yeah. Spit it out, and quit fucking with my head."

"The task is simple enough. I want you to guard my niece."

"What?" Riggs's eyes widened, and the broken capillaries over his nose seemed to throb visibly. "You're out of your mind!"

"Not at all. Don't worry, you won't have to deal with her personally. I don't want her to know about our arrangement. I just want you to keep her under your eye at all times. Keep her house under surveillance. Watch her every move. Follow her wherever she goes."

"That's insane! The Cave—"

"You haven't taken a vacation from the Cave in over five years, Edward," Victor cut in. "Arrange one."

Riggs stared at him, aghast. "But I just got promoted! I can't—"

"Of course you can. Don't play the victim, for God's sake. You're a rich man, thanks to your association with me. You have no cause to complain. And this is the last favor I will ever ask of you."

Riggs squinted, disbelieving. "Really?"

"Absolutely the last," Victor assured him. "With this simple task, our account will be closed. You have my word."

"What does she need to be protected from?" Riggs demanded. "Who wants to whack her? And why the secrecy?"

"That doesn't concern you," Victor said.

"It's Novak, right?" Riggs said slowly. "Novak wants to get to you. Through her."

Every now and then the man inconvenienced him with brief flashes of genuine intelligence. "It is not necessary for you to know why," he said coldly. "Just do as you are told. If you should be discovered, you know exactly what will happen if you mention me."

"This is insane," Riggs muttered. "How am I supposed to—"

"Don't whine," Victor snapped. "Do I have to spell out everything for you? A federal agent at the pinnacle of his career, and you need instructions from me as to how to keep your eye on an innocent young woman? Use your dirty mind, Edward. I've seen it at work in those videos, so I know damn well you have one."

Hatred glowed hot in Riggs's eyes. His hands clenched into fists. "Just watching the girl? That's all you want from me?"

"That's all." Victor opened a cabinet and pulled out a hand-held monitor. "Take this. It's already keyed to the transmitters planted in her clothing and jewelry. The device is simple enough so that even you should be able to figure it out. Her identifying icon is a tiny jewel. You must stay within five kilometers for the monitor to work. This enables you to find her more easily should she slip away, but I would prefer it if you kept her physically under your eye. Do you understand?"

Riggs took the monitor, holding it as if it were a ticking bomb. "How long do I have to do this?"

"I don't know yet."

Riggs began to shake his head, and Victor let his voice soften. "Just this one last thing, and it will be all over," he said. "Think of the freedom, the peace of mind. And Edward?"

Riggs turned back from the door, looking hunted.

"I do not want a hair on her head harmed." Victor enunciated very clearly. "At your hand, or anyone else's. If you fail me, I will destroy you completely. Completely. Do you understand?"

Riggs's face twisted. "You're out of your mind, Victor. Why are you doing this? That girl could destroy both of us!"

"Because that girl is worth ten of you, you miserable piece of shit. Now get out of my sight. I can't bear to look at you for another second."

Riggs flinched, lips drawn back in an animal snarl. The mortal hatred between the two of them flashed in the dim room, as perceptible as a drawn blade. "You hate me for doing in Peter, don't you? You didn't have the balls to do it yourself, you arrogant prick. And you hate me for doing your dirty work."

Victor's nostrils dilated in disgust. The man stank of ruin, decay, and violent, premature death. "Don't push me, Edward," he said, from between his clenched teeth. "I'm out of patience."

Riggs's mouth worked. "Remember what you said about betrayal and self-loathing? Look in the mirror, Victor. You spit on me, you're spitting on yourself."

"Shut up and do as you're told. Get out."

Victor listened to the man clump away. He was clenching his fists, almost unbearably tempted to go after Riggs and put him out of his misery, once and for all. In the dark, from behind, as he deserved.

Yes, it was past time to devise a fitting retirement gift for Edward Riggs. Something very special, to pay him back for all his years of loyal service. He had been a walking dead man ever since he had soiled his hands with Peter's blood, but it was clear that Riggs's life was worth nothing anyway. Victor had been squeezing every last drop of usefulness out of him before his sentence was carried out. Waste not, want not.

He knew it was hypocritical. The order to kill his younger brother had been his own, after all. But Victor had given Peter every chance. He had reasoned with him, pleaded, and finally threatened him. A lifetime of wheeling and dealing, of holding his nose and doing what had to be done for the sake of the family. Protecting their interests, insuring their future. All the dirty work he had willingly taken on so that Peter and his family could sit in the lap of luxury, serene and pampered.

After all that, betrayal.

There was no point in thinking about it. Every thought that passed through his mind he'd thought a thousand times before. He poured himself a drink and gulped the liquor down, trying not to compare himself to Edward Riggs. He was not yet quite so reduced.

Ordering Peter's murderer to protect Katya was somewhat bizarre, he thought, with a twinge of doubt. But it made a certain crazy sense. Riggs was the perfect man for the job. For all his personal failings, he was a skilled professional. Best of all, he was expendable. He would do what had to be done, and Mackey was sure to notice that his lover was being followed. His reaction would be swift and predictable.

How amusing it would be if Mackey should end up killing Riggs. So much the better. It would be a fitting end, and it would save Victor the trouble and expense of arranging it himself. And since Mackey would never know who had hired the man, he would remain on guard for Novak or anyone else that Novak might send. It was perfect. Airtight.

But sadly, Riggs had ruined the rare good mood that the party had put him in. It had given him such pleasure to see Katya's beauty polished to a high gloss and displayed in a proper setting, out of Alix's long shadow at last. But Riggs had pried open Pandora's box. Ugly memories were fluttering out like bats.

The door behind him opened, and he recognized Mara's perfume, an earthy, alluring blend of essential oils. She made no sound as she padded across the cream-colored Aubusson carpet. "I saw Riggs out," she said. "Charlie took him back to the mainland."

"Thank you, Mara."

He almost dismissed her then and there. He knew from bitter experience that sex could be disastrous when his mood was so precarious, but he had his weaknesses, too. He turned and looked.

She had changed her clothing. Gone was the black evening gown slit up to the hip that had been chosen to set off an exquisite antique, a Japanese pearl and lapis headdress that she had worn over her braided coil of dark hair. She had taken down her hair. The braids had left soft ripples in it, giving her a softer, more vulnerable look. She was wearing a short tunic of white silk, simple and stark, which showed off the length of her bronze thighs. The toe ring was gone.

She met his gaze, her topaz eyes unreadable and paced silently over to stand in front of the bank of monitors. She studied them for a moment, and pointed to the blank one. "Malfunction?"

Victor shook his head. "My niece's lover likes his privacy."

She nodded, unsurprised, and turned her gaze back to the monitors. "Those two look good together," she commented.

He stood up, feeling a warm shimmer of anticipatory heat. Amazing. He approached her from behind, bending down to inhale her perfume, to touch her shimmering chestnut hair. "Was it you who picked out the Dolce & Gabbana for her?"

Mara's slender shoulders lifted in a tiny shrug. "It was the obvious choice. It wasn't hard to make her look good. She's stunning."

"So are you, my dear," Victor said. "So are you." He lifted up her hair to admire the curve of her back, the whorl of fine dark hairs at the nape of her slender neck. "Lovely."

Mara smiled from beneath her thick, sooty eyelashes, then turned back to the monitor. She took the mouse next to the keyboard and clicked on the icons with expert swiftness until one of the images on Monitor #17 enlarged, obscuring the other windows. She enlarged it again, until the image filled the entire screen.

It was Sergio, the curator, tangled in a complicated knot with two beautiful young Asian women and a muscular blond boy, creating a writhing configuration that Victor would have sworn was anatomically impossible for a man of Sergio's age.

They watched it for a moment. Mara clicked onto Monitor #9. It was the celebrated cardiologist, Dr. Wade, giving his own heart a strenuous workout. They watched a lithe, coffee-colored woman in a black bustier apply a pink unguent to a certain part of the renowned doctor's anatomy, and then, very slowly, introduce a formidable sex toy into said part. To the august doctor's evident delight.

She clicked idly across the other centers of activity, lingering on the image of a beautiful young brunette, clad only in scraps of lingerie, rocking back and forth on her hands and knees. She was sweaty and flushed, eyes half closed, as a local software mogul belabored her vigorously from behind.

Victor had little interest in what was on the screen; he had gotten bored with it lifetimes ago. But watching Mara watch made his own sexual energy uncoil, slow and sinuous as a snake waking up from its winter sleep. "You like to watch, Mara?" he asked softly.

She shifted until she was leaning back against him, a light, warm, silken weight. "I like a lot of things," she said.

He put his hand upon the fine-textured skin of her thigh, and slid it up beneath the short skirt. He discovered, with pleasure, that she was naked beneath it. Depilated as well; her mound was smoothly shaven with just a flirtatious little puff of hair shielding her clitoris. She widened her stance, opening for him with a sigh. He delved deeper and found that she was already aroused. She moved her body with feline grace against his hand. Hairless, silky and slick. Delicious.

He bit her neck, savoring the reaction rippling through her slender body. "You're a naughty girl, aren't you?"

"If I wasn't, I certainly wouldn't be here," she said. Her voice choked off into a gasping moan as he thrust his hand more deeply, unfastening his trousers with the other. She braced herself against the edge of the table and arched herself open.

"True enough," he agreed.

He drove inside her with a violence that surprised them both. She cried out and stumbled forward, catching herself against the table, and then braced herself more firmly. The room was a haze of glowing images, the bank of monitors with their assorted scenes of pleasure and depravity, Mara's perfect buttocks, the silk tunic pushed up to her delicate ribs, his penis gleaming as it thrust in and out of her.

He barely heard the grunts and gasps, the slapping sound of contact. The cool, detached part of his mind that always watched was well aware that it was his fury at Riggs that fueled this brutal rhythm. He didn't want to hurt Mara, but he paid lavishly enough for her services to indulge in his baser instincts without needing to ask either permission or pardon. He was so aroused. More alive and aware than he had been in years, not since his brother, Peter—

No. He pushed the thought away before it could unfurl, before it could detach him from the intensity of this delightful experience. The tight, slick depths of Mara's perfect body exciting him beyond measure as he caressed her trembling buttocks, giving into the hard, driving rhythm.

Erotic heat roared through him and carried him over the brink. He spent himself in a long blast that blotted out every thought in his mind.

When he moved to withdraw, Mara made an inarticulate cry of protest and shoved herself back against him. "Wait," she gasped. She came, long and shivering and totally unexpected. Delicious to watch, to feel. Her lingering pulsations milked and massaged his still-erect penis.

They were sticky and wet, but the architect had not planned the room with spontaneous sex in mind, so there was no adjoining bathroom. He withdrew himself, closed his pants and waited for his heart to slow down. Mara sank down onto the carpet, her legs sprawled out beneath her, as limp as a rag doll. She was still trembling. With her back hunched over like that, she looked fragile and vulnerable. He put his hand on her bare shoulder. It was hot and damp. She looked up at him. He felt a shock of startled recognition as their eyes met.

The sex had genuinely excited her. A fascinating discovery.

He held out his hand, pulled her up onto her feet. "Thank you, Mara. That was a revelation," he said. "You can go."

Her face convulsed. "Don't dismiss me like that!"

Another moment of blank surprise. "I beg your pardon?"

Mara looked suddenly unsure of herself. "I said . . . don't dismiss me," she whispered. "Not after we've just had sex. Like that."

"My dear, I can do anything I want with you," he said gently. "You agreed to that when you were hired. Remember?"

Her wide mouth trembled. She stared him in the face, eyes wide and glittering with unshed tears. "Don't," she repeated.

He was taken aback, almost touched by her daring. Under the circumstances, that gesture took both courage and honesty. Both of which were in short supply in his life.

Ordinarily he would never permit a member of his staff to make personal demands of him. But tonight was a night for rule-breaking, for risk taking. Tonight, he would overlook this breach of protocol.

The girl was shivering. Her taut, dark nipples were clearly visible through the delicate fabric. He would not mind seeing those breasts again, he realized, with a fresh wave of lust. He saw her in his mind's eye, naked on the bed, her hair fanned out across the white linen. Those topaz eyes, filled with genuine need.

Yes. It would be good. It would work. He was hard again. Already. He gave her a brief nod. "Come along, then. Let's go to my suite."

Victor stalked down the corridor, watching as Mara scurried ahead of him, her bare feet silent on the cold flagstones. She cast nervous, wide-eyed glances back over her shoulder at him, as well she should. She was an intelligent girl. She had good reason to be nervous.

He opened the door with a predatory smile and gestured for her to enter. Mara was hungry for something, too. And in appreciation for her charming honesty, he was going to see that she got it.

As much of it as she could take.

Chapter

19

Riggs swerved on the dark road, correcting just in time. It was bad tonight. Ever since Jesse Cahill's death, his ulcers had been flaring up to the point of burning agony. Medication didn't do much good, mixed with bourbon, but he needed booze to take the edge off the knowledge that he was an unredeemable piece of shit. Survival lay only in keeping that knowledge from Barbara and the girls for as long as he possibly could.

He thought of this morning; how she'd pressured him to see a therapist with her. "You have to face your feelings, Eddie," she said, with that goddamn *look*, that anxious, furrowed-brow look that made him so crazy with rage and shame, he wanted to smack it right off her face. He hadn't sunk that low, not yet, but it was a near thing.

The girl was a lot like Alix, in spite of the clumsy clothes, the glasses and the scraped-back hair. Alix's billowing mane had always been perfectly coiffed; Alix had worn clothes that would have cost him a month's salary for a single outfit. He'd never had a woman like her, a drop-dead, blaze-of-glory woman. Barbara was lovely, but she was a good girl. Too good for him. He'd met her in college, and had been attracted to her ladylike manners. Barbara was an obvious choice for a wife, the perfect mother for his two girls.

But when he met Alix, something had detonated inside him, blowing everything he thought he was to pieces. A man could die happy fucking a woman like Alix. She was feral in bed, a bitch in heat. A couple of lines of coke snorted off her perfect tits, and they'd gone at it for hours, doing things he'd only heard of but never dreamed of trying. Things he could never imagine with his sweet, quiet Barbara.

He'd held himself together during that hallucination of a summer back in '85 by keeping his two worlds separate. Even Haley had never gotten a clue, thank God, since he himself had been the one infiltrating Lazar's operation, not Bill. Barbara had inhabited one segment of reality, safe and sane and sensible with her cardigan sweaters and her smooth dark bobbed hair, all meatloaf and babies and breakfast cereal. Alix had ruled another segment. Naked, wide open, burning for him.

He'd had a pretty good life once, before that bitch had spread her legs and welcomed him into the gates of hell. Victor's hooks had sunk into him so insidiously that he'd barely noticed them. Riggs was so far out of it that when the order came down, when he found out how deep in shit he was, he'd *wanted* to kill that worthless, whining bastard Peter Lazar. He wanted him the hell out of the way so he could have Alix, *really* have her, all for himself. . . .

Riggs cringed, thinking about how gullible he had been. The world had exploded in his face, and when he sifted through the rubble, he was left with the knowledge that he was not one of the good guys, like Barbara believed. Maybe he never had been. Maybe he had been a piece of shit all along. Victor's creature, belly-down in the mud.

There had been long periods, years sometimes, when Victor hadn't called on him, and he'd begun to fancy himself a normal person again. But the call inevitably came. If Victor Lazar should ever find himself in trouble with the law, those videos would be mailed to his family and to the local media. Details of certain deposits to offshore accounts would be made public. The circumstances of Peter Lazar's death would be recounted to one and all. The same thing would happen if Victor were to die in a suspicious manner. If Riggs was to maintain some semblance of a life, no matter how fictitious, Victor had to stay healthy and happy. Cahill and McCloud had acted on their own. Goddamn mavericks, both of them. They had almost ruined everything.

His eyes fell on the monitor that lay in the passenger's seat. If only he'd drowned the little bitch along with her father. She'd seen him today, and if she hadn't recognized him yet, she soon would. Those bright eyes had witnessed his transformation from a man into a crawling thing. He wanted to close those eyes. Forever.

He saw the sign and swerved. A roadhouse. He stumbled into the dark interior and ordered a shot of bourbon and a glass of milk. It was as much as he dared allow himself, in his current state. He could drive after a single shot, if the pain in his stomach didn't make him pass out. He popped a handful of antacids and chased them down with milk, a trick that had ceased to work about eight months ago, but he kept it up out of force of habit. He thought about how it would be, to pass out and run into a tree. It didn't seem so terrible. Just the crunch of breaking glass, the shriek of bent metal, and then, darkness. Then nothing.

He left the money on the bar and lurched out. The puddles in the parking lot rippled in the chilly wind. He got into the Taurus and sat with his eyes shut and his hand pressed hard against his corroded gut.

His mind darted around, like a rat in a maze. But there was no way out, and presently his mind slowed. Just an exhausted, defeated old rat, that was him.

He fumbled the key into the ignition. Heard the squeak of leather against leather. Felt the icy barrel of a gun, pressed against his neck.

"Don't move," someone hissed.

The passenger door opened. A man picked up the small monitor that lay on the passenger seat and got in. A wave of frigid air accompanied him, as if the door to a meat locker had suddenly swung open.

The man gave him a pleasant smile. "Good evening, Mr. Riggs."

He wondered if it were actually possible for things to get worse for him than they already were. "Who the fuck are you?"

The man studied the monitor, playing with it. "We've never been introduced, but we're linked by fate. May I call you Edward?"

"If it's money you want, I don't have—"

"I enjoyed myself carrying out Jesse Cahill's execution, Edward," the man said. "I should thank you for the sport, as well."

His blood froze, and his bowels loosened. "Novak," he whispered.

The other man's smile widened strangely and carved deep shadows into his young-old face. His eyes glowed, phosphorescent in the gloom.

Riggs fought for control of his basic bodily functions. "What do you want from me?"

"Several things, actually," Novak said. "You can begin by telling me everything you know about Raine Cameron."

He was so cold, his body was vibrating. "I don't know about—"

"Shut up." Novak's voice cracked like a pistol shot, and the gun barrel pressed painfully into Rigg's cervical vertebrae. "Sixteen years of licking Victor Lazar's hand, isn't that enough for you?"

Riggs's mouth sagged open, but no sound came out.

"Here is your chance, my friend," Novak said. "Your chance to put it to him right up the ass. Make him pay for making you crawl."

He saw Barbara's face in his mind. The anxious line between his wife's brows was etched so deep now that nothing would ever smooth it away.

"I don't work for Victor Lazar," he forced out, through numb lips.

Novak's eyeteeth glinted like fangs in the roadhouse sign's bloody light. "Of course you don't," he agreed. "Now you work for me."

Riggs let out the breath in his lungs and shook his head. "No," he said. "Go ahead. Pull the trigger. Make my day. Go on, do it."

Novak regarded him thoughtfully, and then made a gesture to the man behind him, who had been silent in the back seat. The pistol was removed. "Very well," he said briskly. "Let us put matters in a different light."

"You can't control me. I don't give a shit anymore. I won't do it."

Novak held up his hand, fluttered it impatiently. "If the prospect of punishing Victor and saving your own miserable life is not sufficiently motivating, then let me tell you this. You may not be aware of the company your daughter Erin is keeping."

Riggs had thought it impossible to feel more afraid. What an idiot. Fear was an abyss that had no bottom, and he was falling. Down, down.

"Remember Erin's ski trip? To Crystal Mountain, up on Mt. Rainier? With her girlfriends . . . Marika, and Bella, and Sasha."

"Yes," he replied. His voice was reduced to a rasping thread.

"Erin met a young man yesterday, while drinking hot chocolate by the fireplace. A dashing fellow, with a romantic foreign accent and long blond hair. Georg was the name he gave her."

"No," he croaked.

"The young lady is surprisingly resistant, to her credit, and yours, if I may say so. But Georg is confident in his powers of seduction. He will eventually make it into her bedroom. He will take her to bed. And you, my friend, will be the key to the quality of that experience for her."

"You can't."

"Oh, but I have. You decide, Edward. It could be just a bittersweet memory of new love found and then, inexplicably, lost . . . or with one short call on my cell phone, it could become something else entirely. Something that a loving father should do absolutely everything in his power to spare his innocent child."

Riggs closed his eyes. He saw Erin, in the wading pool. Helping him rake the leaves. Curled up in the window seat with her journal. Sweet, quiet Erin, who always tried so hard to please, to be good.

"By all means, take your time," Novak said softly. "Think about it. There's no rush. Georg is very aroused by Erin's maidenly reluctance. She is a beautiful girl. This is his favorite kind of assignment."

"Don't you dare touch my girl." His words were flat and hollow, followed by Novak's soft chuckle. "Oh, God," he whispered. As if God gave a damn about him, after what he had done, after what he had become.

"One phone call." Novak's faintly accented voice burned like corrosive acid against Riggs's nerves.

The bloody red roadhouse light wavered in his watering eyes. "If I cooperate with you, this man won't touch Erin?"

Novak laughed. "Oh, I can't promise you that. I'm afraid that depends upon Erin herself. Georg is very attractive, very persuasive.

What I can promise is that if you cooperate, she will have nothing to complain about. Georg is a skilled professional. No matter which way you decide, he will carry out his duties with enthusiasm."

"Promise me he won't touch her, and I'll do it." Riggs hated himself for the hoarse, pleading tone of his voice.

"Don't be foolish. Erin must take her chances with sex and love, like every other woman. And if you are considering calling the Cave, be aware. My men are watching Crystal Mountain very carefully. I have spared no expense in my planning. The slightest wrong move, an intercepted phone call, and poor Erin's fate will be sealed in a heartbeat. And I have not yet even begun to devise something special for your other daughter, little Cindy. And there is your wife to think of, too." He sighed, shook his head. "An infinity of details."

"No," he repeated stupidly.

Novak patted his shoulder. He was too numb, too cold, to even flinch away. It was almost as if he were dead already.

"Come now, Edward. Let's move ahead. Raine Cameron. Out with it. Tell me everything, my friend. Everything."

"Not your friend," he mumbled.

"Eh? What was that you said?"

He took a deep breath. "I'm not your friend," he said more clearly.

Novak gave him an approving smile, as if he were a dull child that had just gotten a difficult math problem right. "That is absolutely correct, Edward," he said. "You are not my friend. You are my slave."

Jesse was standing on the boat, wearing Seth's black leather jacket. He knew it was his jacket because it was far too big for Jesse. The shoulders drooped off Jesse's narrow shoulders, the sleeves hung down all the way to his fingertips.

He was very pale, freckles standing out sharply against his skin, his green eyes somber. "Be careful," he said. "The circle is getting smaller."

In the dream, Seth understood perfectly what that meant. "How small?" he asked.

Jesse held up his hand, thumb and forefinger touching in a circle. Then he was a child again, dwindled down to the size of the five-year-old he had been

when he came to live with them. The jacket now hung down past his knees.
"Very small," he repeated, and the water behind him glittered as a bolt of
sunlight pierced the clouds. Something was dangling from Jesse's little-boy
fingers, flashing green and blue fire. Raine's grandmother's necklace.

Seth slid into waking consciousness, fixing the details of the dream in his mind as he registered the luxurious sheets he was tangled in, the flower-petal softness of Raine cuddled in his arms. She stirred, trying not to wake him, and he feigned sleep as she dropped a kiss on his shoulder. She slid out of his arms. The door to the adjoining bath opened. The toilet flushed. The shower began to hiss.

He had resisted sleep to the very end, but Raine had been as fierce and demanding as he was; and after hours of wild lovemaking, sleep had finally claimed him. He stretched, enjoying the remarkable comfort of the huge bed until the bathroom door opened, then the armoire. He heard a gasp, and opened his eyes.

Raine was standing in front of the closet, wearing nothing but a towel. Her wet hair hung all the way down to her perfect ass, and he was relieved to see that the curls were back in full force. He tried to see what had alarmed her, but all he saw was plastic-wrapped clothes.

"What's the problem?" he asked.

She smiled over her shoulder at him, but her eyes were anxious. "Those bastards took my glasses! And my clothes are gone, too! I left my suit here, and my shoes, but now there's just . . . this other stuff."

"So? Those glasses were pretty weird anyhow, sweetheart. You've got the contacts you wore last night, right? No problem. Pick something out of the stuff that's there," he suggested. "I'm sure it's all for you."

She rifled through the clothes. "Lord. I can't take these. Armani, Gianfranco Ferré, Nannini, Prada . . . there's a fortune in this closet."

"Does that surprise you?"

She scowled at him. "I don't like being shoved around, Seth! I want my cheap blue suit back. I paid for it, and it's mine."

The movement had caused the towel to slip, catching on the top of her nipples. His morning erection throbbed urgently, as if he hadn't spent the night having the hottest, most prolonged sex of his whole life. He threw the covers off and lunged for her. She backed away, but there was no place to run, and he was all over her, dizzy with the fragrance of soap and shampoo and Raine. Honey and violets. Good enough to eat.

"I'm too nervous to make love again, Seth," she whispered.

He stared over her shoulder into the mirror at the graceful curve of her back and cupped her round, rosy buttocks in both his hands. "Don't be nervous," he urged. "It doesn't matter what you wear. You always look gorgeous. I like you best stark naked anyway."

Her arms stole around his waist, and she nuzzled his chest tentatively. "I can't go out there stark naked."

He tossed her down onto the rumpled bed. "Sweetheart, your outfit is the least of your worries this morning."

She took his words more seriously than he had meant her to, and her face clouded with real fear. "You're absolutely right," she said. "Seth, I'm not sure if I can—about the—"

He kissed her hard and put his mouth to her ear. "Not one word."

Her mouth trembled. She closed her eyes, and two crystal bright tears squeezed out between her lashes, flashing down her face. "But—"

He covered her mouth with his hand and kissed the tears away, trying to communicate without words that it was a done deal, no going back, no longer negotiable. She stared into his eyes. Her breath came in short, panting gasps, trapped beneath his weight.

It seemed as natural as breathing to push her legs apart and start petting her. She moved against his fingers, getting slick and wet for him almost instantly, and he eased the head of his cock inside her, kissing her as she tried to speak again. He thrust his tongue into her mouth, muffling the cry she made as he forged into her. The almost scalding heat of her body shocked him. He hadn't put on a condom.

But it was so good. Amazing. Just a few strokes, careful and controlled. He wouldn't come inside her, just enjoy some unprotected bliss for a few delirious moments. She loved it, too. He could feel her soft body quiver beneath him. But the intensity of his bare flesh inside hers was driving him out of his head. His thrusts grew harder, deeper.

She was trying to speak again. He kissed her words away, didn't want to hear them, wanted to stay in the spell. But she was shoving him, pushing his face away. "Please, don't," she said.

Seth stared down at her, horrified at the tears trembling in her eyes. He could have sworn she'd liked it. "What?" he demanded.

"Don't use sex to control me." Her voice shook with anger.

He was dumbfounded. He studied her for a long moment. "I didn't know I was doing that," he said. "I just wanted you."

"You're good at manipulating. You use whatever weapon comes to hand. But don't use sex against me."

He was shivering, even though he still felt as hard and hot as a brand inside her. He withdrew from her clinging heat, flopping onto his back and staring up at the ceiling. All his past relationship fiascos paraded through his mind. The air felt cold and inhospitable on his dick, which lay, wet and disconsolate against his belly. He tried to think of something to say, some way to convince her that it was different than she thought. No words came to him.

"I'm sorry," he said finally, just to say something. Anything.

Raine pulled herself up onto her knees and looked down at him silently. She laid her hand on his chest. "Thank you," she said quietly.

"For what?" His voice sounded gruff and ungracious, but there was nothing he could do about it.

"That was a very nice apology," she said. "I liked that there were no ifs, ands or buts attached to it. It was very simple and effective."

"Oh." He squinted, bewildered. "I'm, uh, glad you liked it."

For the first time, he'd gotten something like this right, but not by intelligence, or sensitivity, or technique. Just by pure, dumb luck.

The thought was not a comforting one.

"So you're, uh, not mad at me anymore?" he asked cautiously.

Raine smothered a laugh with her hands, and shook her head. She leaned over, and placed her hands on either side of his head, gazing into his eyes with searching tenderness. Her hair hung around them like a perfumed tent and her breasts dangled like lush, ripe fruit above him. All he wanted was to seize them, stroke them. She leaned down, dropped a kiss on his lips, a light, brushing touch.

He thought that was his cue to pull her closer, but he got it wrong again. She stiffened, pulling back with a nervous murmur.

He let his arms drop and opened his hands. Afraid to speak, afraid to breathe. *No threat*, he tried to say with his body, with his eyes. *No moves, no agenda, your call.* He couldn't bear to feel her flinch away from him again, so evidently frightened.

She gave him a tremulous, uncertain smile, and he let out a sigh of relief, which turned into a gasp when her hand slid down and seized his cock. "Lie still," she whispered.

She twisted her hair into a loose spiral behind her neck and seized him in both hands, stroking and pulling with a bold caress that made him gasp and jerk up onto his elbows. A drop of moisture formed on the end of it. She bent down and licked it off.

"God," he muttered. "What is this, Raine? Are you trying to prove something? Trying to get back at me?"

"No," she whispered. "I want to give you pleasure."

The warm brush of her breath against his cock as she spoke was the sweetest caress he'd ever felt, until she put her mouth to him. It was so wet and soft, deliciously tender. Her eager tongue darted and swirled, under, over and all around. Oh, God, he was in for it.

She had lost all her awkwardness. She cupped his ass with one hand, pulling him even closer to her luscious, suckling mouth, and the other cradled his balls, rolling them tenderly around in her fingers. She licked around and over the head of his cock, then up and down the whole length of him until he was slippery and wet; and then accompanied her mouth with her hand, gripping and sliding as she took him in. Her hot mouth clutched and pulled, tongue swirling lazily as if she were savoring something very good to eat, then sucking him into another long, gliding caress.

He'd gotten plenty of blow jobs in his time, and he'd thoroughly enjoyed every one of them, but this was different. This was so tender and intimate, it was almost agonizing.

He couldn't afford to feel so vulnerable. Not in Lazar's house. He slid his fingers into the cascading tresses on either side of her face and stopped her.

She lifted her head. "You don't like it?"

The irony almost made him smile. He tried to speak, but his

vocal cords wouldn't connect. He took a deep breath and tried again. "It's incredible. But I'm wide open. I can't take it. We've got to get away from here. Try this wild, sexy stuff once we get to someplace safe."

Her eyes were soft with perfect understanding. She reached across him and seized a foil packet from the bedstand. She knelt beside him and smoothed the condom over his cock with tender, careful strokes. Still, he waited, afraid to make another wrong move. She seized his hands, lifting them up and pressing them against her breasts. "You can touch me now," she said shyly. "I've calmed down."

He touched her as carefully as if she were made of fragile glass. He couldn't afford to mess up again. Raine had to make all the moves this time.

She lay down alongside him and tugged his body on top of hers. "Let's go back to our tropical paradise, Seth," she whispered.

He poised himself above her so that the whole surface of his body was in light, kissing contact with hers. He let her do it all. She was the one who opened up and adjusted herself, she was the one who reached down and guided his penis into her body. He even waited until she grabbed his ass and pulled him in before he took the plunge.

They wound their arms around each other. At first it was slow and careful and tender, then it melted like a spring flood and rushed them over an endless fall, united body and soul. He finally understood the futility of trying to batter his way towards the fusion that he craved.

They clung to each other for a long time, until Raine began to disentangle herself. She sat up and perched on the edge of the bed. "There's a ship on the horizon," she said.

"Huh?"

She looked back over her shoulder. "One morning the pirate queen and her sailor stud are making love on the beach. They look up, and there's a full-rigged ship on the horizon. Their idyll is over. You can't run away from the world forever. Sooner or later it always catches up."

He sat up, chilled by a sudden feeling that something precious was slipping away from him.

She got up. "I need another shower."

"I'll shower with you." He reached out for her.

She dodged his hand. "No, you will not."

They got ready in absolute silence. She chose some stuff from the armoire, which of course looked great on her. Everything did.

They were dressed and ready. There was no putting it off any longer. Seth took the kit out of his bag and fished out the transmitter. She took it, turning it over in her hands. She started to speak, but he put his finger over her lips, and shook his head.

Raine's lips pinched into a quivering line. She slipped the tiny transmitter into her pants pocket.

He shrugged on his jacket, suddenly thinking of his dream.

The circle is getting smaller. He didn't know what it meant, but he could feel it happening. Like fingers tightening around his neck.

Chapter

20

Raine picked at her breakfast, acutely conscious of the clothes on her body. A blue cashmere sweater by Armani. Boots by Prada. It seemed ungracious to complain when the clothes were so beautiful and fit so much better than her own, but they still made her nervous.

Seth sat down across from her and set down his third plate from the breakfast buffet, loaded with a seafood omelet, bagels with cream cheese and smoked salmon, fried potatoes, sausage and biscuits. He dug in his fork and nodded at her plate. "Eat, Raine," he said quietly. "Hanging with this crowd really burns those calories."

"You're the one who makes me burn calories," she murmured.

Seth's gaze focused over her shoulder. She turned, and saw Victor shaking hands with the museum curator she had talked with at dinner. Sergio. She waved and smiled at him, and he waved back.

Victor got himself a cup of coffee from the urn and came towards them, beaming. "Good morning, my dear. How lovely you look in that color. I trust you both slept well?"

Raine blushed helplessly.

"Well enough." Seth forked a bite of sausage into his mouth.

"And what is your agenda for the day, Mr. Mackey?" Victor asked.

"Raine and I will be going back to Seattle."

Victor sipped his coffee, his eyes calculating above the rim of the cup. "Actually, I planned to spend some time with Raine this morning. I'm sure you'll understand. I'm coming back to the city myself this afternoon, so it will be no problem at all to bring her—"

"That's OK," Seth said. "I can wait. She can go back with me."

"I hate to think of your valuable time being wasted."

"No problem," Seth said. "I've got my laptop. I can amuse myself just fine while you guys have your family bonding experience. If you want, I can design a more up-to-date surveillance system for your guest bedrooms. A lot of the stuff I dismantled last night was pretty passé."

Victor's gaze hardened. "How kind of you to offer, but please don't trouble yourself. Stone Island is for relaxation, not work."

"Suit yourself." Seth gave him a cheerful grin.

Victor turned to Raine. "Have you finished your breakfast?"

She pushed away the yogurt and fruit and got up. "Yes," she said.

Seth's hand shot out and caught her wrist as she passed. He pulled her close and gave her a hard, possessive kiss. She blushed, flustered by the amusement on Victor's face.

"There's a bit of sun today," Victor said. "Shall we go outside and take advantage of it?"

She followed Victor out onto the porch and down the path. They stood side by side at the dock, watching the sun glitter on the water. "You used to be afraid of the water," Victor remarked. "Remember when I taught you to swim?"

She winced at the memory. "You were ruthless."

"Of course I was. You didn't want to learn. You didn't want to learn to ride a bicycle, either. Or shoot. But I insisted."

"Yes, you most certainly did."

The bicycle episode had been particularly awful. She'd been scraped and bleeding and blubbering, but Victor had been pitiless. He'd forced her to get back on the hellish thing until she finally mastered it. It had been the same with the swimming. He'd yanked her head above water, sputtering and flailing, to let her grab a breath of air and some advice. "Pump with your legs," he ordered calmly, before letting her drop back down into the green liquid underworld.

But she had not drowned. She had learned. Even to use the pistol, although she had hated the noise, the violent kick, the bruises it left in her small hands. The concentrated violence in the small object had terrified her, but she had learned. He had given her no choice.

She turned away from the water and met Victor's eyes. "You thought it was your duty to toughen me up," she observed.

"Peter and Alix were lazy and soft," Victor said. "If it had been up to your parents, you would have ended up a sniveling coward."

It was true. She had Victor to thank for that crazy, joyful feeling of accomplishment, when her body finally understood the trick of equilibrium on the bike. And when she'd emerged from her first wobbly dive, Victor had applauded briefly, and then told her to get right back up onto those rocks and do it again until her technique was better.

Alix and her father hadn't even bothered to come down to watch.

She gazed at the water, lost in memories. She had worshipped and feared Victor as a child. He had been unpredictable. Demanding and mocking. Sometimes cruel, sometimes kind. Always vivid and engaging. The direct opposite of her drifting, absent father, sipping his cognac, lost in his dreams and his melancholy reflections.

"I thought for a time that your mother had succeeded," he said.

"At what?"

"Turning you into a sniveling coward. But she didn't quite manage it. The Lazar genes breed true. She didn't quite manage it."

There was fierce, exultant pride in his silvery eyes. He could read her mind, follow her thoughts as if they were projected on a screen. He could understand her like no one else. Something inside her responded to it. The rest of her recoiled, horrified. She could not let herself bond with him, or care for him in any way. Not after what he had done. She groped for a way to break the spell. "Where is my father buried, Victor?"

"I was wondering when you were going to ask. He's buried here."

"On the island?" She was startled.

"He was cremated. I buried the ashes and raised a monument to him here," Victor said. "Come along. I'll show you."

She was unprepared to confront the reality of her father's grave in Victor's company, but there was no escaping it. She followed Victor up the winding, rocky path that led to the crest of the island, trying to breathe. There was a small valley hidden in the windswept rocks. It was a velvety bowl of green moss, bare of trees. A tall black marble obelisk stood on a pedestal in the middle of the hollow.

Identical to the one in her dream.

She stared at the obelisk, almost expecting blood to start trickling from the words etched on the gleaming stone.

"Are you all right, Raine? You're very pale all of a sudden."

"I've dreamed of this place." Her voice sounded strangled.

Victor's eyes lit up. "So you have it too, then?"

"Have what?"

"The dreaming. It's a Lazar family trait. Your mother never mentioned it to you?"

She shook her head. Her mother had complained about Raine's crazy nightmares until Raine had learned never to mention them.

"I have it. Your grandmother, too. Vivid, recurrent dreams, sometimes of future events, sometimes the past. I often wondered if I passed it on to you."

"You? To me?" she faltered.

"Of course, to you, from me. I would have thought that such a bright girl would have figured it out for herself by now."

He waited patiently as she gaped. She finally found her voice again. "You're saying that you—that my mother—"

"Your mother has many secrets."

She felt as if the earth was opening beneath her feet. "You seduced her?"

Victor snorted. "I wouldn't go so far as to call it that. Seduction would imply a certain amount of effort on my part."

Raine was so stunned, she barely registered the insult to her mother. "Are you sure?"

Victor shrugged. "With Alix, nothing could be sure, but from your looks and your dreams, you are certainly either my daughter or Peter's. And I, personally, am convinced that you are mine. I can feel it."

Mine. The possessive word echoed in her head. "Why?"

He made an impatient gesture with his hand. "She was a beautiful woman," he said casually. "And I wanted to make a point with Peter, I suppose. Not that it worked. My brother was soft. I spoiled him, did all the dirty work for him. It was a mistake. I thought he could protect my innocence for me, and in return, I would spare him the ugly side of life. But it didn't work. He went looking for it anyway. He found it in Alix."

She held up her hands in protest. "Victor—"

"He needed someone who could appreciate his sensitivity." Victor's face rigid with old anger. "Not a money-hungry bitch who would spread her legs for any man who could stare her down."

"Enough!" Raine shouted.

He jerked away, shocked at her tone.

She forced herself to meet his blazing eyes, horrified at her own daring. "I will not tolerate you speaking of my mother that way."

Victor applauded softly. "Brava, Katya. If that had been a test, you would have just passed it. Alix doesn't deserve such a loyal daughter."

"My name is Raine. Please do not mention Alix ever again."

Victor scrutinized her stiff, averted face for a moment. "This place appears to upset you," he observed. "Let's go back to the house."

She followed him down the path. Over and over, she considered the enormity of his revelation until her mind reeled—and gave up, unable to comprehend it.

The path ended at the veranda that stretched the length of the back of the house. He opened the door for her, and gestured her to precede him down the stairs. "I promised to show you my collection," he said. "The vault is in the cellar. After you, my dear."

The tiny transmitter in her pocket was burning a hole in her mind. She thought of Bluebeard's castle, and her stomach clenched. Don't think of it, she reminded herself. Just do it. She was swimming with sharks, a dagger in her teeth. She'd promised Seth. She had to at least try.

Victor opened a metal plate on the wall next to an armored door, and keyed a series of numbers into a glowing silver wall panel. "Oh, that reminds me," he murmured. "This morning I changed my personal computer access code. I change it, on a daily basis, usually. I call the password my 'divine override.' It lets me into any part of the system."

She nodded politely, as if she understood.

"One word. Minimum number of letters, four. Maximum number of letters, ten. The key is . . . what I want from you."

She was bewildered. "You mean, you're telling me your code? But what do you want from me, Victor?"

He snorted. "Oh, for God's sake. You know me better than to ask such a question. If I tell you, it means nothing. If you figure it out for yourself"—he smiled, almost wistfully—"you are divine."

He keyed in another string of numbers. The big, heavy door popped its seal and swung open. "After you," Victor murmured.

She walked into the room. The humid, climate-controlled air closed around her like a possessive, suffocating embrace.

Victor put away the sixteenth-century stiletto, placing it in its case with the others. He took a wooden case from a high shelf, laid it on the table and opened it. "I was told that this rapier delivered the death blow in a famous duel in seventeenth-century France," he said. "Over an unfaithful wife, if the documentation is to be believed. The outraged husband is said to have murdered both the lover and his wife with this blade. Often these stories are fabricated to inflate the value of such items, but I have reason to believe that it's true. The papers are in antiquated French, but that's no barrier to you, of course."

Victor watched her reaction as she inspected the rapier, the delicate tremor in her hand, the faraway look in her eyes. She really was his offspring, he exulted silently. Her dreams were solid proof.

She hefted the rapier, sliced it through the air, and turned to him. "Yes," she said decisively. "I think it's true, too."

She felt it too, just like him. It shouldn't matter, but it did. What a pleasure it was, to show his beauties to someone with the capacity to understand why he valued them.

"You feel it, don't you?" He reached for the rapier. Raine relinquished the thing with obvious relief.

"Feel what?" Her eyes were wary.

"The stain. I would say 'vibration,' but the term has been so overused in New Age parlance as to become practically meaningless."

"I'm not sure I know what you mean."

He patted her shoulder. "You will, my dear. If you have the dreams, you probably have other sensitivities as well. That is the price you pay for being born a Lazar."

"I've already paid enough," she said.

He laughed at her, pitiless. "Don't whine. Power carries its price. And you must learn to use power in order to appreciate its gifts."

She looked dubious. "Bad dreams can be useful?"

He hesitated for a moment, and pulled a set of keys out of his pocket. He unlocked a drawer and pulled out a black plastic case.

"Knowledge is always power, if you are strong enough to face the truth," he said. He laid the case on the table. "Take a look at this, my most recent acquisition. I'm curious to see the effect that it has upon you. It isn't ancient, or beautiful, or rare, like the other items."

"Then why do you have it?" she asked.

"I did not acquire this for myself. It's for a client of mine."

Raine stuck her hands in her pockets. "What's its story?"

He popped the lid open and beckoned her closer. "You tell me. Let your mind empty. Tell me what rises in it."

She stepped closer to the thing, looking pinched and frightened. "Please don't watch me so closely," she said. "It makes me nervous."

"Excuse me." He stepped back.

Raine reached out and placed her hands on either side of the gun. "It feels different than the rapier. The . . . the stain is very fresh."

"Yes," he corroborated.

Her eyes were blind and wide, as if she saw far beyond the gun. As, indeed, she did. He felt a pang of sympathy. So much crashing down on her young head all at once. But she had to face it.

"A woman, murdered," she whispered. "By a person . . . no. A thing. A thing so dead inside, it isn't even human anymore. God."

She doubled over, choking as if she were about to retch. Her hair coiled and draped across the plastic case. She shuddered violently.

He led her to a chair and pushed her into it, alarmed. She hid her face in her hands, her shoulders shaking so hard it seemed that she was weeping, but she made no sound. He poured her a glass of the cognac he kept on the shelf. "Katya. I'm sorry. Are you all right?"

She unfolded. He pressed the glass into her hand, and she held it, as stiff as a doll. "What is that thing, Victor?"

He was taken aback by her flat, hard tone, by the bluntness of the question. "It's a piece in a game I'm playing," he said, feeling defensive. "It's a stolen murder weapon. I am sorry, my dear. I didn't mean to upset you. I showed it to you to see if you could feel—" He stopped.

"Feel what?" She set down the glass of cognac.

"The stain," he said.

Her eyes looked old beyond her years. "I felt it," she said in a low voice. "I hope to God I never feel anything like it again."

He felt a twinge of guilt. "I had no idea you were so sensitive. I assure you, I—"

"Your game is not worth it. Whatever it is."

"Whatever do you mean?" he demanded.

"That thing is poisonous." Her voice rang with authority, even in the muffled, soundproof room.

Victor was surprised at how uncomfortable he felt. "Aristocrats throughout the ages dosed themselves with tiny bits of poison over a period of years, becoming immune to anything their enemies might throw at them. That's what has happened to me, my dear. Immunity."

She shook her head. "You're not as immune as you think you are. And if you're so hung up on facing the truth, then face that one, Victor. You shouldn't have this thing. Whatever you did to get it was wrong. Whatever you're planning to do with it is wrong, too."

He was so amazed at her gall that it took a moment to find his voice. Her self-righteous tone infuriated him. "And where does this talent for tedious moralizing come from?" he mocked. "Not from me. Certainly not from Alix."

"Maybe it's all mine," she said. "Maybe I found it all on my own, with no help from any of you."

"Ah. The angel of judgment rises above the cesspit of her past. Transcending the sins of her lying, thieving, fornicating ancestors."

"Stop it, Victor."

He snapped the case shut and placed it in the drawer. His hands shook with anger. He hadn't been so furious in years, not since Peter—

No. He did not want to think about Peter.

He slammed the drawer shut. "That's enough shocking revelations for us this morning. It's time to deliver you back into the care of your new guard dog. God knows what might happen to him if he comes sniffing after you in a place so steeped in sin."

"Enough, please, Victor."

The misery on her face prodded at something inside him that was rusty and stiff, better left untouched. The feeling made him even angrier. He swung the door open. "After you," he said coldly.

She preceded him out of the room, holding herself very straight.

He armed the alarms, wondering if he should change his divine override computer access code. But then again, why bother? With the opinion she had of him, the girl would never guess the code, anyway.

Not in a million years.

Chapter

21

There would be plenty of time to grill her later. No reason to bother her if she was feeling silent and solitary, Seth told himself again.

He'd tried to persuade her to sit in the sheltered cabin for the boat ride back to the city, and a mute shake of the head was all he'd gotten for a reply. She'd stared out at the water, heedless of the wind and the cold, whipping rain. When he tied up the boat, she disdained his help and clambered out on her own. It made him nervous.

Once in the car, he fired up the engine and turned the heat up to full blast. "So?" he demanded.

She gave him a confused little shrug.

His patience was wearing eggshell thin. "Hey." He waved a hand in front of her eyes. "Anybody home in there? Tell me what happened."

"It went all right." Her voice was completely flat and colorless. "I did exactly what you wanted me to do."

He was suspicious of the blank, staring look in her eyes. "He told you it was the Corazon?"

She turned away. "Not exactly. It was a Walther PPK, in a plastic bag, housed in a hard plastic case. Recently acquired, and not for him. For a client. He said it was a stolen murder weapon."

"So far so good," he said doubtfully.

"He told me that the stain . . . was fresh."

He puzzled over her halting words. "Stain? What stain?"

"Of violence." Her face was taut with strain.

"Huh." He pondered that. "That was all he told you?"

She shook her head. "I led him, a little. I pretended to sense that it had been used to murder a woman. His reaction seemed to confirm it, so I went for it. I hope I did the right thing."

He could not believe his luck. Literally. "You planted it?"

"I stuck it under the foam, in the carrying case."

"And you're sure he didn't see you do it?"

"My hair was draped over my hand, and I was blocking his line of vision with my body. I'm reasonably sure he didn't see me do it."

He studied her tight, miserable face, his gut clenching with apprehension. "What's wrong?" he demanded. "You should be glad. You want to get this guy, right?"

"I guess so," she said dully. "It's just that I feel . . ."

"What?"

She threw up her hands. "More betrayal and double-crossing. I'm sick of it. I just want to be honest. Clear. With Victor, with everyone."

His teeth clenched at her tone. "Some of us have to compromise our principles just to survive, princess."

"Oh, God, please don't. Please, not you, too."

Shit. She was crying again, and it was his own goddamn fault. They didn't have time for this. He tried to pull her into his arms, but she was stiff and unyielding. Finally he let go and put the car in gear, feeling like an asshole. She sat there, shoulders jerking. Tangled locks of blond hair poked out of her hood. She finally noticed their route, and shoved her hood back, alarmed. "Where are you taking me?"

"Someplace safe," he snapped back. He was grateful she was speaking, in spite of her accusing tone. He preferred her pissed off and snappish to catatonic. Or worse, crying. God, how he hated that.

"I want to go home, Seth. I need some time alone."

"Dream on. No way am I leaving you alone. Not after today."

Her eyes blazed. "Seth, I am this far from losing it." She held up two fingers in a circle that didn't quite close. "Take me home, right now!"

"Home is a piss-poor idea. I can feel it."

"I feel, too, Seth. Too much. But right now I need to lock myself in my room and lie face down on my bed for a long time. Completely alone."

He darted into another lane. "You can lie face down in the hotel."

"Not with you around. You take up a lot of psychic space, Seth Mackey. No. Turn this goddamn car around and take me home."

"You're tormented by the fact that you betrayed your beloved uncle, hmm? And after he gave you that pretty necklace, too."

She stared down at her shaking hands, and clenched them into white-knuckled fists. "My God, you make me angry."

"Truth hurts, don't it?" He was unable to keep the sneer from his voice. "Victor may be your uncle, and he may be rich and powerful, and he may give you presents and treat you like a princess, but he's a murdering scumbag who deserves everything that's coming to him. So if you're having a crisis of conscience, hold off. Wait till we get to the hotel. You can have it in the bathroom, where I can't see you."

"Fine." She unsnapped her seat belt and shoved her door open.

He was too busy braking on the rain-slicked pavement to grab her. "Where the hell do you think you're going?"

"Someplace where you can't see me."

Raine slammed the door shut behind her and darted into the traffic.

The light went green. Horns blared and traffic surged around him. He tried to follow her gray-clad figure out of his rearview mirror as she climbed over the median and darted across the opposing line of traffic.

He was losing her in the gloom, two lanes too far to the right to turn after her with all these goddamn cars in his way, and by the time he managed to get over to the left and turn around, she was gone.

He was screaming obscenities into the windshield, and other motorists were giving him nervous looks. One was eyeing him while talking urgently into a cell phone. He lunged for his own and fumbled with it, hitting the sequence for Connor.

Connor picked up instantly. "It's about time you got back to me," he snapped. "I've left you six messages already, and we have to—"

"Connor, do me a favor. Open up the X-Ray Specs on Raine's house. Now, quick. Don't take your eyes off them until I get there."

There was a startled silence. "The shit must have really hit the fan for you to be calling me Connor," he said slowly.

"No time for wise-ass bullshit. I'm tailing her home, but she's got too much of a head start on me for the sick feeling in my stomach."

"Gotcha," Connor said, with a businesslike air. "Later."

The phone clicked off. Seth grabbed the handheld from the glove compartment. There she was, five kloms ahead, almost out of range, blipping away. He dropped the monitor to his lap and concentrated on driving too fast, a skill at which he fortunately had a great deal of practice. He wove through traffic, ignoring the cacophony of offended horns, hoping like hell that no cops would spot him.

The cell phone rang. His stomach sank lower than he ever knew a stomach could go. "Yeah?"

"It's a bad scene at Templeton Street." Connor's voice was hard and tense. "Your lady's got company in the garage. Black ski mask and gun. You're closer than any of us. Floor it."

She'd thought that getting away from Seth's taunts and jeers would make her feel better, but surprise, surprise . . . she felt worse.

She shivered in the back of the cab. Just the short dash to the shelter of the bus stop had drenched her. The beautiful Prada boots were clammy from splashing through puddles, but she barely felt the chill. She couldn't register that sensory information and still think about Victor's revelation.

Her father. How was it possible?

One thing was certain. She didn't dare tell Seth. His reaction to learning that she was Victor's niece had been bad enough. She cringed at the thought of his reaction to finding out she was Victor's daughter.

She stared at the lights that blurred through the rain-streaked glass, hoping that Seth wouldn't storm into her house tonight. She didn't have the strength to deal with his anger. It was all she could do to process the shocking knowledge that touching the Corazon pistol had revealed to her.

She had told Seth that she'd faked her reaction to the gun, but she had lied. The gun had vibrated in her hand, like a trapped animal. Both hot and hideously cold. The memory made her queasy. She wrapped her arms around her waist and tried to think of something else. Eagles swooping, snow-capped mountains at sunrise, the ocean.

No image of tranquil beauty was strong enough to cleanse her of the remembered sensation, like a blow to the solar plexus. And the images, racing through her mind: white carpet, spattered blood, tulips scattered across the floor. Screaming. Oh, God. She pressed her hand against her stomach, wondering how long this would last. It was worse than the dreams, because there was no waking from it. She just had to grit her teeth and endure.

Being with Victor on Stone Island had tuned her like a radio to this awful new frequency. She felt raw, torn open. Too much information pouring in. Maybe it was her overwrought imagination, she told herself bracingly. A chorus of sarcastic voices cackled and hooted in her head at the lame attempt to deny reality.

She was Victor's daughter. She had to avenge her uncle against her father, not the other way around. She could go crazy, reasoning it out, but nothing had changed, really. Murder was murder.

The cab pulled up at her house, and she sighed with relief. It would be dark and cold, but at least it would be private. Her stiff hands could barely handle the money. The bills and coins kept sliding from her numb fingers. She got out of the cab.

The house looked desolate, almost menacing. The untrimmed hydrangeas spread out long branches, dripping with rain. The windows that flanked the front door regarded her like cold, unfriendly eyes.

She spun around to tell the cabbie to stop, but his taillights were already receding, picking up speed. Too fast now to chase him down. He turned the corner, and was gone.

Don't be fanciful. Don't be ridiculous. Don't let your imagination run away with you. Alix's scolding tone echoed in her head as she moved slowly up the walk. It was just an empty house, and her car was parked in the garage. If she didn't like the place, she could go in, get her car keys, pack her suitcase and check into a hotel.

That was a great idea, in fact. That was exactly what she would do. She approached the house so slowly that raindrops began to sneak into the collar of her coat, like chilly little fingers.

After today, it would be a miracle if she weren't paranoid, Raine told herself, fumbling with the key. The phone was ringing inside, but there was no use in hurrying. Her fingers would not cooperate.

She had been an idiot to run away from Seth. He might be rude and difficult, but she would have given anything to have him beside her right now, saying something sarcastic and infuriating. His warm, solid presence would drive away any goblins that inhabited this murmuring darkness.

How embarrassing. The first big tantrum she'd ever had in her whole, decorous, polite life; and she had to end up feeling like a fool. She dropped her key for the third time, and almost yelled with frustration.

Finally, she made it inside. It was cold and dark, but nothing jumped out to bite her, thank goodness. She stripped off her coat, turned the thermostat up and flipped on light after light on her way to the bedroom. The phone rang again as she perched on the wing-back chair and started unlacing the soggy boots. She'd left muddy footprints all over the beige carpeting. Should have taken them off in the foyer. She let the phone ring, unable to contemplate talking with her mother.

She peeked at the machine. Five messages.

Strange. She never had so many. It wasn't like Alix to call obsessively, and no one else knew she was here. None of her far-flung friends had this number. Her stomach did a slow, lazy flip.

The machine clicked on, the outgoing message played. The beep sounded. "Raine, are you home? Pick up the phone. Now! Move it!"

She lunged for the phone, weak with relief. "Seth?"

"Christ, Raine, you turned off your fucking cell phone!"

"I'm sorry. I—"

"Never mind. No time. What room are you in?"

"The bedroom," she faltered. "Why—"

"Does the door lock?"

She was shaking so hard she wanted to fall down. "It has a flimsy little lock, yes," she said, teeth chattering.

"Shit," Seth muttered. "Lock it. Get a weapon. A lamp, a bottle, anything. Then get into the bathroom, and lock that, too. Move it."

"Seth, please, what's happening? Why—"

"Get off the fucking phone and *do* it!"

The strength of his will leaped through the wires like a blast of hot wind. The receiver flew out of her fingers like a live thing, pulling the cradle off the table, thudding onto the floor in a tangle of wires.

In the silence that followed, she heard it. The swinging door that led from the dining room to the stairs. The squeak was quickly silenced.

There were no more doors to squeak. The stairs were thickly carpeted. There would be no more warnings.

She lunged for the door. Bright, metallic panic pumped through her body. Step one, lock bedroom door. Done. Step two, find a weapon. Her umbrella was in the basket in the foyer. Her pepper spray was in her purse, next to the cell phone on the table in the foyer. The knives and the cast-iron skillet were in the kitchen. Bedrooms yielded a pitiful household arsenal.

He was coming up the stairs. This was not her imagination. It was horribly real, and she had to react, right now. She rummaged across her dresser. Hair sticks, too small and fragile. She grabbed the hairspray, the hair dryer. Her eyes fell on the bedside lamp, made of brass. She grabbed it just as the doorknob turned. Rattled.

She dove for the bathroom with her armful of makeshift weapons. The stuff crashed to the floor, the bulb of the lamp exploding across the tiles. She flipped on the light, yanked the door shut, locked it.

Three loud, awful, crunching thuds and she heard the bedroom door splinter and give. She was huddled on the floor next to the toilet, shaking so hard she could barely move, tears of panic streaming down her face. White, all around her, white tiles, white fixtures . . . it was the curse of the Corazon, she should never have touched the hellish thing; it was speeding through time and space, coming to get her, and there would be crimson spattered all over the bright white—

Raine gritted her teeth and made a choked, growling sound deep in her throat. She was not a sniveling coward. She would not go out like this. She was a Lazar. She hadn't come so far and tried so hard to end up a pathetic victim. She struggled to her feet and seized the brass lamp from the top, so the weighted pedestal would serve as a club.

Monster man was going to have to fight for her blood.

The bathroom doorknob turned, rattled. Her lips curled back in a silent snarl. She raised the lamp high in her shaking hands and waited.

She had to make this split second count. She stifled a whimper as monster man rammed his shoulder into the door. Once, twice, with a grunt and a muffled obscenity. That was a relief. At least he was mortal, not some demon from the beyond. The monster of the Corazon.

Smash, crunch. He burst in, a huge, black-clad figure.

She swung the lamp down with all her strength. He spun around and parried the blow with his forearm, howling with fury. He slammed her against the wall, knocking the wind out of her. She struggled to draw air into her flattened lungs, clawing at the mask that hid his face.

"Fucking bitch," he hissed. His bloodshot dark eyes glared through the eyeholes at her. He stunned her with a sharp backhand blow across the face. With the first gasp she managed to draw, his smell hit her. Old sweat, liquor . . . and fear.

The smell of liquor made her think of her father. Uncle, her brain corrected, inanely. What a ridiculous thought at such a time. She gasped for breath. "Why?" she croaked.

"Shut up." He seized her by the neck of her sweater and spun her around, twisting her wrists up with a painful wrench. He smacked her, face first, against the wall. She felt a bursting, the warmth of blood running from her nose. Then pain. Everything went black.

Seth chambered the round as he bolted for the front door. Locked, of course. Panic was making him stupid. He cursed the lost seconds as he fumbled with the keys Raine had given him. He threw open the door and tore through the foyer, the SIG ready in his hand. He stopped dead at the foot of the stairs, staring up. Time slowed, to a frozen tableau.

A big man in a ski mask was poised at the top of the stairs, gun in hand, holding Raine in front of him. Her eyes were closed, blood was running from her nose, but she was alive. On her feet, and blocking his line of fire.

Ski Mask stared down. Seth stared up. Each waited for the other to turn over a new card.

The world exploded into movement. Ski Mask shoved Raine ahead of him down the stairs. She bounced against the wall, tried to get her balance, toppled and fell. Seth leaped to catch her with a shout. Her weight and momentum carried them down, and they crashed against the newel post, bringing it and a chunk of banister down with them. Raine landed on top of him, bounced and rolled.

Ski Mask leaped right past them, burst through the swinging doors into the kitchen and ran out the garage.

The hunting frenzy inside him screamed for him to give chase, but when he rolled up onto his knees, he saw Raine lying very still on the carpet, the blood on her face hideously bright against her pallor.

He forgot about Ski Mask, about Lazar, Novak, Jesse, everything. Panic wiped his mind clean.

He felt for her pulse, and almost wept in relief when he found one. Strong and steady. He moved his trembling hands gently over her body, feeling for injuries. He understood, with all the raw energy of fear, how precious and unique she was. That what he valued about her had nothing to do with beauty, or with sex, or power. And everything to do with that bright place in his mind that she inhabited; that encompassed the tiny baby she once had been, the beautiful old lady she would someday be. If he had anything to say about it.

Seth's heart swelled and ached as he ran his hands over her, repeating her name, his voice rough with entreaty while an incoherent litany repeated in his mind: *please wake up, please be all right, please don't leave me alone now that I know the truth, please. . . .*

Her eyelids fluttered. They opened, dazed. She focused on him with difficulty. Tried to smile.

He sagged over her like a puppet with cut strings and pressed his face against her chest. Her arms moved. She draped them over his shoulders. Cold fingers patted his hair. He tried not to burst into tears.

He got the number wrong the first six times he dialed it. He needed a drink, to chill him just enough so he could make his big fingers hit the right goddamn buttons on the goddamn microscopic phone. His arm was swelling. The spiteful bitch had given him a wicked crack with that lamp. She was more like Alix than he'd thought.

God, what a fuck-up. He could have shot the girl's lover. Or controlled him by using her as a hostage. There were a million things he could've done, if he'd had the brains and the guts for them.

He finally got the number right, and the ring sent a fresh wave of dread through him. His stomach cramped and burned.

The phone line clicked open. "Yes?"

"Ah—there's been a problem," he stammered. "But if you'd just give me a little time to fix it—"

"What happened?" The very gentleness of Novak's voice made chills crawl across Riggs's sweating back.

"Her, uh, boyfriend got in the way, and I—"

"I am very disappointed, Edward. I chose you for this job for artistic reasons, not practical ones. To have her father's murderer be the one who brings her to me—the theatricality of it appealed to me. Now I regret having been so fanciful. I regret it very much."

"No, no, please. I swear, I have the situation under control."

"I thought that even a pathetic failure such as yourself would be able to handle such a simple task."

Riggs squeezed his eyes shut. "The guy just appeared in her house, out of nowhere. There was no way to get her out of there without killing him, and I thought—"

"Ask me how much I care if you are forced to kill someone, Edward. Go on. Ask me."

"Please, let me try again," he pleaded. "I've still got her on the monitor. They're not moving yet. I've got her cold. I swear to God."

"And her lover? Are you equal to the task?"

Riggs tried to swallow, but his throat just bumped, dusty and dry and thick. He thought of the death that had looked up at him in those glittering black eyes, waiting for him to make a wrong move. The gun, held easily in his hand, the loose-limbed crouch of a trained fighter.

And him, his gut burning like a bed of barbecue coals, his liver shot, no luck left in him at all. Oh, God, Erin. He let his breath out heavily. "The guy's a professional," he admitted. "Either I kill him, or he'll kill me. It's a fifty-fifty call."

And that was a hopeful estimate, he thought.

Novak was silent. A minute ticked by, then another.

"Follow them if they move," he ordered. "I will now give you the number of a certain person. You will call him to communicate your location. You will rendezvous with him. You will lead him to the girl, and you will keep out of his way and let him do his job. Understood?"

"Yes," he muttered. "And—and—"

"What? Speak up, man."

"Erin," he said desperately.

"Oh. The hammer need not fall just yet. Georg is being a perfect gentleman. A maiden's fondest dream. Here is the number. Are you paying attention?"

"Yeah." Riggs wrote down the number that Novak dictated.

"And Edward?"

"What?" He held his breath, clutching the wheel. "What?"

Novak chuckled softly. "Try to relax."

Riggs's arm went slack, the phone dropping out of his stiff fingers. He touched his arm. It throbbed. It hurt like a bastard, but pain didn't matter. Only Erin mattered. If he could salvage her from the wreck of his life, that would be enough. That would be all he asked. As the hours went by, he asked less and less of life. Run, run, run, ruined old rat. He closed his eyes, and thought of Erin's sweet smile.

Don't be an idiot, honey. You might be all on your own with the devil tonight. God help you, please help you. Even if he can't help me.

Raine laughed at Seth's queasy expression and tried to pull the washcloth out of his hands. "It's not as gory as it looks."

"Easy for you to say. You're not looking at it." Seth yanked the washcloth back and dabbed at her face, looking greenish. "Weird. I've seen plenty of blood, and I've never been bothered by it before."

"Give me that." She seized the rag and finished the job, then flung the grisly looking cloth into the garbage. She looped her arms around his waist and lay her head against his chest. "Thanks for galloping to my rescue. My white knight." She turned her head quickly as his arms tightened. "Careful of the nose, please."

"Sorry. God, Raine. You scared me so bad," he muttered.

She pressed her cheek against the slippery cold leather of his jacket. "I'm sorry about my tantrum," she said. "You get to say I-told-you-so for the rest of your life, if you want."

"Yeah, and you better believe I'll milk it to the bitter end." He tilted her face up and glared into her eyes. "Better not even get me started on that. I'll just get pissed off all over again."

"Fair enough, fair enough," she said hastily. "Let's change the subject. Like, how can I tell if my nose is broken?"

That worked like a charm, to her relief. His glare faded. He reached out to touch her nose, very gently.

"Ow! Careful," she snapped.

"Not broken," he said with conviction.

"How do you know?" She touched it, frowning. "It hurts like hell."

"Mine's been broken three times. Believe me, I know," he assured her. "You're going to have two black eyes, though."

She winced. "Ick."

"Could have been worse. Let's get you to an emergency room."

She blinked. "Why?"

He snorted. "Hello! Raine, you're the one who just got attacked by a guy in a ski mask and thrown down the stairs!"

"Where I landed conveniently on top of you." She rose up on tip-toes to kiss his jaw. "I'm OK. Just shaky. And I have a sore nose."

He studied her face with troubled eyes. 'You seem awfully calm."

"I know. Probably it just hasn't hit me yet. I'll fall apart later for sure." She stroked his jaw, running her fingers over the small muscle that pulsed there. "It can hit me whenever it wants, as long as you're with me. Don't leave me alone tonight, Seth. You make me feel strong enough to face anything."

He grabbed her hand, and kissed it. "No way. Not tonight, or any other night. Not in this lifetime. I cannot believe how close that was."

The tremor in his voice moved her, almost to shivering tears. She fought them back, still petting his tense face. "It's strange," she said. "I don't think he meant to kill me. He didn't hurt me all that much, even when I whacked him with the lamp. He knocked the wind out of me, slapped me, and bonked my nose against the wall. That's it."

"That was enough," Seth growled. "And don't forget, he threw you headfirst down a flight of stairs. You could have broken your neck."

"If you hadn't caught me. He knew you would catch me."

He grunted, unimpressed. "And your point is?"

"No point," she said thoughtfully. "Just details. Like the fact that he was afraid."

"Huh?"

"I could smell it," she explained. "He was scared to death."

Seth looked doubtful. "Of you?"

She made a dismissive gesture with her shoulders. "I doubt it. But he was afraid of something."

Seth kissed the top of her head. "He's going to have to have a damn good reason to be afraid when I get my hands on him. Let's get out of here. We've hung around too long as it is." He scooped her up into his arms and carried her out the front door.

"Put me down, Seth. Don't be ridiculous. I can walk."

"Stop wiggling." He deposited her in the passenger side, and stared up and down the street, as if he were smelling the wind. He got into the car and started it up.

"Shouldn't we call the police?" she asked tentatively.

"Police? Sweetheart, do you feel like spending the rest of the night explaining to the nice officer what you've been up to lately? And the many possible reasons why a hit man might have just paid you a visit?"

"I see your point." She stared down into her lap. "Not really, I guess. So you think that man . . . is connected with what's going on?"

He shot her an eloquent look.

Raine twisted her hands together, feeling foolish. "I would never have thought that Victor would hurt me," she said softly.

Seth let out a grunt of derision. "Are you sure he didn't see you plant that thing?"

"Don't condescend to me," she snapped. "I've had a bad night."

"Yeah, tell me about it," he retorted. "One thing's for sure, though, sweetheart. You don't need any help from me in hunting down the ghosts from your past. They're saving you the trouble. Stand still for fifteen minutes, and they'll be right on your ass."

Chapter

22

He had to assume that the car had been compromised. Time to ditch it and get a clean one. His bag hadn't been out of his sight since the day before, likewise his clothing. Raine had to get rid of every stitch of clothing that Lazar had provided, and they could look for someplace to hide and rest. He stared at highway signs, trying to orient himself. He saw signs for a mall, and flicked on the turn signal.

"Seth, how did you know that guy was in my house?"

He'd been dreading that question. He shook his head, considering and abandoning various lies and prevarications.

She waited. "You planted your spy stuff in my house, didn't you?"

Her still, quiet voice revealed nothing. That made him extremely nervous. He let his breath out slowly. "Yes," he admitted.

"Why?"

He turned off onto the strip mall that led to the neon signs for the mall, noting with relief that there was a car dealership right down the road. "It had nothing to do with you at first," he said reluctantly. "Victor's mistress was the previous occupant of your house. We were watching her. Then she disappeared, and you showed up."

"And you watched me," she finished.

"Yeah." He pulled into a parking space and cut the motor. "I watched you. After a while, I couldn't stop watching you. Not if you'd put a gun to my head. I don't regret it, and I won't apologize for it."

He braced himself to withstand fury and outrage, but none was forthcoming. When he dared to peek, she was gazing out at the Home Depot across the parking lot, her face misty and perplexed. She turned to him with worried eyes. "Have other people seen us make love?"

"No way," he said emphatically. "I saw to it."

She looked down. "That's good. I wouldn't like that at all."

"Me neither." He reached for her hand. "What's mine is mine."

She looked down at her slender wrist, engulfed in his big hand. A laugh exploded out of her. "Conan the Conqueror," she murmured.

He shrugged and just sat there, holding her hand in the dark for forty or so precious seconds that they could not afford to waste.

Her fingers wiggled inside his. "I've told you everything, Seth. It's time for you to lay your cards on the table, too."

"Truth time has to wait. We've got to shake off your ghosts."

Her eyes widened. "You think we're being pursued?"

"Let's just say we should definitely cover our asses."

She bit her lip and stared down at their clasped hands. "Do you promise me that once we get somewhere safe, you'll tell me what's going on?"

"I promise," he said rashly, popping the locks open. "Let's go."

They ran hand in hand through the rain to the nearest clothing store. He flagged down the first salesgirl he saw. "We're in a serious hurry. Bring us a pair of jeans, a T-shirt, a wool sweater, underwear, socks, hiking boots, and a winter coat. Size six. Quick."

The girl took one look at Seth's blazing eyes and Raine's gory, bloodstained sweater. Her jaw went slack with alarm. "Don't you, uh, wanna pick the stuff out yourselves?" she faltered. "Colors, and stuff?"

"No time!" he barked. "Move it!"

She backed away. "Um . . . lemme call the manager."

"Never mind." Raine cast an irritated look at Seth. "I'll pick them out, but stick close so you can ring them up right away, OK?"

A flurry ensued, of grabbing things off the rack, checking labels in breathless haste. Then he spotted the underwear bin. He grabbed a random handful of thong panties. See-through lace, in awesome, lurid colors. Black, hot pink, purple, lime green, lipstick red. He flung them on the counter. "Put these on the tab."

"Those are thongs," Raine said, blushing.

He leered at her. "Yum."

Raine was busy struggling into a navy blue parka when he spotted the nightie. It was a peachy color in a clingy knit that would hit her just above mid-thigh and show off every curve and hollow. And it would peel off. Stretchy, just like he'd always wanted.

He yanked it off the hanger and flung it onto the pile in the salesgirl's arms. "Ring that up, too. Hurry up."

"Yes, before he finds something else he likes," Raine snapped.

He paid out of his thick wad of emergency cash. As soon as they were back inside the Toyota, he was yanking clothes out of the bags and biting off the plastic label tabs. "Off with your clothes, babe. Quick."

Raine looked at the cars driving past, and back at him, appalled. "Right here?"

"Every stitch. I can feel them breathing down our necks."

She hesitated, looking bewildered. He grunted and yanked open the sash of her trench coat.

That jolted her into action. "No, no, I'll do it." She tugged her boots off with a wistful sigh. "These boots were so beautiful."

He pulled his knife out of his pocket while she was peeling off her jeans and underwear and slid his knife beneath the sole of one of her discarded boots, managing at the same time to keep an eye on the tantalizing nest of ringlets at her crotch. She pulled on one of the thong undies. The hot pink one, he noted with unquenchable interest.

"These things are not comfortable, Seth," she grumbled.

He gave her a wolfish, unrepentant grin. "Sorry, sweetheart."

He peeled back the upper. Bingo. He pulled out the tiny chip with its dangling antenna. "Check this out."

She stopped in mid-shimmy, her new jeans halfway up her thighs. Her jaw sagged in horror. "Victor?"

"Hurry, Raine," he said grimly.

She needed no further encouragement. In moments, she was freshly clothed and ready.

"Leave it all there on the floor," he instructed. "Let's go."

"We're just leaving the car?"

"We'll get it later, if we can," he said indifferently.

He grabbed the bag that held his laptop and his X-Ray Specs gear, and pulled her through the pelting rain at a dead run, expecting every set of headlights to veer towards them, for someone to lean out and open fire. They darted across the highway, to Schultz's New And Used Cars. Fifteen minutes later his emergency cash wad was a hell of a lot slimmer, and Samuel Hudson, one of his alternate identities, was the proud owner of an only slightly dented bronze '94 Mercury Sable. Not what he would have chosen, but it was the best of the lot for the cash he had on hand.

After forty minutes of winding torturously through streets and back roads, Seth was reasonably sure they weren't being followed. He got onto a small highway that began to climb into the hills. The rain got heavier, verging on slush. On the outskirts of a little town called Alden Pines, there was a neon sign that read "Lofty Pines Motel–Cabins–Cable–Vacancy." He pulled into the long, forested driveway and parked.

The desk clerk was a fugitive's wet dream, deeply involved in an old Clint Eastwood movie that flickered on his twelve-inch screen. He was completely unperturbed by Seth's preference for paying in cash, and barely glanced at the fake driver's license before shoving a key attached to a cedar shingle across the scarred counter.

"Cabin number seven," he said, eyes riveted on the screen. "Check-out time, eleven-thirty."

The room itself was musty and cold. Seth fiddled with the antiquated heating device and Raine dragged the extra wool blankets out of the closet. The radiator hummed and clanked. The cracked, brownish lampshade cast a dim light onto the fake wool paneling, the threadbare furniture. The stark reality of the past twenty-four hours rendered them speechless. They stared at each other across the bed.

Raine shrugged out of her new coat and walked over to him. She pushed gently on his chest until he understood that she wanted him to sit down. He did so. The lumpy bed sagged under his weight.

She crossed her arms, adorably cute in her new, raspberry red wool sweater. It clung to her soft, braless tits. "So?" she prompted.

The pink swelling on her face would ripen tomorrow into bruises. It made him clench up inside, to think of how close to the edge she'd come tonight. "Let's get into bed," he suggested.

A half-smile curved her solemn, sexy mouth. "If you think you can distract me from this conversation with sex, think again."

"No way," he protested. "I just want us to get warm." He rummaged through the bags until he found the nightie. "Put this on."

She took the tiny scrap of a thing, and regarded it with deep suspicion. "This is supposed to keep me warm?"

"No," he said curtly. "I'm the one that's going to keep you warm."

She disappeared into the bathroom. He stripped, laid the SIG on the bedstand, got the condoms out of his bag and slid naked into the bed with a harsh gasp. It was like a wintertime leap into Puget Sound.

After a ridiculously long time, the bathroom door squeaked open. She stood, silhouetted against the light for a moment before she stepped out into the room.

She did it to him every damn time. He just couldn't get used to how beautiful she was. The peach thing clung tenderly to her body, showing off the sway of her breasts, the curve of her belly, the soft indentation of her navel. Her eyes had that soft, shining look that made his throat tighten up until it hurt. "Come here," he said, scooting over to the icy side. "I warmed it up for you."

She smiled her thanks and slid under the covers, sighing with pleasure when he pulled her close against his heat. He ran his hands all over her body, needing to reassure himself that she was real, and safe. Warm and soft and right here in his arms. He pressed his aching erection against her thigh and pulled up the brief skirt. She was naked beneath it, her soft downy curls open to his teasing fingers.

She stiffened. "Wait. You promised, Seth. I need to know—"

"Please, Raine," he pleaded. "The adrenaline got me so jacked up. I have to touch you. I was so scared of losing you tonight."

She gave his chest a little push. "You're not getting away with it this time, my love. Adrenaline is no excuse. I had an adrenaline rush, too, you know. I don't know why you're so afraid to talk to me, but you have got to get over it. Right now."

He rolled onto his back and stared at the ceiling. At least she had called him "my love." He would cling to that when it all went to shit.

"It's true," he said tightly. "I don't want to talk. Talking is where I get into trouble. At least when it comes to . . . relationships."

"Trouble? What trouble?"

He rubbed his face with a grimace of discomfort. "You've seen how I am. You saw it tonight. I open my mouth, and things just come out. And I ruin everything. Every time."

"Oh, Seth," she whispered.

"I'm so fucking scared of wrecking this." His voice came out rough and raw. It embarrassed him. He covered his face with his hand.

Raine cuddled closer. "I'm not afraid of the truth," she soothed, stroking his hair. "And even if I get mad at you, it's not the end of the world. I've gotten mad at you lots of times, remember? And here I am."

"Right. I have a hit man to thank for that," he said sourly.

She kissed his nose. "Don't be silly."

He closed his eyes and cautiously allowed himself to enjoy the little butterfly kisses, her fingers stroking his hair. "Easy to say right now," he said. "Wait till one of my moods comes over me. Then you'll see."

"I've already seen you at your worst, Seth Mackey. More than once. And it's true. You can be just awful. Despicable."

He opened his eyes. She wasn't exactly laughing, but he distrusted that bright sparkle in her eyes. "I don't see what's so goddamn funny," he growled.

She pulled his hand up to her lips and kissed his knuckles. "It's so simple, Seth," she said. "You're being sweet to me, and everything works beautifully. It's easy. Just . . . keep on being sweet to me."

He stared down at her pink, amazingly soft lips as they brushed against his big knuckles, covering them with tender little kisses. "I can't always be sweet," he said starkly.

"Why not?"

He pulled her closer, almost angrily. As if someone were trying to drag her away from him. "Because the world's not like that."

Her smile was so beautiful it made his chest burn. Her fingers were so cool and soft, stroking his hot cheek. "Then let's change the world," she whispered.

Breath jerked into his lungs in sobbing heaves. She did not protest when he rolled on top of her, settling his hard weight into the cradle of her hips. Her body softened, clasping him. Accepting him.

Seth was a millimeter away from losing it. The only way to hold his emotions together was to kiss her, with all of himself. All his desperate hunger. Need pounded through his body, but he held it back, trying to express with his kiss everything that was so impossible to say. His anger and grief and confusion, his growing awareness of how important she was to him. How much that awed and terrified him.

If a kiss could communicate that, this kiss would. He would tell her with his lips and his tongue, with every caress, every nuzzle and licking, swirling kiss. He peeled down the thin straps of the nightgown, pulling it down to her waist, and lost himself in the magic landscape of her body, all the secret hollows and hillocks and hidden places.

Her breath fluttered through her, sweet and light, like the sudden flight of surprised birds. He caressed and suckled her until she was just the way he wanted her, flushed and dazed and desperate. He would learn any language she wanted, if she would only give him time, but for now, this was the only language he had. He would be as eloquent in it as he knew how to be.

He touched her between her legs, a love poem of circles and spirals, until she opened up and pressed herself against him in mute pleading, and he slid down beneath her thighs to continue the love poem with his mouth. Her sweet taste was ecstasy, the baby-smooth skin of her thighs clenched and trembling against his face, the folds of her sex drenched and pulsing, crying out in the throes of climax.

She reached down and pulled until he slid back up on top of her. "This is the way I always want you to be before we make love," he told her, grabbing a condom. "Wide open from coming like crazy. Both sets of lips pink and soft from being licked and kissed."

Raine clutched his shoulders and pushed her hips against him eagerly as he entered her. She rested her chin against his shoulder, and he felt the exact moment when something deep inside her body and heart and mind let go, giving herself up to him. He followed her, diving into a new world, a shining place beyond all words. They melted, fused. Her pleasure and his were one single rocking, sighing blur of light and heat.

This time, he wasn't alarmed at all when she melted into tears. He finally felt the rightness of it. Like soft rain in the springtime, rustling on the leaves. A fragrant, healing balm. He vibrated with her, cradling her head against his chest and making sure her precious sore nose was turned to the side.

He stroked her hair and the words just rolled out of him. Halting, and breathless, but he didn't choke on them at all. "I love you, Raine."

She was so startled she stopped crying. When she breathed again, she shuddered and hitched. "I knew that," she whispered. "But I didn't know that you knew it. And I certainly didn't expect . . ."

"Expect what?"

"For you to be the first one of us to say it," she said bashfully.

He waited, squeezing her tightly against him. He could feel the hot wet tears against his chest. She sniffled, her breath hitching. "So?" he said expectantly.

She sniffed, more aggressively. "Hmm?"

"You got something to say to me?" he prompted.

She shoved him over onto his back and rolled on top of him, wiping her face and laughing through her tears. "You want a formal declaration? I love you, Seth Mackey," she announced. "I always have. From the very start."

He tightened his arms around her waist, afraid of the hugeness of the joy rushing through him. "Really?"

"Oh, yes," she said. "Oh, God, yes."

He wound himself around her and stared at her, amazed and

humbled. Words had deserted him again, but he didn't care. He didn't need them anymore. It was enough for him, just to touch her hair, feel her body fitting against his, to stare into her eyes. Two halves of a perfect whole. The wonder of it made him tremble.

He slid into sleep with the thought that he would do anything to protect this. Anything.

Seth was fast asleep, but Raine was still flying. She was so high, she was terrified to look down now and see how far there was to fall.

Her mind raced. So much information to process. Was it possible that Victor had sent someone to hurt her? It didn't make sense, didn't fit her perceptions and memories of him. Could he have been so affronted by her reproof that he was punishing her? She was sure he hadn't seen her plant the transmitter. She would have felt the change in his energy.

Maybe she just didn't want to believe that her own father—how odd it was to think of Victor that way—could order someone to hurt her. What a sentimental idiot she was. He had ordered someone to murder his own brother, after all. And she felt hurt, of all things. She really was a Lazar, as crazy as they come. Someone sends a hit man after her, and her reaction was hurt feelings.

Seth murmured in his sleep and snuggled closer to her. She nudged his muscular chest until his long, curling black eyelashes fluttered up. She poked again, pitiless. Sleep could come later, after he had fulfilled his promise. "Talk," she said succinctly.

He groaned and stretched. "What do you want to know?"

Raine sat up cross-legged, and pulled one of the wool blankets up over her shoulders. "Begin at the beginning. And don't make me pry it out of you, please."

He picked at the satin blanket trimming, staring up at the ceiling. "I had a brother," he said finally. His voice was hard and flat.

She nodded. "Yes?"

"A half-brother, actually. I pretty much raised him. He was six years younger than me. His name was Jesse."

She patted his chest and waited for him to go on.

He stared up at the ceiling, shaking his head. "So Jesse grows up to become a cop, see. Big joke for both of us, considering our upbringing, but Jesse was a romantic. He wanted to save the world. Rescue kittens stuck in trees, babies from burning buildings, that kind of thing. I personally think he watched too much cop TV."

She could already feel what was coming. She braced herself for it. "What happened to Jesse, Seth?" she asked.

He closed his eyes. "He was undercover, investigating your uncle."

"Oh, no," she whispered.

"Oh, yeah. Victor got bored with being fabulously successful in the legitimate business world. In the past few years, he's started dabbling in the dangerous stuff again. Mostly stolen weapons and antiquities, I think. But what got Jesse and his partner all excited was one of Victor's clients, Kurt Novak. Another collector of stolen goodies. Novak is a serious bad-ass. Makes Victor look like a pussy cat. More money than God, no conscience whatsoever. His daddy is a big man in the Eastern European mafia. Novak was the real prize they were after. They almost nailed him, but somebody tipped Lazar off. I don't know who . . . yet. And Jesse was out on the limb when it got sawed off. Novak killed him. Slowly."

"Oh, Seth," she whispered. She laid her hand on his chest, but he was too far away to feel her.

"I should have been there to help him," he said. "I might have been able to change things. But I was too late."

She wanted to soothe and comfort, but she knew that words would be useless and empty. She pressed her lips together and waited.

Minutes passed. He opened his eyes and looked at her. "So that's the story. I've spent months watching Victor. Waiting for him to make contact with Novak. And when he does, I'm bringing those guys down. Lazar, Novak and the traitor. I've been living for that. Just that. I sure as hell didn't plan on . . . something like you happening to me."

She settled against his chest, letting her hair drape over him. "So you and I have more in common than I thought."

He played with a lock of her hair. "I guess so," he said doubtfully.

She stretched out next to him and propped herself on her elbow. "Tell me about Jesse," she asked gently.

He looked startled. "Like what?"

"What was he like?"

He looked clouded for a minute, and then he gave a hard little shrug. "He was nuts," he muttered. "A clown. Incredibly smart. He had these weird green eyes that were kind of too big. Huge feet. Mad scientist hair. When he was too busy to cut it, it just knotted into dreads. And he was a tender-hearted sap. Always in love, always giving away the shirt on his back. He never learned. Never."

She smiled at the image he was creating. "Go on."

His eyes grew distant, and he fell silent. She was about to ask what was wrong when he started up again, in a halting voice. "One time, it was Halloween. He was about eight, I think. Mitch, my stepdad, had locked me in the closet for some reason—"

She stiffened. "Oh, God."

"Oh, it was no big deal, I probably deserved it," he said, his expression faraway. "Anyway, Mitch got blind drunk and forgot about me for about twelve hours. Jesse couldn't find the key, so he got his blanket and pillow and curled up on the other side of the door. He didn't want me to be all alone in the dark. He passed me all of his Halloween candy that would fit under the door. All the flat stuff. Mini Hersheys, mini Nestlés Crunch, all of it. He even squashed his peanut butter cups. I tried to make him go to bed, but he just had to keep me company."

Raine's throat tightened. "Oh, Seth."

He smiled at the memory. "I think I was off chocolate for years after that. But if you're sitting in the dark on top of a pile of stinking gym shoes, and somebody gives you chocolate, you eat it."

He paused. His fleeting smile faded, replaced by bleakness. His eyes flicked up to hers. "So there you go. That was Jesse for you. Satisfied?"

Raine pressed her cheek against his chest to hide her tears. "Oh, Seth. I think I would have loved your brother."

"Yeah, well . . . I sure did." His face contracted. He jerked away from her, rolled over onto his stomach and pressed his face into the pillow.

Raine draped herself over his broad back and absorbed the racking tremors into herself. Covering and protecting him. She had no idea how long they stayed like that. They slipped loose of linear time. She would have stayed years if it could have healed him. Centuries.

He finally stirred, and she lifted herself up. "Seth—"

"No more stories about Jesse. He's dead now. Let him stay dead."

She did not flinch away when he grabbed her and rolled on top of her. "Gently," she said, cupping his face. "I don't want you lost in some tornado in your mind a million miles away. Come back to me."

His body was rigid, his eyes so lost and dark with pain that her throat burned for him. "Think island sunset," she urged, covering his face with soft kisses. "Think garlands of tropical flowers."

He rolled over and pulled her on top of him, gripping her hips painfully hard. "You run it," he said roughly. "I can't control anything. I don't know how to give you what you want."

She kissed away the tears that had trickled out of the corners of his eyes, rubbing her wet cheek against his hot, scratchy one. "Sure you do," she told him. "You always have, from the beginning. You're brilliant at it. You're inspired."

She smoothed the condom over him with a slow, lingering caress, and guided him into herself, sinking down over him, enveloping his burning heat with a sobbing sigh of pleasure. He grasped her waist with a groan as she rose up onto her knees and sank down again, taking more of him. Deeper, bolder. Soothing him with her silken softness.

Raine pried her hands away from her waist and held them out, spreading them wide. She swayed over him in a divine dance of love and acceptance, rejoicing that he finally trusted her enough to be vulnerable; to ask, with arms and mind and heart wide open, for her love and healing. And she could not help but give him what he needed. It would have destroyed her to withhold it.

She wanted to heal all his wounds, fulfill all his dreams.

She wanted to love him forever.

Chapter

23

It was torture to disentangle himself from her velvety warmth, but his back was throbbing where he had slammed it into the newel post, and he was just now starting to notice it, in a big way.

Raine murmured a sleepy protest. "What's the matter?"

"Sore back," he said. "No big deal."

She ran her hand across his shoulders. "Take a hot shower," she suggested, stroking his spine. "It might loosen it up."

He could think of fifty better ways to loosen up, but he didn't want her to think he was a total sex maniac. He reached back with a short wince and massaged it. "Don't tell anybody, but I'm a little old for stunts like the stairs tumble."

"How old are you?"

"Thirty-six in about two weeks."

She kissed his shoulder. "I'm only twenty-eight, you cradle robber, you."

He leered at her. "Want to take a shower with me, little girl?"

She stretched luxuriously under the covers. "I can't face the cold. And I don't think I can move yet. My bones are liquefied."

"That's not your bones that are liquid, sweetheart."

The kiss he gave her could easily have segued into something hot and pounding and delicious, but he dragged himself away. They could always have more sex later. Lots of it. For the rest of their lives.

"Would you like me to call out for some food?" she asked.

His stomach rumbled eagerly at the idea. "Go for it."

"Anything in particular?"

He gave her a goofy, foolishly happy grin. "I'm not fussy."

The water pressure was better than he expected in a dive like this. He relaxed under the hot, pounding spray for a long time, and when he came out, she was asleep. He tiptoed around the room, trying not to wake her. He felt like he was floating. Wanted to laugh and cry at every little thought that passed through his mind. He pulled on his jeans and silently scooted the armchair up next to the head of the bed, so he could just sit there and stare, openmouthed, at how beautiful she was. Every tiny detail fascinated him. The faint, rosy flush that stained her cheek was the most heartbreakingly perfect thing he had ever laid eyes on. He could spend the rest of his life exploring her.

And he would. She might not know it yet, but she was never getting rid of him. He was sticking to her like glue.

She jerked awake when the phone rang. She gave him a sleepy, satiated smile as she reached for it. "Hmm? The . . . oh, yes. Thank you. How much? Ten ninety-eight. OK, thanks . . . we'll be right down."

"Food's here?" He yanked on his boots and sweater, shrugged on his jacket and shoved his SIG into his pants. "I'll go get it." One kiss, to send him high and flying, and he set off down the dark path in a loose, easy lope. The rain had eased off, and the wet pine needles were springy beneath his feet. It smelled good. He was ravenous.

It wasn't sound that alerted him, because the guy was utterly silent. It was a weird rush of displaced air. A shiver on the back of his neck, like the sigh of a lover's breath—but cold, not warm.

He spun just in time to see a cannonball of darkness hurtling towards him. The glow from the curtained window of their cabin glinted across the dark surface of a long blade, stabbing for his gut.

He lunged back, parrying the stab with a chop of his arm, but the guy was in too close. The tip of the blade slashed down Seth's side, a thin, white-hot line. He spun, slammed his elbow into the guy's jaw, felt the jolt, the grunt. Jerked to the side just in time to take the guy's knee in his thigh instead of his balls, fucking ouch, but no time to feel it, no time to grab for the gun. He was dancing back to evade another slash, then another. Ducking back, parrying. Sliding in wet pine needles, going down backwards.

The attacker followed up his advantage and leaped, but Seth blocked his knife arm and grabbed his wrist. He slammed both booted feet up into the guy's stomach, lifted and flung. The guy somersaulted in the air and rolled smoothly back up onto his feet. Seth rolled back over his shoulder, sprang up and yanked out his gun. The guy's leg snapped out, quick as a whip, and kicked the gun right out of his hand.

The light behind him brightened as the porch light switched on. He hoped it would blind the guy and give him a split-second advantage, because he needed one, and fast.

"Seth? What's . . . oh my God!"

The killer launched himself with a menacing shout. Seth spun back sideways alongside him, seized his knife arm at the wrist. Wrenched it up, twisted it back, whipped it down. There was a loud snap. The guy let out a gurgling, agonized grunt. The knife dropped.

There was a small cinderblock structure adjoining the cabin, and Seth opted for the simple and handy expedient of wrenching up the guy's broken arm until he shrieked and bent over, and then slamming him into the cement blocks headfirst. He hauled him back and gave him another one for good measure before he flung the guy down to the ground like the sack of shit that he was. He stared down at the twitching form, chest heaving, and started to shake with retroactive terror. Wow. That had been way too fucking close.

Raine darted towards him, her bare feet flashing over the muddy ground. "Seth, are you all right?"

His breathing was labored. He was pressing his hand against his side, and it was warm and sticky. He yanked up the sweater, glanced at it. No big deal. His sweater and jeans were slashed, and the cut was long and messy, but it looked relatively shallow.

He pushed Raine's hands away, blocking out her anxious questions. He couldn't even hear her, with the unthinkable thoughts pounding at the door of his mind. He would have welcomed another assassin. A whole pack of them, so they could keep him too busy to think, to reason. To use his worthless brain for the first time in weeks and ask himself how the fuck this guy had found them, with all the tricks he had pulled. All the lengths he had gone to. And right after he had confessed every goddamn secret he had been keeping to his archenemy's only heir.

He hooked his foot beneath the guy's carcass and flopped him onto his back. He leaned over with a hiss of pain and yanked the ski mask off. The top of the guy's head was a bloody mess, but his face was recognizable. Short dark hair, mid-thirties. Average, unnoticeable. Close-set, empty brown eyes, staring up. He put his finger to the guy's carotid artery. Nothing. Just as well, though it would have been interesting to question him. Not the Templeton Street guy. This one had been lighter, quicker. Far more deadly.

He straightened, trying not to wince at the sting in his side. He pulled Raine closer and made her look. "You know this guy?" he demanded.

She shook her head, her hands clamped over her mouth.

"How did he find us?" he asked.

She stared down at the cadaver, her eyes wide and blank.

He slapped her hands down from her mouth, grabbed her shoulders and gave her a shake. "Answer me, Raine!"

Her lips moved, but no sound came out. She gasped in enough breath to finally voice the words, on one stuttering exhalation.

"D—d—don't . . . know!" She began to shake violently.

There would be no questioning her until she calmed down.

He retrieved his gun from the bushes and stuck it back into his pants. Raine was standing right where he'd left her, staring down at the hit man, oblivious to the rain beating down on her head and shoulders. She looked lost. The corpse's face was beaded with rain.

He ducked into the cabin to grab his gear, and took her by the arm. "Come on," he said, pulling her down the path. Raine stumbled beside him like a zombie, her bare feet covered with mud.

He scanned the parking lot and counted the same number and make of cars as there had been when they arrived, with the addition of one black late model Saab sedan, the engine still warm. The bluish light of the TV still flickered from the window of the reception cabin. No faces at the window, no shots out of the dark. No sound, just the rustle of the rain. He unlocked the car, shoved Raine into it and pulled out onto the road, driving as fast as he dared.

His cyborg side was back, cold and effective. He could kill a man and leave the body lying in the mud, no problem. He could drag a shivering, weeping, half-naked woman barefoot over rocks and gravel without a qualm. The bright, shining sensation that had invaded his mind and soul, thanks to Raine, could now be observed from all sides with chilly detachment, like the bizarre, dangerous phenomenon that it was.

A silent half-hour later Raine's teeth had stopped chattering. He decided that he had waited long enough.

"That wasn't supposed to happen, was it?" he asked.

"What?" Her voice was soft. Confused. All innocence.

"Me, surviving. Inconvenient, isn't it? Throws off the whole plan."

"Seth, what are you talking about?"

He had to hand it to her. She was believable down to the last detail.

"Come on, Raine. There's nothing left to be gained by holding back. Tell me how your buddy tracked us down."

"You can't think that I—" She stopped, shook her head. Tears glittered on her face, worthy of a highly trained actress.

"I'm clean. You're clean. The car's clean. We haven't used any credit cards. We're in the middle of nowhere, signed in with a fake ID. Sure, they would have found us eventually, but how did they find us so soon? Can you explain that to me, sweetheart?"

She shook her head. "Don't do this, Seth."

"Take a shower, Seth," he mocked, in a sing-song voice. "It'll loosen up your back. I'll just call out for some dinner. Don't you worry about a thing."

"I just ordered cheeseburgers, fries and a soda from the diner," she whispered.

He pondered that. "I should've thought it through," he said. "You're Victor's long-lost darling, right? They tell me the guy's worth a hundred and fifty million or so. I can almost understand it, even if he did whack your daddy. Let's just let bygones by bygones, shall we? What's a little murder? Happens in the best of families."

"Stop it!" she protested. "You saw what happened at my house! That was real, Seth!"

"Yeah, that does confuse things," he admitted. "But a woman like you might have all kinds of enemies. Particularly if you make a habit of treating your lovers the way you treat me."

She had the tears under control now, assuming they were ever real to begin with. "I never lied to you, Seth," she said, in a stiff, dignified little voice. "Where are we going?"

"Someplace where you can't cause any more damage."

She flinched. "I would never do anything to hurt you."

He allowed part of his mind to assess the possibility that she was telling him the truth. He shied away from the thought.

He wanted it to be the truth too badly. It was his weak spot, his Achilles heel. He had to overcompensate for it, even if it killed him.

The pattern taking shape, the one in which Raine sold him out and set him up to die, made perfect sense in the world where Jesse had been tortured and killed. It lined up just fine with a world where a mother could deliberately swallow so many pills that she just didn't wake up the next morning. That was the real world, where any horrible thing could happen. There were no rules at all. No limits to how horrible things could get.

He pressed his hand against his side, lightheaded. His sweater was getting soggy, and the slash throbbed and burned.

Raine saw the blood on his hand. "You're hurt!"

"No big deal. We're almost there."

"Why didn't you tell me? Stop the car, so I can—"

"One more word, and I put you in the trunk."

She stared with burning eyes at the rain pounding against the windshield. Heat poured from the vent, but it was fake heat, it couldn't touch her. She was lost on a glacier. She would never warm up. Pursued by unknown assassins, and the man she loved was convinced that she had set him up to die. Things couldn't get worse than this.

No, not true. If the man at the motel with the caved-in head had succeeded in killing Seth, that would have been worse. Infinitely worse. That would have been the end of the world.

And he'd come so close. She'd seen the blade flash down but she hadn't seen Seth's response, just a dark blur, a crunch, a thud, and that was that. Not like fight movies, where the eye followed every move as if it were a beautiful dance. There had been nothing beautiful about what she'd seen tonight. Just a brusque, lethal efficiency of movement.

There were a lot of things she didn't know about Seth Mackey.

He slowed and turned onto a steep gravel road. The sedan struggled and spun for a moment, but the tires finally gripped and soon they were bouncing along a narrow, rutted road.

The road dead-ended, the headlights of the car illuminating the porch of what appeared to be a large, ramshackle house. A light burned in the downstairs room off the porch. Seth killed the motor.

The porch door opened. A very large man was silhouetted against the light behind him. Seth got out of the car. "It's me," he said.

Seth opened the passenger side and pulled Raine out, wrapping his fingers around her upper arm like a manacle.

"This isn't necessary," she hissed.

He ignored her, and dragged her towards the house. A muscular, hawk-nosed man with a short beard stared at her, stupefied as Seth pulled her through the doorway.

She blinked, taking in a swift blur of images. A big, smoky kitchen that seemed almost tropically warm. A kerosene lamp burning on the table. A card game was laid out, a coffee pot. Glasses and cups, a bottle of whisky. A sink full of dirty dishes. Two men sat at the table. The man with the beard closed the door and followed them in, leaning against the wall and folding massive arms over his barrel chest.

One of the men at the table was smoking a cigarette. He had the same hawk nose as the bearded man, and his big feet were propped up on the open door of the woodstove. There was a hole in the big toe of his sock, she noticed, before he pulled his feet down and stubbed out his cigarette. He was long and skinny, shaggy-haired, his lean face glinting with golden beard stubble. Green eyes, sharp and watchful.

The other man was clean-shaven and extremely handsome, with

a mane of tawny hair pulled back in a thick ponytail. He had similar green eyes, with which he studied her body with undisguised interest.

The skinny guy with the hole in his sock broke the spell. "What's going on?" he demanded.

"I need a room I can lock from the outside, a padlock. A heater. And blankets."

The three men looked at each other. Looked back at her.

"What the fuck do you think you're looking at?" Seth snarled.

The handsome long-haired guy jumped up. "The attic room ought to work. I'll go scrounge up a futon."

"I'll get a padlock out of the shed," the bearded man said.

The skinny one rose to his feet and reached for a cane. "I'll get some blankets." He gave Seth a hard look as he limped by. "Then you and I are going to have a talk."

"Whatever. Let me get her squared away first," Seth said, pressing his hand against his side. He was paler than she had ever seen him.

The skinny guy's eyes widened. "Jesus, man, what did you do to yourself?"

"Later."

They put her in the attic. There was a bustle of activity, which she could not follow. Someone dragged in a space heater and turned it on right next to her, but she didn't feel the heat. The man with the ponytail draped a blanket over her. The skinny guy was speaking to her, but she didn't hear his voice. He snapped his fingers in front of her face, looking worried, and said something to Seth. Seth shrugged.

The men filed out of the room, Seth last. He cast a hard look at her over his shoulder. She closed her eyes against it.

The door shut. Clunk, rattle, and the padlock was engaged.

Connor popped the first aid kit open and pulled out a roll of gauze. "Get that sweater off," he said. "Let me take a look."

"It's no big deal, I told you. Give me some more of that whiskey."

"Shut up and get the shirt off, bonehead. Some antibiotic ointment and some Band-Aids are not going to kill you."

He dragged the thing over his head with a sigh. Davy pulled a dishcloth out of a drawer, ran hot water over it, and handed it to him.

He sponged the blood streaks off, wincing as Connor smeared antiseptic gel over the long, ugly slice and taped bandages over it. Sean tossed him a red flannel shirt, which he pulled on very slowly and carefully. He was too tired to bother buttoning it.

The three brothers plied him with whiskey and pried the whole tale out of him, bit by bit. By the time they were finished, Seth was so wiped out that even their long, speaking glances to each other didn't bug him anymore. The end of his story was greeted by silence, broken only by the crackle of the woodstove.

"OK," he said, bracing himself. "Get it over with. This is the part where you guys tell me what an asshole I am. Go for it. I'm ready."

"Nah," Connor said. He put an oak log into the woodstove, prodding it with a poker until it nested in the coals. "You got it wrong. This is the part where we calmly discuss our options."

Seth gulped whiskey and wiped his mouth. "I told her everything, get it? Lazar's onto me. If we follow the pistol now, it'll be into a trap."

"Based on the fact that the killer tracked you down tonight?"

Seth was startled by Davy's skeptical tone. "It's the only thing that makes sense."

"Not necessarily," Sean said. "Maybe you slipped up. You're not superhuman. Maybe there's something you don't know."

"There are three possibilities," Connor said. "One, she never planted the chip at all, and told Lazar everything from the beginning. Two, she planted it, Lazar discovered it and is onto the two of you. Three, she planted the chip, Lazar doesn't know, and the ski masks aren't Lazar's. I personally don't favor number one. Why would he attack her if she were collaborating with him? It doesn't jive with what I know of her personally, either."

"What do you know about her personally?" Seth said bitterly.

Connor raised an eyebrow. "I enjoy the distinct advantage of not being in love with her, so trust me, my judgment is way better than yours. Why would she call a hit man to whack you right after you saved her life? Come on, Seth."

Seth shook his head. "There was no other way that guy—"

"Shut up and listen for once," Connor said curtly. "I don't like number two, either. Victor's not the type to show his hand by sending an incompetent goon to attack her. He's the type to rub his hands together and wait until you fall into his trap."

"The second guy was not an incompetent goon," Seth said. He touched his bandaged side with a grimace. "He almost got me."

"Yeah, the second guy worries me," Connor said. "Which brings us to number three. The ski masks are Novak's, not Lazar's. We know that he wants her. And he'll go to any lengths to get what he wants."

Seth buried his face in his hands. "She's in on it," he repeated stubbornly. "There's no other way the guy could have found us. And her boot had an X-Ray Specs beacon in it. I sold that shit to Lazar."

"So?" Davy said. "You dusted her stuff too, right? Maybe he just thinks that she belongs to him, like you do."

"And he tagged her because he wanted to keep an eye on her, like you did," Sean added. "'Cause he's a paranoid control freak."

"Like you are," Connor and Davy finished in unison. They grinned and gave each other a high five.

Seth grunted. "Don't expect me to have a sense of humor tonight."

"You don't have a sense of humor at all," Sean observed. "Why won't you even consider the possibility that she's not lying to you?"

Whiskey and exhaustion let the truth just fall out of him. "I can't afford to consider it. I want it too much."

"Ah. So what you're saying is, you're chickenshit," Sean said.

Seth was too tired and depressed to react. "Better to err on the side of being a suspicious bastard. I'll live longer."

"Yeah, maybe. But your life won't be worth a damn."

Seth didn't even bother to glare at him. "It doesn't matter," he said dully. "Whether she did, whether she didn't, she stays in that room until this is over. I'm following the gun alone. I accept the consequences of what I've done, but that doesn't mean you guys have to."

Davy sloshed some more whiskey into his glass. "Don't be a melodramatic asshole, Mackey. It's not up to you what we decide to do."

Seth stared down into the deep amber color of the liquor. "You guys don't have to risk your lives because of some misplaced loyalty to Jesse. He's gone. He doesn't need you anymore."

"No, but you do," Connor said. He leaned over and poked Seth in the shoulder. "It's not just for Jesse. It's for you. Don't ask me why. You're a pain in the ass, and we still need to have that talk about your social skills, but there it is. I'm in this for you, buddy."

Seth choked on the liquor he was swallowing. Coughing to clear his burning throat made his bandaged side sting like hell. "Hey, I appreciate the sentiment, but at this point, I don't even care if it's a trap, see? I just want to end it. Fold my hand and get out of the game. I can't take the responsibility, and I don't want your help."

"Tough shit," Davy said.

"Count me in," Sean piped up.

"Me, too," Connor said, lifting his glass with a grin.

Davy scowled at him. "Not you, pal. You're still hobbling around on a cane. You're not going anywhere. You get guard duty."

"Like hell."

"No," Davy said, in a big brother voice. "I'll tie you down."

"Let's play a hand of poker on it," Connor wheedled.

"Yeah, and you'll cheat, you slick bastard. Non-negotiable, so just forget it . . . "

The conversation degenerated quickly into an energetic fraternal squabble. Seth tuned out the familiar cadences and stared into the fire. The fire of the whiskey warmed him, fuzzing his brain around the edges, and he struggled to follow his own train of thought. Only an idiot with a death wish would follow a transmitter to an unknown destination, to face an unknown number of adversaries with unknown resources. Truth was, he had never meant to involve the McClouds in the actual takedown. He had always intended for that phase to be his own private party.

He broke into the middle of the argument, which had gotten to the shouting stage. "Let me finish this my own way, guys. That way, if it goes to shit, they can't link me to you."

His words reverberated in the sudden stillness.

"Yeah, right," Connor said slowly. "And what are we supposed to do with Blondie? Keep her in the attic like Rapunzel?"

"Oh, God." Seth closed his eyes and rubbed them. "I don't have the faintest idea. What a fuck-up. God. I'm sorry, guys."

The fire crackled and spat for a few minutes. "I know why you brought her here," Connor said quietly. "And you did the right thing."

"Oh, yeah?"

"Yeah. You brought her here to keep her safe."

Seth shook his head. It was not a negation. "I'm an idiot."

"You aren't the first, and you won't be the last," Davy said.

"I were you, I'd go up to the attic and spend some quality time with your lady," Connor said. "She's in a bad way. And you could use some rest yourself. You look like shit. We've got the Cherokee gassed up and loaded and ready to roll. The Specs are set up and keyed to the Corazon transmitter. The three of us will take turns watching tonight. If it starts to move, we'll call you. We can leave on a minute's notice."

"Yeah. Chill," Sean urged. "We need you fresh and snappy when it starts to move. Here, I made a sandwich. Take this on up to her."

"It won't be long," Connor said. "Things are starting to move."

"The circle is getting smaller," Seth said.

The McClouds looked at him. "Huh?" Sean said.

Seth shrugged. "Just something Jesse said to me in a dream," he mumbled. He looked around himself. Three pairs of similar green eyes regarded him with varying combinations of worry and annoyance.

He hadn't seen that look on anybody's face since Jesse's death. He hadn't thought he would ever see it again.

He grabbed the whiskey bottle and raised it, in a silent salute to brotherhood. He grabbed Raine's sandwich and headed up the stairs.

Chapter

24

R aine jumped to her feet when she heard the lock rattle, wrapping the blanket around herself. She was shaking, but not with fear. She had left fear so far behind she didn't even remember what it felt like.

Seth let himself in, dropping the heavy, palm-sized padlock on top of the dresser. He laid a plate next to it, with something wrapped in a napkin. She was relieved to see that his wound was dressed. The white bandage showed up starkly against his golden skin. A threadbare red flannel shirt hung open over his bloodstained jeans. He held an open bottle of whiskey by the neck. He took a deep swallow.

"You're drunk," she said.

His eyes glittered, with a wild, faraway look. "Medication," he said, pointing to the bandage. "This hurts. I brought you a sandwich, if you're hungry."

"You have got to be kidding."

"Suit yourself." He took another swig.

She pulled the blanket tighter. "Are you going to give me some clothes?" She made her voice sharp and businesslike.

He set the bottle on the dresser next to the padlock and advanced upon her slowly. "I don't see the point," he said. He seized the corner of the blanket and jerked it down, frowning when he saw the nightgown. "That thing is still wet, Raine. You'll make yourself sick. Take it off. The room's warm now. Too warm."

"I don't want to be naked with you."

It was the wrong thing to say. She knew it as soon as it left her mouth and saw the hot flash in his eyes.

"Tough," he said. He jerked the thin straps down, his hands lingering on her skin as he shoved the nightgown over her hips. It felt to the floor around her muddy, scratched feet. She forced herself not to flinch back, or cover herself. She straightened up and composed her face. Let him look. She could still be dignified, even if she was naked.

He studied her body with greedy, minute attention to detail. A dull flush was burned deep into his high cheekbones, and his hands scalded her as they clasped her waist and slid up over her ribs. His fingers explored her carefully, as if he were memorizing her.

Despite his unstable mood and the whiskey on his breath, she was absolutely unafraid of him. She placed the back of her hand against his cheek. "You're feverish," she said quietly.

"Tell me about it. Every time I look at you."

"You should take an aspirin, or some—"

"What a joke," he cut her off, as if she hadn't spoken. "The first time I lose my mind for a woman, and it has to play out like this."

She pressed her hands against his burning forehead, trying to cool him down. "You know that I would never do anything to hurt you," she murmured.

"Shhh. We're not going to discuss it."

"But Seth, we have to—"

He put his finger over her lips. "No, we don't. Off limits. Don't want to go there."

She'd crashed into this stone wall before, but it didn't intimidate her anymore. Not now that she had seen what was on the other side; his gentleness, his enormous capacity for tenderness. She slid her hands under his shirt and around his waist, careful not to touch the bandage.

He jerked back and stiffened. His hands fell away from her. "What the hell are you doing?" he snarled.

"Getting warm. You won't give me any clothes, and I'm cold."

He held himself rigid. "Not a good idea. I'm not in control of myself tonight. At all. Don't push me, Raine."

She pressed her cheek against his burning chest, rubbed it gently against his flat brown nipple. "I know you," she said, in a soft, stubborn voice. "You can't scare me, Seth Mackey."

"Oh yeah?" His arms closed around her, his heat scorching her. "Well, you scare me, babe. You scare me to death."

She pulled him closer and twined herself around him. His response was instantaneous, and she almost wept with relief when she felt the familiar flare of heat from him. She needed all of his devouring hunger, all of his volcanic heat to drive away the bleak horror of what she had seen tonight. She caressed the hot length of his erection and unbuckled his jeans, wrapping her fingers around his hard, fever-hot penis.

It all moved very fast from that point. He toppled her onto the futon, pinning her against the tangle of blankets, his boots still on, his jeans shoved down. She stared at the ceiling, wide open, and cried out when he shoved himself inside her. It was too soon; she wasn't soft or wet enough, but she didn't care, she needed this to melt the glacial cold. To make her feel alive again.

It only hurt for the first few rough, awkward thrusts. His breath was harsh and ragged against her neck. His muscles clenched, fighting for control. He drew himself out slowly, surged in again. Already she was softening; he glided more easily with every deep stroke. She twined her legs around his damp, muddy jeans.

His face was a taut grimace of pain. "You're killing me, Raine."

"No." She pulled his face back down to hers. "I'm loving you."

He wrenched away from her kiss. "I want to believe you," he rasped.

She caressed his face, her body pulsing seductively beneath his. The pain in his voice tore at her. "Trust me," she whispered.

He froze, wedged deep inside her. Time stopped. Everything stopped. The two of them were clenched together as tightly as a fist. She held her breath, staring into his eyes.

His mouth hardened. He shook his head and pulled out of her body. "Roll over."

"No!" She tried to pull him back. "At least look me in the face while we make love. You owe me that much."

"It's not love, and I don't owe you a damn thing."

He flipped her onto her stomach. She turned her face to the side and shut her eyes against the intense feeling of vulnerability, the heat of his hands caressing her bottom, his thighs wedged between hers. He shoved her open, his weight settling down on her, and penetrated her, pushing himself slowly, deeply into her body.

"Damn you," he muttered under his breath.

He pushed away the hair that covered her face and pressed his face against her neck. He stayed that way, vibrating with tension. She pried her arm out from beneath her chest with some difficulty, and grasped one of his big, trembling fists that gripped the blanket by her head. She pulled it to her face and kissed it.

A shudder jerked through him. He lifted his weight off, curving himself over her. Warming and sheltering her. He slid his hand beneath her hips, his long, sensitive fingers seeking until he found her tender cleft. He caressed her slick, swollen clitoris with delicate skill.

"You see?" she whispered, pushing back to take in more of him. "It is love, Seth. It's always like this with us. It always will be. We can't hurt each other. It's against our nature."

"Shhh. Hold still." His fingers tightened around her hand. "I'm right on the edge. I don't want to come yet. Don't move."

Raine waited for him for as long as she could, but the wild woman inside her wanted to drive him over the edge and force him to face the truth about the two of them. She arched her back and slid up and down his hard, pulsing shaft, clenching and releasing. She pleasured herself with his body, hungry and bold. Demanding everything he had to give.

Helplessly, he followed her, giving her the rhythm she wanted. He couldn't deny her what she needed for one second, or even try to resist the force that moved them. He was hers, all hers. Fierce joy blazed through her as she pulled him after her, his wrenching explosion of pleasure echoing her own. His body jerked and pulsed into hers, and his cry sounded like a shout of protest

After several breathless, panting minutes, Seth sat up and started yanking at the laces of his boots. He pulled them off, peeled off his jeans and flung them away too. He lay back down behind her, pulling her close so that her whole back was pressed against his hot chest. His penis, still hard, prodded her buttocks. She gasped as he thrust himself slowly back inside her. His arm clamped across her waist.

"Go to sleep," he said. "I want to stay right here. Inside you."

She clutched the thick muscles of his forearm and almost laughed at the ridiculous idea. As if she could sleep in that condition, so utterly penetrated by his body. Then she felt the liquid heat trickling down her thigh, and tingled with shock. "Seth. We didn't use anything."

His teeth sank delicately into her shoulder, dragging across her damp skin. "No. The condoms are back at the hotel. Want to go ask the McClouds if we can raid their stash?"

"No," she whispered.

"I didn't think you'd be into that."

Raine dug her nails into his arm as his teeth and tongue moved their delicate, nibbling caresses to the back of her neck. "It's amazing, without," he said, in a wondering voice. "I can feel every juicy little detail. I want to explode the second I'm inside you. And I thought I had all this self-control." His hips pulsed against her bottom and he swelled inside her, sliding in and out. "I could fuck you all night long, no problem. I haven't done it without latex since I was fourteen. Congratulations. You've reduced me to a state of adolescent idiocy."

She clenched herself around him, dazed by the risk they were taking, and all that it implied. "You'll never forgive me for that, will you?"

"Not in this lifetime."

"Seth, I—"

"Shhh. No more talk."

The flat, hard tone in his voice silenced her. She swallowed down the lump in her throat and squeezed her eyes shut. At least he was touching her with passionate tenderness. His body knew the truth. She felt it in the way his hands caressed her belly, her breasts, the way his fingers fluttered skillfully between her legs while he surged heavily into her from behind in a slow, relentless cadence.

That went on forever, timeless and lazy and delicious, but finally he began to deepen his strokes, his breath sawing harshly into his mouth against her neck. He muttered something incoherent and jerked her up onto her hands and knees.

That was even better; now she could move, arching and straining against him. She cried out with unbearable excitement at his first deep thrust, and he froze into immobility.

"Don't stop." Her voice shook with breathless urgency.

"I don't want to hurt you," he said shakily.

"Damn it, Seth. You're not. You won't."

She incited him with her panting eagerness, and he let go and gave her what she clearly wanted, deep and hard and driving. She braced herself and thrust back to meet him, reaching for her release.

And he gave it to her. Pleasure stabbed through her whole body, as sharp as a fiery spear at first, and then spreading out in widening ripples of sweet, glowing heat. Every cell in her body trembled like wind-ruffled water. He spurted inside her, filling her again with his scalding heat. They sagged down onto the blanket, still joined.

Raine pressed her face into the blanket to hide tears she knew he would not want to see or hear, shaken and moved. She could get pregnant. And she would be glad if she were, no matter what. Terrified, but glad. She had seen death that night, and life called to life, all the messy, confusing heat of it. She would never shrink from it again.

She woke sometime in the night. Her face was sore, her battered feet stung, the wool blankets were scratchy. Seth's heavy arm blocked half of her lung capacity, and his penis, still deep inside her, forcibly reminded her of certain mundane bodily functions.

"Seth. Are you sleeping?" she whispered.

He stirred and kissed her neck with a short grunt of negation. "I'm never sleeping again."

She twisted around. "I have to go to the bathroom."

He pulled out of her and threw back the blanket, reaching for his jeans. "Come on. I'll show you."

She wrapped a blanket around herself and followed him through the dim corridor. He opened a door, yanked a chain to turn on the light and gestured her in, closing the door after her.

The room was so huge the bathroom fixtures looked lost in it. She took care of her business and eyed the ancient, mineral-stained clawfoot tub. It occurred to her how badly she was in need of a wash.

She peeked out the door. "I want a bath," she told him.

"Go for it." He headed back toward the bedroom.

She set the water running. The door opened and Seth entered with the electric heater in his arms. He plugged it in and set it on high, crossed his arms and waited. He was so beautiful, in only his jeans. He dazzled her. Even his long brown feet were graceful and beautiful.

"Would you give me a little privacy?" she asked tentatively.

"No."

He returned her stare, patient and implacable. Water roared into the tub and steam rose up in seductive plumes. Raine gave into the inevitable with a sigh, and let the blanket slide off her shoulders. Seth caught it and hung it on a hook above the heater.

She knotted her hair up onto her head. It needed washing too, but she couldn't face having it wet again. She stepped into the water, wincing as it stung her abused feet. She sank into it, closed her eyes and floated, letting the roar of the faucet fill her ears.

Seth turned the water off when it reached her chin, and she opened her eyes. He sat cross-legged by the tub, gazing at her with unnerving intensity. He took the soap out of the dish and fished out her foot, lathering it. He paid attention to every toe, every bruise and scratch, stroking and petting and massaging her. He lowered the foot into the water, seized the other foot and gave it the same loving treatment. There was no sound in the room but the hollow slosh and drip of water as he caressed her.

Her heart ached with love for him. "I didn't sell you out," she said quietly. "Someday you'll know I'm telling the truth."

He lifted her leg out of the water and ran the soap along the length of her calf. "Oh yeah?"

"Oh, yeah," she said, her voice belligerent. "You're going to feel like a total shit for not trusting me. And I'm going to enjoy every minute of it."

A smile touched his solemn mouth. "Terrifying prospect."

"We'll see how much you like it when it happens," she warned. "You already know the truth, if you'd just let yourself believe it."

He caressed her knee. "Truth is a relative thing," he commented.

"Oh, stop it," she snapped. "Now you sound like Victor."

His soapy fingers tightened and lost their grip. Her leg splashed back down into the tub. He wiped the splashed soapsuds off his face with his arm. "Don't compare me to him. The way things are going, I doubt I'll live long enough to find out."

She jerked up as if she had been bitten. "Don't say that!"

The water sloshed perilously close to the lip of the tub. He was retreating from her. His remote voice made her think of the dream. Her father on the boat, his eyes sunken and shadowy, drifting further and further away. "Please don't say that," she repeated, fighting tears.

"Try not to sweat it," he said quietly. "The angel of death in a black ski mask can jump out of the dark anytime. All you can do is look sharp and seize the moment. Like the moment I'm seizing right now."

He pushed her back down against the curved back of the tub. Raine bit her shaking lip and leaned back, abandoning herself to the love she felt in his big hands. He was right. If this was all there was, then she'd better seize every moment of tenderness she could from him.

She let go and yielded to his tender skill; letting his clever fingers untie every knot, undo her, unravel her. He laved every curve, smoothing her like a potter molding clay. He pulled her up onto her knees so he could wash between her legs, and she held on tight to his muscular shoulders so that she didn't shimmer and melt down into the water. His slick, soapy fingers delved into every crevice and fold, making bold use of his intimate knowledge of her. She braced herself against him, shaking with the intensity of her feelings.

Seth pushed her back down into the water, rinsing the suds away. The water, full of soap, had turned as opaque as milk. He reached between her legs, locking eyes with her, and slid his hand beneath her bottom, pulling her to the surface of the water until he could see the flower of her sex, pink and swollen. He touched her as only he could, a magical sensitivity that always knew exactly when to push, when to retreat, when to insist. He pushed and coaxed and caressed until the power tore through her, unleashed. Huge and terrifying and beautiful. A blaze of love and longing that blotted out fear.

She drifted in the cooling water, feeling newly born.

All too soon, he was pulling her to her feet. He toweled her off, pulled the blanket off the hook over the heater and wrapped her in it. It was deliciously warm. He scooped her into his arms, and she relaxed against him like a sleepy baby, boneless. No protests or arguments.

He laid her down on the futon and shoved off his waterlogged jeans. He crouched over her, covering her with his naked, scalding heat. "OK. It's make-believe time," he said. "This is the part in the story where you show me how much you love me."

She reached for him. "Seth—"

"Please don't. The less you say, the more believable it will be."

She stared up into his fierce dark eyes. This was as far as he could come towards her. They were so far outside the bounds of the normal, ordinary world that she no longer took anything for granted. A million impossible things might be true, another million solid truths might be sheer illusion. But one thing was for sure. She loved him. He had saved her life. He was beautiful, and brave and valiant. He had told her that he loved her tonight, and he had meant it with all his heart. No one else in her whole life had ever done so much.

What was true would stay true, whether he let himself believe it or not. And if he wouldn't let her use words to tell him so, then she would use the only language left to her.

She held out her arms. She would make him understand.

The window was black when the low knock sounded on the door. Seth lifted his head as if he'd never slept at all. "Yes?"

"Showtime," someone said quietly.

"I'll be right down." He flipped on the light and pulled on his clothes in grim silence.

Raine sat up, trying to think of something to say. Seth ignored her, yanking on the shirt. The bandage had seeped blood in the night. He gave it a brief, barely interested glance and buttoned the shirt over it without comment.

Panic uncoiled inside her. "You're following that gun, aren't you? The Corazon?"

He didn't answer.

Images blazed through her mind. Crimson spattered on white, the blood on Seth's bandage. His red shirt. Tulips on the floor. The curse of the Corazon. The words flew out of her, with all the urgency of terror.

"OK, you win, Seth. I admit it. I told Victor everything. Don't go. It's a trap."

He smiled as he dropped to his knees by the futon, but his eyes were somber. "You are a piece of work, sweetheart. I never know which way you'll jump."

"Seth, I—"

He cut off her words with a swift, hard kiss. "Be good."

He grabbed the padlock, and shot her a quick grin; crooked and oddly sweet. The door closed, the lock rattled and clicked.

She heard his light footsteps, going down the stairs, and a faint, faraway murmur of male voices. It was always the same; the panic, the frustration. The boat, floating away, and herself too small and helpless to intervene. The headlights danced across the trees as the car drove away. She buried her face in her hands and wept.

After a long time, she slid back into an uneasy doze. Images melted and reformed in her mind, finally coalescing into the rippling expanse of water that stretched out from Stone Island.

Thunder rumbled, far-off and ominous. Fitful gusts of wind made her father's sails billow and flap. He wouldn't take her with him. He wanted to be alone; always that same apologetic half-smile; sorry, Katya, but I don't have the energy to be cheered up. I need to be quiet and think. Run back on up to the house to your mother, eh? She needs you.

What a joke. Alix needing her, hah. The boat drifted further. He waved to her, and she remembered the dream she'd had that night. She called out to him, blubbering with panic, but he just hoisted sail and drifted further. When she had dreams like that, something bad always happened. And if Alix saw her with red eyes, she would just say, oh, for God's sake, stop whining, Katie, I'm losing my patience.

She curled up beneath the roots of a dead tree that jutted out over the water. Waves had carved out a spot beneath just big enough for an eleven-year-old-girl, small for her age, to curl up tight in a ball and watch that far-away sail bob on the water. As long as she could see it, nothing bad could happen. She didn't even dare blink. It would break the spell.

She heard heavy, clumping footsteps on the dock. Ed Riggs was the only one who walked like that. Katya had never liked Ed, even if he was her mother's good friend. He talked to Daddy like Daddy was stupid, when Daddy was the smartest man in the world except for maybe Victor. Ed pretended to be nice, but he wasn't. And lately, she'd had dreams about him. Like the one she'd had last night.

He stood on the dock in front of her, watching the sail float and bob against the water, as frail and delicate as a white moth. He watched for a long time, like he was deciding something. She was outwardly quiet but her heart was thudding as he untied the boat, put the motor down and headed out. Diesel fumes floated over to her hidey-hole and almost made her sick. He headed right for that white sail, a black dot, receding until he was too small to see. The wind began to rise, and the water whipped and frothed, surging over the pebbles to slosh over her feet. The sky wasn't white anymore. It was brownish, yellowish gray, like a bruise. Thunder rolled, closer. It began to rain.

She kept her eyes fixed on that white moth, afraid even to blink; but the eye spell wouldn't work anymore, Ed had broken it. She pretended her eyes were a rope that could pull him back, but the white moth bobbed and tossed, resisting the pull of her eyes.

The dark speck grew slowly bigger again.

She scrambled out of the hidey-hole, wading over to the ladder of roots. She scampered up to the path. She didn't want to be stuck between Ed and the water, not after last night's dream. It was so dark. Then she realized she was still wearing the frog sunglasses. Duh, of course it was dark, but she couldn't see well enough without them to take them off.

Ed was almost on top of her before he noticed she was there. His eyes went so wide that she could see the whites all the way around.

"What did you do to my daddy?" she demanded.

Ed's mouth dropped open beneath his thick mustache. His hands were shaking. His whole body was shaking, but it wasn't cold outside.

"What are you doing out here in the rain, honey?"

"Where's my daddy?" she said again, louder.

*Ed stared at her for a moment, and then squatted down in front of her.
He held out his hand. "Come on, Katie. I'll take you to your daddy."*

*He smiled his nice-guy smile, but a flash of lightning illuminated what the
smile really was—something horrible, as if snakes were coming out of his
eyes and mouth. Like that horror movie she'd watched on TV one night while
the grownups were partying.*

*Thunder crashed. She screamed and sprang away from him like a race-
horse out of the gate. She was fast, but his legs were long. His hands closed
on her arm, but she was as slippery as a fish. She wrenched out of his grip.
The frog glasses flew, but she kept running, screaming, into the featureless
green blur. . . .*

A knock sounded, and she sat up, choking back a scream. It
sounded again; the same polite little tap which must have yanked
her out of the nightmare. She wrapped herself hastily in the blanket,
her heart still racing. "Come in," she called out cautiously.

The padlock rattled, and the door opened. It was the skinny man
with the cane, holding a wad of limp looking clothing against his
chest. Seth had called him Connor. He regarded her with cool,
somber eyes. "Good morning," he said.

"You didn't go with them?"

His face tightened. "The gimp gets babysitting duty." He indicated his cane. "I'm not happy about it, either, so let's not discuss it,
please."

"Why didn't you just lock me up and go?" she asked. "I'd never
get out of this room."

"Exactly. Totally aside from the fact that two hit men attacked
you last night. If, God forbid, all four of us should get wasted messing with those guys, you would die of dehydration in this room before anybody heard you yelling. We don't have any near neighbors."

She swallowed hard, and looked away.

"Yeah, makes you think, doesn't it? Personally, I thought you'd
already rolled your dice. You should take your chances with the rest
of us. But Seth wouldn't hear of it."

"He wouldn't?"

Connor's eyes flicked over her. "No," he repeated. "He wouldn't."

He laid a pile of clothing on the dresser. "None of us live up here
full time, so we don't have a lot of clothes here. I scrounged up some

of Sean's stuff from when he was a kid. Don't know how they'll fit, but they ought to be better than your nightie."

"Yes, I'm sure they will be," she said gratefully.

"Come on downstairs once you're dressed, if you want. There's coffee ready, and food if you're hungry."

"You're not going to lock me up?"

He leaned both hands on his cane and narrowed his sharp green eyes at her. "Are you going to do anything stupid?"

She shook her head. Despite the cane, she was no match for this man. With that hard, purposeful look on his face, he seemed almost as dangerous in his own way as Seth. All of the McCloud brothers had given her that impression.

"Thank you for the clothes," she said. "I'll be down shortly."

The clothes on the dresser were a threadbare, motley assortment. The best of the lot was a pair of low-slung jeans that were tight in the hips, but had to be cuffed three times to find her feet. Rude anti-social slogans had been scribbled over them with blunt felt-tip markers. The only shirt without too many holes was a shrunken, threadbare black Megadeth T-shirt with the neck ripped out. It did not quite succeed in covering her navel, and stretched perilously tightly across her breasts.

There was a pair of high-top sneakers whose original color was impossible to determine, warped and yellowed with age. They were inches too long, as floppy as clown shoes, and rasped painfully against her sore feet, but she pulled the laces tight and was pathetically grateful for every stitch of the ragged getup.

There was a series of framed drawings and paintings on the wall of the stairway. She slowed down to look at them as she descended. Some were charcoal, some pen-and-ink, some watercolors. They were mostly landscapes, animals and trees. Their simplicity and power drew her in and made her think of the vast, silent mystery of Stone Island.

Connor did a double-take when she walked into the kitchen. "Jesus," he said, turning quickly. "Ah . . . oh, yeah. Coffee's in the machine, right there. Cups over the sink. Cream in the fridge. Bread on the counter, if you want toast. Butter, jam, peanut butter or cream cheese are your choices."

She poured herself some coffee. "Those drawings on the stairs are beautiful," she said. "Who's the artist?"

"Those were done by my younger brother, Kevin."

She pulled a quart of half-and-half out of the refrigerator and dosed her coffee. "Is Kevin one of the brothers that I met last night?"

"No," Connor said. "Kevin died ten years ago. Car accident."

She stared at him, clutching the carton. The refrigerator swung open until it bounced against the wall, rattling the jars of condiments.

Connor gave it a gentle shove. It swung closed with a thud. "That's one of the many reasons we're helping Seth," he said. "The McClouds know how it feels to lose a brother."

She stared at the bread browning in the toaster oven. Her mouth was dry, and her appetite gone. "I'm sorry," she said.

"Sit down," Connor said. "Eat something. You're awfully pale."

She forced down some toast with peanut butter at his urging, and he gave her a flannel-lined denim jacket, the sleeves of which came down five inches past her fingertips.

"I'm going to work here in the office. I'd appreciate it if you'd stay right where I can see you," he said briskly. "There's a couch, and an afghan if you're cold. Books in the bookcase. Help yourself."

"Thanks." She curled up on the couch and stared out the window. Connor was staring into the computer, absorbed, and she realized what he must be looking at.

"You've got X-Ray Specs software running on that computer, right? You're tracking the Corazon!" She leaped to her feet. "Can I—"

"Stay where you are and mind your business, please." His eyes and voice were hard. "Try to relax."

"Sure," she whispered. Yeah, right. As if.

She dropped onto the couch, tucked her feet beneath her and stared out at the fog drifting through the pines. A rent in the clouds revealed a snowy mountain peak across the canyon, glowing a deep, sunrise pink. The shifting colors made her think of opals.

An ugly chill crawled up her spine. She thought of Seth's boat. Slipping the Dreamchaser into his inside jacket pocket. She had forgotten all about it. Seth had never known about it at all. He had no reason to think anyone had tampered with his jacket.

Oh, dear God. It was the necklace. It had to be. It was her fault that assassins had been chasing them, and finding them. She leaped up, her heart in her throat.

At that moment, gravel crunched under car tires in the driveway.

"Connor, I have to tell you something," she began. "I—"

"Shhh." He waved her down with a sharp motion of his hand and limped over to the window. "This is weird," he murmured. "I didn't know he knew about this place."

"Who?"

"A guy I work with," Connor peered out the window, perplexed. "Or work for, I should say, since he just got promoted. Go upstairs. Quick. He might come in for a cup of coffee. Stay up there until I tell you it's clear. And Raine?"

She turned back from the foot of the stairs. "Yes?"

"Do not make me regret letting you out of that room."

She nodded and ran up the stairs for the attic. She edged towards the window that overlooked the porch roof. There was no curtain. Looking out meant risking being seen, and would infuriate Connor. The man was his colleague, for God's sake. His boss; surely not a threat to her.

But Ski Mask's bloodshot eyes and the blank, dead eyes of the motel assassin haunted her. She had learned to take nothing for granted in the past five days. Not looking out the window meant risking something decidedly worse than Connor McCloud's irritation.

She crept closer on tiptoe, keeping back in the shadows, but the men were too close to the porch. She had to get closer. The screen door slammed shut. Connor greeted the visitor. His voice was not particularly friendly, just neutral. Questioning. She could not hear what they said through the double-paned storm window.

The man responded, his voice deeper than Connor's baritone. Goosebumps rose up on her spine. She drew nearer. If he looked up, he would see her for sure. From this angle, she saw only that he was balding, somewhat heavy, bulked out in a black winter jacket.

Glasses. Connor asked another inaudible question. He responded with a shrug.

Connor hesitated, then nodded. He said something else, probably inviting the man into the house, and turned around.

She choked off a useless scream of warning when the man's hand flashed out, snake-swift. The butt of his pistol connected with Connor's head, and he dropped to the ground without a sound. The man knelt beside him for a moment, touching his throat. He stood up, pressing against his belly with his hand. He looked around.

He looked up. Their eyes locked. It was the man she had seen when she had gone to see Bill Haley. Her mother's friend, Ed Riggs. Older and heavier, minus the mustache, but there was no mistaking him. He had tried to kill her seventeen years ago. He was back to finish the job.

He disappeared under the porch roof. She looked around the empty room with a sickening sense of déjà vu. God, stuck again in a bedroom with no weapons. The lamp was useless, a fragile frame of dusty bamboo and muslin. There was the whiskey bottle on the dresser. She grabbed it, hefted it. Almost empty. Only slightly better than nothing.

He was not going to be taken in by her lurking behind a door with a bottle, and there was no point in cowering and waiting for him to come to her. She'd tried that approach, and could say with complete authority that the waiting-and-cowering option truly sucked the big one. Particularly since nobody was rushing to her rescue this time. Seth was off pursuing the Corazon. Connor was laid out cold on the gravel outside. She hoped to God he wasn't dead or seriously injured.

It was up to her. But then again, it always had been.

Raine gripped the neck of the whiskey bottle. Saw the heavy, palm-sized padlock lying next to it, and grabbed that, too. She hid the bottle behind her leg, dragged in a long, slow, hitching breath, and started for the head of the stairs. She was scared to death, but she would pretend not to be. Who knew better than she how to pretend? Her whole life was leading up to this moment. The grand, ultimate pretense.

She did not bother to walk quietly. In fact, she stomped. As much as one could stomp, in a pair of floppy clown shoes.

"Hello, Ed."

Riggs turned the corner at the landing. His jaw sagged.

It was a tableau from a cheap graphic novel. The girl poised at the top of the stairs, looking down her nose at him. Legs planted wide, chest stuck out. In that ragged, sexpot outfit with her hair frizzed out all over the place, he could see why Novak wanted her. Even the bruises under her eyes didn't detract from her allure. She looked like a whacked out fashion model on a cocaine binge, sexy and wild and completely unpredictable.

Eyes on the prize, he reminded himself. This was for Erin.

He lifted the gun and pointed it at her. "I don't want to hurt you."

The contempt on her face did not change. "Then why are you pointing that gun at me, Ed?"

"You have to come with me now," he told her. "If you don't do anything stupid, you won't get hurt."

She took a step down. Before he realized what he was doing, he had retreated back a step, as if she were a threat to him.

"You killed my father." Her voice vibrated with hatred.

He kept the gun trained on her, but she didn't seem to notice, or care. "Old news," he said, sneering. "Besides, that was a mercy killing. Peter was a suicide waiting to happen. I just put him out of his misery. Come on down, nice and slow, Katie. Make this easy on yourself, OK?"

Her eyes were glowing oddly, like Victor's when the mood was on him. Her face was unearthly pale, like a vampire in a horror flick.

"Why should I?" she said. "You're just going to kill me anyway. Like you tried to do when I was a kid. Remember that, Ed? I sure do."

"You were a snotty little bitch back then, too. I remember that," he snarled. "Come on, Katie. Be a good girl. One foot after the other."

"Fuck you. You killed my daddy, you pig."

Her lips drew back from her teeth in a snarl, and her arm

whipped out from behind her, where she'd been hiding the liquor bottle. She let out an ear-splitting shriek and hurled it at him.

He flung up his arm and took the goddamned thing on the same sore arm that had blocked the brass lamp last night. He roared with pain, yelped again at the shiny metal thing that spun out of nowhere right after it, clipping him on the jaw.

Then the crazy little bitch took a flying leap, right at him.

Chapter
25

The bottle shattered. The gun went off, and splinters exploded off of some wooden surface. Raine barreled into him, deafened. They hurtled together down to the bottom of the landing.

Ed hit the wall hard, and she was savagely pleased at the thud, his heavy grunt. There was no time to savor it, though—in a split second she bounced off him and half-tumbled, half-slid down the rest of the stairs, bumpity-bump, thud. She bounced up and sprinted through the kitchen, seizing objects at random and hurling them at him.

The toaster bounced off his shoulder, the blender missed him and smashed against the wall. She darted into the office, spun around and almost got him with a stereo speaker. He ducked and dodged her missiles, screaming something, but she couldn't understand what he said, because she was screaming too, as if pure sound could be a weapon. All the rage she'd ever tried to control came rushing out in a shrill, endless, crazy shriek. She felt capable of any violence, any madness or folly.

He thundered after her into the office. Now he was between her and the other exit. She was boxed in, brainless idiot that she was. No chance now of outrunning him outdoors. She grabbed a sports trophy off the bookshelf and flung it. He shielded his face, cursing as it bounced off his elbow, and charged her again, his face purple with trapped blood.

She shimmied behind the big desk with all the computer equipment, shoving it away from the wall to give her more room. The
wild, manic energy had begun to ebb. Fear was sinking its claws in
again. She threw everything that came to hand: notebooks, software
manuals, a modem. A rain of paper clips and tacks, a handful of loose
CDs. She yanked a handful of pencils and pair of scissors out of a
heavy jar, flung it. He dodged the jar. The pencils bounced and skit-
tered harmlessly off his coat. He dove across the desk, and jerked
back with a shout when she stabbed at his hands with the scissors.

Ed seized the desk. It squealed across the floor as he slammed it
into her hip painfully hard, squashing her against the wall. He
lunged across the desk again, dodging her frantic stabs with the scissors.

"You stupid bitch," he panted. "I'm not going to hurt you."

"No, you're going to kill me," she panted. "And I won't let you."

"Shut up!" he shouted. "I'm not supposed to kill you! If I had
wanted to kill you, believe me, you would be dead! I was supposed
to take you to Novak."

"Novak?" She froze, clutching the scissors like a dagger.

He gave her an evil, openmouthed smile, panting and pressing
his hand against his belly. She could smell his sour, fetid breath all
the way across the wide desk. "Yeah. Novak. He wants you, honey. I
don't think he's planning on killing you, either, at least not at first.
He's got other things in mind for you. Lucky girl. You know, I was
feeling kind of sorry for you before, but it's funny . . . I don't feel so
sorry any more."

He wrenched the desk away from the wall. Raine scrambled
backwards, tripping over the tangle of dusty electrical cords and
stumbling into the corner. "It was you who attacked me last night at
my house, wasn't it, Ed?" she hissed. "I recognize your stink."

A crazy grin split his distorted face. "Ooh, that cuts me to the
quick, honey. What a little charmer." He wrenched the desk out further, and the electrical cords attached to the power strip behind the
desk began to stretch and pull. "Suffering Christ," he muttered, his
lips curling back in disgust. "You look exactly like your slut of a
mother."

Those words gave her the jolt she needed. She grabbed the monitor just before it toppled onto the tangle of cords, heaved it to chest height, and launched it at him with her last burst of panicked energy.

His eyes widened, and his arms flew up. He winced when it hit his chest and stumbled back, trying to catch the thing before it fell on his feet. She seized her chance and reached out, blindly scrabbling for the first thing she touched, which proved to be the fax machine. He was lunging at her again, and she spun around, swinging the thing up in a sidewise arc. Bashing it against the side of his head.

"I am so *sick* of you guys badmouthing my mother," she told him.

He blinked stupidly. The sudden silence was startling. He toppled slowly, like a tree, and bore her down beneath him. She hit the wall behind her painfully hard with her sore shoulders, and slid down onto her butt with him on top of her, his head lolling heavily against her neck. A rivulet of blood snaked down his cheekbone.

She lay there for a few moments, shaking and crying, but it was way too soon to start sniveling and falling apart, with Connor lying still and quiet outside and Seth racing towards a cliff with doom in his pocket, thanks to her. She heaved and struggled and finally scrambled out from under Ed's dead weight, unwinding herself from the tangle of cords.

She clambered over him, recoiling from the necessity of touching his body. She was shaking so hard, she fell down again, almost onto her face. She noticed, remotely, that her arm was bleeding. Quite a lot, but she couldn't be bothered with it now.

First, Ed's gun. She searched through the rubble on hands and knees, sifting through the clutter with trembling fingers. She found it beneath the desk, a Glock 17. She stuck it into the back of her too-tight jeans. It was cold and hard, and extremely uncomfortable.

She stared down at Ed. He was breathing, and he had a pulse, which meant he could come to and attack her again. Villains always did in thriller movies. She'd better not take any chances.

She grabbed him by the feet and dragged him clear of all the fallen equipment, panting and whimpering with the effort it took to heave him out from behind the desk. She stumbled into the kitchen and rummaged through the drawers for rope, twine, anything.

She found a roll of duct tape, and raced back to the office, strapping his wrists behind his back first, then his ankles. She did his knees for good measure, and then bent his knees back and taped his wrists to his ankles. She ran outside, wondering if she might have overdone it.

Thank God, Connor was already sitting up, touching the side of his head with cautious fingers. She dropped to her knees beside him.

"Are you OK?"

He winced at her loud voice. "What the fuck?"

"Your boss hit you with his gun. Then he attacked me. He was supposed to take me to Novak."

Connor gave her a dubious sideways look.

"Believe me, I don't have time to make up stories," Raine snapped. "Come on, I'll help you into the kitchen."

She retrieved his cane and hooked her arm around his waist, steadying him as he got to his feet. "Ed's in the office," she said, guiding him up the porch steps. "I used duct tape, but he's the first person I've ever tied hand and foot, so you might want to check my technique."

"Ed?" His eyes narrowed.

"We've met," she explained. "Seventeen years ago, when he killed my dad. And again, in my house last night. He was the first ski mask."

"Ah," he murmured, as she pulled the door open for him. "You've been busy while I was napping."

There was a bag of cotton balls and antiseptic ointment lying on the kitchen table. She grabbed a wad of cotton, dosed it with gel and picked her way into the war-torn office. Connor was staring at Ed.

"You mummified him," he commented.

Raine parted Connor's shaggy dark blond hair and dabbed at the bloody spot on his skull.

He jerked away. "Ow! I can do that!" He grabbed the wad of cotton. He looked down at Ed, then back at her. "How did you do it?"

She hugged herself, shivering. "I clobbered him with your fax machine," she admitted.

"I see."

"He insulted my mother," she added. As if she needed to justify herself.

"Remind me never to insult your mother," Connor said.

"I have to say, my mother made quite an impression on a lot of men. I'm starting to think she really must have been hell on wheels."

She realized that she was babbling, and forced herself to shut up.

Connor had an odd expression, as if he were trying not to laugh. "Well, uh, if she's anything like you—"

"No, not really," she said. "Look, I'm sorry I trashed your office."

"No problem." He focused on her face, and frowned. "Did you know that you have a cut on your face? Your cheek is bleeding."

She shrugged. "Later." She touched him on the shoulder. "Look, Connor, you're not going to slip into a coma if I leave you here with that bump on your head, are you? I can always drop you at an emergency room on my way to—"

"You're not going anywhere," he said.

"It's too complicated to explain the whole story, but I figured out how the killer found us last night," she explained, through clenched teeth. "And how Ed found me now. Seth has a necklace that Victor gave me in his jacket pocket. That's what's transmitting. It must be."

Connor's face darkened. "You put it there?"

"Yes!" she yelled. "I did! Sorry, OK? I'm an idiot! I had no idea what was going on at the time! If Victor's watching, he'll see Seth on his system. He might think that he's me, but he'll be on guard."

Connor grabbed the phone. He stabbed at the buttons, rattled it. Checked the jack. He lurched swiftly into the kitchen, tried the phone on the wall. "The fucking bastard. He cut the phone line."

"Don't you have a cell?"

"Out of range. We're on the wrong side of Endicott Bluff."

The dream sensation of helpless panic was creeping up on her. "But I have to find Seth before he gets to that meeting."

"How? Even if Riggs hadn't cut the phone, command central was this office, and you just killed it. Davy's the computer geek around here, not me. He or Seth could put this mess back together, but I can't."

She pressed the palms of her hands against her eyes. "I can use the monitor Ed used to find me."

Connor shook his head. "Five kilometer radius. You're out of range. The only way to find them now would be to look them up on a master terminal running X-Ray Specs software that's keyed to the right transmitter codes."

"Victor's system," she whispered. "It's Victor's transmitter."

Connor's face went thoughtful. "Yeah. Victor's system."

"Where are the keys to the car, Connor?"

He shook his head. "Forget it. You're not—"

"The keys, Connor." She yanked Ed's gun out of her pants and leveled it at him. "Now."

He touched his head and looked at his bloody fingers. "And leave me all alone with my possible concussion? I could slip into a coma and die, you know."

She gritted her teeth. "I can stop by a neighbor's house and tell someone to come and look after you."

"Let me give you a tip, Raine. The next time you try to coerce somebody at gunpoint, don't offer them milk and cookies and a nice warm blankie while you're at it. It totally fucks your credibility. Now put that thing down. You look stupid."

Raine sighed and let the gun drop. "So give me a break," she mumbled. "I'm learning this stuff as I go."

"I'll go with you," Connor said.

"No!"

They looked down. The exclamation had come from Ed. He struggled against his bonds. "McCloud, I have to tell you something—"

"Tell it to the judge, Riggs. I'm already nauseous from that conk on the head. Hearing another dose of your bullshit would really make me puke my guts out."

"No, please. This is important. You've got to help me."

"Help you? I've got to help who?" Connor limped slowly around Riggs's twitching form. He braced himself against the cane, wedged his foot beneath the other man and flopped him over.

Blood had run in rivulets across Ed's forehead and under his eyes, like a grisly carnival mask. "Not me," he rasped. "Erin."

Connor's face froze. "What are you talking about?"

"Erin?" Raine asked.

"His daughter," Connor said, his voice almost unrecognizable. "What about Erin, Riggs? Spit it out. We've got things to do."

"Novak's got her," Ed rasped. "That's why I needed the Lazar girl. To do . . . the trade."

Connor's face abruptly drained of all color. "This isn't happening. Tell me this isn't happening, Riggs. Tell me you're shitting me."

"If I can't make the trade, you've got to help Erin, McCloud."

Connor's cane went spinning and clattering across the floor. He dropped down next to Ed and seized him by his jacket, hauling him up with a violent yank. "Novak got Erin, and you don't even call me? You stay quiet to save your own worthless hide? You fuck-up. You don't even deserve to call yourself her father. *Why didn't you tell me before?*"

Ed's eyes squeezed shut. "Too late," he said, panting. "Couldn't risk it. Novak's men . . . watching. The whole thing had gone too far."

"Yeah, well, the whole thing has just stopped. Right here," Connor hissed. He let Ed drop to the floor with a thud, and struggled to his feet. Raine retrieved his cane and handed it to him. He took it, his mouth thin and hard with fury.

Ed opened his eyes again and fixed them on Raine. "Your icon on the system is a jewel," he said. "I got the monitor from Victor. Saw the signal drive by this morning when the car left, but I knew you were still here. Victor wanted me to guard you. Keep you safe from Novak. Fucking joke. Like I could ever keep anybody safe from anything, in my whole life." He panted, swallowed. "Then Novak got to me. With Erin."

"Where is Erin now?" Connor asked.

"Crystal Mountain. With her friends," Ed wheezed. "Lots of Novak's men. A guy named Georg has orders to . . . to hurt her, if I don't deliver the Lazar girl. Please, McCloud. Erin always liked you. Idolized you. Do it for her, not for me. She's innocent. I'm not, but she is."

Connor gestured for Raine to follow him and walked into the kitchen, oblivious to the mess of broken appliances and crockery. He opened a cupboard and dumped loose macaroni noodles out of a plastic container into his shaking hand until a set of keys dropped into it. "Here." He put them into her hands. "It's probably too late, but give it your best shot. Turn right at the end of the driveway, follow the signs for Endicott Falls until you see Mosley Road south. Follow that for ten miles, and you'll see signs for the interstate."

"You're going to go and rescue his daughter?"

His haggard face tightened with doubt. "Davy and Sean and Seth are all three tough sons-of-bitches. They know what they're getting into," he said, as if trying to convince himself. "And you look like you can take care of yourself just fine, from what I can see. But Erin . . . she hasn't got a clue. I went to her graduation party, for God's sake."

She gave him a quick, impulsive hug. "Good luck, Connor," she said. "You're one of the good guys."

"Oh, yeah? What's a good guy supposed to do with that?" He jerked his head towards the office, where Ed groaned and wheezed.

"Lock him in the attic," she said coolly. "He's rolled his dice. He can take his chances with the rest of us."

He gave her an admiring grin. "Spoken like a true heartless adventuress," he said. "You're as tough as nails, Raine, you know that?"

"Not really, but it's sweet of you to say so," she called back.

She found the hand monitor on the passenger seat of Riggs's car. She pulled out on the road in Seth's bronze Mercury, and drove as fast as she dared, with no driver's license and a stolen gun stuck prominently into her jeans. She had to get to him before Victor and Novak closed in.

Seth thought he was the hunter, but he was actually the prey.

Chapter

26

Davy punched the number for the third time, scowling. He snapped shut the mouthpiece. "Line's dead," he said. "We can't get in touch with Connor."

There was a brief, grim silence.

"That sucks." Sean's voice was unusually thoughtful.

"Could be a coincidence," Davy offered.

Seth snorted as he pulled off onto the exit that led to Lazar's usual marina. "Want to bet?"

"Nope," Davy and Sean said in unison.

Seth's mind raced. "If you guys want to bow out now, be my guest," he said. "I'll think no less of you for it. On the contrary. My opinion of your intelligence will rise. Sharply."

Sean gave him a goofy grin and pulled his green ski mask down over his pretty boy face. "Get stuffed."

"Yeah," Davy said. "Ditto."

Seth let out his breath in a long, silent sigh. The McClouds were like ticks. Once they dug in, they were hell to get rid of.

"So? What's the plan?" Sean sounded untroubled. "You can track the Corazon icon from here, can't you?"

"Get my laptop out of the bag," Seth said.

Sean opened up the laptop and logged on. "OK. X-Ray Specs is up and running. I've got the map on screen. Now what?"

"Click the top right button and wait for the prompt."

"Password?"

"Retribution," Seth muttered.

"Oooh," Sean crooned. "That gives me the shivers."

Seth scowled. "You're not supposed to be having this much fun."

"Hey. Just because you're having woman problems, does that mean I have to be all down in the mouth? Lighten up, already."

"Stop being a pain in the ass, Sean," Davy said wearily.

"I'm a little brother. That's what we do best." Sean grimaced, and shot a pained look at Seth. "Oops. Sorry," he muttered.

"Just give me the goddamn laptop," Seth growled. He reached back for it, but Sean kept a tight hold on it, humming cheerfully.

"Wait, wait," he said. "I see the . . . oh, man, bingo! You really do have a romantic streak, don't you?"

"What do you see?" Seth barked.

"The icon. A little heart with an arrow through it. The Corazon, right? One point three kilometers west and moving south, right along with us. We're practically on top of the guy. It's destiny."

The parking attendant in the garage of the Lazar building leaped up when she got out of the car, his face a comical mask of alarm.

"Good morning, Jeremy," she said. "I'm sorry I don't have my employee tags or my parking sticker with me today, but it doesn't matter. I promise I won't be long."

"Huh?" Jeremy's jaw dropped comically. "Who?"

The elevator ride was a trip through an alternate universe. The people that surrounded her stared at her like she had two heads. They were so pressed and polished. Their world was safe and comprehensible and controllable. She wanted to scream at them, warn them that their worst nightmares could materialize and jump out at them any time, with long, dripping yellow fangs bared. Oh yes, indeedy, they could, boys and girls.

She controlled herself with a huge effort of will. It was not her job to warn these people. Thank God her snarled-up hair was so big and frizzy today, long enough to cover up the gun stuck at the small of her back. The skimpy T-shirt certainly didn't cover anything. Her butt was practically hanging right out of the low-slung jeans.

"Excuse me," she said as the elevator door opened, and they all recoiled to let her out first. She could get used to this, she reflected, trying not to laugh. Maybe she should permanently change her look.

The same thing happened in the Lazar Import & Export office. People who had browbeaten and ordered her around all month scurried out of her way, eyes wide, flattening themselves against the walls to give her space. As if she were dangerous. A spark of grim amusement kindled inside her. She'd come a long way from the girl whose knees had knocked when she had to serve melon chunks and mini-muffins to a room full of suits.

Harriet bore down on her like a fighter jet as she strode down the corridor for Victor's office. She blocked Raine's path, her tight, pinched mouth trembling with outrage. "How dare you come here looking like a slut! Have you lost your mind? You've got blood on your face, and you're actually . . . dirty!" Her voice cracked with horror.

Raine swallowed down a cackle of hysterical laughter. "Out of my way," she ordered. "I need to get into that office, right now."

"No!" Harriet held out her arms, prepared to martyr herself. "No amount of intimacy with Mr. Lazar gives you the right to intrude on—"

"He's my father, Harriet," Raine snapped.

Harriet jerked back, her eyes huge and startled behind the frames of her glasses.

Raine advanced upon her. "So get your bony ass out of my way. I'm having a really bad day, as you might have noticed, and I don't have the time or the patience to explain myself to you. Go!"

Harriet swallowed and backed away, her face stiff. "Call security," she said to the cluster of staring, murmuring people behind her.

Security. Lovely. She wouldn't have much time. Raine locked the door and dropped into the thronelike desk chair. The computer was already logged on, the password request up, cursor blinking dutifully.

She seized the phone, punching in Seth's cell phone number. The recorded voice informed her that the phone was out of range. Would she like to leave a message? She slammed it down and rubbed her burning eyes. What was it that Victor had said? More than four letters. Less than ten. *What he wanted from her.*

Damn him. Always a power struggle, always a guessing game. What she wouldn't give to have the power to make people rack their brains trying to guess what she wanted from them. As if. She had to beg for what she wanted on her hands and knees. And she never got it anyway.

Oh, stop it. This was no time for self-pity. She had to concentrate. Victor was a control freak. He liked to control people by. . . .

She typed in "fear." It didn't work. She tried "control." "Revenge."

No go.

She tried "power." Then "respect." Still nothing. She squeezed her eyes shut. She had to think like him. More convoluted, more abstract. Victor was nothing if not abstract. But nothing came to her brain; stress had battered it to a numb pulp. She shook her head to clear it and just started typing in every word that popped into her head.

She tried "trust." "Truth." "Honor." "Justice." "Courage." No. She tried "Mercy." "Forgiveness."

She hesitated for a long time, bit her lip hard and typed in "love." Nothing.

She swore, using some of the brand-new, violent combinations of words she had learned in the past few days from listening to Seth.

The goddamned password should have been "love." That was what she wanted it to be, sentimental idiot that she was, always wanting what she couldn't have, seeking love where it couldn't be found. She wanted out of this screaming madhouse of hate and revenge. She wanted to rescue them all: herself, Seth, Connor, even the unknown, hapless Erin. She wanted to rescue the perfect, precious bliss she had known last night before the killer came and murdered it.

She wanted to go back in time, rescue Peter from Ed, rescue Victor from himself, rescue everyone from their fear and desperation and loneliness. But she was so small and helpless, and the boat was drifting away from her. She needed help, a moment of pure grace from the great mysterious unknown to help her unravel this puzzle, please—

Her hands dropped into her lap. Her swollen eyes stared at the computer screen, frozen in a moment of exquisite, paralyzing hope.

She spun back to the keyboard, and very carefully typed in "g-r-a-c-e." She entered it.

Password accepted. The menu options popped up, inviting her to proceed. She blinked the tears she had no time for, and clicked on the glasses icon. The X-Ray Specs logo flashed up, a catchy blur of animation that her eyes were too watery to follow. She selected, "Last area viewed." Then "Track all."

A map popped up on the screen, showing a large chunk of the residential neighborhood of her Templeton Street house. Tiny colored points blinked all over the place. She wiped her eyes and nose on her grimy, sticky arm. There was a big magnifying glass on the tool bar. She dragged it over the map, letting her eyes relax and unfocus. One moment of grace, she prayed silently. One little moment, and she would take care of the rest.

There it was, a flicker of movement at the bottom of the screen. She dragged the magnifying glass to the point, and selected Zoom, vaguely aware that someone was yelling and pounding on the door.

The jewel icon was on the move southbound on Carstairs Road, a parallel of Templeton. It turned off the main road, and stopped. She knew that place. It had been a timber baron's luxury estate back in the twenties. Now it was an abandoned, dilapidated mansion surrounded by a big, overgrown forest park. She had jogged there, back in the days before she'd gotten too tired to jog.

The office door burst open. That was all the grace she was going to get. A burly man in a security uniform peeked in and eyed her as if she were a rabid animal. "Miss, I'm afraid you're going to have to, uh, come with me now," he rumbled, trying to look stern.

"I don't think so," she said politely. "I've got things to do."

He stepped in front of her, blocking her path to the door.

Damn. She'd hoped to avoid this, but there was no time to waste. She reached back, pulled out Ed's Glock and gave the man a big, toothy smile. "I'm out of here," she said. "Have a great day."

The guy almost tripped over himself to get out of her way, and Harriet squawked in protest. "See? I told you she was dangerous!"

Raine backed away from the horrified faces of the people she'd been trying so hard to please and placate for the last month. The Glock was intimidating, but it wasn't going to take them long to figure out that she would never use the thing.

"Uh . . . I'll see you guys around," she said. "It's been real."

She stuck the Glock back into her pants and ran like hell.

The cell phone rang. Victor checked the number before picking it up. It was Mara, whom he had assigned to watch the monitor in the control room. Memories of what he had done to the delectable, adventurous Mara in his bedroom the night before flashed through his mind. Memorable, yes, but the girl had better have a damn good reason for calling other than pillow talk. He pushed the button. "Yes?"

"Mr. Lazar, the jewel icon is very close to the marina, and moving closer," Mara said.

He was unpleasantly startled. "Are you sure?"

"Yes. It's at the level of Morehead Street. Moving south, at about thirty miles an hour. It's within range of your monitor."

He pulled the monitor out of his coat pocket, entered the password and keyed in the code. Mara was right. Katya was here.

"Thank you, Mara. Carry on." He broke the connection and pulled the collar of his coat higher, chilled to the bone.

Katya wasn't supposed to be here. She should be far out of reach, guarded by both Mackey and Riggs.

He should abort the meeting. Something was very wrong. He could feel it. But if Novak had Katya in his grasp, he couldn't walk away. He had thought himself invulnerable, but Katya was his weak point. She always had been. And he had nothing to bargain with but a piece of cold metal, and images from a nightmare.

They were approaching the marina. The readout on the monitor shifted constantly with the changing flow of spatial information.

He switched off the useless thing and flung it into the water.

Maybe it wasn't Katya. Maybe someone else was carrying one of her tagged belongings. Maybe it was a malfunction. He could only hope.

To think that after all his plotting and planning, that he should be reduced to relying upon something so fragile as hope.

"I have got to get myself a pair of these," Sean said, staring through the foggy woods with his goggles. "I haven't been so jazzed since the last time we burgled that bastard. I can already spot three . . . no, four of Novak's goons with the long-range TI function. Playing with your toys is like having superhuman powers."

"That's the whole idea," Seth said. He handed a pair to Davy and looped his own around his neck. He handed a tiny mike and earphone set to the brothers, identical in their green camouflage gear. They put them on with a swift efficiency that showed such equipment was not new to them.

"So what's your plan?" Davy asked. "March up to the front door and ring the bell?"

"No way to do recon if you don't know the site. I was going to wing it. You guys got any ideas, let's hear 'em."

Davy and Sean looked at each other for a long moment. Their matching sets of perfect teeth flashed through the green ski masks.

"Hunting season," Davy said, popping open the back door of the Jeep Cherokee. "Time to show you the McCloud family arsenal." He pulled out a heavy black case and slanted a questioning glance at his brother. "Do you want the Remington 700 or the Cheytec .408?" He snapped open the case and hauled out a huge sniper rifle.

"You take the Cheytec," Sean said. "You're the better sniper."

"That's exactly why you should take the Cheytec," Davy said with exaggerated patience. "And besides, you're a perfectly good sniper."

"Sure, I don't suck, but you're still better. You're the marksman. I'm the demolitions man." He grinned at Seth. "Too bad we didn't know the site beforehand. God, how I would've loved to bomb the shit out of those assholes. There's nothing so satisfying as a nice big kaboom, know what I mean? Gives you a real sense of emotional closure."

"Focus, Sean," Davy muttered. "Take the fucking Cheytec."

"Nah. The Cheytec gives me performance anxiety. You take it. I like the Remington with my Leupold power scope. We're old pals."

"Whatever." Davy hauled the Cheytec up into position and peered through the scope. "We used to hunt with a bow and arrow when we were kids. For fun." He shot a glance at Seth. "Ever try it?"

Seth stared at the massive rifle, impressed in spite of himself. He focused belatedly on Davy's question. "Give me a break. I'm a city boy."

"Dad taught us how," Davy said. "To prepare us for the inevitable day of doom and judgment when government is overthrown, anarchy rules, and civilization is flung back into the Bronze Age."

"And the prepared, the elect, the chosen ones, would be the dukes and princes of that new world order," Sean intoned. "Namely, us."

"And I thought my childhood was weird," Seth muttered.

"Yeah, Dad was a pretty original thinker," Davy said. "Anyhow, when you hunt with a bow and arrow, you have to get really close to your prey. Sometimes we'd make a game out of it, get close enough to the deer or elk to slap them on the rump and watch them run. Sometimes we shot 'em. Depended on how much was in the freezer."

Seth held up his goggles and peered through the trees that obscured the house. "Do you guys have a point to make with all this?"

"Nah, not really," Davy said. He pulled a bunch of plasticuffs out of his bag, and offered a handful of them to Seth and Sean. "It's just been a really long time since Sean and I have gone hunting."

"Too long," Sean added. "Too bad Connor couldn't come. He was the best of all of us. The original shadow man."

Seth looked down at the plasticuffs, and back at the McClouds. Two sets of disembodied green eyes glowed with hot anticipation out of the ski masks. "You guys are really into this, aren't you?"

"Those bastards put Connor in a coma for two months," Davy said softly. "And they killed Jesse."

"Jesse was our friend, too," Sean said. "We wouldn't miss this party for any money." He reached into the back of the Cherokee and pulled out another case. "Check this out, Seth. You're not the only one with a few magic tricks up his sleeve." He popped open the lid and held the case out for Seth to see.

Seth peered in. "What's this?"

"Gas powered air pistols converted into trank dart guns. With super-fast acting tranquilizer darts," Sean said triumphantly. "I got 'em from Nick, one of Connor's task force buddies. He specializes in just this kind of situation. When a guy wants to even up the odds without having to cope with all the red tape of a full-out bloodbath."

Seth stared at him. "No shit," he said slowly. "You mean to tell me you've already used this stuff? What do you do for a living, anyway?"

Sean shrugged noncommittally, and gave him a bright, impenetrable grin. "Oh, a little bit of this, a little bit of that. I get by. Here. I brought along Connor's for you. A Beretta M92, with a power scope. A laser sight, too, if you want, but I personally think that kind of takes the fun out of it."

Seth took the proffered gun and stared down at it, starting to grin. His mood had unaccountably lightened. "You McCloud boys are a strange breed."

Davy grinned back. "You're not the first to make that observation," he said.

Another man was lying on the ground.

Raine crouched beside the second motionless body, checking with trembling fingers beneath the dark hood to make sure it wasn't one of the McCloud men. She sighed with relief when she saw that it was not. It was a young man with buzz-cut red hair. He was alive, a tiny needle dart sticking out of his neck. Plastic bonds were ratcheted tightly around his wrists and ankles.

She looked around, but she saw no one in the murmuring forest besides her and the unconscious man. It was like the enchanted forest of Sleeping Beauty. Everyone but her had gone to sleep.

She had parked as near as she dared to the abandoned mansion, and sneaked through the woods as quietly as she could, using the monitor to guide her. Seth and the McClouds must be roaming around, taking out Novak's guards one by one. That was heartening.

It had started raining again, but she was too keyed up to feel it.

Her metabolism must be raging like a grassfire. The raindrops that hit her skin felt like they ought to hiss and sputter like water on a griddle.

She huddled by a tree trunk and looked around, clutching Ed's Glock with a white-knuckled hand. Racing to Seth's rescue had seemed like such a good idea at the time, but now, in this silent, creepy forest, doubts were racing back. She was out of her depth, as always.

But it was far too late for good sense or second thoughts. She couldn't just abandon Seth with that necklace in his pocket; and besides, she had nowhere else to go, nothing else to do. Nothing existed but this moment, this place, this task. It pulled at her like a vortex. It was the key to unlock the whole wretched puzzle of her life.

The culmination of everything.

The monitor indicated that the necklace was less than three hundred meters from her to the northeast. If she sneaked along under the cover of those willow trees, maybe she would see—

Something hit her between the shoulder blades with incredible force, knocking her face down in the muddy leaves. Something heavy was on top of her. It moved and breathed and stank of cigarettes.

It pried the pistol out of her hand and jammed it against her neck. An arm slid under her chin, pressing against her windpipe. She hunched her back up with the strength of terror, giving herself just enough space to shove the flat monitor beneath a soggy drift of leaves.

The thing on top of her grabbed her hair, pulled her face around to the side. She saw white-blond eyebrows, pinkish eyes, a hooked nose. The thing grinned at her with big, yellow teeth.

"Hello, pretty girl. The boss is going to be real happy to see you."

Chapter

27

Finally Seth was back in the zone. His concentration was almost back to normal; instincts razor sharp, utterly focused. He was almost to the punchline of this crazy joke, and nothing would keep him from it—as long as he didn't pay attention to that burning cloud that hung in the middle of his mind. Raine.

He wrenched his concentration back with a savage jerk. Nothing existed but here and now. He was on his belly, fifty meters from the house. Cameras were a sure thing, but there was no way to tell if Novak had motion detectors. He doubted it, with that army of sentries on the grounds. Besides, this wreck didn't look like a place that warranted a hard-core security installation. It looked like a creepy haunted mansion. Trust Novak to go for atmosphere over security.

He allowed himself to feel cautiously optimistic. Between him and the McClouds, they'd evened out the odds quite a bit. The monitor told him that the Corazon was in that house. Getting in was going to be an interesting challenge. He wiggled another few feet closer, under cover of an overgrown shrub. The line on the earpiece clicked open.

"Yo, Seth." Sean's voice was strangely subdued. "Hate to tell you this, but . . . your lady friend has decided to join us."

Seth's mind went blank.

No way. She was supposed to be wrapped in a blanket, sipping a cup of herbal tea under Connor's watchful eye. Nowhere near here.

"Where?" he snapped into the little mike clipped to his collar.

"She must've come through the hole I made on the western side. One of the goons has her in a twist. He's taking her into the house."

"Can you get him?"

"Too far," Sean said. "Too risky. I might hit her. Sorry."

"Shit," he hissed. "I can't believe it. I cannot fucking believe it."

"I hear you, man," Sean said sympathetically. "She's a handful. Have to say, though, that chick sure does get around. Wonder what she did to Connor. Jesus. I hope she didn't hurt him, or anything."

"Shut up, Sean. Davy, how's hunting?"

"I've bagged some real beauties," Davy responded promptly. "Trussed up and ready for dressing out."

"How close are you to the house?"

"About a hundred meters," Davy said.

Seth tried to crowd emotion out of his mind, to get back to that perfect realm where instinct ruled. But it was hopeless, it was pure hell, with Raine popping up, getting nabbed, blocking his line of fire, fogging his brain with her beauty. That was her special gift, to turn something that was supposed to be as clear and simple as a rifle blast into something hellishly complicated.

"Get closer," he said. "Listen up. This is what I have in mind . . ."

Kurt Novak stared at the screen that showed him the library where Victor Lazar was waiting. The man was seated comfortably on an overstuffed Victorian armchair, smoking a cigarette. At his ease. Daring to think that he had checkmated the master of the game. How gratifying it was going to be, to watch him grovel and beg.

It was risky to hold the meeting here, but he'd been cowering in windowless holes for too long. Enough. He dialed Riggs's number, one last time. Still nothing. Riggs had failed in his simple mission, even with the assistance of one of the most talented assassins in the area. The girl's lover must be very skilled.

The timing of the game was off. How annoying. He had the cellar room all prepared, and he had wanted the girl right here, so he could play Lazar like a fish on a line. As it was, he would have to improvise. But uncertain outcomes created space for unexpected flashes of genius.

In any case, Riggs would pay for his incompetence. Or rather, his daughter would pay. He began to punch in Georg's number. He wanted Georg to be particularly creative with the Riggs girl.

A radio transmitter beeped. He picked it up. "Yes?"

He listened to what his man had to say, and began to laugh. He turned to the monitor and enlarged one of the images.

Within seconds, Karl appeared on the screen with the Lazar girl. He said something sharp, and wrenched her hair back until she looked up at the camera, her lovely eyes full of defiance.

She looked a bit the worse for wear, but still mouthwatering. Those full, trembling lips. That pale skin that would show every little mark. He hadn't needed the worthless Riggs after all. He had wasted his best assassin for nothing. The girl had come to him on her own.

"Bring her to me," he said. He could hardly wait to conclude this tedious business with Lazar.

Then it would be playtime.

She hated feeling stupid, as well as terrified. Novak wrenched her wrists up behind her and twisted. A blaze of agony flashed through her nerves, and she hovered for a second on the verge of fainting before Novak forced her onward.

Karl, the thug who had jumped her, opened a heavy, carved mahogany door and stood aside to let them enter. He leered horribly as she passed. She could still feel his damp, clinging hands on her body. She wondered if she would ever be able to wash the feeling away.

More to the point, if she would ever have the opportunity to try.

Victor was waiting in the big, shabby library. His face was grim, and he looked unsurprised to see her. Karl and another of Novak's men took up their positions on either side.

"Hello, Kurt," Victor said. "Is this unpleasantness necessary?"

"Most unpleasantness is, Victor," Novak replied. "Please bear in mind that you put me in this position. You have only yourself to blame."

Victor's eyes met hers. A faint smile touched his lips. "Good morning, Katya," he said. "I am distressed to see you here, but not surprised. You have to be at the center of the action, no? You simply cannot stay to the side, where it is safer."

"You saw me on the monitor, didn't you?" If there was one last useful thing she could do, it was deflect their attention from Seth.

"Yes." Victor looked her up and down. "Your sense of personal style is evolving at a lightning pace, my dear. What's this new look you're sporting? G.I. Jane? It has a certain wild, scruffy charm, but I prefer the Dolce & Gabbana, myself."

"I look like this because I've been fighting off Ed Riggs," she said.

Victor's ironic smile froze into a mask. "Riggs attacked you?"

"Everybody attacks me," she muttered sourly.

Novak wrenched her arm up, and she arched back with a hiss of pain. "Stop whining," he said. "Riggs is my man now. He spilled the entire sordid tale to me last night. Seduction, blackmail and murder. What a family, eh? When it comes to squalid secrets, it rivals my own."

She met Victor's eyes. "So it's true."

Victor shrugged. "A small part of a much larger truth," he said coolly. "Congratulations for fighting him off, Katya. I'm sure you were more than a match for that imbecile. You did kill him, I hope?"

White-hot fire flashed through her arm as Novak forced her slowly to her knees. "No," she croaked. "Not my style."

"No?" Victor looked disappointed. "One must make allowances for inexperience, I suppose. For heaven's sake, Kurt, let the poor girl up. There's no need for such theatrics."

"Squeamish, hmm?" Novak pushed Raine's chin up with the gun barrel, forcing her to look up. "You and I are going to play such exciting games," he crooned. "Get used to this position."

She barely managed to shake her head. "Not," she hissed.

"Enough." Victor's voice rang out sharply. "This is vulgar and unnecessary. Let us discuss terms."

Novak pulled her onto her feet with a smug smile. "How unlike you to get right to the point, Victor. Usually you talk in circles for hours. You must be nervous. Ill at ease. Was it something that I said?"

"Enough," Victor repeated, in a stony voice. "What do you want?"

Novak leaned towards Raine and sucked her earlobe between his teeth, biting hard enough to make her yelp. "Everything, my friend," he said. "The gun. The videotapes—all of them. Your niece. Your pride, your peace of mind, your sleep at night. I want it all."

Victor made an impatient sound. "Don't be melodramatic. We've done business amicably for years. Why this sudden hostility?"

Novak assumed a hurt expression. "But you betrayed my friendship, Victor. You played with my most tender sentiments. And now, I am going to play with yours."

Victor did not break eye contact with him. "Katya, I am very sorry," he said, very softly. "You do not deserve this."

Raine wiggled, trying to evade Novak as he thrust his tongue in her ear. She froze suddenly into place when he stroked the underside of her jaw with the gun. "That's for damn sure," she said fervently.

"Your niece is even more exiting than Belinda Corazon," Novak crooned. "Wilder, more challenging. I will be curious to study this videotape, Victor. To see what feelings are aroused, so I can compare."

Their conversation in the vault suddenly flashed back, word for word, and with it, sudden comprehension.

Victor had been bluffing this monster with a dream. He had no videotape to bargain with. She met his bleak gaze, and read the terrible truth in his eyes. There was no need for words. There was no way out of this chamber of horrors.

"Is this what you meant when you told me that the Lazar dreaming could be useful?" she asked.

"This is a fine time to criticize me," Victor said curtly. "I made this deal before you came back into the picture."

"Shut up!" Novak shrieked.

Raine flinched as spittle sprayed across her face. Novak swung the gun around and pointed it at Victor. "Listen carefully, Victor. These are the terms. I have a secret room all ready for your lovely niece. For every hour that you make me wait for those videotapes, I intend to—"

A high, arched library window burst and shattered inwards. One of Novak's men flew through the air and slammed onto the dusty floor, clutching his chest. Then the whole world seemed to explode.

Novak was screaming, Victor was yelling. Novak flung her away and whirled to face the new threat, which seemed to come from all sides. She spun through the air and hit the wall, hard.

Karl shot wildly towards the library door. A single blast responded, and Karl pinwheeled his arms and fell to the ground, clutching the red, viscous mess that had once been his throat.

Another blast, and Novak grunted, knocked to the floor. Time warped into silent, syrupy slow motion as he struggled up onto his elbows and glared at Victor, his face twisted into a gargoyle's mask.

Novak lifted his pistol and aimed it at her. Victor leaped in front of her. The force of the shot slammed him back against her, pinning her against the wall. She felt a hot sunburst of pain in her back. Victor sagged, sliding down against her body. She caught him beneath the armpits. Novak lifted the gun and pointed it at her again, his lips stretched out in a gruesome death's-head grin.

Another deafening explosion, and the gun flew out of his hand. A horrible spray of red fountained out. Novak bent over the ragged mess of his hand, mouth open in a soundless scream.

Another blast. He jerked, clutching his thigh and thudded face down to the floor.

No air. Her lungs were a vacuum. Her heart a burning coal. And the earth was dragging Victor down with a force she could not resist.

Too late. He'd failed, he'd missed. Raine was sliding down the wall behind Lazar and the world had ended, here and now. He skidded to a stop and dropped to his knees in the spreading pool of blood. "Are you shot?" he demanded.

She stared up at him, uncomprehending. He tried to pull Lazar's body away from her so he could see how badly she was hurt.

"No!" Her arms tightened around the wounded man.

"I need to see if you're hurt, damn it!"

She shook her head. "He took the bullet for me," she whispered.

Seth stared down into Lazar's face. His lips were blue. His eyes glittered, still sharp, still conscious. Lazar's lips twitched, but Seth couldn't hear him. He leaned closer. "What?" he snarled.

"You were supposed to protect her," Victor exhaled.

A harsh laugh burst out of him. "I tried. She's hard to protect."

"Try harder," Victor said. "Idiot." He coughed. Blood bubbled from his lips.

"Don't, please, Victor." Raine's voice was shaking. "Try not to move. "We'll get help, and—"

"Shhh, Katya. Mackey . . ." Victor's eyes beckoned him.

He didn't understand why he should bother listening to the dying words of one of Jesse's murderers. But the man had taken a bullet for Raine. He leaned forward again.

"Strength is worthless if you have nothing to protect with it." Victor's voice was a wispy thread of sound.

Seth stared into the dying man's eyes and saw in them all the bleak, empty cold that was waiting for him. He recoiled, enraged at the sheer, fucking nerve of the man.

"Pearls of wisdom from a murderer. Thanks, Lazar. I'll have that printed up on my letterhead. Better yet, I'll have it inscribed on your tombstone. You know what? This is a better death than you deserve."

He just managed to catch the faint, amused smile on Lazar's lips before Raine shoved him away. "Get away from him," she hissed.

He watched her bend over the dying man, murmuring something. Long, tangled locks of her pale hair straggled through his blood. She cried without making a sound, tears streaking through the blood and grime smeared on her face.

Lazar's eyes grew glassy and fixed.

Novak lay face down, twisted and sprawled across the floor like a pile of discarded, blood-stained clothing.

Seth felt neither triumph, nor satisfaction, nor peace.

He felt nothing at all.

Raine stared into Victor's face, using the old eye spell. If she didn't blink, he couldn't slip away from her. She'd only just found him.

But she was crying too hard. She couldn't help but blink. He was slipping away anyway, and no child's spell could hold him. She touched his face, a timid caress that left a smear of his own blood across his high, sharp cheekbone. "I guessed your password," she whispered. "That was how I found you."

"Clever girl." She could barely hear him. "You didn't guess the password. You *are* the password."

"I'm sorry I couldn't give you what you want."

She saw the barest twitch of the corners of his mouth. "Yes, you did. Peter can forgive me now. If you can." His eyes bored into hers.

She gazed back, and nodded. "I can," she said simply.

There were no more secrets or lies between them, just the stately finality of dying, like a boat drifting out into a vast emptiness.

It was like her dreams, and yet different. This time, when the boat drifted away, she didn't panic or blubber or beg to be taken along.

She just held Victor's limp body in her arms, let the tears flow, and quietly watched it go.

Seth was crashing. No way to halt the downward trajectory. Lights flashing, people talking in loud voices, faceless uniforms asking him questions on which he couldn't focus enough to answer. The McClouds were dealing with it, and he was numbly grateful to them.

At some point, he realized that Novak wasn't dead. Close to it, from the looks of him, but medics were sticking tubes into him. They wouldn't bother to do so if he were a corpse.

Great. He'd failed at that, too. Jesse was still not avenged.

But the part of him that cared was buried under a hundred tons of broken rock. He sat on the bloodstained floor and watched Raine cry. There was a yawning expanse between them. Huge and echoing and endless. She was still crying as they zipped Victor into a black body bag, and he couldn't figure out why. The guy was an icy-hearted murderer who had put out a contract on her father and ruined her life. It baffled him so much he had to stumble closer and ask her. "Why?"

She scrubbed at her wet eyes with grimy hands. "Why what?"

"Why are you crying for the man who killed your father?"

The medic was fussing at her, but Raine ignored him. The two of them were utterly elsewhere, locked in a glass bell of frigid silence. Her wet eyes glittered at him with an unearthly silver brilliance.

"He did not kill my father," she said. "He *is* my father. I'll grieve for him if I damn well please."

She reached inside his jacket, rummaging around. He stared down, numb and unresisting. Whatever. She could shoot him or stab him if she pleased. He didn't have the energy to knock her hand away.

Her grubby hand emerged, clutching the glittering opal pendant. "I'll keep this," she said. "As a memento of my father."

He stared down at the blue-green fire that flashed beneath the milky surface of the stone. "That was how they found us," he said.

She nodded and stuffed the necklace into her pocket. "I didn't plant it on purpose. And I followed you because I wanted to warn you. Of course you'll never believe me. Really, I don't know why I bother."

He shook his head. "Raine—"

"Believe what you want. I no longer care what you think," she said. "You're a cold, vicious bastard, but I'm glad you're not dead. I wouldn't want that on my conscience, along with everything else."

The medic draped a blanket around her shoulders and led her away. She didn't look back at him.

They must have given her a shot of something really strong, because everything floated away, leaving her all alone in the white mist. Once she thought she saw Seth, but that had to be a dream, because Victor and Peter were standing on either side of him. She reached out, but her hand fell short and flopped down onto the sheet, limp and useless. "Are we both dead then?" she asked him.

"No," he answered. His eyes looked hollow and sad.

She tried to capture him with the eye spell, as always, but her eyes wouldn't stay open, and it was she who was floating away, not him. She lunged for him, trying to lasso him with words. "I love you. Don't die."

"I won't," he said. She drifted back out into the white mist, clutching that promise like a life raft.

The next time she woke, she knew she wasn't dead, because her mother was sitting by the bed. Her expression was that of a cat lying in wait outside a mousehole. Nothing was more earthly and concrete than Alix when she had that look on her face.

"It's about time you woke up, Lorraine. You scared me half to death. You look terrible. Black eyes, scrapes, cuts, sprains, cracked ribs, a dislocated shoulder, torn cartilage. You are a mess. You just had to run out and do every single thing I've been telling you not to do your whole life! Contrary. Just like your father."

"Which one?" she whispered.

Raine drifted away before she could enjoy Alix's shocked expression.

Chapter

28

He ran the clip back, and played it again.

It was from the Colbit that overlooked the floating dock at Stone Island. He'd sneaked out and collected this batch last night. Ninety-six hours of footage. He'd spliced all the pieces with Raine in them into a montage. This six-minute clip was his favorite bit.

She emerged from the trees and walked slowly down onto the dock. The bruises on her face were almost gone. Her hair flowed long and loose around her body. She was wearing a soft, clingy white shirt. No bra, he noticed. Her nipples jutted out. She needed a jacket. It bothered him that she didn't think to put one on. She never took care of herself. If he were with her, he would insist on a jacket.

A gust of wind blew her hair away from her face. She wrapped her arms around herself and stared out over the water, her face faraway. Like she was waiting for something. Or someone.

He heard a car coming up the driveway. He leaned out the open door of the Chevy and peered down the road. It was Connor's car. He clicked away the video clip and snapped the laptop shut. Comments from Connor about his obsessive pastime were the last thing he needed.

Connor got out of his car and limped over to the Chevy. He leaned on his cane and nodded. "Hey."

"What's up?" Seth was having a hard time feigning interest in the mopping-up details, but he tried, out of politeness.

"I just got a call from Nick, down at the Cave. Novak's going to make it. Sean's shot to the chest just hit Kevlar. Paranoid bastard. And your shot to the thigh barely missed the femoral artery. Bummer."

Seth grunted in disgust. "I should have aimed for his head."

"Console yourself with the fact that he lost a few more fingers on his left hand, thanks to you. That's going to piss him off no end, once he comes to his senses."

"How about Riggs?"

"In jail, licking his wounds. No bail."

"And his daughter?"

Connor's face tightened. "Erin's fine. She hates my guts, of course, but that's to be expected. She told me that Georg never touched her, but I rearranged his face and various other parts of his body anyhow, just for thinking about it. He'll be pissing blood for a while yet." His lips curved in a small, grim smile. "The big house should be a lot of fun for a pretty yellow-haired boy like him."

Seth took hold of Connor's cane, and jerked it out of his hand. "Do you use this thing for show, to get workman's comp, or do you just get off on carrying around an extra weapon?"

Connor yanked the cane back and twirled it with eye-blurring speed. "You can do a lot of damage with this baby if you're quick."

A deer wandered through the meadow, about twenty yards away from them. They watched it stroll by, calm and unconcerned. The world went on. Jesse was still dead. Novak was still alive. The deer munched idly on the yellowed tips of the meadow grass.

The screen door slammed. The buck sprang up and bounded into the trees, swift and silent. Sean sauntered over to the Chevy. "Hi, Connor. Yo, Seth, your buddy Kearn just called, for the sixth time. Call him back, for fuck's sake. He's worried about you."

"He'll live. Besides, I'm leaving. I'll talk to him when I get home."

"Sure you will. You've been saying that for eight days. Not that it's a problem. Stay as long as you like." Sean grinned and stuck his hands in his pockets. "As long as it takes to work up the nerve to go get her."

Seth slanted him a stare that made most people start stammering and backing away. It had no effect upon Sean. He just flashed his dimples and waited.

"Mind your business, Sean," Connor said.

"I've been minding my business all week. I'm bored," Sean said cheerfully. "What's the hold-up? I'd be prostrated in front of that dynamite babe with my tongue rolled out like a red carpet if I were you."

Seth thought of Raine's parting words. "She's Lazar's daughter."

Sean cocked his head, looking baffled, and bounced up and down restlessly on the balls of his feet. "So? What of it? The guy's dead, right? He's not going to bother you."

Connor gave him a pained look. "Sean—"

"Our dad was completely bonkers, but nobody holds it against us," Sean observed. "Or if they do, fuck 'em. Come to think of it, your own daddy wasn't much of a prize either. And we've established that she never screwed you over, right? So?"

There was no arguing with Sean's hammer-blunt logic. He did not feel like trying to explain the anger, the remote, glittering coldness he had seen in her eyes as she looked at him over her father's dead body.

He resorted to simple rudeness. "Piss off, Sean."

Sean's eyes narrowed. "You do still want her, right?"

"That's not the problem!"

Sean snorted. "Nah. The problem is that you're a gutless wuss with shriveled little balls the size of peach pits."

Connor turned away, making a choking sound.

Sean flashed his Wonder Boy grin. "Too much woman for you, huh? Great news. Maybe I can catch her on the rebound. Mend her broken heart. I'll put my all into it, know what I mean?"

Suddenly he was holding a fistful of Sean's faded Mickey Mouse sweatshirt, dangling him six inches off the ground. "Don't even think about her that way," he hissed. "Or I will take you apart. Got it?"

Sean grabbed Seth's fist and hauled himself up so that he could breathe. "Baiting you is so satisfying," he croaked. "Davy and Connor are so jaded, they don't react at all, but you, whoa. You're a sure thing."

Seth flung him away. Sean rolled smoothly up onto his feet and brushed the pine needles off his jeans, unperturbed. A good sport. He had to be, with Davy and Connor for brothers. Something cramped inside him, hard and painful, at the thought. He'd been hard on Jesse, too. Jesse had been a damn good sport. Jesse had forgiven him, even when he didn't deserve it. He turned his back on them and struck out into the meadow. "If Kearn calls, tell him I'm driving back today."

"Chickenshit," he heard Sean mutter.

He didn't turn around. He couldn't handle brotherly banter. He'd rather stare at rocks or trees. After ten months without Jesse, he was out of practice at being nagged and teased. He pushed through the fir trees, cursing as they slapped at him. Goddamn nature. He'd never figured out why people went out and wallowed in it voluntarily. Jesse had tried to get him to go hiking, but Seth had resisted to the bitter end.

The way he resisted everything. Always.

That thought stopped him cold, right in the middle of a clump of baby trees. Their pointy tops were about as high as his heart. They trembled in the breeze. He stared at them, wondering why he'd pushed away Jesse's efforts to help him. Just like he pushed away the McClouds. He pushed away the whole damn world. He beat the world to it, every time, before it had a chance to give him the old heave-ho.

The same way he'd pushed away Raine.

A strong gust from the snowy peaks swept through the grove, setting the baby trees swaying. They sprang back upright, soft and flexible. He shivered without his jacket, but he couldn't go back for it, and face the bright, probing eyes of the McCloud brothers. Not yet.

The van was packed and ready to go. His business needed him, after all those months of neglect. The routine of his life was waiting for him, safe and predictable.

But day followed day, and he kept replaying the same footage in his mind. Every single time he'd made love to Raine was imprinted on his memory. Every word, every scent and sigh. Her textures and colors, her tenderness and courage. The woman was incredible. She deserved better than an evil-tempered, foul-mouthed son-of-a-bitch like him.

Amazing. He was having a pity party. He could hear Jesse sniggering in the back of his mind, telling him to stop jerking off. *Stop playing those old negative tapes*, that was how Jesse had put it when he was in psychobabble mode. God, how that had annoyed him.

Seth stepped out of the trees and found himself on a wide, grassy shelf. It dropped abruptly into a canyon where a waterfall leaped and gurgled. It wasn't a tall, impressive waterfall, but still he stared at it, startled. Almost hypnotized by the milky cascades of foam that spilled down on either side of mossy green fingers of rock. The water tumbled into a churning pool below, where it glowed a deep, transparent green.

For the first time, he got a glimmering of a clue as to why people went out, braving bug bites and boredom, to look at stuff like this. It really was pretty. Spectacular, even.

He wandered closer and stared at it for a long time. The constant rushing, pounding sound of the water created space and quiet in his mind. Enough space to watch a new idea unfurl without flinching from it.

He pushed Raine away because some part of him was sure that she would end up pushing him, sooner or later. He couldn't risk the abandonment, the bewilderment. He would rather skip that part, and cut directly to the frozen solitude phase.

A flash of movement caught his eye. The buck had stepped out of the forest. The two of them looked at each other, a long, cool moment of mutual distrust. The buck melted discreetly back into the trees, drawing Seth's attention to a square, gleaming stone set in the meadow grass. He walked up to the spot. It was a gravestone, set flush to the ground. The grass was cut short around it, and it was scrubbed severely clean of the lichen and moss that decorated the other rocks. He squatted down and brushed away the leaves and pine needles.

*   *   *

Kevin Seamus McCloud
January 10, 1971–August 18, 1992.
Beloved Brother.

A buried memory stirred in the back of his mind. Jesse had mentioned his partner having lost a brother some years back, but the information had been of no interest to him at the time.

Sean was thirty-one, just like this Kevin would have been. He must have lost his twin ten years ago, when he was only twenty-one.

This time, when the ache started up, he didn't try any of his usual tricks to distract himself. Seth just gritted his teeth, and breathed and waited. The decade-old marble slab told a mute, painful story, with the blunt simplicity of stone. He squatted there and quietly listened to it.

It hurt. It shook him. His jaw ached, and his throat ached, and his legs fell asleep. The cold wind swept around and through him. He just kept brushing away the dead leaves and pine needles that blew across the marble and endured the tumult inside him without trying to understand or control it.

When he finally got onto his feet, he stood for a long time until the pins and needles faded. He used the time to scan the meadow grass around him for some color. If there had been any wildflowers around, he would've picked some and left them on Kevin's grave, since nobody was watching. He couldn't follow up on the weird impulse, though, because there were no wildflowers to be found. Just frostbitten grass, red-brown needles, fir cones and dead leaves.

When he could finally put weight on his feet again, the wind was up. It tossed the trees and made the forest rustle and creak. Something had changed. The wind, the weather, the landscape in his mind.

He was going to stop pushing the world away. That would be his tribute to Jesse's memory. And he would start with the McClouds. He owed them, big time. He could never have gotten Raine out of there alive without their help. He would swallow all the irritating, brotherly bullshit they dished out, and be grateful for it. And if he needed them more than they needed him, well, tough shit. That was nothing to be ashamed of.

And Raine. Oh, God, Raine.

Wind swept through the trees with nail-biting, knuckle-gnawing urgency. In the hospital, when she was zonked out on Demerol, she'd told him that she loved him. She had ordered him not to die. That was promising, but he hadn't grown up with a junkie mother without learning Rule Number One. Things people said when they were stoned did not count. Ever.

She might very well push him away. It would be no more than he deserved, after all the shit he had pulled. Spying on her, seducing her, lying to her, manipulating her. And after all that, accusing her of betrayal. The thought made him cringe.

He had to risk it anyway. He would prostrate himself. Grovel and beg until she gave in from sheer exhaustion. She was too sweet and forgiving for her own good, just like Jesse. That might work in his favor, just this one last time, and then he would never take advantage of it ever again.

Nor would he let anyone else do so. He would be her dragon and her white knight, rolled into one. He would spend the rest of his life protecting her, cherishing her. Treating her like the red-hot, gorgeous, adorable love goddess that she was.

Raine was a thousand times too good for him, but what the fuck. He might get lucky. He moved faster and faster through the forest. By the time he burst through the trees into the meadow, he was running like a racehorse.

"The nerve of the man, to make you change your name back to Lazar. Insufferable, arrogant bastard. Condition of your inheritance, indeed. Pah. Pure, vintage Victor. Ever the manipulator."

"I don't really mind," Raine said patiently. "The name seems more mine than Hugh's name ever was."

Alix spun around from the closet she was rifling through, and frowned at her daughter. "You've changed, Lorraine. I don't know where this uppity, know-it-all attitude of yours comes from, but I for one do not like the change one bit."

Raine tugged her comb carefully through the tangled lock of hair. "I'm sorry it bothers you. I'm afraid it's here to stay."

"See? There you go again. Another sassy, uppity remark. I swear,

I'm losing my patience." Alix shook her perfectly coiffed blond head and dove back into the closet, pulling out another garment with a gasp. "Oh, my God. Look at the cut of this gorgeous thing. Dior, of course. A fortune's worth of clothes that murdering bastard bought, and they're wasted on you. Just wasted. Pity they're so small." Alix shot herself an admiring glance in the full length mirror, smoothing her hands over her trim figure. "Two sizes up, and they would be perfect for me."

"Terrible shame," Raine murmured, with a completely straight face. She fished out another tangle to work on. She had been wearing her hair down since she'd come back from the hospital. It hurt too much to raise her elbows high enough to braid or coil it, but when she left it down, the wind whipped the curls into a hopeless tangle.

Alix slanted her a suspicious look. "Don't you get smart with me."

Raine smiled at her. "I'm not, Mother."

For the first time ever, Alix did not protest the title. Her mouth tightened, and she threw the plastic-wrapped jacket she had been admiring onto the bed. "None of this is my fault, you know."

"I know that," Raine soothed.

"No, you don't. I know what you think of me. I know what Victor probably told you. I can't change the past. I made mistakes, as we all do. Maybe I was cold and selfish. Maybe I was a terrible mother, but I did try to do the right thing, Lorraine. I didn't want you to get hurt."

"I got hurt anyway," Raine said. "But I appreciate the effort."

"Well. That's something, I guess." Alix sat down on the bed, kicked off her shoes and scooted behind Raine. "Give me that comb."

Raine hesitated before she handed it over. Hair-combing had never been Alix's forte, and Raine had learned early to brush and braid her own hair. But Alix's hands were gentle, starting from the bottom and working carefully up. "Tell me what happened," Raine asked her.

The comb stopped. "You know most of it by now, I'm sure."

"Not from your point of view," Raine said.

Alix resumed combing. "Well. Victor was making money hand

over fist the summer of '85," she began slowly. "I didn't know how, and I didn't want to know, but we were living in very high style, and I liked it."

She paused, working on a stubborn tangle. When the comb eased through it, she began again. "Peter got very depressed that summer. He said it was all blood money. That the three of us should run away and grow carrots and onions in a hut somewhere. Melodramatic nonsense. I tried to convince him to let Victor deal with the rough side of things. But once Peter got an idea in his mind . . . well, he was like you, that way. Then he told me he was going to put a stop to it, once and for all. Ed Riggs had promised him immunity if he testified against Victor."

"And you tried to stop him?"

"I got an idea," Alix said, her voice uncertain. "I knew that Ed was attracted to me, so I decided to . . . take advantage of that fact."

"You told Victor what Peter was up to. And you seduced Ed."

"Don't judge me." Alix's voice shook. "I thought Victor would bring Peter to his senses. He'd always been able to manipulate him before. I never dreamed that anyone would get hurt. I just wanted for things to stay the way they were."

"I understand that," Raine said. "Please go on."

The strokes of the comb became smoother as the tangles gave way. "You know the rest," Alix said. "I had no idea what Ed was capable of. He became obsessed. He wanted to leave his wife and kids, and run away with me. And then—"

The comb dropped. Raine waited. "Yes?" she prompted gently.

"Then there was that day I came out of the house and saw him chasing you. I knew, somehow. What must have happened. What you must have seen. I saw his face. He was crazy. He could have killed you."

"Yes, I remember," Raine whispered. "I think he almost did."

"I don't even remember what I said to him. I played dumb, of course. I've always been good at that. I made it seem that you were hysterical and overimaginative. That neither one of us was the least threat to him." Alix sniffed. "The only thing I could think of to do was to get you as far away from the whole mess as possible."

"And to make me forget?"

Alix gathered Raine's hair into her hand and combed it from below. "And make you forget." she confirmed. She scrambled around on the bed until she was looking into Raine's eyes. "I never thought that Victor would hurt Peter. Believe me, honey. Victor treated Peter more like a spoiled son than a brother. He loved him."

"So much so that he seduced his brother's wife?"

Alix recoiled. "Raine!"

"It's true, isn't it?"

"It's hardly relevant," Alix snapped. "Or appropriate!"

"Bear with me, Mother," Raine said stubbornly. "Who was my real father? Victor, or Peter?"

"Does it matter now?"

Raine gave her a steely glare. "Indulge me."

Alix sighed and looked down at the comb in her hand. For a moment, she suddenly looked her age. "I don't know," she said wearily. "Go to a genetics lab if you're so curious. It was a very wild time in my life. There are big chunks of it that I don't remember at all."

Raine listened with all the senses that had been honed and heightened in the past weeks. She recognized the ring of sincerity in her mother's voice. That alone was a miracle, and something to be thankful for. She scooted closer, trying not to jolt her sore ribs. She took a deep breath, and a big risk. She laid her head on Alix's shoulder.

Alix froze for a moment, and then reached up and stroked Raine's hair with a tentative hand. "It doesn't matter anymore, which of them it was." She sounded as if she were trying to convince herself.

"No, not to me," Raine agreed. "I've lost two fathers now."

Alix petted her again, her hand stiff and awkward. "Well, you still have a mother," she said crisply. "Such as she is."

An embarrassed cough sounded from the doorway of the room. The little moment of grace was over.

Clayborne fidgeted in the doorway. "Excuse me, Ms. Lazar, but there's something I have to make you aware of," he said nervously.

Raine brushed the tears away from her eyes. "Can't it wait?"

"Ah . . . it won't take long. Mr. Lazar had made very specific instructions as to how to dispose of his worldly remains after the cremation, but two days before the events that led to his death, he changed those instructions."

Raine and Alix looked at each other. Raine looked back at Clayborne. "Yes?" she prompted.

"He requested that you make all the decisions."

Raine blinked at him. "Me?"

Clayborne's shoulders lifted in a helpless shrug. "I'm afraid it's another one of the terms of the will."

The boat rocked gently on the rippling water. She had asked Charlie to take her to the place she remembered seeing Peter's boat seventeen years before. Charlie was respectfully silent as she stared into the water, holding the white box of Victor's ashes in her lap. She was grateful that Victor's staff had taken it upon themselves to look out for her. All except for Mara, who had left immediately. Mara had been inconsolable at the news of Victor's death.

Raine squeezed her eyes shut at the heavy, dull throb of pain in her chest. For some reason, her mind turned to Seth.

He had made it clear that he could never trust her, and her kinship to Victor had sealed his judgment. He would never accept that she had loved Victor, too. But she wasn't ashamed of loving Victor. If she'd learned anything in the past weeks, it was that there was enough to be ashamed of in the course of a messy human life without being ashamed of loving someone. However unwisely.

She had two fathers now. Both flawed, both doomed, but each had given her priceless gifts. She looked into the cold depths that had taken Peter, and silently asked the water, with all its power to cleanse and renew, to accept her other father, too.

The contents of the box were coarser than she had expected, like sand. She took a handful, and cast it on the water.

It was all right. It was appropriate. Peter approved, the whole universe approved. She upended the box, and shook it until the plastic bag inside was empty. The ashes sank. Ripples surged and heaved. She set the box down and turned to Charlie. "Let's go home."

She kept her face to the wind as Charlie revved the motor. The boat leaped and bumped over the choppy water, jolting her sore chest and back, but the pain was a welcome distraction. It made it easier not to think about Seth. Easier to ignore the dark knot of pain in her chest.

She would get through this, she told herself. She wasn't the one who had turned her back on love. She would eventually heal, but he would just fester. And that thought brought her no comfort at all.

The wind was whipping tears into her eyes. She squeezed the tears out and wiped them resolutely away.

"Company," the laconic Charlie said.

She stared at the boat that bobbed by the dock, the hairs rising on her neck. Chest swelling, breath shallow and blocked. Butterflies whirling and spinning. It could just be a similar boat. A neighbor. Someone selling fresh fish. She shouldn't get all wound up when she was sure to be dashed against the rocks again.

It was Seth. A dark, motionless figure against the gnarled tree roots of the shore. His face looked thinner than she remembered. His grim, dark eyes sought hers across the water. They pulled at her, like a rope in the old spell she had dreamed up as a child. The spell that never worked. The spell to make love stay.

Neither of them called out a greeting. Charlie tied up the boat. He gave Seth an unfriendly once-over and shot Raine a questioning glance.

"It's all right, Charlie. Thank you," she said.

Charlie clumped away, shaking his head.

"I see Victor's staff has adopted you," Seth commented.

She couldn't interpret his tone, so she braced herself for anything. "They've taken good care of me," she said. "It's been a tough week."

"Are you OK?"

"I'll be OK. I'm still stiff, but it gets better every day."

"I don't mean just physically."

She tore her gaze away from his penetrating eyes. "How about you? Did your wound heal all right?"

He frowned. "Don't change the subject."

"Why not?" she asked. "There's nothing more to say."

Seth dug his hands into his pockets. "Isn't there?"

"You tell me, Seth." She tried to copy his trick, the eyes that took in everything but reflected nothing.

Then something happened that shocked her. He looked down, breaking eye contact. He shifted from foot to foot. He swallowed, visibly.

He was nervous. She had made Seth Mackey nervous.

"I think . . ." He scowled past her at the water. "There's a lot to say. So much that, uh, it might take the rest of my life to say it all."

Raine wanted to scream with joy, but she kept her face composed, as if her whole heart wasn't hanging on what he said in the next few seconds. "You told me you didn't have a romantic, lyrical side."

Somehow, amazingly, her voice came out cool and steady.

His eyes flicked up. "That was before I started hanging out with you."

"Oh," she whispered.

He smiled cautiously. "Hanging out with a pirate queen is bound to shock a guy's latent romantic creativity to life."

He stood there, looking expectant. Waiting for her to make the next move. He didn't dare to show his hand, any more than she did.

Well. If that was the best he could do, he could suffer to the bitter end.

"I have a proposition for you," she said. "A business proposition."

His eyes narrowed. "Let's hear it."

"I want to hire your firm to do Lazar Import & Export's corporate security. But only part time."

"Part time?" He frowned.

"That's to leave you free for your real job. Full-time love slave."

He blinked, and looked away with a muffled snort of laughter.

"Kind of like the setup you suggested after Victor's party," she continued. "Clueless muscle-bound stud brought to island hideaway to fulfill my every erotic whim. We never did explore all the possibilities of that scenario. We got distracted by the pirate queen and her insatiable appetites. And other things. Murder, revenge, betrayal and whatnot."

She waited to see if he would ignore the mockery in her tone—or echo it.

"Interesting," he said slowly.

"I thought you might think so," she said.

"I have a counter-offer. I'll tell you the job description I really want."

Raine's throat tightened in frustration. If he was going to keep it on this level, it was up to her to force them to the next one. As always.

Seth looked down at his feet. She saw his Adam's apple bob, once. Twice. He met her eyes, with the look of a man who was facing the firing squad. "Full-time lover," he said hoarsely. "Father of your children. Companion in adventure, champion, guardian, protector, helpmeet, mate. Love of your life. Forever."

Her heart eyes stung and burned with tears. Her heart thudded against her sore ribs, and her throat shook. "Oh. But I'm afraid, um, the love slave clause is non-negotiable," she whispered.

"Fine. I'll be your love slave, I'll be your white knight, I'll be your sailor stud, I'll be your frog prince, I'll be whatever the hell you want. Just tell me you still want me. Tell me quick, Raine. You're killing me."

She finally understood the trick of the eye spell. It had to be mutual to work. It pulled her like a rope, until she was wrapped around him, pressing her face against his chest. "God, yes, I want you. And I need you. I missed you so much," she said.

He stroked her back as if she were made of glass and buried his face against her hair. "Me, too," he said roughly. "I'm sorry I made you wait. I was embarrassed. It was stupid. So, uh, about my offer. It's official, then? I can relax? Done deal?"

She pulled her wet face away and stared searchingly into his eyes. "You're sure?"

"I love you. Why wouldn't I be?"

Her eyes flew to the place on the water where the white moth had drowned, where Victor's ashes had mingled with it. "Because of who I am. I'll never turn my back on it. I'm a Lazar, Seth."

He took her face in his hands. "I love who you are," he said, dropping soft, reverent kisses, on her cheek, her forehead, her jaw, her lips. "I want to celebrate it, and protect you and adore you. What you are is beautiful, Raine. There's no one else like you in the whole world."

The world softened and widened as she gazed into his eyes. The final glow of sunset rippled over the surface of the water. A golden eagle swooped over their heads. Then another; a mated pair. The muted whoosh, the shadow of their vast wingspans was a solemn benediction. Another moment of grace. Life had more of them than she had thought. They would spend the rest of their lives making those moments together, and rejoicing in them.

Seth's eyes were full of love and cautious hope. There was a fine tremor in the big, strong hands that cupped her face so tenderly. "So? he asked. "Will you marry me?"

She wrapped her arms around his neck, her heart bursting with a joy too big to contain. "In a heartbeat," she whispered.